Cosmic Heart

A paranormal romantic suspense

Other novels from the
Maverick Hearts collection
by Carolyn Haley

Wild Heart

An Equestrian Romance

Killer Heart

A Vermont Mystery

Cosmic Heart

A paranormal
romantic suspense

Carolyn Haley

Borealis
Books
Vermont, USA

ISBN 978-0-9887191-6-3

First U.S. print edition published as *The Aurora Affair*
Borealis Books
East Wallingford, Vermont, USA

ISBN 978-0-9887191-0-1

First published in electronic form as *The Möbius Striptease*
Club Lighthouse Publishing
Toronto, Canada

ISBN 978-1-897532-82-9

Cover Design: Carolyn Haley with
Leslie Noyes Creative Consulting, Inc.
Bennington, Vermont, USA
www.lmncreative.com
Cover image: "aurora borealis on iceland" (istockphoto)

To Cuz
and T.R.
for the inspiration

Thanks to the Green Mountain Goddesses
for their enduring support

Thanks also to the army of
friends and professionals
who have helped in ways
large and small over the decades

"There is no such thing as the paranormal and the supernatural; there is only the normal and the natural and mysteries we have yet to explain."

—Michael Shermer, Publisher, *Skeptic* magazine

Part One

1
Damsel in Distress

The universe punished me for doubting its powers by arranging a special demonstration. It dropped me, blindfolded and hamstrung, into a room with locked doors, and gave me four weapons: my paints, my doubts, my figure, and a library.

Then it said: "If you can find the right door and open it with the right key, then you can have your heart's desire. Oh, by the way—There's a psychic lunatic running around out there. If you can free yourself before the sands in the hourglass run out, then you can prevent him from corrupting a critical mass of humanity and plunging the world into a new dark age. Have a nice day!"

Okay, the universe didn't actually say this to me. If it had, I would have answered, "Forget it! I'll live without my heart's desire." After all, I'd been doing so for twenty-seven years.

I expected more of same as I backed out my driveway one August evening, heading for New Atlantis. A cryptic call from my identical twin sister, Blanche, had changed my weekend plans. Unaware I was launching on a preordained journey to entrapment and a psychic battle, I zoomed northward in altruism. Two hours later found me steaming along a fire road through the Green Mountain National Forest. Literally steaming: me in a perspiration cloud from heat and humidity abnormal for the Vermont mountains; my convertible steaming from the hit it had taken a few miles back.

It had begun the drive as a pristine vintage roadster—a '66 Sunbeam Tiger, my pride and joy and special toy that had taken me from novice driver to winner in autocross. Now it bled coolant and oil as it limped and thumped on a shredded tire, two bent rims, and damaged suspension. Its V8 motor shook the dense woods around us, as half my custom sport exhaust lay behind in the puckerbrush while the other half dragged beneath the car, carving a trail in the dirt.

Please, please! I chanted internally. Hang in there another mile!

No way would I walk alone through the wilderness in a sundress after dark. Even if the Tiger kept going, at ten miles an hour I'd still be out here when the looming thunderstorm broke and twilight fell. Already, beneath the foliage canopy, I needed headlights. But one was broken and the other gouged out. I could probably hold my flashlight in one hand and steer with the other. Then again, the increasing flares of lightning could guide my way.

Please, please—c'mon, baby, hold it together—

Aha!

The forest pulled back to reveal a stone wall blocking my travel. Front and center loomed an iron gate backed by chain link and bracketed by cameras, set into masonry taller than I could reach. Along the top, barbed wire coiled like a lethal hairdo. Inside the gate, a guard shack squatted in the murk.

"Trespassers Will Be Teleported to a Hostile Planet!" said signs in four languages. And welcome to New Atlantis to you, too! I thought back. I couldn't blame the owner, Dru Montclair, for needing to live in a fortress. That happens when you're a mega-superstar, as was Blanche now that she shared his stage and his bed.

Approaching the gate, I didn't bother braking—the car wouldn't have stopped, anyway—sure that the guard could hear me coming and would be ready on the release switch. Indeed, the gate scraped open when my passage tripped a motion sensor and switched on floodlights within and without.

Once safe inside, the Tiger ground to a halt and expired. I dropped my forehead against my knuckles atop the steering wheel as the gate scraped shut behind.

"Hell of an entrance, Miz LaRue!" came a voice from beside me. I jerked my head up and around to find a guy standing halfway between me and the guard shack, backlit by the floods. My brain, still sludgy from adrenaline overload and dehydration, couldn't manage a snappy comeback. I must have taken too long to respond, for he strode forward and changed his tone to an authoritative calm.

"Ignition off?"

He stood at the driver's door, hand on the latch, ready to pull if I didn't answer.

"Um, no, it stalled."

"Don't try to restart it. Just click off and give me the key."

I obeyed, at loss for words, at loss for thought. When he said, "How many fingers?" I counted three. That seemed to satisfy him. He pulled open the Tiger's door and asked, "You ready?"

"Um, a little gummy in the knees, but I think I'm okay."

I pivoted in the cockpit and stuck out the legs that had earned me a six-figure income. The rest of the package emerged disjointedly, making me glad that Blanche the Dancer wasn't around for comparison. The gate guard noticed everything without reaction, just offered a hand to help me stand.

At that, my synapses resumed firing. Those hands! Oil-stained fingers with nicked knuckles, curved around palms callused and thickened from years of turning wrenches. A mechanic! At New Atlantis! Oh joy, the day's bad luck had just reversed!

I leaned against his solidity, vaguely noticing that we stood the same height, as he walked me across packed dirt to a log bench outside his guard shack. I flopped my weary derriere atop it while he nipped in and came right back out with a water bottle. I took, gulped, then poured the rest over my head, neck, and chest.

"Ahh. Thank you. I had a gallon in the car, but it went into the radiator."

"And right back out, from the look of things."

"Oh god, I hope the engine hasn't seized!"

"Mm. We'll see."

He stood before me and finally asked, "What happened?"

I wiped my wrist across my mouth.

"Deer. Two. Right in the middle of the road."

He returned to the Tiger and walked around it, scowling. "Doesn't look like you hit them."

"No. I missed them, that's the problem. Landed in one of those rock-lined drainage ditches along the road. Took out half everything underneath, and punched out the lights on a boulder and a sapling on the other side."

He nodded. "How'd you get in that deep, then get out?"

"In? Overconfidence, and being mad at my sister. Out? A winch."

His brows jumped and he stopped circling the car to stare at me.

"A come-along," I amended, pleased to demolish his expectations. "Between that and jacking the nose I got the rear tires on the ground and was able to back out of there. That messed up anything left that hadn't been crunched."

He continued to stare, reminding me of a hawk with his expressionless intensity. Then he returned to the bench and sat at my side. The lights caught his eyes, revealing a clear, sky blue often found in pilots and sailors. They regarded me so frankly, so honestly, that I did a double take and looked straight in.

Instantly, a familiar and dreaded rippling began in the atmosphere around us, until his visage was overlapped by a face I knew but had never seen before, with a voice I'd never heard before yet recognized and which warmed my heart. My vision heightened and blurred at the same time, with a golden shimmer around the edges, forming into white and silver curtains like an albino aurora. An ache resonated through my body, swelling until I was paralyzed. I recognized him. I loved him. He belonged to me.

Then the scene snapped back to the wooded gateyard of New Atlantis.

The guard stood and stepped away.

Panting, I shook off the vision and wondered how many seconds had passed while I'd been overcome. The flashes I normally experienced were as quick as the lightning still blinking above us. A big vision like this one, which had occurred only once and not for a decade, warped time enough to alert other people that something was awry.

He had noticed, judging by his stiff stance at arm's distance and that stare through his hawk mask. Now he stood lit so I could see that he was not only my size but my age. He wore scruffy cut-off jeans and a holey T-shirt. His hair, unevenly trimmed, brushed his neck and jaw. It gleamed a tawny bronze, as did his skin over lean muscle. He was a perfect specimen for the Men At Work series I was painting for a gallery feature. However, this was not the moment to invite him to my studio!

After regarding me in turn, his eyes veiled and he pulled us back into the moment. "I'm supposed to tell them when you get here."

He escaped into the guard shack, almost long enough for me to recompose myself, swatting at mosquitoes. Upon return he declared, "Dru said—this morning—that if you weren't here by eight-thirty I had to go find you."

He waited for me to gush, "Oh, Dru must have had a premonition!" When I didn't, he added with a twitch that could have been a suppressed smile, "You missed by two minutes."

"Damn. You mean I could have just sat there and the cavalry would have come?"

"Well, just me on an ATV. If you weren't anywhere on the fire road, we'd've sent somebody out your route with a truck and trailer. No cell reception 'til a coupla towns down."

He paused for a beat then spoke the question that was bugging him. "What the—heck—were you doing out there in the race car?"

I stifled a knee-jerk anger. Of course he knew the Tiger was a competition car. Who didn't, when the tabloids tracked your sister's every move, including her estrangement from an eccentric twin?

So I answered, "Trying to avoid the groupies at the front gate."

"Nobody told you about the road conditions out back?"

"Blanche said it was 'rough' when she gave me the bar-gate code a few years ago, but only the first mile to discourage sightseers." I snorted a laugh. "It looked more like a landmine field after everything had exploded!"

"She's never been out there herself. Neither has Dru."

"I doubt she's even driven since she moved here. And she sure doesn't know anything about suspensions!"

"And you don't know much about tires if you went off like that on dirt!"

Throughout this exchange, we played peek-a-boo with our gazes, trying to catch the other out around our facades. I welcomed the earthbound topic, though, and rewarded him with the embarrassing truth.

"I was practicing four-wheel drifts."

Again he stopped and stared. I explained. "That nice smooth stretch after the landmine holes but before the two-track? The ess-turns? They're perfect."

He kept staring until I finished, "There's an autocross tomorrow I was hoping to win, which would have given me my first championship. I was planning to get up early and drive there from here."

Awareness of lost achievement and huge expenses settled like a cement cloak around my shoulders.

He concluded, "So you tried your nice, wide tarmac tires on nice, slick dirt then came around a corner sideways and met Bambi."

"Yep." I sighed. "Giving me the fun choice of a bucking bronco ride off the shoulder, a bloody hood ornament, or a cockpit full of guts and hooves."

He dropped his gaze and shook his head, then grinned and barked out in laughter. It changed his face so dramatically that my breath stuck in my throat. I almost blurted, "I've got to paint you!" but he pressed onward with reality so I swallowed back my words.

"I'll check it out tomorrow." He gestured at the car. "But for now we gotta get you to the show. It's already started."

"I figured."

I glanced at my wristwatch, surprised to find a shattered face. I hadn't felt my arm hit anything during the bronco ride, though surely bruises would emerge by tomorrow. Already my sternum ached from slamming against the belts. And my dress was sweat-soaked, with oil smears augmenting its floral pattern. Thankfully, I had packed two changes of clothes along with tools and driving gear for the event-not-to-be.

When I looked morosely at the Tiger, the gate guard said, "It will be safe here."

"I know. Better put up the top, though." I glanced at the sky, still grumbling and flaring above the treetops. While I might make it to the amphitheater after all before the storm broke, I doubted the show would run its course. No point changing if I was going to get wet again.

Stiffly I rose while he stepped inside the shack to set gadgets on automatic. Movement chased away the hollow feeling in my limbs, and the simple tasks of unfolding and securing the top, extracting and organizing my baggage, freed me to replay the vision he had stunned me with minutes before.

My mind still reverberated like a bell that had been walloped by a sledgehammer. The visuals had already melted away, but the lingering . . . certainty . . . struck as hard as it had the first time, with Buck. Back then, the vision had convinced me I'd found my soulmate after millennia of reincarnation. Subsequent years of emotional torture had proven me wrong.

I was cured now, though sometimes I saw past people's skin to their true colors in a snapshot moment that seemed supernatural. But after Buck had left I'd figured it out. The artist's eye I'd been born with simply interpreted my five senses in textbook intuition. Blanche, however, considered it a sixth sense, which she called "soul-seeing" to avoid annoying me with the term "ESP." Nevertheless, my gift was why she had called me here tonight.

Nothing strange or sparkly happened when the gate guard approached me again. I wanted to ask him, Why you? Why now? What for?—but he kept us firmly on task.

"We figured you'd drive yourself in, so all I've got is an ATV. If you want, I'll call a car down to take you to the amphitheater. Or the house."

A polite way of asking if I would I turn into New Atlantis royalty and refuse to ride a spine-jarring open vehicle up a rough road in a dress.

I chirped, "I'm fine," and followed him to the ATV, mounting it behind him. I just had time to wedge my tote bag between us before he took off so fast I almost tumbled off the back.

What remained of my French twist unraveled as we churned uphill, spitting dirt behind us, the machine making a prolonged flatulent noise. Too soon my driver slowed, when our road merged into another that linked the compound's main driveway to its residential lodges, The Glen and Valhalla. These I recognized from my previous visit.

Tonight the dirt loop served as a parking lot, with one-way passage between cars jammed along the mowed shoulder. We rode through sounds that shaped into music, then stopped at the loop's reverse point where sawhorses and traffic cones marked an opening into the woods.

"Here ya go!" he announced with a heartiness that rang hollow.

I swung off the ATV then paused for a long look at him, which he returned without blinking. Who are you? I wondered at him. He didn't answer. Of course he wouldn't. Couldn't. But a new thought blossomed: Might this be the person Blanche wanted me to scope?

In her call, she had said only, "If you know why, Madeline, it won't work. Just come to the finale and tell us what you see and feel. We need to know if it's real or I'm hallucinating. The finale is our last chance."

Click.

I couldn't call back because she had timed her lure for the last moment before stepping on stage in New York City. That show had run until midnight, followed by parties, interviews, then hours of travel to New Atlantis for rest, rehearsal, and the finale underway right now.

Her only other words, disrupted by people dragging her away from the telephone, had been, "I need—tomorrow—back gate—please—"

—leaving me to think she'd offered "back gate" privilege in delayed remembrance of my vow to never run the front-gate gantlet again. Now I wondered if she'd directed me here in order to "see" this guy. If he were hired security for the tour, then this would be his final night on duty. If he lived at New Atlantis, then tonight's show would be the last chance—for what?—forever.

I could already tell her, thanks to the vision, that he had a lion's heart, a warrior's courage, an artist's passion, an artisan's skill, and a teenager's hormones. If I were in the market, he would be an intriguing replacement for Buck. Blanche probably thought I was still looking, since we had stopped confiding after Dru entered the picture. So was her drawing me to New Atlantis a matchmaking mission in disguise?

Pah! As Buck had taught me, cosmic visions did not identify a soulmate. I was still waiting to find out what did. Blanche had spotted hers on TV when she was twelve and redirected her song-and-dance interests into music videos until she was in the right place when Dru was producing. They had mated instantly. No such luck for me.

I had been celibate, other than a few smooches and gropes with select autosport buddies, since Buck had dumped me three years ago. Yet my appearance and former career led people to assume I slept with a different guy—or three—each night. In truth, I had abandoned hope that anyone would make my loins quiver again. So why had this gate guard triggered a vision just like the one I had with Buck?

For now I could only translate his face and physique into blocks and planes to sketch later. Then I waved him away and applied myself to the next ordeal.

2
An Enchanted Evening

Obstacle number one stood just beyond the sawhorses: a wooden Indian.

Correction: a white wannabe with a good suntan, who didn't breathe or blink. He wore no headdress but otherwise played the part with a breast plate over bare chest, fringed leggings, and beaded moccasins. His dark hair was cut short save for a skinny braid down his neck ending in a turkey feather. Like my gate guard, he was lean and muscled. I presumed he served as a bouncer, since he also carried a spear.

The spear remained upright as I passed. Beyond him, torches led toward a glowing crater. From within it came a cacophony shot through by a banshee wail. I recognized the band's heavy-metal satire from their *Millennium Magic* album. That award-winner had borne my first cover painting, and won me an award, too. Enough commissions had followed to launch my true career.

The path leveled to become a gravel walkway rimming the amphitheater. Marble logs separated it from the first tier of seats. I observed this from the wrong side of obstacle number two: a rope barrier between trees. Here a nymphet with jaw-length black hair and Asian eyes intercepted me. Despite my credentials, she inspected my bag for booze, drugs, weapons, or cameras, while stage lights danced a kaleidoscope across our clothes. She wore a scarf tied into a halter top over fluid, translucent trousers. Must be nude night, I mused, marveling at the amount of skin I had seen since arriving. For once it was somebody else's skin than mine.

We both shuddered at a crashing chord that made my fillings hum in the pause before the audience erupted. Applause and whistles rang for minutes, during which the girl pulled aside the rope and directed me down one of four aisles radiating from a vertical half-shell at the bottom. The amphitheater could seat a thousand but that would come later. Tonight three hundred Chosen clustered in the terraced wedges opposite the shell. VIPs sat under a striped canopy in the center. A seat among them waited for me.

One had to be very VIP to attend this concert. Tonight the Dru Montclair Band was retiring from the road for good. After a career starting in a ghetto basement and ending in the stratosphere, Dru could retire from the world if he wanted. For now, it was business as usual while the band shuffled instruments and sipped water before the next number.

Initially, I had tossed my invitation without RSVP-ing. I had loved Dru as a voice on the stereo, but couldn't accept him as a reincarnated Atlantean prince with psychic powers, fated to lead the world into the next golden age through his mystical music and model community. Because Blanche had bought the package, I had endured a visit to the compound, attended any performances within an hour's drive—including the tour launch nine months ago—and maintained contact through vague e-mails. Clever Dru had hired me to paint his portrait and album covers, enabling me to change careers without crashing and rebuilding.

Yet I declined his invitation to live in their ivory tower or travel the world with them on tour. And I would have skipped this finale because it impinged on tomorrow's autocross. But after Blanche's SOS, I had fished my invitation from the trash.

No sign of her distress now as she posed beside a woman as ebony as Blanche was golden. Blanche burst into a grin upon seeing me, which I returned, forgetting my pique. She looked fantastic—an hourglass sheathed in turquoise from mid-thigh to cleavage, her hair a gleaming gold cap. Stage makeup enhanced her tapered eyes and bow lips and sculpted cheekbones. If she wiped off the paint and donned a long auburn wig, we would be interchangeable. But I could never match her presence or dance in three-inch spike heels, even though I'd worn them on many a photo shoot.

We could do nothing more than exchange signals as she received her cue for the next song. The fanfare diminished, and the four players and two backup singers took position. Dru whipped back his hair and stepped forward to the lip of center stage. The lights dropped, Dru gestured a countdown, and Pete Davidson started a kick beat on his drum set. Then Adam Hillary added an under-rhythm on his bass guitar. Troy Powers sprinkled synthesizer notes during each cycle of the introduction. Finally Dru, clutching lead guitar, fingered the theme then began to sing.

His voice sprang forth like an arrow and pierced my solar plexus. That voice, even though rasped raw after countless performances, struck true every time. Whether he was snarling or crooning, he vibrated and I resonated. My heart filled my body. My body craved his touch. My mind opened until I saw energy crackling around him—a charisma few could see but millions felt.

I sat back on my bench, grateful to be cocooned for a while. During the next two numbers, Dru acknowledged me with a wink and a nod. So did the other players. All wore a slender headset with microphone above jeans and a three-inch gold medallion against bare chest. Given that the troupe had worn opera-scale costumes for the tour, I presumed the finale's theme to be Revelation. Dru even revealed his natural hair color. I had never seen it in a hue that came with the human gene pool. Now cornsilk flew around his neck and jawline, sweeping back and forth across his eyes.

He strutted across my view, his fingers blurring on the guitar strings and skin gleaming from sweat and drizzle. The other performers and equipment were shielded by the shell or smaller canopies, while he postured on the exposed strip of stage. Lightning strobe-flashes froze his moves for half a heartbeat; seconds later, cloud kettle-drums drowned out his voice. Between numbers, he eyed the sky warily. The audience urged him to carry on.

Nonetheless, he shortened the program, as I could tell from glances and nods among the performers. The music became gloomily romantic, prelude to the closing: a mythic anthem describing a man's transformation from suicidal loser to supercharged healer—*Atlantis Rising,* Dru's autobiography, a fact he denied. The symphonic album sharing its name had taken him so far beyond the top of the charts that the record industry had created a new category for him. "Quadruple Platinum" no longer served. The devotees around me gushed adoration at him. He absorbed it, enhanced it, and sent it back.

I marveled that he had kept sane under such pressure. Not bad for a man who put his pants on one leg at a time.

As passion filled the amphitheater, my mind switched back to where it belonged. *Okay, Blanche . . . I'm here and my eyes are open. What do you want me to see?*

I scanned the amphitheater as she danced. Dru traversed our line of sight. Throughout his saga-song, spotlights featured the players during solos, the beams tunneling through a thickening mist. Three men directed lights from around the amphitheater, while a fourth ran a console a few tiers behind me. The remaining lights were automated and bolted onto trees. All were connected by underground cables. This allowed the New Atlantean cameramen to dart around speakers and amplifiers. All crewmen covered their bodies with jeans and T-shirts. I guessed we were supposed to ignore them as in a regular show.

That was hard to do when one of them looked so much like Buck Williams that my heart did a fandango. I squinted at him through the shifting colors, hoping, fearing . . . no, it couldn't be him. Bluegrass-Buck hated Dru's music and had worn a beard since he could grow one and wouldn't look like that without facial hair. And he knew my twin lived with Dru—she would report him instantly if he stuck his head above her horizon.

Wait a minute. She wanted me to verify something she wasn't sure about seeing. A beardless Buck would qualify. Given the odds against him becoming a roadie for Dru Montclair, she would not believe her eyes if she saw him. Only I would recognize him anywhere. And if she told me he'd turned up at New Atlantis, I definitely would not put a toe inside the place.

So I had been right! A matchmaking venture was in process, only not with any gate guard. Blanche had somehow uncovered the missing Buck and lured me here to give us another chance!

My head snapped up and I glared at her, lost in her minor-key harmonies. Then I beamed the thought: *You duplicitous, conniving . . . !*

I jumped to my feet, ready to yank her off the stage and shake her. That popped my head into a spotlight so I plopped back down. Still sputtering, I grabbed my tote for a hasty departure. Stopped halfway through the motion, recalling I had no vehicle to depart in. Arrgggghh!

I boiled in my seat while everyone around me grooved to the crescendo. Presently I came aware of a cold prickle in the center of my back. I shrugged the clammy dress off my skin; the chill persisted. Ick, must be insects or raindrops crawling in. I levered my arm to brush them away, feeling no bugs or droplets. But my hand passed through a draft, as if I were seated in front of a vent discharging cold air.

My skin puckered into goosebumps. I peeked over my shoulder, wondering if the guy behind me held a battery-powered fan. Nothing there except bodies and packs and coolers and umbrellas, plus the console, backdropped by forest and roofed by flashing clouds. I couldn't see every seat because of the canopy angle, but most people sat in range or boogied in the aisles. Whatever had set the chill on me shut it off when I twisted around.

Turning back to the stage, I tried to attend to the merging musical themes but couldn't focus. The cold prickle locked on my back again, swung to the side and above, then returned, like a searchlight. It seemed to be tracking Dru. Dear gods, was it some high-tech aiming device, like an invisible laser? Should I stand up and shout? Was there anyone near me in security? How could someone get a weapon past the gates and the bag search? And why would they bother trying?

I stared at Dru, willing his attention. His gaze skipped over me across the audience. Before, he had panned smoothly, holding eye contact, to personalize his message. He had the better viewpoint to scan from but presented a bull's-eye for anyone with good aim.

I turned again to search the tiers. People behind me cursed and shifted to watch around me. I peered between them, seeking any oddness among the rapt figures.

Finally spotted it on the last tier before the canopy cut off my view, next to an aisle. Not a refrigerator exhaust pipe, but a void in the lineup. Not an empty seat, but a darkness shaped like a man.

What the . . . ?

Lightning etched jagged afterimages into my retinas. Before I could blink clear and relocate the weird silhouette, lightning flared again. Between flashes I saw a black shape emanating blackness. I stared until my neck cramped and people commanded me to settle down. I faced forward just as rain began a tattoo against the canopy. Suddenly I felt cold inside and out.

Both Dru and Blanche caught my eye, to signal query without changing expression. They performed on automatic pilot, eyes no longer glazed from stage-high but jumping to me when a glance could be spared.

I realized then that Blanche's mystery contained a subplot. They must have been feeling this thing in the audience during the tour.

No wonder Blanche had been cagey. At her description I would have said, "That's what you get for living with New Age fruitcakes!" But if I saw for myself, she knew, then she could rule out hallucination. Which didn't leave appealing options.

I glanced at the light man who looked like Buck. Maybe, maybe not . . . how could it possibly be?

But if it was him, either he was linked to the weird blackness or his presence was one of those flukes that tempt people to believe in destiny. At least I could check out the spook without disrupting the show. A trip to the portable toilets near the sawhorses would take me right by it. Also to a guy with a spear.

The people I squeezed past, bumping with my tote bag, were happy to lose me. I got as far as the aisle before the brewing storm reached a climax and preempted my plan.

Cannon fire, electric tridents, and a deluge erupted. The wind surge sent me staggering and battered me with my dress and hair. Whirling gusts ripped umbrellas inside out and shattered spotlights with projectiles; snapped cables from their moorings; toppled limbs out of trees. The main canopy billowed, popped its stakes, then flapped upward like a Portuguese Man o' War. Two of its spiked tentacles snared the drum set and cartwheeled it into Pete's chest.

A resounding crack stunned us into statues as lightning reamed a tree along the upper walkway. When the splintering fireworks subsided, screams rose in the blackout as people stampeded. I found myself on the stage shrieking, "Blanche! Blanche! Where are you!" with other audience members right behind me. We lurched through the dark bellowing for our loved ones, trying to unscramble our senses from flashing, cursing, scorched sap and ozone, sparking wires, shouts and splashes, elbows and upended gear.

"Madeline—over here!"

I followed Blanche's cry and nearly tripped on Pete, still entangled with cymbals and guy wires. Then I collided with someone helping him, who grabbed my arm before I stepped on Adam, out flat from a power spike through a cable. Another lightning bolt illuminated us for sizzling microseconds. In them I saw Buck's face at the end of the arm clutching mine.

No mistake this time—with our eyes bugged and pretenses shattered, we knew each other at the same instant. Then a roaring black waterfall killed sight and sound.

Buck thrust me aside and shouted for someone to help him lift the drum set. People elbowed me out of the way since I couldn't move.

"Mad, where are you?" came Blanche's voice behind me.

Buck's voice in front: "C'mon Pete, easy does it."

Then Adam at my ankles: "Jeez, what hit me?"

From out in the tiers: "I thought it was a bomb!"

Dru commanded, "Blanche, get to the car—I'll find her."

That released me. I whirled and flailed between people, through jumping flashlight beams, until finding Blanche. When I grabbed her wrist, she fell into me to hug, but I pushed her back, hissing, "You bitch, you tricked me!"

"What—?"

"C'mon girls, get moving!" yelled the band's manager.

"We're taking the scenic route," I snarled at him, tugging Blanche off the stage. We landed with a splash. Blanche yelped as her ankle turned. "Damn it, Mad—I've got spikes on!"

"Kick them off. You must have six-inch calluses on your feet by now!"

Her curses were cut off by a thunderclap so close it warped the air. Wind whiplashed the trees and machine-gunned us with hail. We followed the pack up the tiers in a dazzle of blue-white zigzags. Some people continued down the slope to the driveway loop, others sheltered under trees. Not a good idea, considering the toasted maple beside the walkway. Raised veins snaked from its base where voltage had boiled the root system beneath the gravel. Fortunately, the closest tier had been empty. In a full house, people would have gotten hurt or killed.

The storm subsided as abruptly as it had started. Rain settled back to a patter, and the booming and flashing moved on. The dripping woods filled with voices, and tree trunks and bushes became shadowy people. Flashlight beams flicked in all directions. Torches along the trail were relit and some carried sputtering back to the amphitheater. Camera flashes declared that rules had been blown away with the show.

Blanche and I skidded down the trail then fetched up short at the bottom. The loop now resembled rush hour in New York City. Men in slickers waved lights and shouted; among them I saw the Indian hip deep in traffic, and a woman on horseback herding people on foot. Good thing this was a small, invited crowd, else mayhem would become a riot.

Pedestrians divided into a down-loop flow to the parking area and an up-loop flow to the mansion. Only passholders could get inside the house. The rest watched from their cars, creeping through a cloud stained red by taillights. We passholders would leave them behind when the loop joined a paved drive that continued uphill toward the mansion or downhill to the front gate.

A sloppy half-mile hike between here and there—we needed to regroup, first.

I gestured Blanche into an empty parking slot on the verge and thumped my tote bag onto the hood of a bracketing car to signal, Right here, right now.

She slicked back her hair and demanded, "What do you mean, I tricked you? I only—"

"What the hell is Buck doing here!"

"What!"

Her astonishment stalled my next outburst. We stared at each other like two fighting cats that had been doused by a hose.

I slumped against the nearest car. She shook her head. "Buck? Here? Where?"

"In the amphitheater. He's one of your stage crew, Blanche! How could you miss him?"

Her face puckered. "Are you sure? I mean, the lighting could've—"

My expression answered.

She wiped away makeup streaking down her cheeks. "I can't imagine—I have nothing to do with arrangements, Mad. We could hire King Kong for all I'd know! But I did hear . . . there was one new guy—turned out to be Pete's cousin. Some hard case they tripped on in Montreal but I never met. We paid off the roadies after last night's performance. I thought tonight's crew was New Atlantean."

"Well, Buck would die before joining that club. I can't believe you missed someone traveling with you for two weeks! Granted he shaved, but—Blanche! He used to cook breakfast while we sat at our table in bathrobes. I've had him plastered all over my walls for a decade. How could you not recognize him!"

"Sorry, Mad, but we don't travel with the crew, and on stage I don't notice them. And I haven't seen Buck in so long I doubt I'd recognize him with or without a beard. He's got nothing to do with why I asked you here. But him popping up makes it a lot more interesting!"

I inhaled to retort then bit it off as a background sputtering grew into the sound of an ATV. It stopped then backed up after the gate guard spotted us. He unholstered a radio, muttered into it, then drove into our niche.

"Hey, ladies. Your presence is requested at the manse."

He dismounted. I tensed, half expecting him to shimmer. He looked me in the eye and asked, "You know how to drive one of these?"

"Sort of. I—"

"Good." He gave me a five-second overview then ordered, "Take her up to the house. Leave it in the circle with the key in the ignition. I'll catch you later."

His slicker flapped after him as he plunged back into the traffic jam. I stood with my mouth open then clapped it shut.

Blanche paid him no heed. "So did you see anything besides Buck?"

I approached the ATV and fiddled with its controls. "Yes. Just before the storm broke."

She nodded, wide-eyed, hoping for more.

"Okay, you've got yourself a talented practical joker disguised as a spook. I don't know how he did it. Is that what you want?"

Blanche closed her eyes, tipped her head back, and mouthed, "Thank you!" to the sky. Then she leveled her head and opened her eyes. "Did you see who it was?"

"No, I was hoping you'd tell me!"

She shook her head. "I've got my suspicions. If you can ID him alone, then I'm right."

"I know him, then?"

"By sight and name."

"So you're not going to tell me the story?"

"Not yet. You should see now why I can't lead you."

"Yeah. But tell me this: Is that gate guard part of it?"

"Who, Kit? No, he's just staff."

"Didn't tour with you?"

"No."

"Did you assign him the back gate because I was coming?"

"No. What happened, Madeline?"

"Who did? Or did he volunteer?"

"I don't know. Ask Mark—he handles security. What happened with Kit, Mad?"

"I'll tell you my secrets if you tell me yours!"

I shoved my tote into her hands and straddled the ATV. Blanche, after rolling her eyes, mounted with the bag clutched in her lap. "You driven one of these before?"

"No." I lurched and stalled to prove it. Blanche squeaked at each jerk.

Presently I figured out the controls and zoomed off, dodging cars and trees and people. Having something within my control settled my pulse. Traffic thinned as the line inched uphill, then split at the paved intersection. More New Atlanteans sent the stream toward the gate; a second Indian pulled aside sawhorses and directed a trickle toward the house.

I bypassed them by heading across sloping turf in a straight line. The ground leveled to become a landscaped prelude to the marble mansion. It regarded us through yellow-lit panes. A chain of solar walk-lights connected the manse to its carriage house, off on the left from our viewpoint. Opposite it across the driveway stood a stone circle like something in ancient Britain. In front of the house, at least twenty vehicles including a bus packed a crushed-marble driveway. This circled from the slope crest, through a porte cochère, then back to where we idled on the ATV.

"House or carriage house?" I asked over my shoulder.

"Carriage house. I'm freezing."

I nodded then putt-putted across the lawn to Dru and Blanche's private dwelling. Other New Atlanteans roomed in the mansion or houses around the estate. For tonight many had doubled up to make guest quarters available. Out of the hundred now converging on the mansion, two dozen would stay for the weekend, while some family would linger into the week. Eventually core members would be left to their own devices. Last I'd heard, thirty-five lived here full time.

"We've still got a press conference to get through," Blanche said as we parked, "then the bus'll get out of here. After that it's a few hours playing hostess and tucking people into bed."

I followed her into the squat timber-and-stucco cube footed with marble. We entered at basement level beside a garage originally used for carriages that now housed exotic cars amassing investment value, half buried under stacks of junk.

Narrow stairs took us up to the apartment, whose eclectic clutter was overlaid by unicorns and pyramids and crystals. Plus a cork-walled bedroom devoted to photographs of Dru Montclair and the Sisters LaRue.

Blanche strode past it all to fling open a wall-length closet. "Here, what do you want—sweats? A caftan? Jeans?"

"A towel and a drink will do."

"There'll be booze in the ballroom, towels in the bath. You'll have to help me out of this dress, it's stuck."

She continued jabbering while tossing clothes over her shoulder. This explained the open luggage spilling garments onto the floor, bed, and chairs.

I extracted a micro-fleece zip-front hoodie and yoga pants from my tote, guessing that the temperature would drop another ten degrees in the next hour. Then I stepped into the marble bathroom to effect repairs.

Blanche managed, while I was in there, to peel off her Lycra tube and wrap herself in a bulky lemon sweater over matching leggings. She was freshening her face and hair when I emerged.

"How long can you stay?" She watched me in her mirror.

"Whenever. I trashed the car in the forest, avoiding deer."

She pivoted on her vanity bench and fixed emerald eyes on me. I looked back through a pair just slightly more hazel. These, plus larger hands and feet on opposite sides, and "inny" versus "outy" navels, comprised our only physical differences. Yet somehow her skin looked better with blonde hair while mine looked better with our natural red-brown.

Internally, our differences rose from whatever gene controlled intro- and extroversion. But we both knew that once we scrambled over our barriers, we'd be twins again and not stop talking for hours. Tonight, unfortunately, her public waited. One more night, then she would be free to talk for months.

We tacitly agreed to let this night play out and start fresh on the morrow. Blanche rose to hug me and put it into words. "I'm so glad you came, and gladder you're staying. Sorry it's costing you—let me know how we can help. For now, we need to put Dru in the picture."

"And pose for a few while at it, I suppose!"

She grinned. I returned it, then shouldered my tote strap and followed her into the moist but clearing night.

Engine noise in the background confirmed my guess, prompted by a blinking clock in Blanche's bedroom, that generators had kicked on after lightning blew out the power. The solar walk-lights carried on undisturbed. They led us into the porte cochère—a glorified carport made of marble—toward the main entrance. Blanche, back in heels again, took two strides to my one.

With music and voices within earshot, we refrained from talking. As we started up the front stairs, a man stepped out of shadow so that the door lights revealed his face.

"Evening, ladies," said Buck without expression.

We halted in step and gaped at him. My heart congealed into a rock and clunked to my feet. Then Blanche exclaimed softly, "By god, Mad, you're right. Hello Buck, nice to see you again."

Turning to me she commanded, "Meet us in the ballroom," before marching inside.

3
Prodigal Lover

We waited in silence until a door closed behind her. Then Buck opened with, "So . . . fancy meeting you here, I guess."

"Hah!" escaped me, and suddenly I could speak and move. "Given that my sister lives here, you can't be too surprised to see me!"

"She didn't even notice." He rolled his eyes after her.

"She's got better things to do. Anyway, that was a cheap shot, expecting her to pass word to me. I see you haven't lost your cowardice!"

Anger rushed in where sensibility feared to tread. Buck ignored it. "I figured you'd hang up on me. Or your brother would run me off. I decided that if you didn't show up tonight, maybe I'd try to contact you."

Gack! What would I have done if he had surprised me at the cottage? All those paintings I had put up after he left . . . a shrine to what had been, what could have been, and what would never be. I had even portrayed our reunion, images ranging from me as a dragon roasting him with breath of fire until he was a charred and mewling penitent, to him as a winged god swooping me away to eternal bliss. Either would be better than this chat with a stranger.

I pushed it along. "You must be the hard case they picked up in Montreal."

"Yeah, I was in town when the band passed through, so hitched a ride."

"How'd you get there from Colorado?"

His voice hardened. "It's a long story."

"I'll bet. And an even longer road to here. I remember comments about deluded do-gooders and hating all rock music 'cause of too much drums."

"They're still true."

"Then—"

I broke off at the sound of laughter. A raft of people approached from inside the door. Buck dropped his voice. "This isn't the best place to talk."

"Forget it, I don't have anything to say to you."

"No? C'mon, I'm sure you've stored up some fabulous curses. Step into my parlor . . ."

He gestured across the lawn to the stone circle. At that moment, five visitors streamed out the door around us, calling farewells. We waved them away and stood immobile until their taillights disappeared down the hill.

Into the quiet Buck asked, "Coming?"

No, no, no, I instructed myself. There's nothing you can accomplish here, Madeline. You got your wish: You've learned what became of him. Move forward now!

I tilted my head to look him in the eye while refusing. Instead, I just stood there and looked. Light from the door lit half his jaw and shoulder. I had not seen that corner of throat and wedge of bone for ten years. The cheekbone above them I had drawn many times, as well as drawn my fingers across it, and traced that upslanted indent from the corner of his eye. His hair, still straight and chestnut, was cut shorter than I had seen it. Like the performers on stage, he seemed to have stripped down to basics. His white T-shirt and weathered jeans downplayed yet highlighted his physical fitness.

He took my hand and towed me across the lawn, bisecting light bars that stretched from the mansion windows but didn't reach the circle. Unlike Stonehenge and its ilk, the New Atlantis circle carried no capstones and was not aligned with the sun. Dru had scavenged twenty-one flawed marble blocks from quarries scattered throughout the state and set them upright in a circle. Presto! New Atlantis became known as a sacred power point.

Tonight it was lit from within by gleaming marble and from above by emerging stars. Distant thunder still drummed and distant branches rustled. I could hear blood rushing inside my head. Buck stood closer this time, though I could barely see him. He released my hand and turned away.

"I sort of hoped you'd come tonight," he said toward the stones, "since I take off tomorrow. After mopping up the amphitheater, it's back on the road."

I went hollow. All the questions I wanted to ask jammed in my throat. The worst one to voice broke free before I could stop it. "Back to your ski bunny?"

"Not unless I want a load of buckshot in my face!"

"Ah, so that's why you were in Canada—evading a warrant?"

"Not quite. Just . . . touring."

"Sure. So how come you never told me Pete's your cousin?"

"Because I didn't know. Well, I knew he existed, but on opposite coasts—I never met him 'til two weeks ago. And even if we'd been buddies all along, I wouldn't have said anything. With your sister screwing the big guy, who cares if my cousin plays drums in the band?"

"Ten million groupies would find that good enough!"

"Yeah, but you're not one of them. Though I see you're doing covers. Hell, I see your portrait of Dru everywhere I go!"

I wanted to tell him how that portrait and the album covers had bought me a sportscar and racing, plus horseback-riding lessons shared with my brother, Colin. But memory of the ruined Tiger and a glowing gate guard checked the urge.

Buck showed no sign of glowing. Part of me wanted him to, while the rest of me hated both him and Kit for doing it in the first place and scrambling my perception of the world.

I brought my mind and mouth back to the present. "So you've worked your gig and now it's back to aimless drifting?"

"I don't know about aimless." His tone sharpened again.

"Then what are you doing besides chasing babes?"

"Tilting at windmills, what else?"

"Hah! Then why not stay at New Atlantis?"

"Not invited."

"Trade places with me—they're holding a berth I don't intend to fill."

He chortled. "You'll have to, for a while."

I hesitated then exclaimed, "My, news travels fast around here!"

"Why not? Up 'til that cloudburst, you were the most exciting thing to happen tonight!"

"What do you mean?"

"Blanche's evil twin finally deigns to put a toe inside the compound! The only outsider allowed in the secret entrance!"

I laughed. "No wonder you shaved your beard and played roadie. If someone remembers you and hooks us together—oh god." I could see it in the tabloids. Good thing Buck had taken off before Blanche officially linked with Dru. Actually, the two events had occurred in the same month, but there had been a lag before the press recognized my interest value. Buck had made it out of sight before the paparazzi zeroed in.

I pulled my face back to sternness, even though he couldn't see the expression. If I relaxed and enjoyed the encounter, he might feel he had gotten away with hurting me to my core. I couldn't begin to forgive him until he accounted for himself, and apologized.

He sensed the demand coming and raised his hands. "Don't get any ideas, Mad—I'm outa here pronto. This is hello as well as goodbye."

"Nice of you to say so this time!"

"Maybe that's why I'm doing it, to make up for before."

"Not much consolation. You didn't even contact me, or even your mother, to say you're alive! Wanna know how many times she called me? In the end I had to call her, to tell her I'd heard through the grapevine you were heading for the hills astride a ski bunny. I really appreciated that one. And all I can say to that is, Fuck you, Buck Williams. I hope those three years were hell!"

"They were. I hope that makes you happy."

His voice was soft but cold. I stood with heaving chest then whispered, "An apology would make me happier."

He snorted, turned away, then reversed. "I'm sorry, okay?"

His voice held an unfamiliar note I interpreted as sincerity. It melted my knees but I held myself taut. "Better than nothing, I suppose."

"You wouldn't have gotten much better if we'd stayed together."

"I'm sure. So . . . have a nice life, I guess. You told me all I wanted to hear."

"And that's all I've got to say."

He jammed his hands into his pockets and turned away, but didn't go anywhere. Neither did I. It seemed pathetic to end like this. The real question was, Did we want it to end?

He must have felt the same doubt, for he peeked back over his shoulder then pivoted to face me. I looked up to his eyes but in the dark couldn't see them, just like those other nights when we had groped and gasped together, blind. I welcomed the darkness this time because it hid the tears that had welled despite my resistance. We'd been through so much, for so long, for nothing. Fruitless to go backward, no place to go forward; if he'd just kiss me goodbye, I could walk away.

I nearly vibrated from the effort of suppressing this desire. He must have sensed it, for he reached out and pulled me against his chest. He was still damp from the storm beneath a clean, dry T-shirt. A change of clothes but no time for a shower, so he emitted the scent I once knew. It stirred me in places I couldn't control by willpower. I could only back out, or lift my face from the thudding heartbeat beneath my ear and touch the lips I knew were waiting.

He saved me the choice by bending and crushing me closer. I fell into his kiss as I always had. Since the day we'd met, alienation evaporated on contact, as if I'd been lost in a foreign country unable to speak the language, then someone stepped out of the crowd and welcomed me in my native tongue. With Buck, touch became a language in which we communicated fluently. In his arms, I felt the only sense of belonging I had ever known.

My heart launched into the "Hallelujah Chorus" while my body commenced heavy breathing. I wallowed in the heat of his tongue, his lips, his skin, his hands. But then, abruptly, something inside me unhinged and the whole picture shifted. My mind escaped my skin and perched above us on a marble shoulder. From there I watched Madeline LaRue and Buck Williams twine together, almost grappling in their urgency. At the same time, I felt every sensation. The dichotomy confused me; sent images reeling; made sensations flit in to and out of my consciousness like bats.

I was rolling across a mattress with the gatekeeper. No, I was with Buck in the marble circle on New Atlantis's front lawn. No, the sheets were satin, this hadn't happened yet—wait a minute, what was happening? How many men were in my arms?

Temperatures and scents—so familiar. Complexions all the same. But mass and contour, all different—it was déjà vu in parallel worlds with the same, different man. Good god, such spiraling and blurring . . . what had I eaten today? I gasped at a vision of flames and screaming horses, Dru's face contorted in agony—then Buck's lips dragging down my throat and hands massaging my breasts.

Spotlight! No, a headlight slicing between the menhirs. We jerked apart, reliving lovers' lanes and cop flashlights. When the beam swept past and settled in the porte cochère, we separated and peered between the stones. An ATV taillight blinked out while voices arced between porch and driveway. I recognized some, realized Kit had returned from traffic duty. Oh lord, when would this bad acid trip end?

The interruption returned us to the present. Buck straightened and stiffened as an invisible wall rose between us. I knew better than to bash against it—our moment had passed. Poetic justice demanded that I leave him yearning. I would have pronounced, "Goodbye forever!" if my throat hadn't been locked so tight.

We stood apart, mirroring the boulders. Together, we turned and jumped as our psychic wall gained visible form. He saw it, too, I could tell by his sudden rigid stance and a gleam from rounded eyes: a shimmering sizzle, like a diffuse electrical field, hovering between us. I gasped; he blurted; I froze; he bolted. His passage left a glowing imprint on the nearest stone.

Marble, I knew, was not phosphorescent. So I dared not move until all glows faded, upon which I burst between the menhirs. Behind me, something crackled the grass, from the opposite direction Buck had run.

No one was abroad to see me dash across the lawn to the empty carriage house. I flung myself into Blanche's bathroom to wheeze and sob until I could draw a full breath. At that point I realized I was crouching in the dark, so I stood and groped the walls until my fingers found a light switch. Twenty globes surrounding a mirror came on like a supernova. I squinted past them, taking stock of tangled hair, swollen lips, unzipped top, trembling fingers. My pheromone contrail surely glowed in the dark.

I fumbled for my bag, found it no longer attached to me. Oh great—must be somewhere in the circle. Now I had to go back to paw the trampled grass and demon stones. My big flashlight, of course, was still in the Tiger. How I wished my car was parked in the circle and ready to blast off on ignition! Instead, I had a psychic bulldozer blade shoving me toward the edge of a cliff.

No, no, no—I refused to plunge into the abyss below me. Down there lay the cop-out of believing in untruths. How easy it would be to explain spooks and glows and coincidences as supernatural—even as karma, given how hard chance had worked to restore my lover to me. Most New Atlanteans would attribute my strange visions tonight to psi phenomena. But not me.

I never forgot that early humans thought fire was magic. Until mere decades ago, no one could imagine walking on the moon. Life still contained things we couldn't see, things we didn't know, that affected our reality.

So if I happened to be suffering from an unprecedented string of unbelievable events in one place within a few hours, there must be an explanation. Something rational and comprehensible, and some reason they seemed to revolve around me.

Logic insisted that these aberrations were connected. Foolish of me to let Buck run away. Again. I should have found out when and how he was leaving, and grilled him about his time with the New Atlanteans. Well, the night was not over; he was somewhere on the compound; I might as well search for him. I could forgive his panicked sprint since I'd done the same—characteristically, in opposite directions. All the more strange that we'd both ended up here!

In a final moment of farce, the carriage house door resisted opening. I shouldered hard and stumbled out over my tote bag. Wait a sec, did this place have gremlins as well as demons? Who had been following and now mocked me with this favor?

I glanced around. People loitered between door and driveway, but none near me or observing the carriage house. My gremlin must have been Buck. He alone knew I had been in the circle. Why had he gone back, to check out those glows? To apologize again, thinking I was still there?

Nah—one apology in a lifetime was all he was good for. Perhaps he too had added up factors and figured we shared current problems worth discussing.

So why hadn't he knocked? Or had I not heard him from the bathroom? Then, in lieu of carrying my bag around all night looking for me, he left it where someone would find it. He probably didn't want to face me again, so when I proved unavailable he abandoned chivalry and returned to his business. Whatever that was. Yes, that scenario made more sense than anything else that had happened tonight!

The rest of it had to make sense, too, which made it time for me to stop dithering and start investigating. By now all key players should be in the ballroom; so, after tidying my hair and dashing on some makeup from Blanche's arsenal, I headed across the lawn to the mansion. Somewhere in there I ought to find a clue!

4
Portents

No one outside in the now starry night recognized me, and vice versa. I actually made it through a few minutes and few hundred feet without event. The main entry promised grandeur with carved oak double doors propped open by an amethyst geode no man could carry. A fanlight greeted visitors with the band's unicorn/pyramid logo in stained glass.

I passed through a pair of teal doors framing leaded glass into a hall with chandelier and central staircase curving up to a gallery. A corridor on my left was roped off and darkened. To my right, lights beckoned down a hall faced with closed doors. I followed puddles across chessboard marble then footprints down carpet to the ballroom. There storm refugees clustered around food tables. The band, backed against a tapestry, fielded questions from the press.

I took a deep breath and straightened then plunged in. Eyes spotted me and lenses immediately followed. However, nobody approached, as all were conversing with each other or the band. This was the first time media reps had been allowed inside New Atlantis, and they had a lot of ground to cover with the clock ticking. Only the lottery-picked two dozen would stay over and physically cover ground on tomorrow's tour.

The band and their mates signed autographs and bantered while New Atlanteans passed out organic hors d'ouvres. Only the four musicians still had bare skin showing; everyone else had covered up. Their fashion statements ranged from grunge to chic, with a bias toward costume and a ubiquitous New Age theme: yin/yang tattoos. Peace-sign earrings. Crystal necklaces. Gaia T-shirts. A unicorn carved out of ice on the buffet table.

Blanche's gaze flicked toward me but she sent no other signal, given that she was talking into a reporter's vidicam. My eye moved on to Dru, who also talked with animated face and hands. He seemed to have antennae bristling from his head, scanning the room around him. Certain he was aware of me, I kept moving lest I draw his direct attention. Or anyone else's. The interviewers would soon exhaust their questions and start sniffing for fresh game. I wove between reporters grilling family members, and music-industry bigwigs nursing cocktails. A trail of empty glasses led to an open bar along the back wall. There, a knot of musicians—I recognized the Plate Tectonics' keyboardist, and the singer Apollo—laughed and drank together. We exchanged nods as I passed. One of them whistled.

I turned my back to them at the bar, where a burly New Atlantean wearing an earring mixed me a double scotch and soda. His lumberjack body poured into jeans, like the gate guard's fighter physique and mechanic's hands, would fit my Men At Work project. This series of figure studies celebrated male beauty, power, and competence—a reminder for those who needed it that men had built the wonders of our world as well as ruined so much. A reminder, also, that while American culture was plastered with erotic female images, many of us pined for a similar quantity and quality of males.

I planned to do something about that imbalance. But not tonight.

After memorizing the bartender, I secured my back against a wall and scanned the crowd. I didn't know many in Dru's entourage, having attended concerts and visited backstage only twice, and New Atlantis only once when painting Dru's portrait. I knew the band well enough for small talk, including Adam's girlfriend Leslee, a dancer whose place Blanche had usurped on stage. I also recognized Troy's wife, Allanna, a Native American, who vibrated with purpose in the background, along with the two Indian wannabes and the amphitheater girl. Others looked familiar but I couldn't tag them. No sign of Kit or Buck.

People returned my survey with leers and winks or just sparkling-eyed curiosity. I held no one's gaze and acknowledged no gestures, just knocked back a drink and abandoned my glass.

While sidling across the ballroom, I noticed that no New Atlanteans held liquor glasses and all wore identical medallions—the same chest-thumping disks sported by the band. This might help narrow down my spook search. Since it/he had been in the audience, not on stage or working as crew; and since his effects had only manifested during the tour, as I deduced from what Blanche had told me so far; he probably wasn't an official member. That eliminated a quarter to a third of the people in the room.

A flash pierced my thoughts as a photographer snapped me. I stepped behind a pillar of ornately cut stone. My eye could not resist following it up to the ceiling, inspiring me to wonder how those original friezes, left untouched by Dru, had been crafted, and who had painted the murals and woven the tapestries. How much money the whole represented. That crystal chandelier dangling over the center of the room? Worth thousands, if not tens of thousands. The marble tiles, blocks, edgings, and facings? Uncountable worth. Real Art Deco sconces sprouted from walls and pillars. Every place my gaze touched revealed a lovingly detailed masterpiece.

While I gawked, the press conference changed gears. I came back to Earth as reporters regrouped around the band, or fanned out to buttonhole relatives and visiting dignitaries. I slipped behind the nearest tall stranger then emerged along the wall near the hallway exit. The band, meanwhile, inched toward the same door.

I pulled up as a man in black jeans and polo shirt passed between us. A dark haze outlined his figure and a chill followed in his wake. I stopped and blinked then pinched myself, yet still felt the chill and saw the hazy aura. Damn it, damn, damn—he hadn't been a bad dream!

The spook was right there in front of me, I couldn't deny it. We were in a fully lit room free of thunderstorms. He carried nothing. I saw no projectors, no accomplices, no alien objects. Yet a man just walked in front of me who glowed black like some cliché occult bad-guy. Oh god. I pressed my forehead, hoping to find a bump there from smacking the Tiger's windshield. Nothing. And not enough time had passed for my cocktail to hit.

The spook edged around the crowd surrounding the musicians, his back still toward me. People greeted him with smiles and stepped out of his way. I could not see whether he wore a medallion. No one else seemed to notice his aura. Perhaps I had merely lost my mind. It was bound to happen someday . . .

He stopped when Dru's naked shoulder gleamed about two arm lengths distant. I understood with a jolt that the spook intended to touch him. No way! I might be nuts, but no creep was going to lay a hand on my sister or her soulmate!

I wormed between bodies as fast as I could without shoving. Blanche slipped her arm around Dru and grinned. During the photo frenzy that followed, my quarry wriggled into the innermost ring around the band members. I drew close enough to yank him out backward or kick him in the balls.

He must have sensed me coming, for he swung to face me with rifle-barrel eyes. They caught me and sucked me in with the speed of a motorized zoom lens. Just as fast, my viewpoint zoomed back again, presenting a fanged gargoyle with glowing reptile eyes.

Yow! The image knocked me breathless. An eyeblink later, in the same place, I saw a lean olive-skinned man with coiffed black hair. Raoul Lamont!

I staggered back a step. This was the band's publicist! I recognized him from photos and parties—one of those oily parasites I had met often in my modeling days, who gravitated toward celebrity. Usually they were harmless; in this case, lauded for his role in Dru's success. This man couldn't be aiming to harm his meal ticket! On any other day, I would have retreated in shame.

But normal days didn't bring horrific visions! Although Blanche had primed me to suspect someone of mischief, and my rattled brain might have conjured a demon to explain a threat I could sense but not explain, I could not ignore this aberration. Here was trouble trying to happen. The embarrassment I might suffer if wrong seemed puny against the horror if I was right.

Holding my breath, I shouldered past Raoul into the circle. He reached after me, missed, but caught Dru's arm. I grabbed Dru's other arm plus Blanche's and wriggled between them. Tugged Dru free of Raoul's grasp and presented us to the nearest camera with a deranged grin.

"Why Madeline, how nice of you to join us!" Dru said archly. I stood on tiptoe to give him a showy kiss, pecking close to his ear and whispering, "I need to talk to you right now."

When I stepped away, Blanche hissed into my other ear, "What are you doing?"

I gave her the same kiss and whisper. She and Dru slapped on smiles and, in turn, bobbed close to me and muttered, "As soon as we get rid of these guys."

Ten minutes of beaming and posing passed before we could move. I answered questions with half my mind and tracked Raoul with the other. He had withdrawn from the circle; and, if that haze zigzagging to the door was any indicator, quit the scene. I cursed myself for panicking. I should have followed him, tried to engage him and learn something useful. Another "should have" to add to the list.

Dru said something that brought a group laugh, then stepped behind me to hook my arm in his left and Blanche's in his right. "That's it for now, guys—have some eats, look around, we'll talk again later. I've got business to discuss with these beautiful ladies."

He propelled us into the wall of bodies, which backstepped to form an opening. Blanche and I smiled and chitchatted while he steered us into the hall. A reporter followed with vidicam on his shoulder but Dru said, "Not now, Larry—we'll be back in a minute." Larry faded backward. Other people stepped aside as we strode along three abreast.

Blanche's heels went thut-thut-thut along the carpet, then clack-clack-clack across the entry hall. On the far side she paused to step over the velvet theater rope barring the corridor, then led us along it to a conservatory featuring a grand piano.

I shoved the door slab closed behind us. "Does this thing lock?"

"Of course not. There's no need—"

I shocked her silent by grabbing the nearest chair, jamming it against the door, and flopping into it. Dru observed with cocked eyebrow and folded arms.

"Blanche, I found your spook," I declared.

She exchanged looks with Dru then found an armchair and slid into it. Dru remained standing.

Blanche asked, "Who is it?" then closed her eyes when I answered, "Raoul Lamont."

Dru scowled but said nothing. I continued, "I don't know how, but he generates a black aura. You can't miss it. At least I couldn't—but nobody else seems to see. But I saw it in the amphitheater before the storm then just now in the ballroom. It's like a dark nimbus around him, or a void or something, abnormal—like a vampire throwing no shadow. I thought it might be a hologram. But it throws a cold draft."

I shook my head, still incredulous. How could it be?

Dru cleared his throat. "You sure?"

"Yes, unless I've got the wrong name attached to the face."

I described both appearances the spook had presented to me. "That's him," Dru said after hearing the standard description, followed by a low whistle and headshake after I conveyed the demon vision.

"I wasn't kidding," Blanche said to Dru, "when I told you he scares me!"

"But you've never seen anything like that!"

"No, I don't see images, I can only sense atmosphere." She shifted to include me. "I try to give everyone benefit of the doubt, but the way he looks at me . . . I can't hold a positive thought about him. I know he's . . . waiting. I feel all slimy when he touches me."

"It's never been inappropriate," Dru defended.

"It should be never, period, if that's what she wants," I butted in.

"I'll speak to him again." Dru set his jaw and kept his arms folded.

"On his way out the door—for good!" I unfolded my arms and waved one. "Dru, there are only four possibilities here. Either I've gone stark raving nuts, or this guy is a magician, or a special-effects wizard, or really knows something about the black arts. Maybe he's a satanist: I felt he was trying to pass something to you, or take a hair from your body for something voodoo. I don't know. But that's why I shoved in, so he couldn't do it. He took off right away."

Dru broke pose and paced. "There's got to be an explanation. I've known him for years. We've never quarreled. He helped me to the top and has made a good living off me. Why would he turn bad?"

"Maybe he was bad all along and you never noticed."

Dru stopped and flared his nostrils. "I notice things like that."

We glared at each other. He softened his tone. "The fact she sensed something and I couldn't is why we called you in."

I discarded several responses before saying, "When did it start, and where?"

They looked at each other and shrugged. "Couple weeks ago," both said.

"Before or after Montreal?"

"Around the same time," said Blanche. "I've always been turned off by Raoul but never scared of him. He joined the last leg of the tour and it seemed he was focusing on me more, making opportunities to be near me, brush me . . . I always felt naked in front of him and started worrying when I was alone."

"Did he say anything specific?"

"No, he rarely speaks to me. Just lurks and leers."

"Him and every other male above puberty," Dru sneered. "You should know about that better than most, Mad."

I certainly did. And understood how no one could do anything about it so long as the lurkers and leerers behaved within social bounds.

"So you started feeling . . . uncomfortable . . . during the shows after Montreal?" I prompted.

Dru rubbed his jaw and looked inward. His eyes, I noticed, were a pale gray. I had thought them to be blue-violet, especially after a long portrait sitting. Did that chameleon swap between tinted contacts as well as dye his hair every month?

"Yeah, that's about right," Dru answered my spoken question.

"It was always fleeting," Blanche added. "But suddenly got intense tonight."

"So what was different about Montreal?" I asked Dru, shooting Blanche a look that commanded silence.

He studied me before saying, "We picked up a new guy."

Blanche and I waited. Dru looked back and forth between us. "Pete's cousin from California. He was having hard times. We gave him a job. He came back with us. He did excellent work and we'll be sorry to lose him."

"But?"

"But I sensed something about him. I can't identify what. Just . . . something."

"Keep trying."

Dru focused on me so hard I knew he was seeing more than I chose to project. If Raoul lusted after Blanche with that intensity, no wonder she sweated!

"His aura," Dru stated. "It was unbalanced, spiking, showing great pain."

Ah, I thought. So this was Dru's psychic power. I tossed a look at Blanche, who braced herself for my protest. I gave none, for I believed aura perception to be a normal human ability. It resembled my soul-seeing—the subconscious mind's ability to process mixed inputs then project a picture into the conscious mind. In that case, I had just seen Raoul's soul.

And Dru couldn't.

Blanche experienced a more common sensitivity: hyperawareness of atmosphere. Dru might have a talent akin to mine, but I wouldn't label him psychic unless he could engage it at will. Seeing an aura around Buck didn't count; Buck's inner turmoil was obvious to anyone paying attention, whether they perceived it visually or viscerally. I opted against pointing this out.

Instead I asked, "Who else's aura have you seen?"

Dru shrugged and looked at Blanche. "Most everyone's."

"How about mine?"

He laughed. "Constantly."

I filed that for future reference. "How about Raoul?"

"That's the problem. He's always been a stable, monochrome glow."

"Even tonight?"

"Always." His voice hardened.

I sighed through both nostrils. "Look, there's no point continuing this conversation unless you accept that I can see Raoul's true colors and you can't."

"It's not that simple," Dru said, finally sitting. "I'll accept that we all perceive differently and it's not a case of your word against mine. But I don't accept this knee-jerk condemnation of Raoul. You could be picking up Blanche's anxiety and revulsion. As twins, that's likelier than my friend being a satanist! Or another party has been stirred into the mix and is triggering incomplete images, or overlays. Why should I be worried about Pete's cousin, Madeline?"

I looked at Blanche. She nodded.

I lifted my chin. "Because he was my lover since senior year in high school. He dumped me about the time you and Blanche moved up here. He hates your music and laughs at your mission. And he's the only person who ever . . . um . . ."

"Triggered visuals?" Dru suggested.

"Yes. That is, until tonight."

"Raoul, who triggered an evil, ugly image," Dru supplied.

"No, I mean earlier this evening. Entirely good."

Blanche sat forward. Dru kept his gaze on my face. "Who?"

"Your gate guard."

"Kit Douglas," Blanche translated.

Dru laughed. "Of all people! What's he got to do with it?"

I shook my head.

He continued to himself: "Quite a cast of characters we've got here! I've always known this place was a power point, but I never thought it would affect folks not seeking enlightenment. I wish we could publish this—all those people who don't believe me . . ."

He faded off into his dream. I used the moment to exchange looks with Blanche. She said to him, "We have to keep this quiet 'til the press goes home. Everything could backfire if you lose your credibility just when we're banking on it to support us for the next decade!"

"You're right, babe, don't worry, I won't say a thing." He flashed her his warmest smile, which she returned. Straight-faced again, he turned back to me.

"How long can you stay with us? If you're the only one seeing anything, you'll need to do most of the scoping. We'll help sort it out. Your ex, now, that's an intriguing development! Can you persuade him not to leave tomorrow?"

"I don't know. I don't even know where to find him."

"Probably the amphitheater." Dru rose and held out a hand for Blanche. She allowed him to hoist her up. "If they're done down there, try The Glen. That's where we bunk single guys. I can have Mark radio him and give you a ride to wherever he is."

"Thanks, but I don't want to attract attention. For all we know, he's already gone." Buck had, after all, made a hasty exit from the stone circle!

I was tempted to recite that event but resisted. I needed to keep a few cards to myself. And if Blanche and Dru didn't get back to the ballroom soon, people would ferret us out.

"I'll make sure he has something to do in the morning," Dru said, "and we'll deal with him tomorrow." He steered Blanche toward the doorway.

I removed the barricade. "Since I don't share your host duties, I'm going to retreat for the night and think this through." Turning to Blanche I added, "Is that tower suite still available?"

"It's yours for however long you want."

She dodged my eye by opening the door a crack and peering into the hall. Voices flowed into our room. She closed the door and fluffed her hair with her fingers. "We'll draw their fire. You wait a few then go upstairs."

I obeyed. Blanche and Dru cut a swath through the minglers, distracting them so I could saunter toward the staircase. I trotted up the curve, chuckling at the contrast of cheap, indoor-outdoor carpeting over marble steps as wide as I was tall. On one side ran a polished railing supported by carved banisters, and on the other loomed a stone-block wall. Along its face, sconces designed for candles but which now held compact-fluorescent lightbulbs lit the way to the gallery.

There the carpet runner switched colors and split to continue down dim hallways in opposite directions. I remembered from my other visit to turn left for the south wing. This hallway, slightly warped as in old hotels, led to the tower. Along the way, doors hung with message boards, hand-drawn nameplates, or mystical icons gave the feel of a college dorm. The only blank door, on the left at the very end, opened into the tower suite.

It wasn't much: an anteroom, a bedroom in the tower, and a bathroom in between, all empty save for mismatched basics. Dru's fortune had not been wasted on decor. Instead, it had bought and modernized the finest construction available in the days before income tax. What joy it would be to decorate these chambers! I squashed that thought and forced myself to merely be thankful that I was safe and warm for another night.

5
Surreality

While waiting for the claw-footed bathtub to fill, I parked on the window seat watching lights and shapes move along the driveway. Somewhere out there was Raoul Lamont. Was I hallucinating about him, or was there really something supernatural going on? Now I understood why Blanche had called me. I needed to do same with our brother Colin. No supernatural thing would get past his analysis!

For now, I would treat it all as a waving yellow flag on a racecourse, which meant: Keep driving, but slow down, use caution. There's something happening up ahead that you can't see.

Putting "how" and "why" aside still left a growing list of questions. When would Colin get back from his trip so I could call him? How would I get the Tiger back to the shop in Massachusetts? Any chance, any chance at all, it could be repaired before the competition season ended? Should I just find another car—maybe this one prepared with a full roll cage?

Meanwhile, where was Buck? Should I track him down and ask what he knew about behind-the-scenes New Atlantis? Had he experienced any surreal events besides what happened between us in the circle? Did he know anything about Raoul?

And what about that Kit guy? He was probably still on cleanup. Since I no longer heard generators, he or whoever must have gotten the power back on. No lights flickered in my tower suite, and the water rising in the tub was steaming. I stepped into the bathroom to check it; ahhhh, deep enough to justify slipping in. I felt safe now, for the first time since leaving the cottage in the Berkshires I shared with Colin. A long soak might help me relax, as well.

I stripped and dipped a toe to test the temperature, just as someone rapped knuckles against the anteroom door.

"Who's there?" I blurted, scrambling for a towel.

"Kit Douglas," came a muffled voice.

Yikes! I jumped back into my clothes, calling out "Just a second!" During that second I considered greeting him naked. But the consequences would be more than I could handle.

He was rattling the locked door handle by the time I released it. I swung open the door to find him standing in jeans and chambray shirt, with a basketball-sized egg tucked under his arm.

"My helmet!" I exclaimed, astonished less by Kit's arrival than by the fact someone here had understood that a racing helmet was valuable and retrieved it from my car. I hadn't told him that my track bag with helmet, driving shoes, and paraphernalia were locked in the Tiger's trunk. Maybe I should consider being in the market for a new guy.

"Thank you!" was all I could say.

"You're welcome." He dropped the helmet into my grasp as he sidestepped me into the anteroom. At mid-floor he turned and announced, "We got the Tiger under cover."

My mouth flapped. "Already? How?"

A corner of his lip tweaked. "Popped a pair of wheels on the front, winched it onto a trailer, and towed it up to my garage."

My shoulders dropped a notch. "How bad is it?"

"Expensive but not fatal."

"Any chance you can you fix it?"

"Yeah, but not for a while."

I twisted my mouth then walked past him to the bathroom to turn off the water before it flooded. En route, I popped into the bedroom to unload the helmet. Kit called after me, "If you're willing to wait, it'll cost a lot less than hauling it home or buying another one. I can give you a lift back if you're stuck here."

I returned to regard him through the door frame. He stood with less confidence than he had shown on his own turf. What had made him glow at me the first time? And what had he felt in the same moment, making him share my anxiety now?

I yearned for a normal, pleasant encounter with no undercurrents. Too bad his eyes were so brilliantly blue. They made distracting things happen in my blood and organs.

I collected myself and gestured toward one of two stuffed armchairs. "Have a seat. I'd offer a drink if I had anything."

He hesitated, then reached back as if to withdraw a wallet from a rear pocket. It proved to be a hip flask. My eyebrows arched. He flashed a grin, revealing a bit of satyr inside.

I sat in one of the armchairs and tucked up my feet. He sat in the other chair and held out the flask. I sipped a schnapps that set my mouth on fire. When I could speak again I said, "I can wait for a while. Turns out I have to. There's stuff going on here I can't walk away from."

"Like?"

I flapped my hand and dodged his eye. "Family stuff. Too complicated to go into. And I'm too tired to try."

But oh, how I wanted to! That vision he had thrown . . . my heart said I could trust him. My head, however, refused to trust gut feeling again. A few times over the years, my gut had been right; but not about The Big One. Now here I sat looking at Big One Number Two and I didn't dare believe.

The dilemma made me sigh. Kit shot me a look but didn't press. Instead he described every detail of damage on the Tiger and outlined my options.

Though I didn't like the facts, I did like his assumption that I would understand the technicalities. Most guys took one look at me and either skipped the information or dropped it to kindergarten level.

"I gather," I said when he finished, "that you're chief wrench around here."

He shrugged. "Close enough."

"Is it a real job? I thought New Atlantis was a co-op, with everything done by members."

Kit snorted. "None of those guys know how to fix well pumps or install solar panels."

I laughed. "So how many people do they employ?"

"Just three."

He took the flask then tipped back a long swig—sharing germs on first acquaintance. "Me, then Julia, who runs the barn. Then a loose cannon they picked up on tour—Pete's cousin, it turns out, who should be taking off now that the traveling's over."

I released my breath as he slid past the subject without any hinting looks. Surely, if he knew about me and Buck, he wouldn't lean back and cross one ankle over the other knee. Unless, of course, he didn't care.

"Do they let you live here?" I asked, thinking of Buck at The Glen.

"Yeah, rent free."

"Really! Blanche said only members or guests can stay on the compound."

He shrugged. "I gotta be here—things break when they feel like it. And Julia was already living here when Dru bought her out."

At my cocked head, he explained. "That horse farm in the valley. Julia's dad bred and trained Morabs. After he died, she kept it going. Dru lets her live there in trade for use of her riding string. His people help with the barn while she helps them hay. She keeps her own money from sales and stud fees. New Atlantis keeps its profits for itself."

A shade of contempt crept into his voice. We exchanged the flask again.

I prodded, "So . . . you were working on the farm?"

"Sorta." He shifted in the chair and lowered his gaze. "I used to fix their vehicles. Julia took me on after her old man died. Then Dru made us both offers we couldn't refuse."

"I see. So Julia must be that woman on horseback herding traffic."

"Yeah." He tensed, waiting for the question I didn't ask. I wanted to yell it—ARE YOU STILL SLEEPING WITH HER?—but restrained myself to a demure, "I guess you guys solved Dru's security problem. Hiring from the general public, or putting that farm up for sale, would open him to too much risk."

Kit cracked a smile. "He might be a dreamer but he's not stupid. Everyone here is connected. He only needs a couple on payroll because the camp followers do other stuff besides music. Dru supports them in exchange. Some, like John and Jake, are here because they're somebody's relatives. They'd be a disaster in the real world, and would cause an internal disaster if Dru kicked them out."

"Who are John and Jake?"

"The other twins."

"Oh, okay. I heard Troy has twin brothers, but I've never met them."

"Then you're in for a treat. You've had one shadowing you all night."

"Shadowing?" I lowered a brow, wondering if a New Age celebrity stalker explained my bag's reappearance. Too bad it didn't account for the demonic effects, too.

Kit's eyes twinkled. "Yeah. You've got yourself a bodyguard. So does Blanche. These guys think they're reincarnated Indians and have made up their own religion out of everything imaginable. A key feature, I hear, is identical twin goddesses destined to be their mates."

I rolled my eyes, then linked a few memories together. "Were they running around in full costume tonight?"

"Yep. I dropped you off in front of one at the show."

I nodded. We exchanged the flask again. He continued, "There's probably one outside the door, making sure I don't violate your purity."

"Too late for that!"

His gaze sharpened, seeing my body under its clothing. I resisted the urge to wriggle but granted him a moment to look. Then I said, "I suspect you've never seen me with this much skin covered."

He blinked and straightened, then accepted my challenge with a grin. "Well, you did drape yourself across a lot of motorcycles and hot rods . . ."

"Got one of the calendars in your shop?"

He flicked his eyes to the side. "Who doesn't?"

Then his gaze swung back. "And some of the bodice-rippers Julia reads have a broad who looks like you on the cover."

"Hey, you're sharp. Most people don't notice those. They never get past the poster!"

Or the swimsuit specials that ran in national magazines, or the naughty underwear catalogues that circulated the world. The poster, though, is what had sealed my reputation before my twin took up with Dru Montclair and made me tabloid fodder forever. It had also pushed my bank balance so high that I could retire at twenty-seven and paint for the rest of my life. But if I wanted more, like sportscars and horseback riding, then I had to earn it by selling my art.

"There's one of those posters down at The Glen," Kit said. "And I hear Pete's cousin has an eight-by-ten in his guitar case nobody's seen before."

My face froze. Kit noticed, even though I kept my tone casually curious. "You mean, a print?"

"I don't know, I haven't seen it."

Hopefully you never will, I prayed. Please, Buck, go away so we don't have to include you in this equation.

I dodged with, "When you see it, let me know if it's a paparazzi shot at an autocross. I want one of those."

"Me too. So what's the event you're missing tomorrow?"

I sighed. "Series championship. I'm high enough in points that all I had to do was show up and finish."

Now my rival would get the title. The two of us had battled all season, the first women in the series to run in class against the men. Only club league, but that didn't matter. Being good mattered, as did proving I wasn't a rich bimbo trolling for men, but a competent human being seeking skills and thrills on a budget like everyone else.

Kit grunted sympathetically, watching color flood my face as resentment pounded in my bloodstream. For the first time since the crash I had opportunity to feel it. So much for sleeping tonight.

Fury eased when I realized that, for the first time outside my car club, I didn't have to explain autocross and time trials to my listener.

Kit's grimy fingernails didn't come just from mechanics. He had raced, too, which info slipped out when he suggested how to rebuild the Tiger for next season. The New Atlantis walls around us disappeared as we moved into track talk. I described how, in the past year, my skills and car prep had suddenly come together to make me competitive. He recited a progression from go-karts to dirt bikes, then autocross and rallying, graduating to road-course racing. Before I could ask for specifics, he glanced at his watch and returned to the present.

"Even if I had the parts, there's not enough night left to fix the car and make your gig tomorrow. And nothing here in your class to borrow."

"I'm surprised you don't have something sassy and snorty parked behind a barn off-compound!"

He scowled and looked away. I thought I detected a flinch. "Naah, what's left is here. I gotta bunch of different stuff but nothing track-worthy right now."

I took that as a Keep Off sign. "Thanks for the thought. But I'm resigned to taking care of my business here. For that I really need a hot soak and good sleep."

He gave me a sly look then flicked his gaze away. "I ought to leave you to it."

He sat forward, coming aware of the flask that had been resting in his hand. Before closing it, he held it out to me with a smile. "Nightcap?"

I hesitated, certain that if I accepted the flask he would stay a while longer, maybe even attempt to stay for the night. If I rejected it, he would see a red light and back off. I therefore took the flask and sipped again. He settled into the chair when I returned the flask.

At my prompting, he described each race car he had built and driven, failing to mention whether he had been a winner or a back marker, whether he still competed, or what he drove today. As his tale moved closer to the moment, his eyes moved away more often. This told me, obliquely, why he was hiding out at New Atlantis. I figured I'd have to get his pants down before I'd learn what had knocked him off course.

Not tonight! Maybe after we solved the Raoul thing . . .

When he faltered to the end of his story, I let silence fall until his unease became palpable. Then I said, "Can I ask you a personal question?"

He stiffened. When I followed with, "Will you sit for me?" he dropped his hawk mask for a full second.

I restrained a laugh. "I mean model. I'm on the other side of the lens now and working on a project you're perfect for. Would you be willing to sit for a portrait?"

He composed his face back to indifference. "Er . . . with or without?"

I laughed. "Half and half." Then explained the Men at Work studies.

"I, um, I guess so. When?"

"Don't know." I stood. "Since I was planning to drive not paint this weekend, I didn't pack materials. But keep it in mind?"

"Sure." He stood up beside me. Too close. Stepping to a more comfortable distance would flash one of those red lights. I would have preferred to step closer. But exhaustion was tapping me on the shoulder, reminding me of cold bath water and psychic mysteries. The time left before I had to face those mysteries again was shrinking fast.

I crossed the anteroom, hoping he would follow. He did, though when I stopped at the outer door he didn't reach for the knob. Instead, he stopped too close again and looked at me in calculation. I struggled to return his gaze. He proved the truth of the saying "He who hesitates is lost" by acting on my hesitation: In one smooth move he pinned me to the door in a kiss.

Other than a startled squeak, I didn't resist him. Or move a muscle below the neck. He pressed close without grinding, his hands I don't know where but not on me. We just kissed, and kissed, testing and teasing, until I forgot about Buck exploring the same territory mere hours ago, and went so gooey inside I had to break away.

Kit eased back, smiling. I smiled back until recovering my voice.

"Kit, I needed that like a second appendix."

He laughed. "And I need you like a hole in the head!"

"Then let's not complicate each other's lives any further."

"Why not?"

I couldn't answer.

"In that case, see you tomorrow." He dropped a kiss on the tip of my nose.

In turning away to pull the door open, he suddenly became an archer in full draw. As if a shutter had closed across my vision: click, one Kit Douglas in chambray and denim; click, one faceless archer in green tunic and leggings. Back to denim with a final click.

All so fast, he didn't spot my attention break. I was still standing agape when he swashbuckled away. When the door latched, I pressed my hands against my temples and squeezed shut my eyes to hold back a scream. What was happening to me? Why these visions? Was I sleep-walking and dreaming? Why Buck, why Kit? Why now?

I had suffered a lot of stress today, but that had never spawned delusions! And booze on an empty stomach? I was no greenhorn—I knew the difference between tipsy, drunk, and pink elephants. Tonight I hadn't reached tipsy, and hadn't touched recreational drugs in years. Yet I was seeing black auras, glowing bushes and gargoyles, green archers. Pink elephants! What the hell was going on!

Visions, while not unheard of in human experience, normally followed starvation, concussion, or chemical upheaval. Not applicable here. Only Raoul—and Kit—appeared abnormal. If I were going crazy, wouldn't all of my perceptions shift?

Or had they done so, and I just couldn't tell?

Before bolting the door, I opened it to check the hallway. When Kit left I had spotted a block of color from the corner of my eye. Bright color that hadn't been there before, out of place in the hallway. It proved to be a stack of extra bedding, folded towels, and clothes. My gremlin again, delivering what I needed without knocking. Blanche would have signaled her presence even if she left me alone. I didn't like being stalked, but better an adoring protector than a ghoul out to get me. Thank goodness the door locked, for what that was worth!

Even so, I wedged a chair under the knob before retreating to the bathtub. The water had cooled. I released some then turned the hot tap to full open. Melted muscles offered the only hope of sleeping tonight.

6
Twilight Zone

I woke at the edge of daybreak, sweating and trembling, from dreams of burning buildings and panicked horses. I dozed again but kept waking, from a limb going numb or another bad dream. Afraid to go back to sleep but unwilling to rise and shine, I hovered between gray dawn and white noise . . .

. . . until blur expanded into clarity, as if I had fallen asleep and wakened at the same time. I saw myself lying on a couch before a TV broadcasting test patterns. Suddenly they came alive.

That you, Madeline? Dru shimmered into focus wearing a lilac robe.

I jerked. The screen went blank. I mentally replaced it with a blank canvas and tried to re-create Kit upon it. The exercise calmed me back into a drowse.

Dru returned. *I thought so. I knew you could do it! Don't worry, we're only having a dream together. Relax—*

I forced myself awake. Yes, I lay on a padded slab in the tower suite at New Atlantis. My wish for a magic carpet ride home had not come true. Which made Dru just another hiccup of my weary mind. If only I could relax, as my body begged me to, I would drift back to—

That's better, you're getting the hang of it. Welcome to alpha state, Madeline—we can talk here without anyone interfering.

Asleep or not, I wasn't talking to any spirits! The Dru-spirit laughed. *How long can you deny the evidence of your senses?*

No evidence, I thought back at the spirit. *You're a hallucination. I was wrong about Raoul—it's me that's gone bonkers. Go away! I want to go home!*

He disappeared.

My eyes popped open. Outside, almost enough light had bloomed to justify rising. I let my eyelids sag and started counting off minutes until the breakfast buffet might open. Then I would . . .

Hello!

Eek! Get out of here! Leave me alone! I've had it with you goddamn spooks!

Take it easy, Mad—I'm a good guy.

How am I to know that? Your buddy Raoul's a good guy, too, remember?

He ignored me, intent on transforming his outfit from lilac robe to cowboy-hero whites. *See? Up here you can do anything. Stick around—you'll like it.*

I clung to whatever I was feeling, afraid to shift lest I wobble and plunge like a novice tightrope walker without a net. Dru grinned and extended his arms, luring me on by flashing through different costumes. I had to laugh—at which release my mind's eye cleared and I felt curiously mobile. The distance between us sailed by. Dru gave the solid yet sparkly impression of a hologram. My dream-arm reached out to touch him but the hand passed through. Behind him, a silver twinkle looped away to a diffuse horizon. I recognized it from my readings as the cord that binds body to soul. Presumably, I was also attached to one.

We must be in the astral plane!

Something like that, he replied. *I've always called it the "glittery void."*

Visit here often, do you?

The Dru-image shrugged. *It was years before I realized not everyone comes here. At least, the alive ones.*

We soon had company: a frigid, black presence. Dru's ethereal jaw dropped and eyes bulged. When the fog-wave passed, Dru's essence diminished. However, he lasted long enough to project: *How did he get in here?*

Same way you broke into—

Dru evaporated as I fell back to Earth, reeling into daylight. I sat up as if jabbed and rubbed my eyes hard. Sparks danced until I removed my hands and blinked my vision clear. I was still in the tower suite, still alone, still trapped in weirdness. Outside, clouds glowed radioactive pink, making the birth of a new day look like the end of the world. Oblivious, a songbird fluted and trilled while sparrows and finches chittered in the shrubbery. Another day in artist's paradise.

Make that Hell.

I rolled off the cot with joints snapping and muscles groaning like rusty hinges. Then I crossed the room naked to look out at the carriage house, half expecting to see Dru staring up at me. Or was he still asleep and trying to reconnect with my mind?

"Don't worry, we're only having a dream together," I mocked. Dream, my ass! He had just performed the mental equivalent of slipping through my bedroom window and seducing me, leaving the window open for anyone inclined toward rape. Naive, dangerous fool! He had somehow learned to access a mind through the same back door used by hypnotists, without knocking first like a professional. And hypnotists used conventional techniques, like the spoken word. You could not be hypnotized against your will, they said—but apparently you could be penetrated despite it. How dare he! I should storm down there and kick him in the balls.

Unfortunately, he might still in bed with my sister. Scrap that plan. Focus, Madeline, on the clue he just gave you about how visions can happen while you're awake.

My empty stomach tried to detour me into wondering when I had last eaten. I couldn't remember. What time did they set up the buffet downstairs? Must be dawn for the farm folk—but I dared not go down, dared not leave the room, lest something out there confirm that what I'd just experienced with Dru existed outside my head. Please, let me be insane, let that dialogue be a dream. If he had truly found a way in . . .

. . . then Blanche and Dru and all those lunatics might be right!

My stomach suddenly, violently twisted and propelled its acids up my throat. I barely made it to the bathroom to retch into the toilet until I slumped shuddering on yet another marble floor. No, no, no!

They could not be right. It could not be true. If psychic phenomena were real, then . . .

. . . then that beautiful, rationally mysteriously incomprehensible reality I had always trusted was now an alien world.

My stomach lurched again but nothing came up. I crawled back to the cot and buried myself under the covers. For only an instant I wished that Kit or Buck were snuggled there with me, to stop the shivering. Then I spat out that idea, for they were the ones who had started it all. One logic said they would be the best to turn to; other logic said the worst. I couldn't risk the wrong choice. Maybe I should corner Blanche and Dru and interview them until cross-eyed, until I knew for sure. But how could I tell the difference between their fantasies and facts?

The last thing I needed was to suddenly become a believer. I needed someone unflappable who could look at all viewpoints and help me assess what was really real. Only one candidate qualified: Colin. My brother and surrogate father. Who was currently on the last day of a business trip to Chicago, hence his absence from this affair.

But danger lurked there, too: He might simply drive up here and snatch both me and Blanche back into his sphere of protection before pausing to listen. I had to keep my mouth shut and eyes open for a while before I acted.

My stomach again interrupted, this time begging for input instead of output. I disappointed it again by collapsing into deep, dreamless sleep.

I awoke to a buzzer repeating itself every few seconds. An alarm clock? No clock in the room. It must be that intercom I noticed last evening. Still half asleep, I stumbled into the anteroom and poked at buttons on the wall until the next buzz was cut short because I had opened a channel.

I leaned close to the speaker. "Um, yeah?"

"Mad?" came Blanche's voice, electronically flattened.

"I'm here. Where are you?"

"In the dining room, where you're about to miss breakfast."

My stomach almost screamed aloud. I said on its behalf: "Save me some eggs, I'll be right down."

In the pause before she responded I added, "Is Dru with you?"

"No."

"Anyone else?"

"Well, there's people around but I've got my own table."

"Give me five and I'll join you."

I really didn't want to, not yet, maybe not ever. But what else could I do?

Needing fresh clothes to face the day, I took a T-shirt and jeans from the bundle delivered last night by the gremlin. Then, after sucking in air and walking the anteroom until steady, I abandoned my chambers.

Along the upstairs hall, doors remained closed to my curiosity. Downstairs, however, rooms bustled with strangers, New Atlanteans, and half of Adam's huge family, talking and laughing. Anyone looking toward their open door watched me pass. I nodded or waved if they looked familiar, likewise as I threaded between tables in the dining room. Everyone in there watched me progress down a sideboard heaping my plate from chafing dishes, crocks, and baskets. I felt eyes from all directions until I joined Blanche at a table against the terrace doors.

She personified freshness in a turquoise sundress with Aztec border design, her face scrubbed and hair shining. I hated her in that moment, while welcoming the normalcy of blue sky and yellow sun outside the glass behind her.

The room recovered from my novelty and returned to flapping newspaper pages or peering into handheld computer screens while discussing last night's show, this morning's write-ups, and damage from the line of storms that had passed through the region.

Thus covered by background chatter and kitchen racket, I said to my twin, "Thanks for the wake-up call."

"I figured you might need one."

She poured me coffee from a brushed-steel carafe, not meeting my eye. "Did you sleep okay?" came the verbal question, covering the unspoken one: Did you sleep alone?

"I slept on and off with bad dreams, then a rude awakening."

She looked up. Her eyes reflected the creases on her brow. "More visions?"

"No. Well, I suppose it qualifies."

I burned my lip on delicious coffee. Its searing familiarity moved me to challenge her before I succumbed again to fear. I would probably get further by accepting her frame of reference than by confessing that my own had been shaken. In deference to the audience so casually ignoring us, I kept my voice hushed and expression neutral.

But not my words. "Your boyfriend dropped by on the astral plane to visit me this morning."

She didn't blink. I prodded, "Are you aware he can do that?"

Now she blinked, then smiled. "We connect there sometimes. Why do you think I fell for him?"

I didn't answer, wondering if those visions with Buck and Kit had actually been semiconscious connections in the astral plane.

Then I shook my head clear. "What matters is that Raoul can visit there, too."

Her poise wavered. "What do you mean?"

"I mean, while Dru was trying to impress me with his virtue, a black presence broke our connection. I think it's the same thing that revealed itself yesterday. Has Raoul gone home?"

Blanche considered. "He left but didn't go back to the City. He's staying somewhere around here and is due back for the cookout."

Her hand stirred her scrambled eggs. She looked down at it, and it stopped.

"I hope you understand," I continued, "that by violating my mind—in bed—he crossed a very dangerous line with both me and you."

She kept her chin down but rolled her eyes up to meet mine in a glare. "I understand more than you think, Madeline. For instance, I know his secret fantasy is to get us both in the sack. I also know you sensed that a long time ago, and it's part of why you cut me off."

After a stab of surprise, I welcomed seeing the sister I used to know. The feisty one with whom I had exchanged a childhood pledge to deemphasize our twinness and never pursue the same beaus, so that we could always be certain we were loved for ourselves.

It had worked a little too well.

"I also know," she said, "it's rude, if not downright dangerous, to enter people's minds without permission. And I don't appreciate him playing psychic footsie with you while in bed with me!"

"Maybe he wasn't. What time did he get up this morning?"

She shrugged one shoulder. "Not sure. Early. He was gone when I woke up. Went down to the studio to edit last night's video."

"Well, his visit was around dawn, so he probably transmitted from there. That is, if I didn't dream the whole thing. Would anyone have been with him?"

She pointed her chin at Troy and Adam. "Those guys are heading out now. Otherwise I think he's been alone."

Drats. I'd been hoping for something more concrete, like, she had seen him in an odd trance state, or he had been working with others then withdrawn, and I could ask them about his behavior.

Any other prospects? I scanned the dining hall, noticing no Pete and saying so to Blanche. Then I added, "Have you seen Buck yet?"

"No. But I think Dru plans to round him up before the cookout."

"That'll make his day." Perhaps make mine. Buck was the number one person I needed to talk to aside from Colin. In their absence I queried, "Anyone else had funny experiences I ought to know about?"

"None I'm aware of," Blanche said, "though Allanna's been bugging Dru for a while about danger in our midst. I figured it was Raoul, but on the normal physical level, like, he might jump me."

I shuddered. Then: "Who's Allanna again?"

"Troy's wife. You know, the Iroquois woman."

"Oh yes." I withheld comment, remembering what I had heard about this one. It figured—the only Native American here would be the group's shaman. I wondered what her people thought about that. I really wondered about Troy, with his Indian wife and faux-Indian brothers.

"By the way, Blanche, did you ask one of those twins to bring me clothes, or did he help himself from your closet?"

She smiled. "Don't worry, I sent him. And I told Kit where to find you, too."

She lifted a brow as if to say, Anything interesting happen there? Back in our teens, I would have told her everything. Now, since she had more than once referred to my car friends as "grease monkeys" and my horsey-set friends as "dykey snobs" (no doubt to retaliate for my calling New Atlanteans "tree-hugging wingnuts" and "artsy-fartsy parasites"), I no longer confided details of my social life.

She didn't get the idea, anyway. Having always attracted people she liked, she suffered no rift between personality and appearance. Likewise, athleticism came easily to her, so she only needed to practice, not train. She considered the use of horsepower to be "cheating," not grasping that it added challenge: more variables to master and higher risks to manage. Colin, who galloped horses over four-foot fences in timed trials, understood the appeal of sport-driving. As a three-piece-suit guy, he shared my need to do something lively outdoors with unpretentious buddies. Blanche got everything she needed from New Atlantis and the stage.

I therefore told her only that Kit had informed me about our twin bodyguards. She smiled again.

"They're okay, Mad. Really."

"And isn't that what Dru says about Raoul?"

She scowled.

"Anyway, Kit and I had a nice gab about cars, then he threw a vision at me on his way out the door."

I described the green archer. Blanche responded, "No wonder you didn't sleep last night!" then poured us refills. "This gets more interesting by the minute!"

"I call it scary! Wait 'til your fears start coming true!"

"It sounds more like your dreams coming true. A chance to reconcile with Buck, a new guy in the wings, your psychic powers blossoming so strongly that the doubt that's plagued you all your life—"

"All I wanted to do was win an autocross this weekend!"

My voice penetrated other people's conversations. They looked away and resumed talking when I glared at them.

Blanche and I hunched over our coffees and lowered our voices. She said, "Will horseback riding do, instead?"

"Together? Don't you have to give a media tour all day?"

"Just a few hours. And we're riding."

"What! Are you guys so anti-fossil-fuel that you can't even take guests around a huge estate on wheels?"

"No, no—some of them want to ride, and claim they can. The rest will tour in cars. We've got a couple of those hybrid thingies. You could go with that group if you want. Or else run sweep with Kit."

"Sweep?" I imagined whisking brooms across floors and driveways.

"To make sure everyone's off the grounds," a new voice said. We looked up to find a Valkyrie entering off the terrace. I recognized her at once as Julia the horsemistress. Though no taller than me, she looked it, all leg and high bust and straight posture, toned and tanned. Paprika freckles all over matched her thick hair, drawn back from her round face, which showed no weathering despite an outdoor lifestyle. If Kit wasn't sleeping with her, I'd eat my helmet.

I must have looked blank, for Julia plunked into a chair and explained. "Our walls are so spotty, and there's so much land, that anyone could stay lost until they got hungry. Who knows what's left over from last night. You know how to ride?"

Her voice was cheerful and friendly but her eyes held a cold, appraising glint. I responded levelly, "Horses, ATVs, or motorcycles?"

"Horses. We've got plenty of babysitters for the motorized troop but need more for the riders. You offer the bonus of a useful distraction."

I slid my gaze toward Blanche. "So this is an edited tour?"

"Very."

I turned back to Julia. "Yeah, I can ride."

"Good." She pushed her chair back. "We're meeting at the stable at eleven."

After a stabbing glance at me, she departed as she had come, through French doors onto the terrace. Blanche and I watched her stride out of sight, then we exchanged looks and sighed.

More breakfasters arrived before we could resume conversation. This set was bold and pulled us into their chat. I wanted to ask whether they had noticed any spooks last night, or experienced freaky visions, or had bad Raoul encounters, but a stern look from Blanche kept my mouth shut. I opened it only to insert more food, hoping that a dose of carbohydrates and protein might normalize my blood sugar. Maybe that would stop me from seeing things that shouldn't be there.

7
Power Point

At the appointed hour, Blanche and I drew up at the stable in an electric golf cart. Julia, tapping her foot and scowling, plus the impassive Allanna and her twin brothers-in-law, stood with horses in hand. Two print reporters and an independent video guy were already mounted. A worker led a pair of saddled mounts out of the stable for us. When he stepped from barn shadow into sunlight, I recognized Buck.

Sunglasses masked my blink of surprise from onlookers. Whatever look he returned got masked by the sunglasses he promptly donned. Blanche set herself to relaxing the visitors, knowing that any hint of interest in him would put her on the front page of the tabloids ("Blanche LaRue Has Secret Lover! Dru Montclair Suicidal!"). Likewise, I treated Buck as so much farm equipment to avoid a tabloid nightmare of my own ("New Atlantis Love Triangle!" "Sleazy Sister Sex Shocker!").

Buck gave Blanche a leg up, aloof and silent. In the same manner, he boosted me aboard a vigorous gray gelding, then tightened straps and adjusted stirrups. Throughout I fought back memories of riding the beach with him in California and pack tripping into the mountains. Damn Dru for choosing this as Buck's "something to do" to keep him around!

Once I was safely astride, Julia hustled us into formation. The moment everyone shifted to follow her, Buck lowered his glasses to look over them at me. I could have sworn I saw glowing bushes in his eyes. Then he pushed his glasses back into place, wiggled his eyebrows cryptically, and returned to the stable.

I pivoted my horse to join the tour group. We set out along the valley road riding two or three abreast, Blanche and I up front. We added mischief by wearing identical clothing. With our hair concealed under matching red baseball caps, our faces half hidden by sunglasses, our figures identical in "New Atlantis" T-shirts and designer jeans, we could have been clones.

That ploy got foiled by unmatched horses. Hers was a bright chestnut with white blaze and stockings, a flaxen mane and tail—close to palomino but copper, not golden. Mine was a dappled gray with black muzzle, mane, tail, and legs.

We chatted with the guests and answered or evaded questions. One by one I let the reporters pass me, so that when we turned off the road to ride single file, I eased to the rear and let Blanche manage the show. We clopped along between hay- and cornfields, sweating in the sun then dried by the breeze. The Powers twins, on mismatched pintos, casually shifted their own positions until one rode within response range of me, the other in reach of Blanche. Ahead of me, Allanna sat with her back as straight as her hair, oblivious to hovering insects. Behind me, Julia's gaze bored holes into my back.

The trail rose into the woods. At viewpoints or trail crossings, Blanche paused to talk about New Atlantis's size (a thousand acres, abutting the Green Mountain National Forest so it seemed like a trillion); previous owners (a Vermont marble baron and descendants, then a short-lived religious cult, then a bank); self-sufficient organic farming and maple sugaring (covered by popular and industry press). Then she passed the lead to Julia, who described her breeding program (Morgans + Arabians = new horse breed combining the best of both, the Morab) and how this subsidiary, along with crop production and cottage industry, shared resources and revenues with New Atlantis. The reporters nodded or asked questions, halting to scribble notes or fiddle with recorders. The cameraman raised and lowered his equipment, laughing in thanks that he rode a docile horse.

During Julia's spiel, Buck rode into view but kept behind us. My heart sped up, hoping we could cut from the herd at the next fork in the trail.

I knew from Blanche that the group would divide, which was why so many New Atlanteans rode along. I was to join her and the video guy on the promontory loop, while Julia and Allanna took the print reporters to view the hemp fields. Dru's legal cultivation of that plant for industrial use was well documented; still, he did not want anyone photographing the site, so Blanche would lead the video guy to other photo ops. My presence offered compensation. The plan, however, soon went awry.

Blanche and cameraman turned uphill as intended, with both Powers twins following. Buck then overtook me to peel off with Julia and the print reporters along a ridge.

That left Allanna barring my path until the rest moved out of sight behind the foliage. Once she had my attention, she set her horse up a third trail I had not noticed.

I reined in, at first confused, then irritated. The Indian tribe had just set me up! What for?

I pressed my heels against my horse's ribs and pursued, needing answers more than the gratification of snubbing anyone. For once I faced only a simple physical barrier. A copse of staghorn sumac, its maroon spearheads in their fuzzy state like the young antlers that had inspired its name, swung closed behind Allanna's passage. I crouched over my saddle horn and pushed through until undergrowth thinned beneath the forest canopy. There Allanna waited, still expressionless, still silent.

I matched her then followed through mixed hardwoods and evergreens, scolded by chickadees. Early autumn color shot through the trees like random flames. Yesterday's steam bath had given way to freshness. Allanna seemed content to soak it up as if I weren't there.

When we emerged in a slanted meadow, she pulled back until I rode beside her. We gazed down on the valley, across which a river sparkled on a rough diagonal traced by purple loosestrife. The spike blossoms appeared a brilliant magenta seam across a mustard and gold carpet. The green-gray-brown mountains surrounding it suggested silhouettes of abstract women lounging at ease. Above, clouds congealed into cutters sailing across an inverse blue ocean; below, a yellow slope of grass, goldenrod, and black-eyed Susans brushed our horses' bellies. Their bits jingled as they snatched and sampled. I itched for my paints.

Allanna alternately studied me or sat tall and scanned, relaxed and vacant. I imagined her extending antennae and reading energies that I couldn't perceive.

"But you can if you want to," she said, almost startling me out of the saddle. "Just open and calm your mind, and let the life force flow through your senses."

I sputtered, unable to seize any of the exclamations that swamped me. She smiled. "I'm sorry, but you broadcast at deafening pitch!"

"Broadcast! Have you been reading my vibes or something?"

She looked smug. "Ever since you arrived."

Out here, I felt no need to censor my reactions. "Since when does reading minds give you the right to skip common courtesy? Introducing yourself and saying, 'I'd like to talk to you' would work a lot better!"

I kicked my horse away from her. The gray—named Riyadh, in honor of the Arabian side of his pedigree—stepped out exuberantly. I gave in to emotion and let him run.

Allanna caught up when forest stopped us. "You can't escape your destiny. Better to face it—and learn, and grow."

I yanked Riyadh around and glared. "Do Not Give Me That Karma Crap."

"If you truly believe it meaningless, you wouldn't be here. Part of everyone's karma is free will."

"And I came here of free will, to help my sister."

Allanna shook her head and nudged her horse after Riyadh. "You were drawn here as helplessly as the tides obey the moon. You have business to finish and a destiny to fulfill. You are the one who will stop Evil."

That stopped me with a jerk. Riyadh pulled against his bit in protest. "You'd better explain that, Allanna."

"No explanation necessary. You know what I mean."

She pushed forward. I jogged after her. "How do you know I know, O Wise Shaman?"

"I have seen."

"Seen what?"

"Seen Good and Evil fighting, as dogs over a bone, for New Atlantis. You will be our champion, and vanquish Evil."

I slapped my forehead. "I have now heard everything! Get real, Allanna. You've been watching too much TV! Evil is not some guy I can run through with a spear and presto! Utopia. Even if he were, I'm not the person to do it!"

"Why not?"

"I—because I'm an artist, not a hero. My job is to observe and inspire and maybe change a soul, not the world. People might follow me around, but that's for my body, not my charisma. Besides, there's too much evil in the world to get it all. And I'm not going to kill myself trying to erase it alone!"

"You won't be alone."

"That's not what you said two seconds ago!"

"No, I said you would be our champion and vanquish Evil. The rest of us will be beside or behind you all the way."

"Just like generals sitting back and directing while the troops get slaughtered! Sorry, Allanna, I'm not that stupid."

"Neither am I."

I shot her a look. "I never said you were. Just . . . rude as hell, and . . . misguided."

"How do you know that you're not the one who's misguided?"

Oh, that old existential riddle: Am I a man dreaming he's a butterfly or a butterfly dreaming he's a man?

I snorted then resumed. "Doesn't matter. But I know enough to keep asking questions. And to analyze and reject the shit you're handing me, until you dish up some proof."

"How about the evidence of your own senses?"

Poor Riyadh got jerked up short again. Allanna had repeated the phrase Dru used in my dream. I had not quoted it to Blanche, who'd had no chance to pass it to Allanna. So either Allanna really was psychic or Dru was a blabbermouth or that line was cliché spiritualist lingo and she had just scored a lucky hit.

I drew myself up and looked down my nose. "Senses provide information that the brain processes and the mind interprets. That leaves a lot of room for error and multiple possibilities."

"Then how do you explain the vile one who haunts your visions?"

My skin goosebumped despite the sun. I had to clench my teeth to keep from shouting, How do you know about that!

Blanche had mentioned Allanna pestering Dru about evil. Perhaps this woman saw the same things I did. Now that I had a chance to learn something, I wanted to kick it away because I loathed her attitude. She and her ilk were part of why I refused to Believe.

I calmed my voice. "First of all, Allanna, my visions are none of your business. Second of all, the evidence of my own senses doesn't qualify as evidence. Ever heard of scientific inquiry? 'Extraordinary claims require extraordinary proof.' The burden of proof lies with the claimant, and all that. Any visions I might have are meaningless unless I am medically examined from stem to stern and have the same experience under identical, verifiable, and controlled conditions."

I should have left it there but added, "And whatever visions you might have don't impress me, either."

Before she could respond, I impelled Riyadh forward, letting him pick his path while I scrambled mentally. Allanna rode back a pace to let me think.

Who was correct here? What were the limits of reality?

Regardless, she had no right to thrust her credos on me. If she could indeed read my mind, she should realize I did not appreciate shock tactics! And if she felt compelled to bring some awareness to me, I retained the right to reject it. Besides, as a spiritualist—whatever her stripe—she was obliged to honor certain behavior codes if she believed the tenets. I ought to know: I had studied the full spectrum before switching my fealty to science.

Together with Blanche, I had studied Taoism, Buddhism, Hinduism, Druidism, shamanism, and Christianity. Then, under Dru's musical influence, we had explored spiritualism and the occult. This had led to meditation, yoga, past-life readings, and astrology. The Tarot and I Ching, Egyptology, channeling and healing, magic crystals, sisters of Wicca, and a taste of the black arts . . .

"And after all that," Allanna intruded, pulling alongside me, "when nothing changed inside or out, your dreams became hazier and seemed even more distant."

Her accuracy chilled me. I bit back a protest: What would you expect? My soulmate dumped me and my twin ran off with a guy who thinks he's a reincarnated Atlantean. Why shouldn't I be depressed?

Allanna finally smiled, her teeth bright against ruddy skin. "Don't looked so shocked—you're not that transparent. Simply treading a well-worn path."

I muttered an obscenity, looking away.

"After a while," she continued softly, "you quit in disgust and pursued the tangible with fierce passion, dismissing all spiritualists as kooks and occultism as bunk. With nothing mystical to believe in, you started feeling hollow. You bored yourself, stopped caring what happened, and began living through your artwork—which changed character, I'll wager, surprising you with what sprang from your fingers instead of your planned designs."

I could only wag my head. Allanna finished, "So now, when you least want and expect it, strange things start happening. Your resentment overrides your fear. You had opened a door to another world, peered in, then walked away thinking you had only to close that door and lock it to dismiss what you'd seen inside. That belief allowed you to empty your mind and relax in a way not possible when you were trying so hard."

"But why now, why here?" I hated myself for engaging, but my questions outmuscled restraint. "It makes no sense, I can't believe it!"

Riyadh jigged beneath me, sensing distress.

Allanna shrugged. "Because New Atlantis, like Stonehenge and the Great Pyramid, is situated on a power point. Everything you were born with is more powerful here."

Ah. A possible geologic explanation I could research. My blood pressure subsided.

"Thank you, Allanna. That explains a lot. But it doesn't tell me what I need to know. Like, how long have you been sensing evil here—enough to bug Dru about it?"

Allanna slung me a glance then looked forward between her horse's ears. "Since we moved here, something lurking, but only recently did it waken."

"How recently? And were you here all along or with the tour?"

"I traveled with them off and on, but it was during the Toronto to Boston leg that I realized something had changed. Then I came back here to help prepare for the finale."

"Did you notice anything then?"

"Oh yes." She slid me another loaded glance. "You arrived, and energy fields began shifting like plates in the Earth."

"So I'm the trigger?"

"No, you're the champion."

"Forget that. I can't be a champion until I know what I'm vanquishing!"

And if I'm acting out some destiny, I didn't add, then what do Buck, Kit, Raoul, and Dru have to do with it?

As we rode, the undergrowth fizzled out into a coppery pine-needled carpet. On gaining a plateau near the amphitheater, we passed between sap-dripping trunks whose branches interwove into a green, bristly ceiling. Allanna steered me onto a trail that led to a birch grove overlooking a reservoir. There she dismounted to rummage in her saddlebags, reminding me that sandwiches had been provided for the teams.

Between bovine chews of Vermont cheddar, organically grown garden-fresh lettuce and tomato plus sprouts on a home-baked, whole-grain roll, I resumed my interrogation. "So do you know who the Evil One is?"

"No, only that he dwells among us."

"Dwells? Literally—he lives here?"

"I don't know. But his presence is constant. It ebbs and flows."

"Are you sure it's a he?"

"It's a male energy, I don't know what form its flesh takes."

"What's going on when it ebbs and flows?"

"People coming together. Worse than ever when you appeared."

"So why do you believe I'm not part of the evilness?"

"Your own energy. While you're hostile, you're not evil. I can't explain it, but I can tell."

Interesting. If I could glimpse souls and Blanche could feel atmosphere and Dru could see auras, then this woman probably could sense energies. She seemed to be more consistent about it than the rest of us. She also shared Dru's habit of probing into other people's minds uninvited.

Allanna collected her wrappings with a crackle that brought the horses' heads up. They had been cropping grass a few yards away, dappled by sunbeams through the canopy.

"To shield," she said, "visualize a barricade. Hold your thoughts close, as if you're gathering a bouquet, then place them in a vase at the center of your being."

I imagined steel walls shooting up through a floor to clang into a barricade. If that didn't keep her out, then nothing would.

"Excellent! You truly are gifted. The other thing you must do is choose a place of refuge, where your spirit can hide."

That drew foreboding. I thought of the original Atlantis, long beneath the sea.

Allanna responded, "When you're alone, you must meditate. Learn to relax and regenerate, so you'll always have the power you need, on tap. You're the only one among us with natural psychic ability. Mine is cultivated from years of study and practice. And Dru—well, Dru has it, but he's like a little boy with a saber. It's fifty-fifty every time whether he'll fence brilliantly or cut off his foot!"

Allanna's stoicism finally crumbled. She peeked at me around her hair with a little smirk.

I ignored it to ask, "What about Blanche?" as we caught the horses and repacked our saddlebags.

Allanna thought for a moment. "She too carries latent power. However, her innocence, and her instinct to support Dru not overwhelm him, keep it suppressed. But she lacks the doubt that inhibits you so doesn't require counsel and discipline. As in all other things, your abilities complement each other. You must learn to rely on her, not compete."

"How can an apple compete with an orange?"

"How can two fruits not vie to be the more sweet?"

Allanna swung into the saddle with a great flap of hair. I mounted less dramatically, hampered by too-tight jeans borrowed from Blanche. If my sixth sense had awakened a day earlier, I would have packed riding togs. Damn! If only, if only . . .

"Look at it this way," Allanna summarized as we skidded down the trail to the valley. "Just as a horse or car will follow where your eyes are pointing, your mind will adopt the direction your body takes."

A statement one could interpret literally or figuratively. What I hated about mysticism was the arcane undertone it gave to facts. True, I had improved as a rider and driver once I started concentrating more on where I was going than what I was doing. But since arriving at New Atlantis, my mind and body had launched down different tracks. Would the twain ever meet again? Leaving New Atlantis didn't assure it. Running away wouldn't erase my memory, and leaving Blanche would inflame guilt. Best to stay at this funny farm and try to find sense in it. The smartest thing I could do was draw Colin into the game.

Miles to go before I could act on that intention, so I shifted to ease budding saddle sores for a long ride back.

Where was everybody, anyway? A hundred trespassers could have frolicked by and I would not have noticed. For that matter, more than a dozen guests and residents were buzzing around out there and we had not spied a one. Good thing my companion wasn't dangerous, as far as I could tell, since my Powers twin bodyguard had failed in his duty. Or performed it too well, assuming he obeyed Allanna's command over my unspoken wish. Not everyone around here was psychic—I hoped!

For now I was stuck with one, unless I belted Riyadh and galloped the remaining distance. Both mind and body were too drained to attempt it, even if I knew the trails and didn't mind ruining a horse. I let him follow his nose and closed my eyes, turning inward, reinforcing barricades. Allanna rode behind.

Upon resurfacing and opening my eyes, I observed a raven perched atop a dead tree. Definitely a raven—too big and coarse for a crow, with the raspy, metallic caw I knew from backyard bird-watching. I half expected the raven to pronounce, "Nevermore!" then to wake from a dream that I had been caught in an Edgar Allan Poe story. Allanna seemed to think we were in one: Upon seeing the bird, she pulled up beside me with a gasp.

"What's the matter?" My body hairs prickled. Riyadh rattled his nostrils and pranced.

Allanna's stare served as a pointed finger. I looked again at the raven, which returned our attention, lifting its wings to an air current and wobbling.

"C'mon, Allanna, it's—"

Allanna fell so still that I thought for a second she had died. Before I could react, she recovered with an energy surge I felt from four feet away and saw as rainbow spikes jutting from her skin. Both horses whinnied and plunged; the raven flapped away toward the mountains. Its fading squawk echoed over the landscape as Allanna crumpled from the saddle to the ground.

I yelled and jumped after her. She came to upon impact and gained her feet as I reached her side.

"Are you all right?"

Her complexion resembled muddy water. "Yes. I just—fainted, it's such a drain."

I grasped her shoulders. "What did you do? What was it?"

She looked around for our mounts—which hadn't gone far, since Julia trained her stock to ground-tie.

"A familiar. A spirit servant in an animal body. Keeping tabs on us. The Evil One must be nearby."

I looked around, seeing unchanged scenery. Allanna collected her horse. Shaking my head, I gave her a leg up into the saddle. "C'mon, Allanna, people can't mind-control animals!"

"Why not? They can mind-control humans. Haven't you heard of subliminal advertising, hypnotism, and brainwashing?"

She gathered her reins with square hands still trembling. I caught and mounted Riyadh. "Hypnotism requires a willing, cognizant subject. You can't just hypnotize creatures passing by!"

"No, but you can capture their attention indirectly then condition them. And if you're an accomplished psychic, you can project your mind anywhere you want."

She jogged away, maintaining a brisk pace until the barn came into sight, at which point we walked the sweating horses. Throughout, I contemplated Dru's astral projection and Allanna's psychic powers. Could she in fact read my thoughts, or was she an exceptionally keen observer and shrewd guesser? Much of what she had told me about myself she could have deduced or learned from others. Certainly, she wasn't reading me now; because I had "shielded" or because she had no such power?

That raven could have left on its own accord from proximity to humans, not Allanna's mental repulsion. The field I had seen around her could have been supplied by my imagination, just as Raoul's black aura could have been autosuggested. And my telepathic chat with Dru surely had been a dream brought on by suppressed desire.

I needed some objective feedback, fast.

For the last part of the ride I pondered how to contact one of those teams that investigate paranormal phenomena. Or labs that test psychics. To date, no one had produced valid results. One renowned magician held a million dollars for the first person who could perform, on demand, a bona fide psychic act. If Allanna could earn that check, then I would believe anything!

The fact it had gone so long uncollected, by thousands of candidates, convinced me that orthodox science correctly interpreted the universe. Everything I had experienced in the past twenty-four hours must fit somewhere within that realm.

I conceded to whomever—whatever—might be watching that there's more going on in the universe than I understood. No problem: I'd known that all along, just failed to comprehend the degree.

Okay. I would learn. But nothing, none of these flakes, was going to convince me that their juju-voodoo-stupid-romantic surreality had the right of it. If I had to meet them halfway, I would come at it from my own direction.

This resolution calmed my spirit and allowed me to enjoy the return route. The other riders awaited us outside the stable, watching our approach from a half mile away.

Julia stood inside the paddock that housed her stud horse, Nova, who could have passed for Pegasus minus the wings. Blanche still held her copper gelding, named Suliemann. He and Nova, juxtaposed, triggered a snap similar to Kit changing into a green archer—except that this time I saw horses rearing and screaming against a backdrop of night and flames.

The picture reverted before my gasp escaped, to Blanche handing Suliemann to Buck, and Julia splitting hay sheaves for Nova. One frame had been snipped from a mile of film, nothing more.

"We were just about to send a search party after you!" Julia greeted, showing her teeth. Buck led Suliemann into the herd paddock without glancing at me.

"I gave Madeline the grand tour," Allanna replied, cool and pleasant, as if the world were the Hudson River School painting that sunlight made it appear. Golden rays slanting through unpolluted air vivified the hills, pastures, and buildings. I would have gone home and painted the scene myself if I'd had the choice. Thanks to whatever, I was stuck amid a gaggle of curious reporters and psychic weirdos.

Upon dismounting, I led Riyadh after Buck but Julia intercepted. "Members and staff only."

"I'm perfectly happy to—" I started, but she tugged Riyadh's reins from my hand with eyes flinty and nostrils pinched. I bit hard on my lip to keep from snarling, What's your problem? I could think of several possibilities but didn't want to know.

Turning away, I pulled off my cap to release my hair. The video guy trained his lens on me. I gave him the finger. He tilted down the camera and grinned. "Now now, Miz LaRue, is that any way to treat your fans?"

I walked away before saying what I really thought and headed for the mansion, a mile back along the valley road. Nobody, even the cheerful barn dogs, tried to follow.

8
Paranormality

Golf carts passed me on the road a few minutes later. Blanche and company waved but did not slow down. I considered backtracking to the barn, barging past Julia, and demanding that Buck talk to me, but rejected the notion. Better to rest, eat, and try again when composed.

Blanche's clothes and towels strewn across her bedroom told me that she had changed personas and headed for the cookout. I followed suit after a shower, choosing a sleeveless denim tent dress from her closet. This not only suited the temperature, but showed enough skin to interest Kit, whereas Buck would grind his teeth knowing I wore nothing underneath. Raoul would have no curves to ogle, thereby reducing the chance he might decide that two Blanches were better than one. I left my hair down and added sunglasses.

A great Oriental gong crashing then reverberating over the compound announced my cue to join the crowd. The gong doubled as a fire alarm—and probably started a riot every time the fans outside were reminded that something was going on beyond the walls.

I followed other stragglers to and through the mansion's dining hall. We exited onto the terrace, via the French doors Julia had used that morning, to find at least three dozen people already gathered. The media folks had been sent home, leaving some friends, associates, and family scattered among the New Atlanteans. Kit stood at the grill flipping franks and burgers. My heart clenched then relaxed at the sight of a species from my own planet. He looked up and stared at me briefly, conveying a smile without actually moving his face.

Interesting trick, I thought, comforted, then continued my reconnaissance.

John and Jake Powers sat with Troy on the terrace wall shucking corn. A toddler climbed Troy's leg while another viewed the world from his father's backpack. A young girl helped New Atlantean ladies place bowls on picnic tables on the lawn. Everyone else spread across the grass and flagstones, some in chairs, most standing in groups, all exchanging jokes and stories or panning with video cameras. Neither Raoul nor Buck moved among them.

Dru's cornsilk hair stood out as the hub of a circle. Blanche occupied her place inside his arm. I shied from joining them but forced myself to do so since avoidance would draw attention. With ease born of a thousand photo shoots, I strolled up to their group smiling.

"Greetings!" Dru called, with an I've-got-a-secret twinkle in his eyes. "How was your ride?"

"Enlightening," I replied, holding my lips and cheeks in a smile while baring my teeth.

As he groped for a response I sent a message: *At first opportunity, I'm going to blast you with both barrels!*

The sass faded from his eyes. Blanche, catching the flash of steel in mine, inserted, "Hi, Mad, have you met everyone yet?"

She flipped a hand to remind me of the audience. I turned to the first stranger she introduced, enduring a round of "How do you dos" and "Nice to meet yous" with Brian, the carrot-topped medic who had helped Adam after the lightning strike; his bouncy wife, Alexis, who matched his hair with her own carrot mop; Adam's mother, whom I had met previously; and a bespectacled-nerd type named Gene, whom I had glimpsed last night after the washout.

Beyond him, people I already knew—Cassandra the cook, in a Hawaiian-print muumuu, and Jim Casey the stagehand, sporting a sling from last night's tumble down the tiers—paused to talk then continued in opposite directions. As they separated, I saw Julia and Buck beyond them sitting on the terrace wall.

Buck waited to catch my eye while Julia chatted with a couple I didn't recognize. I looked for a place to sidle off to and meet him but was intercepted by Mark Lester, the band's manager.

"Ah, so you're still with us!" he greeted. "Have you met everyone?"

"Only just started."

"Well, let me add a few more to your list. Drink first?"

"Please!"

I turned my back on the group, tossing out "Excuse me" for my sister's sake, and followed Mark to a folding table where he offered herbal iced teas from pitchers, fruit punch from a cut-glass bowl, or spring water in fancy bottles.

I accepted a punch, disappointed to find it unspiked—noting in peripheral vision that Buck had started edging through the body maze to position himself for an "introduction."

Mark apparently didn't feel Buck merited my attention, for he twirled me instead between other faces as if we rode a revolving horse on a slow-motion carousel.

There went Cornelius, a friendly nebbish and thriller writer I knew of by pseudonym, who worked in the kitchen between chapters. There went Rob, furry and round, who split duties between grounds and stage. Both wore the New Atlantis medallion. So did Irene and Jeff, who lived in Hill House, formerly Julia's family farm. Julia now occupied a trailer near the stables.

Irene, with her long center-parted hair and trailing black dress, could have been a blonde Morticia Addams. She managed the gardens. Her husky, bearded husband was the resident veterinarian. They formed an agrarian household with Troy, Allanna, and toddler son; the other couple with children; and the girl who had admitted me to the amphitheater: general farm assistant, Lu.

"About half our people work the farm," Mark said after sniffing hard through red nostrils and rubbing red eyes. "Damn ragweed. Anyhow, the rest of us split between maintenance and business, though everyone helps anywhere during peak needs."

"Like harvest?" I asked, to prove my attention—which in fact followed the chestnut hair and teal eyes that kept appearing between heads and shoulders.

"Or the show," a mellow voice inserted, accompanied by a lime scent. I swiveled to behold Raoul, today sporting the playboy yachtsman look in crisp white with navy and gold accents. I flinched, waiting for a lewd gesture or an assaulting vision. Nothing happened.

Mark said, "Hey Raoul, how ya doing. You met Madeline yet?" He sneezed.

Raoul ignored him. "Actually, I thought this was Blanche wearing a wig."

He smiled, showing perfect teeth framed by Mediterranean good looks. But the smile didn't crinkle the skin around his eyes, and no warmth glowed within them. His irises, so dark brown they hid his pupils, served as shutters over—instead of windows into—the soul.

I met that opaque gaze through my mirrored sunglasses, into which he projected his frozen smile. For a second I felt my dress dissolve and fingers crawl between my legs. It took all my will to resist a gasp and shudder. Like Blanche, I could accuse him of nothing yet felt threatened and defiled.

Mark, sensing bad chemistry but not sure why, stepped in. "Well, Mad, this is Raoul Lamont, our publicist. You might have seen him—"

"We've met." I frosted both men with my tone.

"In a fashion." Raoul narrowed his eyes. "I believe we bumped into each other after the concert. Quite a pleasure seeing you and Blanche together after all these years."

I'll bet, I thought. Maybe he enjoyed having two Blanches to look at, but I bet he resented the reminder that she was not unique. Not his. Not attainable. Now another obstacle stood between them: a sarcastic inversion of his goddess, who not only found him as transparent as he found her dress, but who made his loins ache. Or so I suspected; I didn't glance down to check.

"Will you be joining our community after all?" he inquired.

"Just visiting," I said airily. "Couldn't miss the grand finale!"

"It's not the end."

Raoul dropped his eyelids halfway and flattened his voice. I knew he wasn't referring to Dru's concert schedule. Mark thought he was, so prodded Raoul into his routine about New Atlantis's future. Then he turned away and blew his nose.

Raoul stepped a pace sideways and visibly forced himself to relax. Then he explained how the band had decided it could best reach its audience through electronic media, a better use of resources than touring. From here on, live performances would take place only in the amphitheater, with tickets available by subscription or lottery and the proceeds donated to humanitarian and environmental causes. New Atlantis lifestyle solutions would be the product as much as Dru's music, and go on forever as a template for others to copy and enhance for the new age.

Blah blah, I had heard it all before, even read articles Raoul had written about Dru's philanthropy and meetings with world leaders. I had watched Raoul on television describing the New Atlantis mission to take the best of old and new, mix it with global consciousness, blend with spirituality, and create a profitable, ecologically balanced community. Throughout these presentations, Raoul had been sincere and engaging. In person, he made no attempt to charm. His dark eyes stayed on my sunglasses as if he could see me through them. I wished I could perform Allanna's trick, wondering anew how—or if—she had repelled that raven. For that matter, how had Raoul directed it—if he had—and what might he be conjuring now, which I couldn't perceive?

I saw no field around him, felt no temperature change. His necklace, rings, and belt buckle—all show-off gold and onyx—bore no satanic motifs like horns or pentacles. Any tattoos were concealed by his clothing. He stood there manicured and chic, reminding me of Colin. In fact, Raoul appeared more a multimillionaire than his clients, who looked like gypsies, yuppies, movie extras, woodsmen, punks, or hippies, content in their favored era while the world moved on. Dru's music, drawn from all periods and genres, accounted for this mixture. Yet despite the free style, Raoul failed to blend in, his normal visage as jarring as the spook had been in the amphitheater.

Unaware of this impression—or faking it, he finished his pitch. "Sounds great," I lied. "I'm sure you'll all do a great job."

Raoul smirked. I turned to Mark, fluttering my lashes. "Shall we finish our rounds? I want to meet as many folks as I can while I have the chance."

The truth: Get me away from this guy!

While it always helped to know one's enemy, I couldn't risk arousing Raoul's interest. Nor could I sustain the bimbo act for long. I was streaming with sweat out of proportion to the temperature. Too bad I had stopped smoking when I retired. This would have been a perfect moment to light up and exhale into his face.

"Thanks, Raoul." Mark clapped him on the shoulder.

"Nice to meet you," I followed, waggling my fingers in a "ta-ta!"

I didn't like exposing my back to him but felt sure he would no longer try anything in public. For him, the word "occult" applied in its true meaning: hidden, secret. He had gotten overconfident and alerted a few sensitives. Henceforth he would operate under deeper cover. But toward what end, and who would believe me when he stopped doing anything I could see and report on? What did he know that the rest of us didn't, so that he could generate creepy effects?

I mentally slapped myself in the face. Some rationalist! I had leaped to the conclusion he was the culprit based solely on subjective experience. I'd never get to the bottom of things if I kept on in that vein.

Mark thwarted my attempt to keep track of Raoul by spinning me through the next contingent: a sinuous black man and a bearded bohemian, who introduced themselves as Greg, house manager, and Daniel, livestock overseer. Their earthy eccentricity calmed me. Daniel had offloaded his child to his wife, Karla, who rounded up the girl and retreated to the kitchen. They returned moments later leading a train of serving-bowl carriers, whose gaiety spurred the rest of us to cluster around tables and grill.

Buck had been reclaimed by Julia. She held him in the food line performing a hostess routine of her own. Interesting that she had latched on to him. Was she a closet psychic and knew about us, was now trying to compete with me? Or was she done with Kit as Buck was with me, leaving them two single people who liked horses and found they could work together, and maybe get something going while at it?

Kit, a car guy, would prefer his horsepower on wheels. With him employed at the grill, I couldn't read the chemistry between him and Julia. Buck seemed to find her company a safe harbor. He and I exchanged final glances, in which he rolled his eyes to convey a shrug of resignation. I replied with lifted eyebrow then turned to pursue a more profitable course.

The end of the food line would do. That let me monitor everyone and have a reason to stand around doing so. Raoul snaked through the guests without stopping long anywhere, his mouth always smiling, and his eyes always returning to Blanche. She appeared oblivious but I felt her tension from across the yard. She and Dru mingled by staying in place, letting people circulate around them. Raoul never passed within range to exchange a word.

He also held distance from me and Allanna. She regarded me with the same inscrutability she bestowed upon everyone, a sage Indian act that added her to the list of people I wanted to avoid. Our only exchange came after I had removed my sunglasses and our gazes crossed between passing people, and she held mine too long as if trying to communicate. I turned away to talk to the woman in line ahead of me, Adam's partner Leslee, who appeared to have just come from dance rehearsal. Adam, beyond her, joined our chat. People behind me hailed him over my head to ask about the DVD in progress. I kept an ear tuned, for I would likely be doing the cover art for that release.

As the line shuffled forward, the Powers twins abandoned Troy to the corn cauldron and separated, one to stand in line a few places behind me and the other to carry corn to Dru and Blanche's table. Tonight the twins provided a means to distinguish between them. Though both wore Indian brave costumes, the one heading for the table had symbols I didn't recognize tattooed on his left arm.

"That's Jake," Adam provided, following my interest. "It's a little easier to tell you and Blanche apart!"

We grinned then he turned to select from the grill options. I glanced back at the other twin, John Powers, and surprised us both by intercepting his gaze. His costume and role seemed to vanish as I recognized an aware human being. Although his eyes were as dark as Raoul's, John's contained warmth—nay, fire—and an intelligence that seemed to vibrate instead of calculate. He prevented me from seeing more by veiling his eyes with lashes a model would covet. I resumed forward position, feeling oddly safer, just as Leslee accepted her fare from the grill then joined Adam at a table. I stepped forward to face Kit.

"Soy burger or turkey dog?" he asked in a deadpan.

"You're kidding, aren't you?"

He rolled his eyes and twitched his mouth. I laughed. Back to deadpan, he leaned close. "But I've got some juicy red steaks back at the gatehouse. Some real booze and ice cream with fudge sauce, too."

"You're on! Then give me one of those turkey dogs. I'll save you a seat at our table."

He selected the most evenly browned frank and bun, dropped them onto my ceramic plate, and then, after a loaded glance I couldn't read, repeated his offer to the next customer. Still smiling, I crossed the lawn to the head table and sat opposite Blanche. She sat beside Dru, knees touching while they conversed in opposite directions. Once I had settled, she met my eyes, flicked hers toward the line where Raoul stood, then looked back at me, nonverbally asking, Anything happen?

I returned a slight nod before looking at Dru. He had followed our exchange as if it were a tennis match, smiling down at us from his reedy height. His eyes, even paler in daylight, looked into mine, through mine, to the images boiling inside my head.

"How'd your day go?" he said, playing at normal.

"Very interesting." I glared up from under my brows. "And yours?"

"Quite productive."

"Here, pass me your plate," said Troy from the end of the table. He waved tongs then plucked an ear of corn from a pyramid of same as the table's centerpiece.

I obeyed, watching salads and deviled eggs get added on the way down and back as Troy continued, "I understand you'll be staying with us a little longer than expected."

Uncertain whether anyone had briefed him, I launched into my car story while everyone began stuffing themselves. Kit arrived midstory, stepped over the bench, and squeezed in beside me, resting his thigh against mine. Our companions—Troy, wife, and toddler, plus brother Jake; Dru, Blanche, and Seth the grounds manager—interjected questions and suggestions. Kit explained what a bent control arm meant and why big exhaust systems aided both fuel economy and horsepower. Jake Powers, who had stayed silent, left the table to man the grill, while his twin took the seat he had vacated and consumed his meal.

I joined the banter at our table, or watched the twins watching everyone else, or spied on Raoul as he schmoozed with Adam and Leslee and flirted with Julia. Daniel and Karla's daughter plucked his clothes for attention. I wondered how he could deceive so many, so easily. Or did only twins and Indians read him wrong? No, Buck glowered at him from opposite Julia. Did that glower come from Julia's interest in Raoul or dislike of Raoul himself? Might Buck see strangeness in him, too?

I sought to catch Buck's eye without anyone noticing—a feat akin to juggling plates while riding a unicycle, given how many people we both had to look at and respond to in different directions while passing bowls and eating. The prospect of telepathy gained appeal.

But how? What was the right combination of relaxing and focusing that allowed psychic exchange at will? My mind could expand and wander when I was alone in my studio, or think fast and concentrate when in motion, but I could not process many variables at one time, especially when under pressure. Perhaps meltdown from this sort of stress caused my visions, exacerbated by sitting on a power point. What was that, anyway—a confluence of magnetic fields in a certain kind of rock? A combination of people in a certain environment? What kind of energy did it generate?

Enough to set off hallucinations, I answered myself, as people around me began to shimmer.

My eyes widened and jaw went slack before I could restrain them. Dru felt my surprise and cocked a brow. Blanche felt us both and looked on. I ignored them, amazed by the ghostly extra outline that had appeared around everything alive. The auras ranged in colors and intensities, depending on individual and backdrop. My blinking didn't erase them. Jeezus! What had brought this on?

I glanced around for Raoul but couldn't find him. *Hey Allanna, look up, something is happening.* She kept eating. Some psychic. I snorted and looked at Dru, who waited to catch my eye. I wondered hard and loud: *Can you see it?*

He dropped his lids halfway in a pseudo nod: *Yes.*

Lordy, he heard me! And Blanche looked perplexed, Allanna now suspicious. The remaining men seemed as oblivious as the child. Mustn't be the cookout fare, or else more people would be gawking. I collected my poise right as Kit realized I had lost it. I yearned to ask him what he saw but didn't dare.

Time, then, for a rational experiment. If I moved around, would the phenomenon follow?

After asking for directions to the nearest restroom so no one would join me, I gathered my dirty dishes and stepped over the bench. No hope of catching Buck, who was helping clean up the grill within a nimbus. He appeared, for the first time, to be enjoying himself. His aura agreed; none of the unbalanced spiking Dru had described. Nobody, in fact, appeared agitated. So if I had any second-sight companions besides Dru, they were either used to it or concealing awareness.

Earlier I had noticed people wielding vidicams. Too bad they weren't shooting now. I would like to see what the cameras captured. Unfortunately, until Dru and Blanche cleared me to discuss our affairs with the populace, I couldn't borrow a vidicam without a reason. I didn't have the wit to fabricate one now.

I headed for the house, dodging kids who had escaped their parents and cavorted on the lawn with the house dogs; weaving between groups on the terrace; following a parade through an herb garden into a scullery where we had been instructed to deposit our dishes. Before nipping inside, I spotted Raoul heading away around the south wing of the mansion. He alone emitted no aura—not even the black one I expected—which made him stand out the way a film actor looks wrong against a cartoon background. This convinced me I hadn't become fevered or taken in some drug giving me LSD effects. Were that true, everything would be distorted the same way.

The auras faded as I left people behind and entered the dining hall. I recalled a TV show I had seen about forensic science, which had described a new fingerprinting technique. Apparently human sweat generated some chemical that, when dusted by some other chemical, became visible under laser light. This allowed investigators to find fingerprints invisible to conventional methods. The sweat chemical had been likened to phosphorescence. Perhaps science hadn't discovered yet that the chemical became visible to the human eye under other conditions. If living organisms generated electrical fields—a fact well proven—then why couldn't some people perceive them? Might I be one of them? If so, why—and why now?

My bare feet slapped the dining hall's parquet floor then went silent on carpet. The corridor between dining and entry halls seemed a dank tunnel despite the residents' art, framed and lit. The original of my portrait of Dru outshone them—a perfect likeness, only the eyes in color. I had filled them with a mix of all the colors I had seen in them, and had fought long with myself not to do same with his hair. I ought to sneak back in the night and add his aura! Too bad my art supplies lay out of reach at home.

In the water closet just off the entry hall, I peered at myself in the mirror. Same old face looked back at me, with no halo in view. Hmm. Was it possible to see one's own aura? I stalked around the first floor until I found a solarium, in which no plants were glowing. Okay, either my mental switch had closed or the house shielded power or the energy came from people interacting and I had moved too far from the source. Damn it, I needed help with this!

Halfway back to the dining room I found Mark's office. It contained a desk and filing cabinets, two chairs, four computers, and a land-line phone. I lifted the handset, punched three nines, and was rewarded with a dial tone. Tapped in my number. Colin answered on the second ring.

"Oh Colin, am I glad to hear your voice!"

"Er, hi—this Mad or Blanche?"

"Madeline."

"You still at the race? I thought you'd be home by now."

"So did I. But I'm not going anywhere for a while."

He growled. "What did you do, blow the engine?"

"No, I stuffed the car in a drainage ditch on the fire road to New Atlantis."

Silence. Then he sucked air through his teeth. "I don't want to know, do I."

"No, especially when you hear the whole thing!"

"Do I get to hear it now?"

"Not until I can arrange a private line and location."

"Uh-oh. Is everything okay with Blanche? I saw the papers and checked the website, looks like you had a mess last night but no catastrophe."

"Correct. But we've got a mysterious subplot, potentially dangerous, and need your brain. Can you get up here any time soon?"

Pause, while he rustled through his datebook. "Couple of days, or tonight if it's a true emergency." I could see the scowl that surely matched his tone.

"I'd prefer tonight but can't claim it's urgent. The situation has been developing for a while and has picked up steam, but there's nothing to suggest a looming crisis." I hoped I hadn't just uttered famous last words!

He sniffed, then sighed. "What about your car?"

"I think I can get it fixed here, or arrange something if not, and get a ride home on demand if I don't go with you. But I'm probably here for a while." I rattled off a list of clothes, toiletries, books, favorite pictures, and art supplies for him to bring from the cottage. I lived there as caretaker while he worked in New York City. It was big enough that we could share it on weekends without strife.

"Jeez, I'll need a truck! Didn't you swear you'd never go back there?"

"You'll understand when you hear the whole story. Shall I call you tonight?"

"If security is an issue, hold on 'til I get there."

"In that case, get your investigator pal to scare up some background on Raoul Lamont and bring it with you."

"Lamont? He's Dru's publicist!"

"Well, he's also a problem. So is Buck Williams. If your guy can find anything about where he's been for the past three years, that might help."

"Buck? Your Buck?"

"Believe it or not, he's here."

"Hoo-boy. The plot thickens."

"Treacle and molasses. Sure you can't make it tomorrow?"

"I'll do what I can."

After signing off, I returned to the corridor, feeling better. A telephone in my hand, my brother's familiar voice, his grounding in reality . . . I almost felt silly, as if I'd overreacted to some ordinary stress. Perhaps my recent experiences were just a convergence of extremes, allowing me to see, through what seemed like extrasensory perception, what had always been there. A unique combination of too much emotion, too strange an environment, too upset a body chemistry was allowing me to perceive through new eyes, the same way some Native Americans used pain and fasting to open their minds to vision and insight.

I ought to ask Allanna about her tribal customs. Or John Powers, who emerged from another doorway to trail me back outside. Too bad he couldn't—or didn't—speak; he probably knew about such things. I didn't have the gumption left to initiate conversation before we were back amid people. He drifted to the edge of sight range as Kit met me on the terrace with a questioning look behind his smile.

I said, "Did I miss dessert?" noting that he and everyone else had stopped glowing. Why? Damn it, what triggered this! Why wouldn't anything stand still so I could study it?

"Fruit and yogurt over there," Kit said, gesturing at a table and cooler near the French doors. "And my stash at the gatehouse. Want anything?"

Yeah. You! The thought leaped out before I could repress it, and his return gaze signaled receipt of the message. Oh no, was he psychic, too?

"Everything you were born with is more powerful here," Allanna had said. Did the Earth pulse sometimes, or concentrate pockets of energy, boosting us all into psychics—or lunatics—every now and then?

I averted my gaze and said, "No thanks, maybe later. I'd like to just stroll around for a while."

He offered his arm: tough skin over cable, surprisingly warm. His strength radiated along with the heat, enveloping me in security. Maybe there really was some god watching out for me, providing this stabilizing gift while I stumbled after the truth.

We stepped down the backyard, which resembled a giant's staircase. Terrace dropped to groomed turf set up for croquet, which dropped to wildflower meadow extending to a cliff that fell away to the plain. Each tier was broader and deeper than the one above it, sweeping away from the house like ripples from a shoreline. All looked out on the mountains, now purple beneath salmon-streaked clouds.

We followed marble steps then a slate path to the cliff edge. The valley we overlooked seemed a cauldron of liquid gold. Within it floated Hill House—a farmstead with porch around three sides and outbuildings telescoping off the rear. Its residents owned no electronics or luxury appliances. Atop the house, solar collectors reflected sunset, and atop a tower behind the wood piles, a wind generator idled in the evening calm. I couldn't see any battery bank but trusted they had one, since Vermont weather spawned more cloudy days than sunny ones and wind was unreliable in a valley. On one of those distant four-thousand-foot peaks, however, they could probably generate enough power to sell.

Horses, sheep, goats, and fowl browsed on the scrubby slopes and in the pastures. Had I been commissioned to paint a rural advertisement, I would have created a similar scene. But turning away from it screwed the elements into a different picture. Something in the switch from far to near focus—maybe my exhaustion or flayed emotions—shattered images into a kaleidoscope and flung my feet into the air.

Suddenly I was lost in a reverse dream of falling. Instead of waking at the downward jerk of my leg, I spiraled out of awakeness into descending cartwheels, with screams echoing down the funnel with me.

Kit's outcry penetrated from some place distant. It caused a regret so fierce that I kicked free of the vortex and jerked back inside my skin. I came to in the grass with my dress hitched and twisted. Kit crouched beside me with an ashen face.

"Are you all right?" He pressed fingers against pulse points.

I blinked back dizziness then sat up. John Powers stood ready to grab or gallop.

"Get Brian!" Kit snapped at him.

"No!" I braced on an arm while waving the opposite hand. "No, I'm—fine, really. Don't bring any more—I must've just—tripped on the wall." I attempted a smile. "After all, the view is engrossing!"

Kit scoffed. "Don't bullshit me, Madeline!"

His harshness gave the same jolt his terror had. How interesting, I thought, almost understanding. Something in adrenaline could be stronger than the quirk in my mind.

The twin unwound but continued watching. "Then get water or brandy," Kit amended. As John obeyed, Kit helped me sit on the retaining wall and propped me against him. "Sure you're okay? Yeah, here comes some color. Jeezus, Mad, you're gonna kill me. It's even spookier when you know it happens to Dru!"

I stiffened. "Same thing?"

"Three times I know of, in the past couple weeks." He shook his head. "He calls it vertigo, Brian says burnout, Brian's twitty wife thinks epilepsy, Allanna calls him possessed. All I know is he keels over mid-sentence after turning white as a sheet."

I barely heard him, distracted by the yelling inside my head: Oh god! Why didn't they tell me? Oh no—how complicated is this going to get?

"So . . . are you epileptic or something?"

"No, just exhausted and dehydrated. But—"

Approaching footsteps interrupted. Kit and I looked up to face Adam and Dru. They unconsciously formed a fashion statement: phantasmic Dru, tall and stringy, in white T-shirt and drawstring pants; swarthy Adam, in a black, sleeveless jumpsuit that accentuated his chunky build, dense chest fur through half-zipped front, and chocolate eyes and hair. Both emitted spectral glows.

Dru spoke. "What's happening." A demand, not a question.

"You bastard, you already know!"

"No, I don't," he said quietly, squatting to my level.

"And I sure as hell don't!" Adam flung up his hands.

"What did you see?" Dru persisted.

"Nothing, this time . . . at least, nothing clear."

"Then what happened just before?"

"Nothing." I pushed to my feet. Kit withheld assistance. "I was enjoying a few totally normal moments for a change! What were you doing?"

Dru stood opposite me. "Exactly the same."

"Then where's Raoul?"

The three men looking on flinched in surprise while Dru stared me down, trying to extract what I might be hiding. I stared at his aura, marveling at how easy it was to accept such things once over the shock.

Dru, from within a steady flicker, answered, "I don't know," then turned to Adam. "Find out."

He turned back to me. "I'd say it's time for another confab." He glanced at Kit. "You too."

"Wouldn't miss it," Kit said, his own aura a steady gas-burner blue. He slipped an arm across my back and escorted me up the tiers after Dru.

9
Brain Storms

Blanche met us at the middle tier, moving calmly for the audience's benefit but her eyes wide and face pale. She wore a white halter dress enhanced by a rainbow aura.

"What's going on?" Her gaze bounced between me and Dru.

Dru slipped his arm around her and reversed her in one move. "Things are percolating. We need to compare notes and get up to date."

She nodded and fell into step.

We passed through clumps of people, who moved apart. Every face followed us but no one voiced their curiosity. Buck allowed me to catch his eye then turned away, as if saying, Don't pull me into this!

Don't worry, I sent back to him. *But you damn well better talk to me later!* That is, if I could catch him before Dru did.

Just before entering the dining hall from the terrace, we found Allanna hovering in our path. She responded to Dru's chin dip with a nod and joined our procession through the dining hall, out the other side through a courtyard, then on to the carriage house. No one spoke during the trip.

Once in the carriage house's living room, Dru deposited Blanche on one slab of a huge sectional sofa and aimed for the liquor cabinet. Another illusion shattered, I thought. Kit kept an arm or a leg in contact with me as we gathered drinks and arranged ourselves on the sofa, Dru and Blanche on one side, us on the other, and Allanna at the base of the leopard-patterned U.

Allanna, declining a brandy, repeated the favorite question. "What happened?"

Dru sat beside Blanche, sliding his left arm around her and resting his right, balancing a brandy snifter in hand, on the arm of the sofa. "You tell me. What occurred on your ride today?"

After a pause, Allanna recited our dialogue almost verbatim. I cringed at having a confrontation revealed publicly, even to people I would have told anyway. But I would have told them my way, after thinking about it for a while.

I stopped pondering hows and whys and started rehearsing speeches about arrogance and manipulation. The brandy Dru had handed me had disappeared from my glass.

Allanna was quoting her closing remark—"And if you're an accomplished psychic, you can project your mind anywhere you want"—when the downstairs door thumped, followed by ascending footsteps. Seconds later Buck entered the room, flanked by John and Jake. They steered him toward Dru, who welcomed them with facial expression but didn't rise.

Buck scanned the room. His eyes hesitated on me, took in Kit sitting beside me with arm behind my waist, then swung back to Dru. "What's up," he said flatly.

"Thanks, guys," Dru said to the twins, lifting the hand that held his snifter. The gesture looked like a toast but actually meant, Goodbye. John and Jake retreated.

Dru turned to Buck and said, "This is why I asked you this morning to stick around. I'm hoping you can help us clear up a mystery."

Buck cocked an eyebrow. His hands were curled into fists. "Like what?"

"Well . . ." Dru pulled his arm from around Blanche and cupped his snifter in both hands between his thighs. He gazed into it before raising his head. "Since about the time you joined us, we've had some strange happenings. I'd like to know if you personally have observed or experienced anything weird."

Buck expulsed laughter. "Everything has been weird! Can you be more specific?"

I stifled a snort. Dru either didn't hear or ignored it.

"Okay. Two categories. Anything that might be interpreted as supernatural, or any encounter with Raoul Lamont."

Buck glanced at me despite, I suspected, all efforts not to. He needed to know if I had mentioned the glowing field in the stone circle. I couldn't cue him without everyone noticing so kept my face blank and hoped he would make the right guess. *No, no,* I sent to him silently. *I didn't tell them. I don't want to reveal that. Please play dumb!*

He answered, "Lamont, huh? No, I've never spoken to him, though I get the impression he's a slimeball. And though there's been plenty of stuff I don't understand, or find surreal maybe, I can't call anything that's happened 'supernatural.'"

He paused as Dru nodded and looked at me. Then Buck prompted, "What do you call supernatural?"

Dru shrugged. "Standard stuff. Visions. Precognition. Spooky people. Events defying physical laws." He paused then baited, "Extraordinary coincidences."

Buck failed to bite, probably because he felt that meeting me here was no coincidence.

"Then what about him?" Dru pointed at Kit. "Do you two know each other?"

"Just to show him around," Kit answered after a pause. He and Buck eyed each other. I felt sorry for them, being put on the spot. So far, both were holding up, but their complexions had darkened and bodies had stiffened.

"How about you?" Dru said to Kit. "Anything supernatural, or any contact with Raoul?"

"Why?" Kit returned.

"Because," Dru answered in a matching steely tone, "there's something psychic going on with Madeline, and everyone involved except me feels it centers on Raoul. And the trigger events seem to come from nonmembers. As well, Madeline reported optical effects when she met you. Did you experience anything comparable at the same time?"

The tendons in Kit's neck and jaw flexed. "Maybe."

The rest of us interpreted that as "Yes."

I shivered, only then realizing I'd been shaking since we sat down.

Dru let Kit's answer pass. "You two need to talk. Madeline, bring him up to speed when we're done. Buck, I'd like you to stay on a while longer—make yourself useful wherever you fit, we'll discuss the terms later—make it your job to buddy up with Raoul any time he's around. We're expecting him in and out over the next week—he might still be here, I'm not sure. But as the new guy you're best positioned to engage him. Ask him for more info on what New Atlantis is all about; he knows the drill, I'd like to know whether he's added variations. And try to get him guy-talking about women, particularly Madeline and Blanche. Don't let on that you went to school with them. And for god's sake don't go near the press!"

"And watch it with Julia," Kit warned.

Buck stared at him. Kit stared back. I wondered what testosterone felt and smelled like, for something suddenly filled the air.

Dru interrupted, "That's it for now. If anything happens, I want to know immediately. Contact Mark if you can't find me."

Unspoken was, You can go now.

Buck remained. "And if I refuse to spy for you?"

Dru dropped his lids halfway. "Then you're welcome to stay as long as you need to, but I doubt you'll ever find a comfortable niche."

Buck's eyes veiled and face reddened. He about-faced and stomped down the stairs, letting the door close hard behind him.

The rest of us sat in silence. I studied my hands, noticing a paint stain I had failed to scrub off before leaving the cottage. Only a day ago. I could have been collecting a trophy by now if I had driven east instead of north.

"So anyway," Dru continued, leaning back and re-encircling Blanche with his arm while tossing back his brandy, "let's hear the rest of the story. Madeline, does Allanna's version of this afternoon's events agree with yours?"

"Close enough." I took a deep breath and added, "But I've got to say I object to both of your tactics. Raoul might be doing something to catalyze effects in me, but so far only you two have deliberately violated my mental privacy. Keep it up and I'll not only stop cooperating but I'll have a word with certain reporters on my way out the door!"

Blanche's eyes widened. Dru held his face still. Allanna spoke up, "It was necessary. You needed to be aware of your vulnerability."

"Well, thanks but no thanks. You made your point. Have you been able to read me since we got back?"

"No, you shut me out in the glade."

"Let's keep it that way." I glared at each of them for a count of three, then relaxed my eyelids and softened my tone. "To answer your question, Dru, yes, Allanna reported accurately. But that's not the end of it." I went on to describe the shutter-snap vision at the barn, auras at the cookout, and my vertigo on the escarpment. As I spoke, Kit eased his arm and thigh away from me, while Blanche and Allanna watched unblinking and Dru paled.

"That's the one I get," he broke in. "The fire and the horses—when I'm near the stable or sometimes in the mansion. And I get the same whirling blackouts full of screaming. Oh god."

"Joint visions!" Blanche whispered.

Oh god, indeed, I thought. To delay factoring in that complication, I asked Dru, "How long ago did yours start?"

He shrugged. "Not long before the tour started."

I turned to Allanna. "And you say you've sensed an evil presence all along."

She nodded.

"So where's the common denominator?" I asked the room in general. "If the problem really is Raoul, what caused him to, um, accelerate?"

Blanche, Dru, and Allanna looked at each other.

"How about frustration," Kit offered. All eyes switched to him. "I mean, if whatever bug up his ass has been bothering him for a long time, it could just build and build and then explode. That's what all pressure does unless it's vented."

Dru pursed his lips and nodded. I expounded. "If lust for Blanche is his problem, and she's forever indifferent to him and hanging on Dru, and Dru treats him like a servant and now doesn't really need him any more, then I come along and point the finger at him, well, yeah, that could build up some pressure! But why satanic images? Where did that come from?"

"Opposite of what you guys are into," Kit said. "Atlantis and peace and love and karma and tree hugging, you don't think about the dark side. Plenty of people like the scary stuff better."

"But if Raoul were into dark power, why would he work for me?"

Kit shrugged. "Infiltration. Power for its own sake. Being your front man gives him a lot."

"And . . ." Blanche eased in. "Power is what satanists want. If you judge by our sales and media and crowds, we've got the power to influence a lot of people. So what if we were promoting evil? Raoul's job is to publicize everything we're doing and motivate the world to imitate us. If he's trying to twist the message around without our knowing, maybe his intentions are leaking out subconsciously and our sensitives are picking them up. That could account for some of the imagery."

I looked at her with a slow and thoughtful nod.

Dru shook his head. "He can't control our message without taking over somehow. That would backfire."

"Not if he did it subtly, by corrupting you." Blanche twisted her mouth at the thought. "You're the one who can't sense him, right? If he dethroned or harmed you, the fans and the press would lynch him. But if he turned you into a puppet, and gained my interest, and gradually redirected our purpose . . ."

Dru shook his head again. "Still wouldn't work. People aren't stupid —they'd turn away."

"Hitler did it," Allanna remarked.

"And think of how much subliminal stuff you could put into the videos!" I added, knowing how much mystical propaganda was already there.

Dru continued shaking his head but stopped protesting.

Allanna, still sitting with hands folded on her knees, said, "What bothers me is the satanic element. I've never heard of a serious witch—white or black—operating without a coven. So if he's a black witch, he's a rogue and possibly more dangerous than we can imagine. Or else there's a conspiracy among many that we've completely missed."

"Or this is the first clue, and we're lucky to spot it now," Blanche countered.

"Assuming," Kit sneered, "you consider hallucinations evidence."

We stared at him. He stood and placed his empty snifter on a side table. "Look, the whole thing makes no sense." He addressed Blanche. "If you're the one he wants, and you're Mad's identical twin, why does she get reactions and you don't? Or if Dru's the target of Raoul's lust for power, and you're so close to him and so sensitive, how come he gets the woozies and visions and you don't, and he still won't believe your interpretation? Has Raoul ever made a pass at you? Does anything happen to you at all or do you just float around in a bubble?"

Blanche sipped her brandy for a moment before replying. "All I feel is unease. Raoul makes me feel naked and in danger. When Dru gets his spells, I feel suddenly disturbed. When Madeline gets hers, all I feel is a brief blank, as if she'd been standing behind me and I realized she'd moved away. But that happens any time her mood changes abruptly. When she's stable, I sense her like a subliminal hum."

"I hear her sometimes like she's yelling at me through a megaphone!" Dru said, laughing. "Blanche comes through quietly and steadily, like a whisper beneath surrounding noise."

My companions looked at me. I felt their curiosity, fear, or sympathy in overlapping waves.

Kit stated, "Well, I don't see or feel any of this shit so I'm having a hard time buying it. But I know enough about people to agree this Raoul guy is scum and have always wondered why you hired him. Plenty of other people can do his job. What's he got on you, Montclair?"

"Nothing. We've had a straight business relationship all along. He's been with me since the beginning. We've never been close but always friendly. He knows just what tidbits to drop into whose ears and has played a key role in my success. But he's always been happy with growing paychecks and the perks of fame."

"Or else he's a good long-term planner," I injected, remembering certain terrorist attacks.

Kit crossed the room to smack the intercom panel alive and call the gatehouse. "Hey Gene, anyone come or gone in the last half hour?"

Adam answered, "Just Lamont, in a hurry, a while ago. We just missed him."

"Thanks." Kit turned to look at us. "Was he supposed to stay through the cookout and do anything specific?"

Dru looked shaken. "Not really. Just be here to help anyone left who might be taking home stories, and to stay on top of things enough to write the next batch of releases."

"You might want to talk to the people he's been schmoozing, and intercept those releases." Kit headed for the staircase. "Maybe you've got a problem and maybe you don't. But even if everything in your heads is real, you don't have a real problem until it shows up in the real world. If things are as bad as you say, then it probably has. 'As above, so below,' right?"

On that quip, after a final look at me, he trotted down the stairs and left the group wondering. I just felt bereft and cold.

Ever since he had detached from me on the couch, I'd understood better why so many men came on to me. Meeting one's ideal reversed an internal switch bank: hormones on, intellect off; predatory wiles on, dignity off. With Kit around, I struggled for thoughts and sentences and found everything else boring. I wanted only to be with him. When he walked out, I wanted to follow, to hell with everything else. More, I wanted him to accept my hallucinations regardless of what they portended. My heart knew I wasn't crazy even if my mind still doubted.

Someone was talking to me but I ignored them. Persuading Kit that I was as beautiful inside as outside swelled into an obsession. Remembering just in time to excuse myself politely, I got up without looking at anyone and went outside to find him.

10
Aftershocks

Dusk had fallen, as had the vehicle population in the driveway circle. Lights filled intermittent windows in the mansion. People traversed the grounds in different directions. Nobody was the right size and shape for Kit.

While crossing to the main house, I half expected a Powers twin to materialize and guard me. Not that I needed protection with Raoul off the compound. I did need a sweater, though. Clear sky, a Parrish blue pricked with stars, had released so much heat that the evening felt like October. Fourteen hundred feet of altitude didn't help.

Instead of detouring upstairs for more clothing, I ignored my goosebumps and continued through the house and out back. The dining room and scullery had been closed against mosquitoes. No one lingered on the terrace. In the yard, all tables had been cleared and lights reduced to Japanese lanterns and citronella torches. The barbecue crowd had shrunk to a dozen sitting on blankets around a fire pit on the lower lawn. I spotted Kit silhouetted against them standing with chin on chest, hands in pockets. I headed down to join him, unsure of what to say.

Guitar strumming and sweet harmonies identified the folk and bluegrass contingent, led by Buck on a six-string. The scene hurtled me back through time to a beach party in California, where a teenage Buck had sat in firelight creating minor chords with strings and fingers and entrancing the audience with his perfect pitch. Tonight, as before, another female sat beside him, her knees drawn up with arms locked around them. That night he had left her alone in the sand.

This night he kept his gaze down and stayed beside Julia. I probably could have relived history by joining the circle and seducing the singer away from his groupie and guitar. Instead I stood and wondered, Had this drama been staged to convince me it's over? Were the powers-that-be trying to tell me, Hey Madeline, get it straight girl, your soulmate ain't Buck Williams but that tawny short guy waiting for you over there?

Maybe that's what the visions with Buck and Kit had meant: cosmic neon signs saying, Go this way and learn. Now go that way and learn more. Could Kit help me learn what I needed to know?

He caught my approach and glanced up at me. I halted. When, after a hesitation, he sauntered out of the firelight to meet me on the grass, I wanted to weep in relief.

He stopped out of reach. "Hey."

"Hi."

"Conference over, or do they want me back?"

"Done for now."

"Good. How about we spread a couple sleeping bags and lie under the stars tonight?"

My breath hitched. If his earlier comment to Buck hadn't answered my question about Julia, this offer did. Now I had to decide what to do about it.

A pinprick on my arm helped me delay a little. "Nice idea except for these," I said, slapping my arm.

When he took too long to respond, I tilted my head to look up at the stars. Their vast numbers and clarity surprised a breathy "Wow!" out of me.

"It's even better in winter."

"Doubt I'll be here to see."

"How long are you gonna stay?"

"Undetermined."

We gazed at the cosmos, wondering how to proceed. I decided that bluntness would tell me sooner rather than later whether there was anyplace we could go together.

Still looking upward, I echoed, "As above, so below . . ." then leveled my head and said to his shadow, "You shocked me when you said that back there. I didn't take you for a spiritualist!"

He had moved closer while my chin was lifted. "I've been living here long enough to pick up their slogans. You worried I'm one of them?"

"No. I'm worried about my judgmental capabilities. They seem to have deserted me!"

"Yeah, I'd be worried if I started seeing things you've been. What does worry me is you didn't deny anything."

I sighed. "Can't deny the truth."

"Then tell me this: Did you hit your head when you stuffed the Tiger?"

I ran a quick mental tally. "It's all a blur . . . but I'm sure I didn't bonk my head. The top was down, and if I hit the windshield frame I'd have a shiner by now. All I've got is a sore wrist and belt bruises. And a stiff neck. And saddle sores from today's ride."

"Then there must be some other reason why you're hallucinating. Since you look healthy, and no gossip says you're a flake, I started wondering about that 'as above, so below' thing."

"What could light-years and red giants and black holes have to do with visions?"

"Don't know. Are you seeing any auras now?"

"No, thankfully. In fact, I can barely see you right in front of me."

He closed the gap between us and rested his hands on my hips. "This better?"

Some starlight or firelight glanced off his smile. I returned it. "Yes."

He added a light kiss then turned before I could react and slid an arm behind my back, steering me toward the house. By keeping in its shadow, we could observe the folk singers while remaining invisible to them.

"What it boils down to," I said quietly, encouraged by his warmth, "is either I've gone crackers or something very twisted is going on here."

"Just here?"

"Maybe it's happening outside, but for me it started the minute you let me in the gate."

"Hmm. Do I get to hear about those 'optical effects' you got from me?"

"Maybe."

"And maybe it's got nothing to do with me. Or New Atlantis. You sure those two deer were really there?"

I choked at the thought.

He laughed and squeezed me. "Don't worry, I believe you. I'm just wondering why you plus New Atlantis equals supernatural. I mean, super is a word you add to natural, like para gets stuck in front of normal. Neither means unreal."

"Like extra. Sensory," I returned.

"Meta. Physics. They all connect. You ever seen a Möbius strip?"

I nodded, visualizing a flat ribbon twisted once and its ends linked together, so that a finger tracing its surface would find one continuous face instead of two sides. A mathematical model of infinity.

"Well, somewhere on that thing, there's a transition point between real and surreal. And it probably shifts," he said. "For some reason you're sitting on it."

"Lucky me."

"Gotta admit, it's interesting."

"I might think so if it wasn't so damn scary!"

He led me onward by the hand. "I'd help you if I could. But if I can't see anything that ain't in front of my eyes, and you can't see the otherworld stuff coming, then . . ."

"A bodyguard helps," I said, playing with his fingers. He played back.

"You already got one in John."

"He better not be lurking in the underbrush again!"

"He knows not to when I'm around."

We stopped, out of sight from the world, behind the north wing which housed the ballroom. Kit turned to face me and pulled me in.

"So since we can't do anything about the supernatural tonight, wanna have a super time doing something natural?"

I laughed. "I'd love to. There's just one problem."

"Oh?" He kissed me briefly and gently. I had to struggle not to react.

"Contrary to popular opinion," I said against his lips, "I don't sleep with someone I've known less than a day."

"Who's talking about sleeping?"

"You know what I mean."

"I do. And I also know you're not that kind of girl."

"So why are you trying to corrupt my principles?"

"'Cause you already proved them by shoving me out the door last night."

I laughed again. "You're a cocky fellow!"

He pressed close to prove it, teasing, "Getting optical effects yet?"

"No, but if you keep that up, there might be fireworks."

His hands had sneaked to where they didn't belong without permission. I let him explore for a moment, to torture him with suspense, to make up my mind: Was I a blind fool being seduced by the devil into his den, or had I just been handed a gift I would regret not unwrapping?

A bit of wisdom floated into memory. People on their deathbeds, it was said, always rued what they hadn't done, not what they did. So I stopped seesawing and ventured a nibble.

Kit seemed to swell and focus simultaneously. His hands, with my own still attached unresisting, gathered up my dress until they found skin underneath. My knees dissolved. I locked them to keep from crumpling. Suddenly, as happened with Buck in the marble circle, a swirl of images and scents and tastes of the same, different man passed through my mind like a brief dust devil. Only this time the moment with Buck had become history. Now the gatekeeper occupied present tense.

The mattress we rolled across in the vision, however, had yet to materialize. Needing to know for sure if I had experienced a premonition—not to mention needing this man's strength like I needed air—I wriggled my lips free to offer, "Your place or mine?"

"How about right here?" He eased me down onto humus the at lawn's edge, in a deep pool of darkness beneath a tree.

Though I melted down with him, my mind still resisted. Buck sang not a hundred feet away; Buck, with whom I'd necked in the circle just twenty-four hours earlier; Buck, with whom I always fell into a white light when he pulled me to him, my body savoring the *pas de deux* that followed while heart and soul giddily reunited with their equal opposites, forming one. When we separated, it always felt as if an ice blade had cut some umbilical cord that kept me alive.

I'd not wanted anyone else since he left, although I had forced myself to experiment with guys I liked to make sure I hadn't gone frigid. But those exercises, however pleasant, had left me hollow. All the more bewildering, then, that when just passing by, Kit ruffled me into static like cat fur brushed backward; and now, skin to skin, he ramped up my voltage until I feared we might fuse.

Yet he permitted no fusion, no white light; instead, kept me focused on him by concentrating on me, to banish the memories and mysteries that got in our way. He drove his courage into me and sucked out my fear in cycles, luring me to stay each time I panicked and tried to back out. At last our conflicting urgencies matched tempo and I gave in to trusting him. The fireworks we had joked about overwhelmed us 'til we nearly suffocated trying to not cry out, muffling ourselves in each other's necks. I flashed on an image of what it meant to be an equal partner. Then sank back into thrumming limpness, half wanting to laugh and half wanting to cry.

Afterward, we lay naked and panting atop my crumpled dress, listening to the crickets and people singing around us. The song had changed and Buck's voice no longer led, making me wonder how long we'd been oblivious and whether he had moved away, somehow knowing what went on out there in the shrubbery. What would happen if he found us entwined with twigs in our hair and limbs catching glints of firelight and starlight between the leaves?

Who cared? I was surprised to find I didn't. The kisses creeping up my throat were far more compelling. They found my mouth and stayed there for a while, until Kit eased away and sighed, "Thank you."

Delighted anew, I whispered, "My pleasure."

After a pause, he asked, "You okay?"

"Yes, save for the acorn or whatever I'm lying on."

"Oh jeez, sorry!" He shifted his weight to the side. I drew a full breath and confessed, before I could chicken out: "If you'd been in the amphitheater last night when that lightning bolt hit the tree, you'd know how I feel right now."

He laughed and rolled me to pluck the nut adhered to my back. "I don't see any scorch marks."

"Just the environmentally correct version of rug burn."

We giggled then embraced side by side, until a mosquito whined and stabbed my exposed buttock. I squawked and slapped, which drew another laugh. "Guess it's time to go in." He rose to one elbow. "So, your place or mine?"

"All I've got is that cot in the tower."

"I've got a double in the gatehouse. Walk or ride?"

"We've got to walk anyway to get a vehicle, so why not walk the whole way?" I didn't mention what a treat it was to move around outdoors at night without worry. He took the privilege for granted.

We retrieved his jeans from a branch then helped each other reassemble. After pausing to kiss and fondle for a moment, he led me around the mansion, down the hill, and along the drive to the gatehouse. Its yard light pained like a poke in the eye. We squinted and ducked our heads until safe inside, back in shadows. In deference to Gene, Kit's housemate, we tiptoed and whispered and pressed shut the door. I made a brief racket tripping over some engine part lurking on the kitchen floor, but no lights went on, nobody queried. Kit led through the maze of parts and furniture to his room with a queen-size bed and door that locked with a reassuring snap.

He switched on a bedside lamp, providing light to see while leaving a cozy dimness. I glanced around the room—typical bachelor typhoon aftermath—then turned to look at him. He awaited my gaze with dilated pupils and tensed shoulders. His shirt hung open over half-zipped jeans. I yearned to paint the paradox of stud and child. Brushless, I took up his hands.

"So now what. Physics or metaphysics?"

He smiled and relaxed. "You get comfortable, I'll get ice cream."

He disengaged his hands to reach for the door. "You like chocolate?"

I would have preferred a whopping-strong drink but nodded with a smile. He left without another sound.

I turned to peruse the walls, remembering how Buck would relax so far after lovemaking that he almost became another person. Then, as if I had done something repulsive, he would rewrap himself in layers of mask and chill me out until I backed away.

Kit, I learned in seconds, had left me to learn what I could about him, without him. The room assaulted me with history. No photos of family or girlfriends, no diplomas, just walls and shelves groaning under the burden of trophies with gold-plated cars on top; marble chunks engraved with crossed checkered flags; pewter plates and ceramic mugs bearing dates up to four years ago, along with car club logos and placings—all firsts and seconds. Polished wood plaques proclaimed championships and series. A shiny piston stood on a block of wood. Screws, bolts, washers, tools, and coins littered the horizontal surfaces, while the verticals held photographs of race cars: stop-action or blurred, Kit popping up from cockpits grinning, sheet metal plastered with decals, and one car crumpled into a smoking wreck.

"Oh god . . ." escaped me as I stepped closer to study it. As I knew from events and listening to drivers' anecdotes, the safety equipment required for racing allowed drivers to walk away from horrendous crashes. Most of the time. In this instance, I suspected a hospital aftermath. Kit confirmed it upon reentering the room and catching me at the crash photo. When I turned to face him, eyes loaded with anguish, he answered, "Too many months."

"Have you competed since?"

He shook his head and handed me a bowl of ice cream. For lack of choice, we both sat on the bed.

"Too broke," he said, "and I kinda lost motivation."

"How badly were you hurt?"

He shrugged. "Broken bones and burns. Some internal injuries. But I'm better off than the guy who hit me."

I dared not ask for more. He didn't provide it, and his gaze had withdrawn. We settled back on pillows against the headboard and lapped the chocolate in silence. I felt surprisingly young and innocent for a woman who had just fornicated with a virtual stranger in her host's backyard. Must be the ice cream, I mused, along with empathy. Kit might not be my soulmate, but I could recognize a shrine to loss when I saw one. His display reminded me of my Buck exhibit back at the cottage. Photos, drawings, paintings, mementos . . . things I had better pull down before I let Kit through my front door!

"So Madeline," he said, depositing his bowl on a tower of magazines and manuals on the nightstand. "How long have you been seeing things?"

I handed him my empty bowl for the stack. "Depends on what you mean. I'm an artist, Kit. I've been 'seeing things' all my life. Whether I'm a genius, a fool, or a madwoman depends on who's looking at my depictions of what I see."

"That's not what I mean."

"I know. But it's relevant, because it means I'm capable of seeing things that aren't there. Or putting a different spin on them from everyone else."

He leaned back and folded his arms behind his head. "Okay. Then what's the difference between artistic vision and hallucination?"

"Sometimes not much! When people hallucinate but have no outlet, they're considered crazy. If other people have the same hallucinations but make something out of them, they're considered artists."

"So . . . ?"

"So, in my case, there are visions I conjure up on my own and turn into paintings, then there are images that seem to come from outside me—and feel like they're imposed on me—and don't have anything to do with my own world and thoughts."

"Like?"

"Raoul. And, well . . . my outside visions come in two forms. I've always been able to see people's souls. Not everyone's, and not often. But now and then, when I least expect it, and for no reason I've yet been able to figure, I see through every layer of pretense or façade a person carries and get a good clear view of who they really are or what they really want or fear. It's so intense, it feels like an epiphany! Almost religious in flavor. But it happens mostly with men, so there's probably some sexual link, especially when you factor in the big ones."

I darted a glance at him. His face was set in that hawk mask of unblinking attention.

"Twice now my random soul-seeing has come with special effects: overlying visuals, sounds or music, fancy lights—bowling me over! The first time, I thought I had found my soulmate. That proved bogus, so when it happened again, I didn't know what to think. But I had sex with the guy anyway because I knew I could trust him. Right now, with everything shape-shifting around me, I need someone to trust more than anything else!"

Kit sat a long moment without replying. When he relaxed and dropped an arm across my shoulders, I continued.

"The second type of outside vision started right after I met you, in the amphitheater."

I recounted the sequence from spook at concert to vertigo at cliffside, repeating what he'd heard at the confab in case something had gotten missed. Again I omitted the tumbled sheets and sizzling glows with Buck in the circle. If those proved important to the puzzle, I would share them with people who must know. At present I couldn't see any value in telling Kit about Buck, especially since he stayed mum about Julia. I prayed to whatever might be listening that all mysteries would be solved in another day, setting both Buck and I back on our separate courses.

A short-lived hope, for Kit said, "So who was the other guy?"

"Doesn't matter," I evaded. "It was a long time ago."

"Funny, I would've thought it all overlapped. Then some of this might make sense. Sex, power, and money are the only things that make people crazy. Like if you and Blanche were both in love with Dru, or you'd had an affair with Raoul that ended bad, or you wanted either one of them but both wanted Blanche—or even something real far-fetched like a guy you went to school with showing up here ten years later, with a special picture of you in his guitar case. Maybe he was your first love or something, and now he's in cahoots with Raoul to bring you all down . . ."

Kit's gaze was unrelenting. I could have been standing on a window ledge being asked if I would rather jump or be pushed. "I don't know, Kit," I said eventually, choosing to dangle off the ledge. "I just don't know."

At least that was true.

He remained stiff and silent. I hedged with other truths. "I've run into old schoolmates in airports and restaurants, once even in a department store restroom. Finding one in Dru's entourage isn't too strange. I'll bet if you raided the camp outside, you'd find plenty of pictures of me you've never seen before—and possibly another old schoolmate. There were two thousand in my graduating class, after all."

"Yeah, but that was California. This is Vermont."

"And that restroom was in Minneapolis, and one of the airports was in France!"

He laughed. "Point taken. But you gotta admit, there's usually some cause in the past. Like when a part fails prematurely, it can be from a manufacturing defect or a faulty installation. When people turn strange, there should be a reason why. You're the only one in this with a history element, so—"

"What do you call Raoul and Dru?"

Kit conceded that point with a one-shouldered shrug. "What I'm saying is, someone like you with a perfect body is most likely to have some mental flaw that attracts the wrong people. Or triggers sick relationships. Or hides weird talents. Or gets stalked by people who've been obsessed with you for years."

I let that pass without comment. "It could be," Kit continued, "that's Raoul's in love with you, not Blanche—but Blanche is in his life in three dimensions, while you've just been in two, tormenting him with your sexiness, while her bod is running around in front of him all the time . . ."

"That's a gross idea!"

"But it's possible. And it could explain a lot. You two are different enough to appeal to different people, but like enough to be swapped."

"Would you trade me for Blanche?" I had to ask.

"Hell no." That gave me the courage to look up at him. He pulled my free hand to his lips. "Blanche is gorgeous and any guy would be happy to roll her in the hay. But she's . . ."

He shook his head. "When I first heard she had a gearhead twin, I couldn't believe it. And no rumors you had a boyfriend—which nobody could believe! So I assumed like everyone else that every guy was your boyfriend, or else you were so uptight about sex that you were either a lesbian or a prude."

I laughed. "If you could see my portfolio!"

"Don't need to. I saw your portrait of Dru. It practically smokes. And your covers. All those figures, and the mysterious stuff happening between them. Those aren't dreams of a homo or a prude. Then, when you came out of the woods with grease all over your dress and more upset about your car than yourself—"

He looked at the ceiling, wet his lips, and clammed up. My eyes got hot and leaky. How I wanted to tell him everything! But that meant sharing why he differed from Buck despite the initial effects upon meeting. And mentioning that I recognized the bed we lounged upon, which was not covered with satin sheets. I had advanced two-thirds through what threatened to be a real premonition. Until I learned whose bed the satin sheets belonged to, I had to hold back.

But I could express my feelings honestly without compromising either of us. I snuggled close and kissed him again, followed by a long, tight embrace.

When he eased back for breath, smiling, I said, "What we should have done was leave my car in the woods and jump in yours and head back to my place. My daily driver's in the shop for service until next week. We could—"

"—drive back up here because you'd still have Blanche's problem stuck in your mind."

I shut my mouth. Kit went on: "You got it right the first time. Either you've gone crackers—and conned me into it—or there's something twisted going on at New Atlantis. I wouldn't leave my sister here without figuring out which."

He gave me a shock of fear by rising to disappear behind a closet door. A water closet, I deduced upon hearing the patter of liquid in a toilet bowl.

My muscles unclenched. I slipped in to the bathroom for my own pit stop as soon as he came out. I considered inviting him into the shower with me, to make up for the lost opportunity in the tower suite, especially after I saw the notorious poster of me pinned to the inside face of the door (not quite hidden by too many towels on the hooks). Several magazines I'd posed for were piled on the back of the toilet, well-thumbed. Very interesting. Very gratifying. I wished I'd known him for as long as he'd been aware of me.

I stuck my head out the door to lure him in, but bit my tongue upon seeing him extended on the bed, naked, arms folded up behind his head. He might as well have hung a "Love me!" sign from the ceiling above him. I emerged from the bathroom to oblige, nice and slow.

11
Pandora's Boxes

In the morning, he ignored the chores and repairs that demanded his attention, and I ignored the mysteries and people who required my attention, in order to draw Kit's portrait.

First we slept late, then scratched together coffee and breakfast from the gatehouse larder. I was giggly and girly in a way I'd never behaved before, but then, I'd never spent a night making love with no strings attached, no subplots, no mind games, no white lights, just sheer animal joy and friendship between boy and girl.

Though a tad raw upon waking, I felt loose and healthy, with a strange sensation I suspected might be happiness burbling inside my rib cage. I knew that if I lived to old age I would look back on this night as a highlight of my life.

All that led to one of my best drawing sessions ever. Kit posed for a set of figure studies that I dashed off with a ballpoint pen on a grid pad he used for technical drawing. Like most of the amateur models I recruited, he had to be directed or placed into position, and struggled to hold it for the minutes I needed to capture his image. Unlike most others, he didn't get twerpy from exposing himself to a woman who studied and recorded him as an object. He only balked when asked for poses that showcased his scars. I had to kiss them all and promise not to include them. Then he relaxed and fluidly displayed his virility in pose after pose, inspiring a series I knew would win awards if I could only exhibit them.

Soon I became too stimulated and had to move from paper to flesh. The session ended predictably. We finished with another shower.

Finally we emerged into muggy, metallic sunshine that promised sweat now, thunderstorms later. I wore one of Kit's T-shirts and cut-offs, unwilling to go out in clothes worn the day before. Years of being assumed a slut made me touchy about advertising I had spent the night with someone. Kit cared only that he was clean and dressed.

We stood in the gatehouse yard to examine the Tiger. He worked the repair into his schedule, not rushing it, since I seemed to have lost my desire to get home.

By then it was nearly lunchtime, so we strode hand in hand up to the mansion to help the kitchen crew prepare soup, salad, and sandwiches, then sat down to eat them with fourteen others. No Blanche, Dru, Buck, or Raoul. The New Atlanteans eyed us with interest but either chit-chatted as if we belonged there or left us alone with our starry eyes.

At the front entrance, Kit tore himself away to earn his paycheck. Something tore open inside me as he did. The wrenching shocked me rigid and froze my hand in the air reaching after him. He sensed the change and turned back, his own mask dropping for an instant when he saw tears glinting in my eyes and my throat bobbing as I tried to swallow the uprush. He stepped close again and took my suspended hand in both of his.

"Hey," he said softly, curling my fingers closed. "What?"

I continued gulping but could breathe again and used my free hand to wipe my eyes. My nose, however, had filled and threatened to dribble.

"I'm sorry."

"S'okay. Are you?"

I nodded. Shook my head. "I—don't know . . . what hit me."

"Another vision thing?" He tucked an arm around me, kissed my forehead. I inhaled roughly and started to calm.

"No. Just—suddenly—I was petrified."

He sat us on the steps. "It happens."

"Not to me!"

"Maybe that's why it finally did."

"I guess." I swiped the back of my hand across my nostrils. "I guess when you left I realized I had to face reality again, and since it's a reality with all the rules changed and I'm completely over my head, I just . . ."

"I don't have to go right now."

"No, go. I'm okay. There's things I need to do."

He shifted, looked me over, then rose. "Okay. I'll see you at dinner." He gave me a quick kiss and a breast tweak. "Call if you need me—I'll have a radio, you can get one from Mark."

He saluted then went off on an ATV.

I returned to my suite to freshen up then meditate on the problem of the skeleton in my closet and my white knight occupying the same place and time. Then, wanting action but still feeling insecure, I called my twin.

Thankfully, she, not Dru, answered the intercom. "Hi, no, nothing's wrong, we're just taking a day off. How you doing?"

"Better than yesterday."

"Oh? Did you finally get a good night's sleep?"

"Didn't get much sleep at all."

"Hmm. And whom weren't you sleeping with?"

"You mean, it's not obvious, and eight people haven't reported to you, and Dru wasn't watching from the astral plane?"

She laughed. "We're not that bad! I mean, I can think of three possibilities."

"Three!"

"Yeah—Buck, Kit, and John Powers."

"I forgot about him. I generally talk with people before I sleep with them, and that one appears to be mute."

Blanche ignored my tartness. "I'm told they speak but I haven't heard one yet. But they're so devoted, you can't be sure you're not going to find one when you pull back the covers!"

"In that case, I might have faked him out by sleeping in the gatehouse."

"Ah."

"Yes. Let's say . . . I'm more interested in hanging around than I was before."

"I'm glad to hear that."

"But I've still got to sort things out with Buck, so I'll be running him to earth this afternoon."

She suggested places to look for him. In return, I informed her about Colin's pending visit. She replied, "We're not going anywhere for a while, so it doesn't matter when he gets here. I can't wait to see him. And I'm glad to have a day without Raoul scheduled to be around."

My mood darkened. Nonetheless I said lightly, "Does that mean I might have a day without psychic excitement?"

"No guarantees, but if he's off site, you're less likely to get scary visions. Keep me informed, though, of anything that does happen."

"You're in retreat for the day, I take it."

"I sure hope so! Do you realize it's been two hundred sixty-four days since I didn't have to sing, dance, travel, work out, make plans, or interact with people? Do you realize that I don't have to wear makeup today? I don't even have to put on clothes! And no one's going to take my picture!"

"I remember the feeling. Enjoy."

I switched off before she could reply, knowing that seconds of privacy counted.

This left me with a day to rearrange my life around new priorities. Number one: Solve psychic mysteries. Didn't need to quest after a soulmate any more, because that mystery was solved. The visuals I had once believed to be cosmic signposts to my special someone were in fact nothing more than mutual hormone overload. If there were such a thing as a soulmate, I had stumbled upon him in Kit. Someone like enough to be comforting, different enough to be bracing, with whom honesty was possible on most levels, with whom one could either be serious or have fun. A person who would take a long time to know, who could operate inside New Atlantis's walls or outside them. Someone who could be a plain, old-fashioned, steady boyfriend—a relationship I had never experienced. And one I couldn't wait to get underway!

This thought train sent me off on my search. Buck was an interfering loose end that had to be tied up. I started on the main floor of the mansion, opening every closed door I passed from dining hall to ballroom. Found closets and utility rooms, along with the conservatory, screening room, bathroom, a rec room, laundry, solarium, library, salon, and parlor. Light and muted nose-blowing came from Mark's office, where I found him in glasses scowling and muttering at a screen.

He looked up at my "Hi" around the door frame, then sat back and pocketed his specs.

"You won't be happy," he opened. "I've been digging up anything on Raoul to support your suspicions, but aside from having no living relatives, he comes up smelling sweet as a rose."

"I'm not surprised," I said, in fact surprised to have Mark in on the picture. He didn't look the type to be Dru's confidante. Always dressed in plaid and khaki or corduroy with pockets, shod in wool socks and hiking boots despite the season, he struck me as a career hiker not manager of a twenty-first-century rock band. Then again, Raoul looked like a jet-set gigolo and I looked like an X-rated inflatable doll.

Stepping into the room, I continued, "If Raoul is serious about what he's doing, he won't leave any traces."

"So what's he doing?"

"I'm not sure yet."

Mark crossed his arms over his chest. "You realize it's your word against years of Raoul's devoted service."

I met his eyes, which were dubious but not hostile. "I know. I'm open to other scenarios but he's the best choice so far. How much did Dru tell you?"

"Enough. Then asked me to vet all the press releases and check Raoul's records. All we've got is standard personnel stuff—an old résumé, some articles, and notes from the background check we did when Dru hired him. All as textbook as you could want."

"May I see them?"

I peered over his shoulder. Mark blanked the computer screen. "Sorry, Dru didn't mention opening files to you."

"I see. I'll have a word with him. Meanwhile, do you know Raoul's schedule this week? We need to talk with him."

"Good luck. He was supposed to meet me for lunch. Hasn't shown, hasn't called, doesn't answer his cell phone or pager." Mark glared as if the whole thing were my fault. Maybe it was.

I shuddered, aware of a new range of potential. Mark fed it by saying, "So I made some calls, and though I got no whiff of satanic connections, I did find some morbid details . . . like, a lot of his clients are dead or druggies. As of today, he's representing three in dry-out clinics, one who retired to make babies, and a few lounge acts with lots of empty seats. In other words, Mister Lamont doesn't have too much publicity to arrange these days. So you'd think he'd be hanging on us like a drowning swimmer instead of skipping stuff he's committed to."

"Maybe he's just sick of working and has invested well enough to live the high life for a while. Maybe he thinks New Atlantis can coast along fine without him."

"You got that one right. Between you and me, and the lamppost, I didn't expect him to last the year even before this funny business started. Now? Well, assuming we ever see him again, I think his job is history."

"Maybe we'll get lucky and he'll just disappear."

"I'd rather he show up once more so I know when to terminate his pay and where to send it! Knowing Dru, he'll let that drag on unresolved for months."

Shaking his head and putting his glasses back on, he returned attention to his screen. When I didn't take the cue and leave, he looked over his rims at me and said, "Something else I can help you with?"

"I was just wondering . . . where did Raoul come from in the first place?"

"He was working in the City, and came to us on recommendation after our original guy fell under a subway."

I laughed.

Mark scowled. "What's funny about that?"

"The convenience. A satanist would excel at murder that looks like suicide or accident, don't you think?"

I left before Mark could comment and resumed my prowling, although this time with flagging confidence. Music drifted after me or across my path like mixing air currents, either live notes from a distance or canned melodies from hidden speakers. It seemed to run twenty-four hours a day. The only rooms in which I had not heard it were my own and Kit's, where the speakers had been turned off.

Ubiquitous electronics reminded me of how easily one could learn anything these days. We no longer had to bury ourselves in the back stacks of libraries, or belong to special societies, in order to learn ancient or forbidden lores. Just about everything could be found via computer, if not books, television, videos, or seminars. No coven required any more to study the black arts.

I shuddered and went outside to resume positive action. Find Buck, for starters, which meant reconnoitering the grounds since I had forgotten to ask Mark for a radio. Didn't feel like telling him why, anyway.

But clouds had moved in and started rumbling. A round trip of the compound, even in a vehicle, could take an hour. Should I fetch weather gear, or take my chances? Or go back inside for an overdue nap?

While I dithered, Colin's blue BMW crested the driveway and crackled into the circle. Both its front and back seats were packed to the headliner, and a bungee cord held shut its overstuffed trunk. He nodded but didn't wave as he passed, pulling to a halt in the porte cochère. Blanche and Dru emerged from the carriage house and approached via the pathway. We all caught up as Colin opened the car and stood.

Before he uttered a syllable, I knew something was wrong. Normally, Colin wore a tailored suit or immaculate casual wear. The last time I had seen him in grubbies was the day I had moved into his cottage from New York City. While he might have worn them today to pack the car, he would have changed before departing. Instead he looked as if he had spent all night in the same clothes then blown town at a run.

Glancing between us, he half smiled with a sheepish "Hi."

"Hi," Blanche said, her face uncertain. Dru hung back while I lunged straight to the point. "Colin, what happened?"

He raised his hands. "Don't shoot the messenger!"

We didn't get the message for minutes, delayed by a welcoming committee assembling on the stoop and Kit riding up on his ATV. Cassandra, Mark, and Brian herded us into the parlor for drinks and munchies. Colin came along after ducking inside the car to grab a large envelope.

"This was lying on the porch when I got back from breakfast this morning." Although he spoke to me, he reached across me to give the package to Dru, who cocked one brow and extended a hand.

I craned to see the label: "drew montclare" in childish block letters. Delivered to the cottage? Oh-oh. Sure enough, a dark haze shimmered around the envelope. Reflex took over faster than thought.

"Drop it!"

I karate-chopped Dru across the forearms. The envelope flipped up and over, ejecting its contents through the end that Colin had slit open. The last thing I saw was a glossy reproduction of my Dru portrait drifting downward like an oversized leaf, with his heart cut out and X's crossed over the eyes.

Then bloody fire—starbursts of shrapnel—agonized shrieks and pummeling hoofbeats overwhelmed my senses. I screamed and thrashed but couldn't escape the roaring whirlpool, which spun faster and faster, full of hideous faces looming then receding like ghouls. One had fanged jaws, dripping saliva in jubilation as they clamped over my arm—

—with pressure that didn't hurt. Human fingers, I realized, compressing my skin. Hands gripped my arms and legs, squeezed under my back, lifting and carrying, although I didn't feel my body weight until it collided with padded ground. The impact chased away the demons. In their place came a light show of colors and sound.

It went on until I cried for it to stop, then the music and colors faded. I sailed, still spiraling, through a silent void. Presently I coalesced on the stairs of a roofless temple and heard birds singing. Above and behind, pillars reached upward like gilded sequoias; before me, grass undulated in a breeze. All was color, stretching in riotous bloom to the horizon. I saw no buildings or people but knew where I was.

Though aware I was in a dream state, I couldn't break it. Nothing mattered but to sit and bask. At last I was safe; here was where my purpose lay. In fact, it floated toward me across the meadow, another formless essence like myself. His glow rekindled a dormant fire in my center, which flared and extended. Our bodies materialized after our energies fused, placing me nose to nose with my beloved, looking into his eyes from within his arms. I transmitted joyous thought with a smile. Buck returned the sentiment then closed his eyes to kiss me. Instead of his lips, I met an icy wall.

Sputtering, I blinked—and the vision vanished, replaced by Blanche's face and her upraised hand holding an empty glass. Water dribbled down my chin.

"Blanche! What the f—"

"Jeezus, Madeline, where were you! You wouldn't snap out of it for anything!"

Colin's face entered the picture, leaning close to see through me with wild eyes. His hands cupped my jaw. "Madeline—what happened!"

His demanding voice contained a waver. I seemed to be the only one undisturbed. Frowning, I thought, This won't be easy. Then I sighed. It's never easy being weird.

"C'mon, Mad, wake up!" He shook my shoulders. As my head bobbled, I recognized the gray and mauve parlor, realized I lay on its sofa, looked upon by Mark, Brian, Kit, and Cassandra, stood over by Colin, Blanche, and Dru.

"Jeezusmuthafuckingoddamcrist!" Mark exploded. "What the hell was that?"

"Possession," Dru stated. "Also known as mental rape."

"Looked pretty physical to me!" Colin straightened and scraped a hand through his hair.

"Madeline, what was after you?" Blanche begged. "Where did you go?"

"Must've been Atlantis." My voice sounded gravelly. "I don't know how or why. But what chased me there came out of that envelope."

"What are you talking about!" Colin bent forward to grasp my shoulders again. I swatted his hands away. He regained self-control, touched my cheek, then stood and turned to Dru. "Explain this!"

While Dru scowled in thought, Brian pushed by Colin to check my vitals. Beyond his shoulder, Kit watched through slitted eyes.

"I would guess," Dru said slowly, "that Raoul knows Madeline has blown his cover and is trying to scare her off."

"By delivering your hate mail to her house?" Blanche exclaimed.

Colin's gaze snapped back to me. "Is this what you were trying to tell me on the phone?"

I nodded, dragging myself upright against couch pillows. Brian returned stethoscope, thermometer, and blood pressure cuff to his kit and moved away.

Colin said, "I think I'd better hear the whole story."

The rest of us looked askance at Mark, Brian, and Cassandra, who would have to be levered out of place to exclude them. Dru accepted them with a nod. I mentally set a timer to track how long before both the inside and outside worlds learned of our situation.

As Colin sat beside Cassandra on the loveseat, Dru, Blanche, and I described our experiences and theories. I inserted the info Mark had provided earlier but continued to withhold the story of Buck in the circle and now on the temple stairs. Those were just too . . . personal. Also, I suspected a second layer to this affair, which might be about me alone.

Brian summarized what had been shared. "So these visions are either a demon, some flaming tragedy involving people and animals, or an idyllic scene of an ancient place. Interesting." He turned to Dru. "Precognition and retrogression triggered by the same entity!"

Blanche shook her head. "Could both be past-life recall. Madeline might have lived peacefully in one incarnation and died horribly in the next, both in situations involving this person, presumably Raoul."

"And we're sucked into it," Brian suggested, "through ties to other people and lives. A score of different fates accumulating to be resolved all at once!"

"Hold it, hold it, hold it!" Colin stood and sliced the air with his arms until we fell silent and looked at him. He lowered his voice.

"Your imaginations are running away with you. Look underneath your feet. This power point you claim you're sitting on, which boosts your creativity. What if it enhances any special talent someone has? Everything abnormal has only happened here, right?"

"Yes. So?" Brian prompted.

"So think about it. Raoul slipped up and can't risk coming here any more. Yet he wastes his time sneaking up to my house to deliver threatening messages to Dru. What did that accomplish?"

"Making me feel safer here by reminding me how vulnerable I am at the cottage," I realized aloud.

"Persuading the rest of us of the same thing," Colin concluded.

Silence as we contemplated what could happen to me home alone, with pregnable doors and windows. I broke into a cold sweat and the shakes.

Mark said, "I don't get it. If Raoul really wants to scare us, all he has to do is back down so Mad will relax and go home, then send her a grotesque mutilation of her own picture, or a nightmare vision in her own bedroom. Or just mug her or rape her on her front porch. Or bide his time until Blanche and Dru come to visit, then nail all of them together."

"But if he doesn't want to hurt us, what does he want?" Blanche almost whined. "He knows we're all more powerful here. Why wouldn't he want to defuse and disperse us?"

"Sport," Kit muttered under his breath.

"Weakness," Colin declared. "Sounds like he's got control, knows exactly what he's doing, while you guys flounder. Isolated here, you can scare yourselves into a lather."

Nobody argued. He resumed. "Or if this power point thing is real, it helps overboost your imagination so he can control you with simple psychological tricks. Make you think he has real power. If he actually does have it, maybe he needs to be plugged into this energy source, too. On the other hand, if he's working remotely and drawing from your energy, he needs you all to be here, all the time, all charged up. This is guesswork, of course, but it has some logic."

"Not really," said Dru. "Doesn't take into account when my visions started."

Brian turned to him. "But it does. We know you've been psychic since puberty. And Blanche and Madeline, like classic twins, have a hypersensitive connection with each other and the world. So where's the surprise that you were able to sense Raoul when he started focusing on you more intensely? Then, when everyone else gathered here, the energy level jumped through the roof! Put together that way, it all makes sense."

"If you read history," Cassandra said into the pause, "you'll find that every folly or tragedy has made as much sense as every triumph. You can rationalize anything but that doesn't mean it's true."

A long pause followed. Colin gazed at her with such admiration I thought I heard wedding bells.

"That's my point." He resumed sitting beside her. "Ordinary human conditions are getting blown out of proportion."

He held up a splayed hand and ticked off fingers. "First, you've got a guy who wants everything Dru has and no way to compete on the same footing. Second, he knows how to prey on your faults. What better way of hurting you than ruining your self-confidence and credibility? If New Atlantis fails, there goes your mission, your sales, your reputation. He might even slip in some bad publicity to help it along."

We mumbled and shrugged.

"Then Blanche," Colin added, "who he surely thinks wants Dru just because he's rich and famous, will abandon him in disillusionment. Won't Raoul and his goodies seem more attractive when Dru is shamed and broke?"

"But—" Dru started.

Colin overrode him. "Consider this. I checked him out a little yesterday. He's done pretty well for himself investing in eastern Europe. While letting his client list here deteriorate, he's been building contacts in their entertainment industry. Capitalizing on his New Atlantis ties, meanwhile snapping up stocks and properties. If everything bombs here, he can skip out tomorrow. But he'd probably prefer arriving a bigshot with the fallen queen of New Atlantis on his arm."

Blanche looked green; I could feel her nausea. Dru resembled a wooden statue of himself. Kit folded his arms across his chest and reeked, I told you so! Mark gnawed a cuticle, scowling.

Brian and Cassandra inhaled as they turned to Colin. Brian got his question in first. "But how does that explain the visions? This kind of greed plot happens every day. But it doesn't cause people to share mystical visions!"

"Mystical?" queried Colin. "I haven't heard anything yet about gods or religion. Your descriptions sound more like mismatched bits of a premonition of New Atlantis burning down!"

Dru leaped to his feet as he finally realized that sick, angry people can come up with bombs.

Brian clamped a hand onto his arm and pushed him back down. "Easy does it. Remember, premonition is what could happen, not what will. If two of you are receiving identical warnings, it's probably because events are in process with disaster as their likeliest outcome. Consider yourselves lucky! You have a chance to redirect the flow."

"Like how?" said Kit. "You can't just arrest the guy!"

"No," said Colin, looking at him closely and wondering why he was sitting by me with a proprietary air. "But you can see the writing on the wall and be prepared to act defensively, meanwhile starting to build a case."

"But what about the Atlantean imagery?" Mark insisted. "And that green archer business? You're formulating theories without using all the facts!"

I cringed as Blanche turned to him. "Madeline's trip to Atlantis was reflexive. It's a memory of haven, where she escapes during fear. Allanna told her to find a place of refuge. Looks like she did!"

Blanche looked at Dru. "You couldn't follow her, could you?"

He shook his head, rubbing the bridge of his nose. Turning back to Mark, Blanche finished, "Madeline basically dives into a vault and locks it behind her when she goes to Atlantis. Not even developed psychics can penetrate such a shield."

"But what about the archer?" Mark persisted.

I ventured, "Allanna made a big noise about a savior from outside. Maybe she was wrong about it being me."

We all looked at Kit.

"Whoa no!" He extended his hands with palms forward. "This is your game. I'm just trying to help!"

"Forget it for now," ordered Colin, who turned back to Dru. "What happened when you took the envelope from me?"

Dru hesitated. "Nothing at first. But just before Mad hit me, I got a brief, stinging headache." He rubbed his temples.

Colin nodded. "When I took it out of the car, my fingers got burned. But cold, like a dry-ice burn." Now he too looked nauseous.

Cassandra addressed Colin in her soft, alto voice. "You forget that the envelope could have been dropped off at your house by anyone who knows you're connected to Dru and also knows that something so obviously hate mail would never get delivered here. But scaring you with it gives it more clout—maybe even some press coverage if you freaked. Sickos often want attention more than anything."

She turned to address the group. "Raoul has always been more sophisticated. Unless it's a blind, I wouldn't expect him to pull this kind of stunt. Has anyone talked to him yet? I will if none of you feel neutral. It seems that too much centers on Madeline, who's noted for her imaginative paintings. How do we know it's not entirely her problem? Why can't she be triggering reactions in the rest of you?"

This speech stilled the room. I agreed with its logic, even while burning from the insult she had just dished out.

Colin gazed at her then turned to me. "Have you been taking drugs?"

"No."

"Could anyone be slipping them to you?"

"No," pronounced Dru.

Colin shot him a dirty look. I answered, "It's extremely unlikely."

"In that case," Dru said to Colin, "we have our first physical evidence of a hostile party. It appears to be aimed at me but willing to take pot-shots at my family and friends. But Kit's right, we don't have enough to take to any authorities, and I sure don't want the kind of publicity this will bring! All I can offer is sanctuary here for both of you until we sort it out. At least Raoul is off compound and we can control his access."

"I agree," said Colin. "It's not a problem for me 'cause I'm in the City most of the time. But Mad is completely exposed at the cottage. Which is why I brought as much of her stuff as I could carry."

While my mouth hung, the group nodded in satisfaction. I shook my head. What a way to go down in history: the first person to be conscripted into New Atlantis! Never mind that I had planned to stay for a while. Choosing to do a job and have an fling differed from being forced into hiding! Paintings spitting resentment were already composing themselves in my head.

Out of my mouth burst, "Damn it—you can't keep me here!"

"Of course not," Dru oozed.

Brian added, "But I'm sure you can see the sense of it."

"And I'm sure you can see the sense," Colin said to him, "of giving these people thorough physicals. We'll all look pretty stupid if any brain tumors show up!"

"I don't have that kind of equipment," said Brian.

"You can cover the basics, can't you?"

"Of course."

"Then you take care of that while Dru and I rustle up private investigators."

"Line up some psychiatrists and neurologists while you're at it," Cassandra said.

I glanced at Kit, who was already looking at me. *Your place or mine?* I thought into his eyes. He neither blinked nor responded, and I ached at the silence. At the same time I sensed Dru and Blanche tuned in.

Mark bleated, "So what am I supposed to tell people who ask me what's happening? We won't be able to stifle it internally much longer. Most people already know something's up."

Dru didn't move but his face seemed to age while we watched. "I don't know yet. But I'll think of something. Let's have dinner, first."

He swept from the room, eyes downcast and preoccupied. Blanche, after pausing in the door frame to look back at me, followed. Cassandra paused likewise to look at Colin, then returned to her kitchen. Brian hung back to ask me, "Sure you're all right?"

"Nothing a little food, a stiff drink, and a new life won't cure." I flicked him a smile and waved him away. He took the hint.

Mark didn't. "Can I help you unload?"

"As soon as I pull the key from the ignition!" Colin said, trotting off to do so lest I beat him to the car and hurtle it through the front gate.

Mark followed him, saying, "If we hustle, we can get everything in before the storm breaks."

Kit and I, left alone, looked at each other. Outside, thunder growled a little louder, reminding us of our first encounter at the back gate.

Engrossed in our thoughts, we set to work heaving and hauling my baggage. I was impressed by how much Colin had packed into his sedan. John Powers showed up so the unloading went quickly. I sent my helpers off to dinner and went down to close the car, passing Kit heading up with a final armload.

On the front step, I registered what he had been carrying: a clutch of framed paintings interleaved with towels. Panic froze me for an instant, then I spun and raced upstairs. Grasped the door frame to slingshot myself through the open anteroom, leaping over boxes and heaped clothes to stumble into the bedroom where Kit stood beside the cot.

Before him lay three framed canvases with the towels peeled back to reveal Buck as an Atlantean prince; Buck and I on horseback cantering through surf; Buck alone in a nude figure study. Kit stood like a man who had lifted the lid on a booby-trapped trunk and been shotgunned in the chest.

I reeled backward myself, feeling his hot, blinding shock then cold anger like a percussion clap from an explosion. The air sizzled as he fought himself against lashing out. He didn't look up at me, or acknowledge my presence, until he turned and walked past me. Then he slashed me once with eyes like razor blades. The muscles in his back and neck bulged through his damp shirt as he walked down the hall, down the stairs, and out into the weather. I heard his ATV snarl awake before he drove out of my life.

Part Two

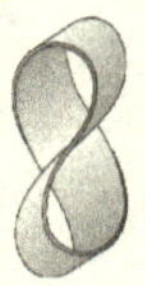

12
Alienation

Equinox morning I skipped breakfast rather than face anyone, and spent the morning on the balcony in a negligee, drying my hair in the sun.

The landscape before me was burnished with autumn. In four weeks the season had turned without my notice; during the same time I had aged a decade and cared not a whit for the flaming maples I normally would have cruised the countryside to paint. Nor did I look forward to the party scheduled for this evening. In protest, I planned to skip my chores.

The sun penetrated stiffness like a dry heat pack. It also melted emotional control. I hadn't cried since Kit had packed his old Land Rover and driven away in a downpour. Now tears dribbled down my face as if I had sprung twin leaks.

On the balcony overlooking the driveway, I could blubber in private. New Atlanteans went about their business, whistling or singing while they worked. Below me on the lawn, a man raked and a woman pruned shrubbery. After the concert, only grounds adjacent to the house had been maintained. Most service personnel moved to gardens, fields, and outbuildings during fall, racing the sky to finish harvest and projects before the season changed.

This year, I'd heard many times over meals, we'd gotten lucky. No frost yet; none of the cold rains or surprise early snows; foliage was late and great, good news for the state's tourist industry. These joys passed me by, lost as I was in an endless-loop question: Which of us committed the greater wrong, me for trying to protect myself, or Kit for not giving me a chance to explain?

Behind me, two men banged and thumped on the south wing's steep rooftop, wrestling with solar collectors for a hot water system. Another of Kit's projects, like my Tiger, left undone.

Their unmusical background blended with the rasp and snick of tools, and crunching footsteps. I startled alert when Dru appeared from the wooded path between studio and carriage house, scuffing leaves. In drawstring denims under a knee-length black vest flapping open, his wispy hair in a ponytail, he could have stepped out of the '60s. Instead of pausing to chat with the workers, as he normally did, he continued barefoot toward the mansion. I didn't move or make a sound but he glanced up, as if expecting to see me. More likely, he had sensed my gaze—or intercepted my thoughts. Just because he hadn't "visited" me since the first night didn't mean he couldn't read me. I had no way of knowing if he did.

By the time he stepped through the French doors onto the balcony, I had dried my eyes and settled into a canvas sling chair. He stood between me and a cloudless turquoise sky, returning my stare.

"Perhaps my news will clarify things for you," he opened, then waited.

I broke first. "What? What! Is he back? Has he called?"

Dru shook his head and crossed to the balustrade I had minutes earlier considered jumping from. Only one story high, it didn't offer a fatal plunge.

"Nothing that dramatic. I just thought you'd like to know you're free to go."

"Huh?"

"You can leave. Goodbye. The gate will open as you approach it. Take my Ferrari. Have someone drive you. Push your Tiger. Call your brother. Walk. Fly. Go find Kit if you must."

My mouth gaped then snapped closed as I scowled sideways at him. "Why?"

Dru leaned his rump against the balustrade, resting interlaced hands slack against his thighs. "Because I have no right to keep you. Nothing's happened for a month. Raoul has not been seen or heard from. No one has reported strange visions. All physicals proved normal, your cottage remains unwatched and unharassed. You, meanwhile, are starting to look like a caged cheetah. Gaunt, pacing, going through the motions of adapting but in truth biding your time until the caretaker gets sloppy and you can bite his neck and escape."

Dru fixed his clear pale eyes on me, open and patient. Inviting me inside to swim around. I kept my mind vaulted, as I had since that envelope had violated me. Maybe I couldn't help projecting, but nothing was going to slip in my back door!

Now the real back door—and front door—lay open. I should have sprung to my feet and skipped off to pack. Instead, I sat there as if I had grown a tap root, gazing over the grounds.

New Atlantis offered so much more beauty than our tourist village in the Berkshires. Those hills had seemed enough after the City, but once I had started exploring, then traveling into horse country with Colin, I recognized what I had been missing. Even in the crowded northeast corridor, natural splendor endured a surprisingly short distance inland. And for hundreds of miles the terrain folded and rolled into larger and larger hills—spine and offshoots of the Appalachian chain, at their most glorious in central Vermont. I found, the more I looked at mountain vistas, that they strummed my heartstrings. I didn't want to leave them. I didn't have to. But I should, since the person who made it worthwhile had abandoned me here. Then again, my deceit would have lost him anywhere, so I might as well stay. Neither Dru nor Colin nor fate had imprisoned me; they had forced me to make up my mind.

"So it looks like we made much ado about nothing," he continued. "Allanna still insists that Evil is alive and well among us, but it's not manifesting. I've come to think she's been sensing the evil latent in all our hearts, which was more focused when Raoul was around. I can't insist you stay in the face of facts, although I'm uneasy about having no closure. Of course, you're welcome to stay if you want."

I remained silent, contemplating a vow of silence forever. It would go well with a celibate retreat behind walls.

He probed me with his gaze, now challenging instead of inviting. I visualized bricks, steel doors—any tool that might protect my mind, still unsure whether shielding worked or if anything existed to shield from.

"Before you decide," Dru said, shifting his eyes away, "you ought to know that Buck's staying, too."

The surprise made me gulp. "Why?"

"Because we need someone to cover for Kit until he comes back."

"What makes you think he will?"

Dru met my eyes again. "Same reasons I gave you before. He left his stuff here except for camping gear, and he's disappeared before when he had to work something out."

"Like what?"

"Don't know. I didn't ask, he didn't confide."

"Then what did your aura reads tell you?"

Dru scowled at my caustic undertone but let it pass. "The first one had something to do with Julia. Another was about what to do with the rest of his life. I gave him a big raise when he came back from that one, hoping to persuade him that helping a bunch of appreciative New Age fruit-loops—" Here he winked. "—would pay better than returning to the track broke with his confidence damaged."

I sat in a pile of roiling, contradicting emotions, through which the first upwelling of hope emerged. But then it died as I realized we'd be back where we started if Kit returned and Buck stood in his place.

"So did you invite Buck or did he volunteer?" I asked after a long pause.

"A little of both. He's been evading me, expecting an ultimatum, while easing into Kit's duties and impressing the guys with his skill."

I lifted an eyebrow. Dru looked down at his finger tracing patterns on the balustrade. "So I cornered him last night to make a firmer arrangement. He was interested in picking up Kit's slack until he learned that you might be staying, too."

He paused for effect. I drummed my fingers. "So?"

"So it's the first time I've heard him talk in paragraphs. By which I learned that you two go pretty far back. Like, teenage beach parties in California. And you followed him east, and tormented him through college, and beyond. He said there was always something scary about you, though it wasn't until he met you here that he knew what it was."

"And what was it, pray tell?"

"He said you began glowing that first night."

I burst out laughing. "So he did see it! I wasn't sure. Funny, everything was sparkling and flaring around me all night, yet I managed to function!"

"You had the advantage of understanding what you saw."

"Not really. But it doesn't help to freak out!"

"I think you're both doing well under the circumstances."

"Yes, walking miles out of our way to avoid each other." I hesitated then realized aloud, "I suppose three miles is better than three thousand!"

Dru grinned. "What drove you so far apart?"

"The bigger question is, what closed the gap?"

"He wouldn't tell me. I'm hoping you will. The odds against coincidence of you two meeting here are off the scale."

"If you say one word about destiny, I'll claw your eyes out!"

"No, curiosity is my only motive."

I looked at him askance then gave in with a sigh. "I don't know why he came here. His story struck me as lame. He ran it by like a rehearsed excuse the first night and I haven't talked to him since. Which convinces me he's not here to win back my heart."

"He's made no effort to see you?"

"No. In fact, I get the impression he's sleeping with Julia."

"Well, as far as he knew, you were sleeping with Kit."

"Who's been gone long enough to answer that question! No, Buck and I are history, just like me and Kit. I made the same stupid mistake with both of them: Believing a vision held any truth. And that sex can bind two people's souls together."

I snorted. Dru said mildly, "Then how do you explain me and Blanche?"

"I don't bother trying! How do you explain any couple?"

He shrugged. "I have explanations you're not willing to hear."

"It doesn't matter. Even if I have another chance with Kit, it's shot if he comes home to find Buck in his job after thinking he lost his girl to him, too! If you truly want Kit back to stay, then either Buck or I have to go."

"I would prefer all three of you in happy resolution."

"Me too, but unlike you, I don't believe utopia is possible."

"Then you're leaving?"

"I didn't say that."

"Then will you please stop fencing with me and tell me what's on your mind."

His voice was calm yet backed with iron. I recognized an indirect apology and atonement for butting in uninvited before, so I capitulated.

"My mind is stuck on one thing. 'Fool me once, shame on you. Fool me twice, shame on me!'"

Dru recognized the old adage but cocked his head to show he didn't understand why I quoted it. So I explained, "Kit thinks he got deceived, but the bigger dupe was me. Twice now I've fallen for the same delusion. I thought those special visions were pointing to a soulmate, but all I got was runners—two men who bonded me to them then skipped. For some reason I keep reading those signals backward. What they really mean is, Run, fast, the opposite direction from this guy!"

"So why are you still here?"

"Because I can't bear the thought of being home alone in case the Raoul-type visions come back. And can't risk a surprise attack from Raoul in the flesh." I paused then added, "And I can't face the real world any more."

"You're not just waiting for Kit?"

I couldn't answer. Dru ruminated, then said, "Okay. What about Buck?"

"Can't you get by without him?"

Dru lifted his palms. "I need someone in Kit's capacity, and Buck does double duty at the stable and can help in the studio."

"I think you just like the melodrama of us all packed in here together!"

"I'd rather learn what's behind the melodrama and turn it into creative energy and peace."

I turned away and gnawed at a finger, wishing for one of my long-ago cigarettes. No New Atlantean would give me a ride into town to buy the evil weed. Nor could I filch a compound vehicle, even though all parked with keys in the ignition, because I had not been granted permission and would be stopped at the gate.

"What's behind the melodrama," I sneered, "is nothing more than jealousy and deceit."

"Too easy," Dru countered. "You could say that about Raoul, also, but we know it's more complex than that."

"For sure, we've all got our neuroses adding variety, but the core problem is plain. Kit and Buck both wanted a sex goddess who could bear all their sorrows and prop up their egos. I wanted a sex god who could do the same thing. But with everyone wanting to get, not give, no decent relationship is possible."

"Very profound, but also a crock of bull. If you really felt that way, you'd be speeding back to your old life to prick-tease your racing buddies until the next sex god came along. Or else you'd lock yourself into the cottage and paint yourself into madness. Instead, you're pining so bad for Kit that you can't lift a brush or even look at your car, and you'll fall at his feet the moment he turns up. In the meantime, you're playing chicken with Buck—seeing who can hold out longest before cracking—and both of you hiding information relevant to Raoul. All this," he added while my face changed color, "I can figure out with my two eyes and my brain, no psychic probing at all."

Tears veiled my vision. "Damn it, what do you want from me!"

He continued in the same matter-of-fact tone he had been using. "I want to know what you're hiding. I need to know why your affairs are connected to my life. I want to know why you can see things I can't. I need to understand why you and your twin are so different. And I want to know why Raoul has been quiet while Kit's been away."

Seconds ago, I had been sweating in the sunlight. His last question turned me cold.

"I hadn't made that connection."

He nodded. "I only just connected those two dots this morning. Too busy puzzling over you and Buck to see anything else."

I stood and walked to the corner of the balustrade, giving him my back. After a long pause, gauging distance and air currents to determine whether anyone might overhear, I turned, fixed my voice into a low monotone, and began.

"I can't answer any of your questions. But I can fill in some blanks. About Buck: We met at a beach party, end of junior year. We had friends in a group from several schools counting down days to graduation. Blanche and I were set to move east on a modeling contract so could have graduated early, but Mom insisted we run through the normal program. And she only let us go at all because Colin was already in New York, at college."

Dru said nothing. I could feel his observation of my form and wished I wore something more than a filmy house gown. I felt as sexy as a plank. Fortunately, he threw no lust vibes, being as engrossed in the mental landscape as I was.

"All the girls wore eensy bikinis. Blanche was rehearsing the moves that would get her into commercials and videos—even then determined to plaster herself across the media until she got your attention. I wanted to crawl under a rock, but knew I had a very short window in which my looks could earn me big bucks, and I was committed to grabbing as many of them as I could. So I practiced looking like I enjoyed it. This wasn't a problem on a shoot—in the commercial world, people understand you're a commodity and can turn a persona on and off at will. But in a crowd of teenage boys, well, they didn't get it. I couldn't wait to leave them all behind and go professional. As far as men were concerned, all I wanted was to be loved or left alone."

Dru made a sympathetic noise.

"Anyway, in the evening we built bonfires. The group split into loud drinkers dancing around an old boom box, and quiet smokers sitting around a guy playing guitar. He sang my favorites in a beautiful baritone. And he and I were the only ones who weren't high. So I was astounded when he illuminated before my eyes as if a celestial spotlight had found him, and his guitar sound changed into orchestral music and the words of his song were overlaid by something older, and deeply personal and true, and someone who was him but didn't quite look like him sang them just for me. In the seconds this lasted, I saw a soul full of kindness and passion and honesty and integrity, courage and pain and loneliness. Then the imagery shrank back to a lanky kid I'd never seen before. But he was mine and I had to have him. In an eensy bikini, that wasn't hard to do."

Dru laughed. I tossed a look at him. He had stretched out atop the two-foot-wide balustrade, leaning on an elbow to prop up his head with the heel of his hand. I returned to the vista of lawn and trees with bluish mountains peeking over the tops of them. My mind's eye, however, was back on a California beach.

"He felt something, too, though he never told me what. But it bonded us, as did deflowering each other that night in the dunes. He had a car so drove me home but we parked along the way, and—well, seventeen-year-olds have a lot of steam!"

This time Dru and I both laughed. I fell into reflection until he said, "Go on."

"That one fantastic night was the high point of our relationship. After exposing his emotional underbelly, Buck went out of his way to prove himself unmoved. It took days to get back to conversation. Eventually he loosened up and we went out. But every time we had sex, he dissolved in the aftermath then frantically distanced himself from me and put up walls. I'd go after him with chisel and jackhammer until he cracked open again. And so began a cycle that went on and on . . ."

To my dismay, I felt tears coming again. I sucked them back then pivoted to face Dru. "The trouble with soul-seeing like that is once it happens, you expect your relationship to go from there. I couldn't understand why Buck kept pulling away from me. In bed, we were golden. In everything else, we were out of sync. He moved through the layers of his personality faster than I could follow, or in directions I couldn't anticipate, which left me confused and hurt. I questioned and challenged but he couldn't answer me. He didn't understand what had happened between us, and the conflict drove him nuts. He wanted an easy, companionable girlfriend who would fuck him senseless and leave his soul alone. But he got me, who kept catching his soul with its pants down every time he dropped the real thing. When I couldn't take the torture any longer and handed him an ultimatum, he jumped on the nearest willing body and rode her into the sunset. Then got a long lesson in what loneliness really means."

Dru waited with the stare that made me squeamish: eyes wide and fixed on my face, looking through me, while seeing something else in his mind. Probably Blanche. She had come to him not a virgin, having studied the sexual arts with a host of lovers so that she would be a goddess to Dru when she reached him. The press had not yet caught wind of this irony, still believing Blanche to be the girl next door who had saved herself for her hero, and Madeline to be the round-heel who could never hope for more than a cast-off sidekick.

"So anyway," I finished after a deep inhalation, "Buck distorted things by telling you I followed him east. Blanche and I went first, on that modeling contract. Buck came to Boston the following fall. We went through our cycle at longer intervals, while he played musical colleges and I flapped between Connecticut and New York. He jilted me about the time you and Blanche got together and moved here. Our fallout got lost in your fanfare. Since then, for all I knew he was dead until I ran into him at the finale. He waited for me afterward and apologized for treating me bad. Beyond that, we had nothing to say—

until we jumped each other in the marble circle. Then those years of separation disappeared."

Until, as I described, my vision of rolling lovers interrupted by Kit's headlight. Then the energy field that both Buck and I saw.

"So you were in the circle!" Dru sat up. "No wonder. Blanche and I made love there one night—full moon on the solstice—and it was unbelievable."

"But you knew it was a power channel. We had no idea, and it scared us half to death!"

"Buck still doesn't know. He ascribes the effects to you. And they probably come through you, since you were already having psychic moments in your teens. I'd say you two are here to resolve past-life issues, except you'd probably hit me."

This was the moment to tell him about the kiss on the temple stairs. I couldn't do it. If I accepted that past lives were involved, then I had to tie them to Kit and Raoul and further redefine the universe. Easier to investigate the power point phenomenon and compile a map of such sites around the globe and events that had occurred there through history. I had already started reading up on power points, magic circles, and ley lines in the library.

"You're right—I will not discuss any of this in terms of destiny or karma. But you can think that way if you'd like. Have I told you what you needed to know?"

"Too much and not enough." He slipped off the balustrade and dusted off his rump. "But plenty for now. I've got stuff to do before tonight. When is Colin due?"

"When he gets here."

Dru nodded then stepped close to peck me on the forehead. "Thanks for the story. It helps me. And do me a favor: Spend some quality time with your sister. She's worried about you."

"I'll try, but it's hard. We don't live in the same world anymore."

"You do now!"

Dru grinned and waved himself back through the French doors.

13
Triangles

I stood for a moment, seeing nothing, as my mind changed gears. The decision to stay, which had sneaked up on me, constrained and released at the same time. My steps back to the suite were tentative, almost mincing, as I looked around with new eyes and thought, Home?

Sure ain't no hotel when you're the one collecting garbage!

After my first week at New Atlantis, I had graduated from guest to hanger-on so was assigned the lowliest duties. Everyone split the housekeeping load in mandatory rotation each month. For freestyle, unscheduled chores, only cataloguing the library had been available. I took the job to take advantage of its resources, which included password-free computer access to the Internet. The combination let me update my knowledge of the paranormal. I also got better acquainted with my co-residents through the books they had warehoused when they pared down from houses and apartments upon moving in.

In case I forgot the world outside, the media reminded me daily. If not ruinous weather and global warming, then bombings, overdoses, and gunfire battles; assassination, starvation, epidemics, toxic ruin. How anyone could maintain hope for humanity taxed my imagination. Any bright spot, such as a saved patch of rainforest or two enemies shaking hands, expired under the next dark flood.

Yet New Atlantis sent forth upbeat press releases and video teasers describing its operations and policies, to be followed by a photo spread then the finale concert video for Christmas. Everything published triggered demands for more. Raoul would have been obsolete as a publicist.

New Atlantis steamrollered through public awareness just fine on its own.

Raoul's old writings, in which none of us had found any slanting or insinuations, were being outclassed by the new materials sent out by inspired New Atlanteans. Cornelius had done a terrific write-up of the cookout after Raoul failed to submit anything. He had become our lead promoter when not working on a book.

Nonetheless, I worried. No counterattacks appeared in the media aside from the usual Dru-Montclair-as-pagan-wacko jabs. Maybe Colin was right and Raoul had cut his losses and left the country. In that case, why weren't the paparazzi spotting him? Anyone associated with New Atlantis got photographed or mentioned if they stuck a toe into public places, as well as many private ones. With his track record as a hobnobber, Raoul should have turned up by now.

Private investigators reported that he had moved from his apartment with no forwarding address. His car registration remained linked to the old address, but the vehicle itself hadn't been spotted.

The office team kept an eye out for mention of him as they combed the Internet and worldwide papers and television between fielding inquiries, updating the New Atlantis website, and managing Dru's foundations, businesses, and trusts. Their electronic equipment, along with the studio as the band developed next year's releases, made a bad case for off-grid living. I left everyone to their New Atlantean paradoxes, retreating to my den to secretly paint.

Dru's ignorance of this practice gave me security. Although he had read me right about the cheetah, he had misinterpreted the rest. I didn't need the cottage to paint myself into madness; a tower suite served just fine. And I had several times visited the Tiger in the gatehouse garage, making and discarding plans for it, each time deciding to wait one more day to see if Kit would show up to fix it.

During one visit, I pulled my club-sized flashlight and a can of pepper spray from the car. With these I returned to the stone circle late at night. I first wandered around it, touching the menhirs, then sat in the center until my teeth chattered, watching constellations track by—brilliant as spotlights without the ambient light that clouded cities, making the flashlight redundant.

The beauty gave my mind a vacation as I pondered how to mix paints to capture moonlight. Those thoughts got pushed aside by sexual fantasies, incited by a tremendous need to copulate that built like magma seeking release from the earth. If John Powers had chosen that night to shadow me, he would have been a lucky man. I ran back to my suite before I transformed into a howling predator seeking flesh.

Unnerved, I avoided company even more for the following days. The New Atlanteans, having deemed me in grief since Kit's departure, continued giving me space. I knew that Blanche, Dru, or Colin would eventually confront me so had to return to the circle before then to test a hypothesis. Had my lust-wave been a mix of monthly hormones and depression, or had it been incited by the circle itself?

At a different phase of moon and weather, I went back, only to find a couple already there trying hard to copulate quietly. Never learned who they were since I backtracked posthaste.

On my third attempt, John caught me leaving the mansion. I pointed the pepper spray at him and hissed. He got the message and backtracked posthaste, too. That gave me the circle to myself, armed with light, spray, food, and blanket. I sat longer than the first time but nothing happened. Perhaps Mother Earth, like her children, also suffered biorhythms.

While this experiment didn't solve my personal mysteries, I did gain insight into the fertility rituals reported for ancient stone-circle cultures. And lost some fear of my co-residents. If New Atlanteans were the nutcases I originally thought, then they would be using the circle for regular group rituals. It appeared instead that while some of them knew about its properties, they only sampled as individuals, and with careful intent.

Elsewise tonight's party would be held out there, not in the dining hall as it was each autumnal equinox, when New Atlanteans chucked propriety and reveled for twenty-four hours. In theory, I could skip the celebration because I hadn't signed the New Atlantis contract. However, having physically moved in then passively—and verbally to Dru—agreed to stay, I obliged myself to pop in on the annual bacchanal.

I shouldn't go, though, because I still seethed. Women who burn to strike back at the universe; to kick men in the genitals; to erase their mistakes from living memory, don't make good party companions! I should lock myself in the tower suite.

But that would be too neurotic. I needed to accept that my duty in life, like everyone else's, was to swallow reality's pills and press on regardless. So tonight I would channel my seething into an outrageous flaunt as a rebound from cowering. This event was safe for such risk-taking, because cameras, journalists, and big-mouths were banned. Party dress could—and would—be outlandish; thankfully, Colin had brought my entire closet, so I had several femme fatale options to choose from.

The idea perked me up. Hmm, let's see . . . the Atlantean princess costume, left over from modeling days when I went by the name Aurora Borealis and Blanche dubbed herself Lady Azilde? That would surely stop traffic. No, I'd rather make every man's eyeballs pop out on springs. That meant the iridescent blue, zip-front jumpsuit edged in turquoise that fit like a second skin, plus full makeup. The combination proved its success when I opened the door to Colin's knock and he halted in the frame and whistled.

"Jeezus, Mad, who you trying to kill?"

"Anything with testicles, although one in particular."

Colin wiped his brow then entered carrying a gym bag. "I'm glad you're only my sister. Will you help me do my hair?"

My mood lightened. Once a year I saw Colin the investment banker go avant garde. Last year he had staggered home cross-eyed. This time he looked ready to do it again. His black stretch pants with red side seams, red shoes, and a splashy shirt left open showed off the muscles he had developed from riding. I sculpted his mahogany haircut into a crest and tipped it with gold and fuchsia, then touched up his eyes, cheekbones, and lips. He came out beautiful without seeming effeminate, and could have passed as my fraternal twin. Certain New

Atlantis ladies would attach to him like remoras when he went downstairs.

Cassandra nabbed him on the gallery landing. The neckline on her flowing dress sliced to her navel, moving Colin to beam like a kid receiving a banana split in a bucket. I left them to salivating at each other, and paused at the bottom to unzip my jumpsuit another notch. The stretchy fabric pushed my breasts into impressive cleavage. It also evoked sweat from standing still. One set on the dance floor would probably kill me. But oh, I'd make a spectacular corpse!

Downstairs, music from the dining hall sent tremors along the corridor. I aimed for the darkened square at its end. Revelers approached me in an erratic stream as I followed others along the carpet. The whole reminded me of driving on an interstate into a storm. People's eyes gleamed like headlamps in flattened daylight, the first cue of impending weather. When I passed into the dining hall, I flinched as if penetrating a rain veil into deluge.

Sound embraced me, implanting a bass beat into my bloodstream. I felt compressed yet adrift in space. The room had become a torch-lit grotto within which costumed savages gyrated in mass ritual—twice the density in half the space of the ballroom, in a fog of conflicting scents. The impact startled my mental shields into collapse, so that bodies bloomed into aura, weaving their motions together. I staggered at the sight, thinking, It's not going to end with Raoul!

Help! I screamed to anyone who could listen. *I can't face this again without Kit!*

None of those so-called psychics heeded. I almost about-faced then saw Blanche sparkle by, in gold lamé pants under a sheer black batwing tunic flecked with gold beads and thread. Beneath it she wore a black bustier as she strutted in black spike-heeled boots, brandishing gold and onyx jewelry. I pressed into the throng after her but never caught up.

Since my jaw was quivering and knees were knocking, I aimed for the bar. Had to rub shoulders with people in order to pass between them, and smile and greet, and elude welcoming hands. A shot of straight whiskey shocked my brain back into operation. As my panic subsided, the auras disappeared.

Interesting.

While watching the dancing and drinking, the laughing and shouting, I concluded that my paranormal experiences had more to do with me and New Atlantis than they did with Raoul or Kit. Something must activate my chemistry with those men when they were on site. This demanded rethinking my choice to stay here. The obvious course was to return home with Colin and see what transpired.

No chance for that until tomorrow, so I settled into the party, alert for anything beyond normal range. New Atlantis and intimates comprised four to five dozen; all had shucked their usual personas to experiment with other selves and new sensations. The main theme seemed to be cross-pollination. Even married couples kissed and fondled others in front of their likewise-behaving mates.

I consumed a second drink then danced with John Powers. He stiffened yet trembled the moment our bodies touched. If the music hadn't been so loud, I would have asked him, Do you think I'm your soulmate? Is your hope as futile as mine? What would it take to make you speak?

I bet I could do it, especially on a night like this. Eeny, meeny, miney, mo—do I tow my love slave upstairs or outside and frolic the night away? Or discard him and pick from the others circling me as a maypole?

I would have chosen Buck, except that he kept the dance floor between us while peeking at me above heads. I even allowed myself the thought of Dru, who swirled across my field of vision in a translucent caftan, naked underneath. What I did was back away from John when the music stopped, kiss his cheek, and merge into the party. When sure I had lost him, I popped outside to cool off.

All doors had been braced open, allowing the party to flow in and out. Along with fresh air, the terrace offered lights, refreshments, and—believe it or not—ashtrays! People stood beside them with orange glows flaring and subsiding in the half-light as they puffed. I recognized the mingled scents of tobacco and marijuana. When I strolled over and asked to bum a smoke, six cigarette packs, two joints, and a pipe were immediately offered. I selected, thanked flirtatiously, then sat on the wall to savor my sin.

Buck came out with Julia and did a double take at me. Julia's stare could have melted steel. I gave her a feline smile then finished my cigarette, wrapped my wits about me like a boa, and hip-waggled back inside, buzzed anew from the nicotine jolt.

This time I regarded the party as an energy supply at my service—opening my senses and inhaling power. Within minutes I could make auras flare and fade as if turning a volume knob. How I did it, I couldn't say; but it felt like biofeedback, when one focuses on a monitor until it behaves as one desires. Thus, I saw a psychic spider web entangling everyone in light filaments. Dru and Allanna, dancing together, paused to project a mini aurora at me. I grinned. Their response was blocked by a passing couple.

I considered trying to tweak people with power . . . like, making Dru's caftan fall open, or tapping Julia on the shoulder from across the room so she'd keep turning around and not seeing anybody there . . . then jolted myself sober upon realizing that such power abuse was the first step toward becoming Raoul. That sent me back against the wall clutching my arms across my chest, shivering. I stayed there, a wallflower in the shadows, until the music faded.

Every ninety minutes, an invisible genie changed the musical mood after a hiatus. During each break, a searchlight skipped over the party to settle on a temporary stage in front of the fireplace, cueing us to assemble for live entertainment. A few breaks ago, Dru and Adam had performed a Gilbert and Sullivan parody. Later, Troy had given a rousing synthesizer solo; a blind New Atlantean I hadn't met had played folk harp, then accompanied Jessie on electric piano for some gut-wrenching blues. Pete's drum solo had moved us to bob and chant like aborigines. We'd then phased back into rock-and-roll without missing a beat.

For this break, a bluegrass set was pending. Buck hauled his battered guitar case to the platform, followed by Rob and Jake. Julia unfolded chairs while the guys began tuning. Someone brought up the lights. The rest of us babbled and laughed, with many stepping outside for private entertainment. Once I could see people's sweat rings and running makeup, and my ears started ringing in the quiet, all extrasensory perception disappeared.

I leaned against a wall between two French doors open onto the front courtyard. Colin appeared from it towing Cassandra.

"Here." He handed me a cocktail. "You might need it."

I took, slurped, then coughed. Dragging my gaze away from russet hair gleaming in the spotlight, I turned to my big brother and his new attachment. Colin raised his glass to us both.

We clinked then faced the platform. The quintet opened with an instrumental, in which Rob sawed his fiddle, Mark rasped on a harmonica, Buck strummed a twelve-string, backed by Jake on banjo. Julia jiggled a tambourine and grinned at stage right in a bib-front minidress over gingham blouse. All stamped their feet in time, soon joined by the audience. At that Buck relaxed and started looking around.

I wriggled forward to catch his eye and was rewarded with a smile. My insides trilled. How long since we had last seen each other flushed and sparkling? As my pulse quickened, I knew it delighted him as much as me. He acknowledged with arched eyebrow, then leaned close to the guitar's sound box. When he tweaked a peg a moment later, I realized a string had slipped out of tune.

My joy rush subsided when the men all switched to guitars and accompanied Julia in a ballad. Her alto voice spoke of love in a country-and-western twang. She then crooned a ditty about sunshine and flowers. Throughout, she bobbed to effect sweetness and truth. Buck smiled at her and nodded encouragement. My skin, I daresay, turned bright green.

At the least I must have emitted sparks, for Dru and Blanche appeared at my elbows. Blanche took my hand and interlaced fingers while Dru draped an arm across my back. I continued staring forward at the negative space around the players. No surprise to find it filled with pink swirls.

The set closed on a mellow number that introduced the next atmosphere. For every five recorded songs that followed, one was lively and four slow. The lights dimmed to near darkness, people paired and slipped off into shadows. Mingling continued among the remainder with a sense of pressure to find a mate.

My options circled me, sharklike, awaiting any signal. I qualified as the prime catch of the day. On the dance floor, Mark struggled to hold my eye with artistic contortions. He failed in motion the way so many models do when they transfer to films. My attention drifted to the peacocks: Jim Casey, wearing jeans and muscles, and Adam as Casanova in a purple satin, open shirt over black tights. Seth's curls and baby blues were set off by his sleeveless shirt displaying chest and neck chains. The twins wore their young-warrior outfits, augmented by paint.

Of them all, I preferred Buck's wrangler look, a taper traced by white piping on his shirt from shoulders to belt buckle, snug jeans to cowboy boots. *Come and get it,* I sent to him while holding off partners, tracking his shape as it weaved toward me across the room and pretending not to notice. Until his tap came on my shoulder.

He grinned as I turned halfway, then dipped into a bow. I placed my fingertips across his palm when he straightened. He closed his hand around mine, stopped smiling, and looked at me hard before leading me onto the dance floor. We held eye contact while dancing apart, posturing like courting birds. Intermittently, rainbow light shimmered around his edges. When the music dropped in tempo and volume, we sagged together in mutual forgiveness.

With only one misstep we found our rhythm. Buck pressed his lips against my neck, slid one hand beneath my hair and the other across my back and bottom. I pressed closer, glad to know I would not be sleeping alone.

That promise ended before the song did. Adam cut in from behind, steered me away in ballroom dance form, and passed me to Dru after a sharp pivot. Buck's glare followed but the rest of him stayed put. My last glimpse showed Julia standing beside him.

Dru drove me away with thigh pressure and a vise grip.

"You just overstepped your limits!" I spat, struggling to free myself.

"On the contrary. I'm doing you a favor. You might even thank me one day!"

He spoke above my head while negotiating between dancers. I came aware of the meager film separating our bodies. Me naked beneath Lycra, him naked beneath gauze . . . my thoughts rocketed along unacceptable lines. I fought them, and him, by swearing and struggling. "Damn it, Dru—you wrote the contract guaranteeing us freedom of lifestyle! How dare you—"

"Ah, but Madeline, you are suffering from warped perspective," he said into my ear. "If you'd only acknowledge a higher power, you'd know this is not the time for you to fuck Buck!"

I pulled my head back. "How do you know? Are you the gods' confidant or something? Assigned to direct our every move?"

"You know better than that! And if your senses weren't so fuddled, you'd know what tonight is really for!"

"I already do. It's for decadence. Getting it out of our systems so we can be good the rest of the year. Which I plan to do, if you'll be kind enough to release me!"

I twisted, seeking Buck and Julia. They had already gone.

Dru gloated. I trod on his instep. "I thought you wanted a reconciliation, you interfering beanpole! That was my perfect chance. Why did you blow it?"

He answered with a spin that took us into the courtyard. My head reeled after a sudden stop in sudden dark. Walls muffled the music to the extent it covered whispered dialogues between couples we couldn't see. But they could see us: Dru's caftan caught every light particle from stars, moon, and windows. He looked like a headless spirit, accompanied by a dull metallic gleam. He therefore propelled me from the courtyard through an arch leading onto flagstones, then diverted through a rhododendron hedge hiding a dirt passage around the south wing.

I halted. "What the hell are you doing! If I didn't know better—"

"You obviously don't."

My mouth clapped shut. Dru laid a finger across my lips and the other hand upon my shoulder, then leaped into my mind. *You'll have another chance with him, but tonight's the only time possible for me.*

But—

His flare quelled my protest. *Very soon Blanche and I will marry. We'll then practice fidelity 'til death do us part. We both wanted one last fling with certain persons. Tonight we can get away with it, so . . . Aurora, I knew you'd never come to me, even at Azilde's request. I won't take you unwilling, but I had to take you when you were willing. Don't you see?*

!!??!?!!???!

He burst out laughing. Abruptly, we were tangible and discrete. Dru waited, holding my hands, as I flung out my mind after my sister. I located her essence, entwined with another, but their minds were shut.

Dru laughed again, softly, and drew me into a light, brief kiss. It affected me precisely as he calculated, releasing reined-in desire as if an ax had chopped a rope restraining a bent-over tree. I leaned into his embrace only to have him resist me. He then beckoned and I followed along the sheltered path ending at the herb-garden wall outside the scullery door.

While unlocking a medieval-looking door beside it, Dru transmitted a final message: *It's legitimate, Mad, really. You were mine in a distant life—didn't you know? You and Blanche are a rare case of soul Siamese-twinship. I'm here to divide you then cauterize the wound.*

The door gave into a musty stairwell behind the kitchen. Dru threw double shadows as we ascended, lit from below by tiny bulbs, like theater aisle lights, in the corners of every other stair. The well narrowed at each landing up to the attic. The attic? I puffed. Why not my suite?

For that matter, why not the circle? The weather was mild and dry. He offered no clue, just produced a penlight key ring at the top landing. He flicked it around until spotting the keyhole, into which he inserted a golden key. This door, unlike the ancient one at the bottom, was a hollow-core contemporary opening into a hallway that stretched to the sky. A crystalline night poured star- and moonlight through ceiling windows. Fresh air and muted music filled the carpeted hall.

We passed five doors, four with light cracks at the bottom, and stopped at the last. Dru again used the gold key, then stepped aside for me to enter. As I pawed the interior wall for a light switch, he spoke aloud for the only time.

"Knob's on your left."

I turned a dimmer. Violet light bloomed to reveal a round canopy bed with satin sheets. A mirror looked down from within the canopy, and lights, stereo, and video controls were built into the headboard. Mini fridge and service doors were tucked between artworks and mirrored panels on the opposite wall. My spike heels wobbled on deep carpet; I gave into it and sank to my knees.

Dru caught me up from behind and carried me to the bed. I squawked as the fluid-filled mattress rippled beneath our weight, then I flopped back, spread eagle, and sighed. Dru twiddled with the console until pan-pipes and organ chords swelled and the lights turned indigo. It reminded me of the astral plane. But in this visitation, my hand met resistance when I touched the hologram. And my consciousness began to toggle between five senses and the light stream of Dru flooding into my mind.

14
The Triumvirate

I awoke to a circular chill between my breasts.

My brain, recalling an unknown coldness in the center of my back, screamed, *Raoul is back! Run!*

Both eyes popped open and all muscles clenched. They relaxed when I registered Dru smiling beside me on the bed, dangling a New Atlantis medallion from a finger. He let the chain slip so that the medallion thumped onto my sternum.

"Good morning."

"Grrk!"

He laughed, holding my gaze without blinking to sustain the night's honesty before I could withdraw. "Thought you might like a souvenir."

I curled my hand around the medallion and sat up. "How many strings are attached?"

"None."

I cocked a skeptical eyebrow. "Last I knew, you had to sign papers and commingle funds to get one of these."

"No, just sleep with the leader." He winked.

"So is that how the band got theirs? And Mark, Jeff, Karla . . ."

Dru grinned and slicked back his hair. From its dampness and a towel around his hips, I deduced he had just showered.

"You're right, normally you don't get a medallion until you've joined. But there are exceptions. Cornelius, for example, is a full member but rejected the medallion. Buck, on the other hand, covets one but won't join. Kind of like your pal Kit."

I frowned. "I have just lost any chance of getting him back."

"So who's going to tell him?"

We looked at each other for a long moment. Finally I said, "If either one of us is seen returning to our quarters . . ."

"Then we'd better get cracking. I don't think too many people will be up at this hour."

He rose and crossed the room to a closet, lifting last night's caftan from the floor on his way by. When he pulled open the closet door, I relaxed upon seeing a selection of loungewear. I wouldn't have to stuff myself back into the jumpsuit, after all.

Dru slipped into a terry robe and belted it. I watched, feeling no urge to draw his whippet physique, which gave me a second sigh of relief. Then I looked down at the disk in my hand.

Almost the size of an Olympic medal, it bore cryptic symbols plated in gold. "Were you so sure of me that you brought this with you last night?" I asked. "Or do you keep a stash of them in a drawer up here?"

"That one's courtesy of your sister."

My eyebrows jumped. He nodded. "She's the one who's sure of you. Before the party she shoved this into my hand and said, 'Tonight's the night.' You'll be intrigued to know it's her very own. We each have a public version in plate, and solid gold ones we gave to each other. There are two more real ones, waiting for the right people."

He let the suggestion rest there. I ignored it. Dru crossed the floor to peck my forehead then headed for the door. "You don't have to keep it, but we both thought you might need some physical evidence."

My eyes stung in sudden, quickly suppressed, tears. "Thank you."

For the first time, he dodged my gaze. After a pause he pointed at a door and said, "Shower in there." Then he tipped his head toward the door he was about to open. "And if you turn left out here there's a staircase that will take you to the gallery. Right will take you back outside. Little elves will clean up after you, and the door will lock behind you."

He glanced at the skylight, through which dawn hinted at morning. "Take your time but don't take too long. And by the way—"

His face opened into the most youthful grin I'd seen on him. "Thank you, Madeline. I love you."

He slipped out and closed the door quietly, leaving me with my mouth open. I pulled it closed and slumped back on the satin sheets to stare at myself in the mirror above, wondering what to do now that I had lived my wildest dreams. Correction: Now that my wildest dreams had been surpassed.

Until he tickled me awake with the medallion, Dru had not spoken verbally all night. Just enwrapped me with his bony body and proceeded to absorb my psyche like a starfish sucking nourishment from a snail. Beyond that first penetrating kiss I remembered no specific movement, only that we had twined together and left the room very far behind.

He had taken me back to the glittery void, this time charged by energy from our melding bodies. It felt as though we swam through a joy fest of invisible people, all tuned in, awash with lights and music. Swirling through it, I had learned Dru's story, along with his fears and schemes and passions. He had gleaned same from me without me uttering a sound. I could not understand how joining flesh allowed us to disembody. Yet we had taken a quantum leap beyond carnal knowledge, to where my self wasn't mine any more but a fragment of a greater whole.

Back in my skin, fully conscious, I felt encased in a leaden suit. For a few moments I feared I had landed in the wrong body. Then I recognized the shell I had occupied for this lifetime, which came equipped with the compulsion to carry on.

A shower rinsed off dried sweat and restored pliancy to my muscles. It also washed away a mental cloud. What I had always wanted—must attain—stood out in neon letters as an imperative instead of a dream: to know my soulmate as Blanche knew Dru. They had shown me how it's done, without the satisfaction. Now I had to identify whether my mate was Kit or Buck or yet another. Figuring that out became my new goal. To hell with psionic mysteries!

First I had to get back to my suite unseen. Hoping the little elves would be Powers twins—how else would this tryst remain secret?—I swiped a robe and stalked downstairs through empty hallways. Phew! Bolted the anteroom door behind me and flopped into my own bed, too exhausted to face the implications of my premonition coming true.

I returned to reality after noon, wakened by an empty stomach. I starved it a little longer while pondering what to wear. The old me would have donned T-shirt and shorts for the mild September day revealed through the window. Overnight, however, I had become third pillar of a triumvirate, which called for a bronze bustier and thigh-high leather boots. Nothing like that in my wardrobe, so I opted for yoga pants and a rainbow-striped stretch pullover. Dropping the medallion inside my shirt felt secretly naughty, like wearing lingerie under a business suit. Thus armored, I went downstairs to scavenge for food.

Most of the late lunchers were lolling on the terrace. I loaded a tray and joined them, jumping inside my skin when Blanche and Dru swung their gazes around to meet mine. Their eyes held curiosity and intrigue but no anxiety. I had expected to find them curtained, not to look straight in. Their spirits held hands while their bodies sat separately. Both greeted me as they would any other day of the week.

I returned a shaky smile and greeted the group in general, then aimed for the only empty chair, next to—oh my god, Buck!

What are you doing here! I screamed—apparently inside my head since no one jumped, though Dru and Blanche must have heard the thought, for they stifled giggles. I amused everyone else with a juggling act involving tray, sliding dishes, and chair arms, which ended when Buck leaned over to steer the chair seat under mine. He didn't miss a syllable of his conversation with Cornelius. Once I'd settled safely into eating, the remaining observers resumed their chats.

Below us, maple cracked against maple as three couples chased croquet balls around the lower lawn. Colin, in T-shirt and sweatpants, his slicked-back hair its normal color, sent his ball through wickets until he overshot into roughage. A glowing Cassandra sent her ball nowhere near where she had aimed. She let her curves hang out in T-shirt and sweatpants, making me wonder about Colin. His previous lovers had all been gem-studded pencils. I promised myself to get to know Cassandra better.

Our group on the terrace watched them for a moment, then Brian tossed out a remark and the rest volleyed. We ended up lounging around the yard all afternoon. Continuing last night's odd pairings, Buck debated global warming with Brian, while Cornelius quizzed me about car racing, and Blanche astonished me by discussing tomatoes with Irene. Dru shared travel tales with Seth and Brenda. As people left or joined us, topics shifted and jokes flew.

Only impersonal topics, I noticed. No outward signs of relationship beyond Dru and Blanche sitting closer than anyone else. At the same time, the air hummed with nonverbal excitement. I felt squished by the weight of curiosity from all directions, and from Blanche's and Dru's casual glances lasting a second too long. Buck, conversely, struggled to meet my gaze with natural frequency then pulled his away too fast. Like us all, he acted jovial and erudite, with breakdowns into silliness. And as we all sidestepped personal subjects, we ignored otherworldly topics, as well.

So of course I started seeing auras again. They came and went as unpredictably as an aurora borealis. This time, unlike at the party, I couldn't control them. Damn it—when would my experiences add up to something? All I'd learned was that paranormal phenomena linked somehow to place and people. That might explain why they had eluded science for so long, but it didn't help me understand.

The bonhomie lasted through dinner, after which Colin climbed into his BMW and rolled southward. Blanche and I waved until he was out of sight. From there we strolled to the carriage house and slouched on the leopard sofa. I opened conversation by withdrawing the medallion and swinging it off a finger like Dru.

Blanche blinked and grinned. "Congratulations! I didn't think you'd accept it."

"I'm not sure I'm accepting it. I might be giving it back."

Her face puckered. "It's a gift."

"For screwing your boyfriend? You're twisted!"

"No, it's for facing what's come between us. Being willing to share it. Needing to know, more than resist."

"Careful, you're starting to sound like Allanna!"

Blanche laughed. "She rubs off on you after a while. But Mad, she's not entirely wrong. There is a reason for us to be here together."

"Would you mind telling me what it is?"

"I don't know. Not even Dru does. But it's something important. I can feel it in my bone marrow. Sometimes it seems to vibrate the air!"

Her eyes unfocused in that look of gazing across cosmic distance. Then they focused on me. "If you really want to know, I needed to test Dru as much as reconnect with you. Now that he knows us both at the same level, I can be sure of his preference. And he prefers me the way you prefer someone else."

I pulled my gaze away to hide the longing. What good preferring someone who had removed himself from choice?

"That's a rough way to do it, Blanche. If you hopped in the sack with Kit, I would kill you."

She matched my stonelike face for a moment. Then she relaxed and looked me in the eye. "That's the real difference between us. I swear, I'm more twin to Dru than you! But with each of you there's a part I'll never share, while you share those parts with each other. I want our differences to unite us instead of wedging us apart."

I looked away and chewed my lip, wishing for a cigarette. Pretty soon I would be walking the nine miles into town to get some, and be back on a two-pack-a-day habit.

"I still have to return your medallion. I can't wear it without drawing questions, and no point storing it when you could be wearing it and keeping your gold one safe."

She shook her head and flapped her hand toward me. "No, you keep it. You need it."

I glared at her. "I'm a big girl, I don't need a token!"

"Oh yes you do! You don't trust anyone as far as you can throw them, and I need you to believe me!"

We stared in stalemate until I looked downward and replaced the medallion around my neck. "Okay. In that case I want to know, How can you stand him? Such intensity every night, every day!"

She laughed. "He's not like that all the time! You got the full treatment for the occasion."

"He blew my mind right out my ears! For a while I thought he might be a soul vampire."

"He could be, if he were evil."

"And only our starry-eyed belief assures us he's not."

Blanche shook her head. "That's something else you know in your bone marrow. I guess the trust gene didn't make it into yours. Believe me, Mad, it gets easier with practice. People live up to it more often than not."

"Not for me." I walked to the window overlooking the driveway. "I trusted Kit. Yet he didn't even give me a chance to explain."

"Well, he trusted you, too, then found out you misled him."

"Yeah, but I'm still here!"

"Would you be if your car was running?"

That shut me up for a moment. Then I rallied. "He could have confronted me!"

"And you could have trusted him with your story. Look, Mad, he only means to hurt you as bad as you hurt him. What else can he do? Ignoring it will make him look weak, and making a stink will make him look childish. He's beating himself up for being a fool, I'm sure. When he gets over it, he'll decide whether he wants to make a stand for you or blow you off—and the rest of us while at it. He's got to come back to do either. So I guarantee you'll have one more chance to see him. Use his absence to clean up your business so it won't get in the way again!"

"My business," I echoed, thinking, Buck. And New Atlantis. How long could I stay before I had to sign the contract? What was the financial fine print? How to handle my accounts, my friends, my agent, my unfinished projects? And my damaged race car in the gatehouse, my street car gathering storage fees in a Massachusetts shop? Could I dismiss Raoul as a fluke, or would he come back to haunt me? What if Buck wanted to get back together?

Blanche joined me at the window. "You'd have less trouble with these things if you believed in the universal mind."

I shook my head. "Dru almost convinced me. It's such a nice idea—we're all points spaced unevenly along the same line, one consciousness in separate containers . . . makes it easier to see how people can connect psychically, and why sex can be sacred. But I'd rather be alone inside my cranium, thank you. And not share lovers!"

"You don't have to do either."

"Then why are you trying so hard to make me?"

"Because I don't want to be alone inside my cranium!"

"Can you at least respect that I do?"

"Of course. But it needs to be an informed choice, not a knee-jerk reflex."

"Hmm."

We watched twilight diffuse the scenery. Without looking at her I said, "Then tell me this: Why do humans bother incarnating if their minds can intermingle?"

"Karma. That's the whole point. You reincarnate to atone for the past and develop for the future. When you've paid your dues and earned your stripes, then you can exist disembodied and enjoy that intermingling. For now, we're far enough along to deserve a teaser, but we still have a long way to go."

"But what do we have to do, to satisfy what masters?"

She shrugged. "Half the battle is believing there's a power to satisfy. The rest is figuring out what to do."

I threw up my hands and rolled my eyes. "Blind faith, in other words."

"Very blind. Very faith. As far as I can tell, the main job is leaving the world better than you found it, and applying your talents toward the betterment of at least one person—a large group if possible."

"Hence, your devotion to New Atlantis."

"Yes. Dru has a gift of communicating important ideas to people: compassion, courage, individualism, altruism. If everyone just took care of themselves and their circle of loved ones, whose circles overlap other circles, then most of the world's ills would disappear. My job is to fill in whatever he lacks to keep him balanced and happy and creative. Your job is . . . I'm not sure yet. But it has something to do with communicating truth, I think."

I stared at her. "Clone of my genes, I barely know you."

She smiled. "You'd be surprised how alike we really are!"

She stepped forward to hug me. I squeezed her tight. "Maybe if I can find my counterpart as you have, I'll find my purpose."

She shrugged. "Some people find their purpose first. Not us. We need to integrate with someone first. For a long time I feared that Dru was the right soul for both of us. Now I know that you need Kit to square you off. When that happens, everything else will fall into place."

"How do I get him back? I don't even know where he is!"

"Maybe that means you have to deal with the one on your doorstep, first."

I sank into a chair, frowning, then told her about my rolling vision in the marble circle with what had turned out to be Buck, then Kit, then Dru.

"What bugs me," I concluded, "is I can't tell if I truly had a premonition. The first part—moving outside my body to watch me and Buck—could have been reaction to trauma. The second and third parts—the jumble of Kit and Dru—could have been pure fantasy juxtaposed with sexual excitement and guilt. It doesn't take much imagination to put blue sheets on Kit's mattress and gold satin on that waterbed upstairs. Besides, I told Dru about this vision yesterday, so he could have swapped sheets."

"He wouldn't do that."

I dismissed her bias. "So I can't use those details to prove psychic foreknowledge. Then the overlay of scents and tastes and textures—well, all three men share the same racial physiotype, and I've been close enough to each to have stored his scent and details in my subconscious. On the other hand—"

I raised open palms. "—if it really was clairvoyance, that means I have to pay serious attention to all the rest of it, which is so scary I can hardly back up to the thought!"

"You know what's worse?" Blanche sat on the arm of my chair. "Whatever you believe is true. If you believe something strongly enough, your mind will find a way to embrace it. But—" She held up a finger. "It can work in your favor. In this case, it doesn't matter whether you had a premonition or a fantasy. Either way, you experienced the same thing. So you need to focus on content and meaning. What do Buck, Kit, and Dru share besides being white guys with light eyes? What have you learned from intimacy with them back to back?"

I sat in frowning silence. Blanche stood and crossed the room to a cobalt vase stuffed with pussy willows and peacock feathers. Lifting the stems with one hand and reaching into the vase with the other, she extracted an object concealed within her curled fingers.

"Here's a New Atlantis bennie for you." She replaced the bouquet and opened her hand to reveal a gold key on her palm. "For whenever you must have absolute privacy. Whatever you do, don't lose it! No replacements for any reason."

She dropped the key into my hand. I examined it then looked up. "Why a purple dot?"

"Matches the one on the doorknob of the room it opens. Only six rooms for all of us. They're assigned randomly on the assumption our needs will be random, since we all have rooms and rarely have guests. Point is, if your room is occupied when you want to use it, tough luck."

"What keeps people from barging in on each other?"

"The dot doesn't show if the door's locked from the inside."

I nodded, imagination racing. It stopped on a recollection. "Were you up there last night?"

Blanche smirked. "Other end of the hall, with Jake Powers."

"Jake! Blanche, does he talk?"

Her lips squirmed in a suppressed smile. "Not directly. But very expressive through his body, and rather noisy when aroused!"

We tittered, regressing to schoolgirl closeness. After a locker room-style discussion of various men's attributes, she returned to Protocol of the Key.

"The other rule is, you use a room, you clean it. Dru took care of that this time. But when the key in your hands opens a door, the room is your responsibility."

I nodded then hitched it onto the chain with my medallion. Just what I needed: temptation and a morality reminder dangling between my breasts! Might as well have a chastity belt and give a key to every man on the compound! The wrong thought on which to go to bed. My well-used body throbbed in reminder and desire. So cruel of Kit to keep away! And why had Buck chosen today to start being friendly? Did my disappearing last night with someone else inspire him to finish the business we'd been interrupted at twice?

I tried to exercise thought power by siren-singing him to my bedroom. If anyone outside the suite heard me, however, they resisted the temptation I could no longer bear.

15
Truth or Consequences

I endured by default: no opportunity, no pursuers. New Atlantis at normal tempo left little energy for affairs. Routine flowed in choreographed streams and eddies. I drifted along, then swirled in circles, then drifted again until snagged.

Although I saw Blanche daily, we didn't interact much. She and Dru devoted their time to satisfying their karma. In long-ago Atlantis, I was told, they had squandered a civilization. This obliged them to help put another world to rights. Through intervening lives they had learned their lessons. On alternate days when I believed this, I felt myself to be lifetimes behind.

Instead of finding answers, I came up with more questions. All applied whether one believed in a single lifetime or many. My unease prevented art or meditation. So I walked at every opportunity, wandering farther afield each time.

One glorious Indian Summer morning, I exited the house by a north wing staircase. That route was as little used as the escarpment trail, which I reached via footpath down the tiers below the terrace. To aid in camouflage, I wore a long rust-colored dress I had obtained from a photo shoot. It made me feel like the heroine of the book whose cover I had posed for, giving me a regal, autumnal look. The indestructible faux suede fit thick and snug through the body, long and loose through the gaucho-style legs, and zipped from waist to neck for adjustable comfort. I normally wore it with tall boots but this time donned leggings and hiking shoes for easy travel. I could go farther and faster on bike or horseback but not unobserved or unintercepted.

So if anyone noticed my departure, they wouldn't expect me to go far because I wore a dress.

I picked my way down the cliff then cut around the shorn cornfields to ford the river. Once across, I took the bridle path into forest. After two miles uphill I gained a rock protrusion overlooking Hill House—the closest I could come to a roofless temple. And I could count on someone uncasing binoculars the minute my form appeared on the ridge!

Nonetheless, the tor gave the illusion of solitude. I settled into a fanny-sized niche in the rock face, drew up my legs, and closed my eyes to the sunlight. Slowly the trembling eased from my muscles, the thud faded from my pulse . . . and I began to contemplate the Möbius strip.

That symbol neatly captured the concept "energy flows, matter cycles"—a slogan adopted by ecologists and a concept accepted, without spiritual angst, by good-old mechanical Kit. Easy to say but hard to pinpoint. On an infinite continuum, where did physics and metaphysics merge? How did the transition between them work?

Science knew a lot about transitions in matter. Ocean to cloud to rain to river. Chicken to egg to chicken, or egg to breakfast to waste that fertilized something else's food. Ashes to ashes, dust to dust, molecules activated by sunlight, absorbed by soil and air and water, and returned to the larger cycle.

All those molecules contributing bits of micro-memory, micro-identity, adding up to organisms—humans—as unique as snowflakes yet composed of the same elements . . . It seemed inevitable that we would "recognize" someone or something or someplace we'd never experienced. As creatures needing a reason for being, we could explain the sensation as memory of past life.

Then again, energy had to go somewhere after the matter that housed it changed form. So what did that energy become? Light? Gravity? Time? Subnuclear electric forces that evolved through the years to power the stars? Or did it hang around in a noncorporeal plane and reunite with matter at another time, thus carrying personality again in a different body?

Forget reincarnation, go back to physics. Newton's first law of motion: An object set into motion will continue unless acted upon by another force.

Okay, if Raoul was that object in motion, and my recognition of his true nature was a force, then his disappearance—a change of velocity and direction—agreed with physics. I could reasonably assume that his mass and composition remained the same. But what about his intent—what was that made of? And what if he was not discouraged or deflected, but enraged and working on a more effective way to get us?

Many ways to harm us remotely. I wished he'd do something obvious, like terrorism or electronic sabotage, so we could enlist the long, strong arm of human law. Here, I suspected, we were dealing with inhuman law, exercised in the form of psychic skills or black magic. Assuming that both were possible, how long would it take to master them, and what would he have to do?

Practice, practice, practice.

Let's say, I hypothesized, that I wanted to shoot someone but had never handled a weapon. It would take weeks to (a) acquire a gun and (b) practice enough—undiscovered—to consistently bull's-eye a target. Then (c) I would have to plan a hit that guaranteed success and escape. The same would hold true for any weapon, including magic. Which left the question: How much could Raoul learn in the weeks since he, and Kit, had vanished?

Another factor to consider was reality's harshness. Although decent people abounded, the cruel and heartless multiplied every year. None of them had ever touched Blanche, so she could afford to believe that everyone lived up to trust if you let them. No such guarantee with Raoul. I had to believe he was out there, conniving. If somebody didn't mistrust him thoroughly, he could blind-side us all.

My broodings were penetrated by an approaching clip-clop. I opened my eyes to find Buck on Nova staring at me from the ledge trail along my left. Our respective heights put us at the same level, separated by a chasm. How symbolic, I thought, as my heart kicked in my chest.

His delay in reacting told me that he too had dreaded a surprise encounter. Now he had to either offend me and embarrass himself by retreating, or give confrontation a try. I remained immobile, chin high against the azure backdrop, with hair and skirt flapping in the breeze.

He nudged Nova upward. I waited on my rock with arms curled around my knees. Buck passed behind me to pick up the promontory access. Moments later he drew Nova to a halt beside my boulder. Our gazes met eight feet from the ground.

"Fancy meeting you here," he opened.

"I suppose it was inevitable."

"You'd think with a compound this size we could avoid each other."

"At least I can finally ask you a question without a dozen people around."

"Which is…"

"Why are you still here?"

"I might ask the same of you!"

"My sister asked me to stay."

"And Dru asked me to plug the hole your boyfriend left."

I started to protest, Kit's not my—but bit it back in time.

"At least I'm working," Buck said into my silence.

"What makes you think I'm not?"

"You really selling your paintings?"

"Not at the moment. But the work I'm building up will pay for my existence for a few years."

Whether it would cover the Tiger as well remained to be seen. I didn't mention the dividend checks that tided me over between sales, or funded racing when I was flush.

"I guess you finally got an ivory tower to do your artsy-fartsy thing in."

"Sure beats modeling! What do you have, a monk's cell in The Glen?" Or Julia's bed? I resisted adding.

"My version of an ivory tower." He patted Nova's neck. "And a damn nice horse."

"I've never ridden him."

Buck stood in the stirrups and patted the saddle seat behind him. "Hop aboard."

Memories overwhelmed me. I shoved them back, saying, "No thanks, I'll try him myself sometime."

"Is that my cue to leave?"

"No, I'm done contemplating my navel for the day."

"I thought you might be recharging yourself for the next glowing session."

I caught my breath. He gave me time to compose a reply by dismounting. While Nova moved to the closest growth and began foraging, Buck scrambled up the boulder to sit at my side.

"How brave you are!" I exclaimed. "I might turn you into a toad!"

He slid his eyes sideways and curled his lip. "I'd like to see you try!"

That shut me up. Buck turned away to watch a red-tailed hawk spiral above the hills and valleys.

I broke the silence by saying, "I wasn't the only one glowing that night."

That caught his breath and earned me a suspicious glance. A long, windy silence ensued. I shivered and hugged my knees closer, wishing Buck would put his arm around me. He just picked at a mica fleck and said, "I think it's time for somebody to tell me what's going on."

"I'd be happy to, if I could figure it out myself!"

"You're involved, I take it." He rolled the mica between his fingers.

"Involved? I'm the centerpiece of the whole affair!"

He looked at me. "Some sort of love triangle?"

"Wrong."

"Then why did Kit leave?"

"Only Kit knows that one. Although I can guess."

"I can make a dozen guesses. What's the most likely?"

I looked down my nose at him. "That qualifies as none of your business."

"Don't give me that crap, Madeline. Everything here is everyone's business. In this case, I'm still here because Kit isn't, and it would be real helpful to know if he's coming back. Especially since I'm stuck with his ex, who's bent out of shape over him missing and takes turn blaming me or you."

"Well, she's right on both counts."

"C'mon, I'm sick of being talked to in riddles!"

"All right—" I broke off to tantalize him. "How about a trade?"

Buck's brows lowered. "What for what?"

"I give you the inside story; you tell me where you've been all these years."

Buck sighed and flung his mica off the outcrop. "I got nowhere, believe me."

"I can tell, but that's not the point."

"Then what is?"

"If you wanna get you gotta give. Something you never understood."

"One thing I'm not gonna give is a chance for you to gloat over my misery!"

"Don't need to. I know you got what you deserved by those lines in your face."

He flushed beneath his windburn and clenched his teeth until his jaw cords protruded. "All right. I lasted six months in Colorado. We fought constantly. She kicked me out. I headed north. My truck died in Wyoming. I stuck out my thumb. Ended up in Alaska, trekked around until I was broke, then worked for a while on an oil spill. Good money, but . . ."

His face darkened as if a cloud had crossed the sun. A long moment later he resumed. "Some of us wintered over. I got into a bar fight so split on a snow machine and cut into Canada through wilderness. Wandered around for a while, heading east, sometimes logging, sometimes playing in bars. I saw just about everything that's wrong with the world and nothing right. I was pretty much at bottom when the band passed through."

I watched cloud patterns shift over the valley. Emotions swirled likewise inside me, never quite catching and holding form.

"Your turn," Buck snapped.

I blinked to attention. "I'm cold. Let's get out of the wind."

Buck glowered then stood and whistled to Nova. The stallion moseyed over and stood beside the boulder. Buck scraped down its slope into the saddle, then jockeyed the horse so that I could inch down and on behind. In the process, my medallion slipped outside my dress.

Buck caught the glint. "Oh-ho! So you signed!"

"No, and don't you dare tell anyone."

With a grunt, I stretched a leg across Nova's rump and heaved onto the blanket behind the saddle, grabbing Buck around the waist until balanced. He clucked and jiggled the reins, directing the stallion up the trail.

"Where we going?" I asked into his neck.

"Where no one can hear or see us."

"Not too far, please—my thigh's getting pinched."

"We can drop the saddle and come back for it later."

"Good idea."

We stopped, dismounted, stripped the horse, climbed on bareback. Much better. In fact, not too far from the painting that had chased Kit away.

"So talk, Madeline. I'm a captive audience!"

"What do you know about Raoul?" I opened.

"Him again? What I said before. He's a sleazebag."

"Well, he's also a satanist or something and has been pulling nasty tricks."

Pause. "Like that envelope on your doorstep?"

"Jeez! Who'd you get that from?"

"Does it matter?"

"Yes, it does!"

"I told you, Madeline—everything here is everybody's business."

Then why doesn't the whole community know about us? I wondered. Or do they already, and I'm the only one in the dark?

"So anyway," Buck broke in, "why you? He make a pass and you blew him off?"

"No, Blanche is the one he's after. And possibly Dru—possibly New Atlantis."

"Good luck. So where does Kit fit in?"

"He doesn't. I mean . . ." I trailed off to chew my lip, unsure of how—or whether—to introduce the central issue.

Nova's hooves crunched through the silence. We had gained the forest and rustled along a leaf-coated path, near the reservoir. I looked around for ravens, or any creature paying too much attention. Deer froze to look at us then sprang away, while red squirrels scurried along branches. Chipmunks streaked across the path with upright tails, chittering their displeasure; woodpeckers interrupted their drumming, nuthatches beeped then departed. If anything watched, we could not see it. Thus, when Buck sighed impatiently, I decided to try what I had learned during psychic dialogue with Dru.

First I said, "Kit did what you would do in his place. Couldn't handle too much truth and too many conflicts so took off somewhere to work it out."

Buck stiffened. "What did you do to him?"

In answer, I slid my hands under his shirt while sending a picture of vibrant sky and marble pillars, ourselves garbed in robes embraced on the stairs.

He twitched and sputtered. "What are you doing?"

I again answered by transmission: a scene from one of the raunchier moments in our past.

Buck twisted and shoved me off Nova. I caught myself on his jeans so landed upright but staggering—and clung to his leg to prevent him from galloping away. Nova skittered and rolled his eyes but Buck held him firmly.

"Damn you Madeline, how did you do that!"

"You asked. There's no better way to explain."

Buck jerked Nova left and right, kicked him forward then pulled him back. "Jeezus! Christ. Jeezus—how long you been doing that?"

"Since the night I got here. And it's why I didn't have to sign to get in."

I relaxed my grip on his calf when his chest stopped heaving. He relaxed his stranglehold on Nova at the same time.

"So that's what Dru was talking about. I suppose he can do it too. And Blanche. How many others?"

"Allanna and Dru are the only ones I know of, but I wonder about the twins. It's called telepathy."

He kicked my arm away. "Don't patronize me. I know what that shit is called!" Then he laughed harshly. "And you're right. I understand just fine why Kit took off!"

"Don't you do it, too!"

He spurred the horse into a trot. "But I should, jeezus, get me outa here!" His voice trailed away through the hoofbeats. "Freakin' cult dancing around their Atlantean prince! I should've seen it coming—jeezus, they're serious. And stupid me thought they wanted to save the world!"

I jogged after him until the trees thinned to meadow. Leaning against a sapling to catch my breath, I saw Nova gleaming white in the sloping field I had crossed with Allanna. Then, the grass had been waist-high and profuse with wildflowers; now it was withered and bent.

Buck lay back on Nova's rump, staring at the firmament. He held one rein in his fists resting on his diaphragm while the other rein trailed Nova's grazing head.

As my footsteps crackled approach, Buck said too calmly, "You know, I could handle this if New Atlantis really was laying groundwork for a new society. Forget the gods—forget mysterious powers—just concentrate on food and shelter and not polluting and getting along. I always thought that if the white man had joined forces with the natives instead of slaughtering them, we'd've balanced progress with respect for nature and ended up with a halfway sane world. But Dru blows it by insisting the golden age already came and went with Atlantis. He might as well claim we descended from visiting aliens!"

"You don't have to believe it." I placed my palm on the fine hairs of Nova's shoulder. "That's his whole point."

Buck sat up and looked down at me. "But everyone here believes something equally stupid. If not reincarnation, then seven days to create the planet and virgin birth. Moon worship and magic circles. Why can't you all accept that we're just the top of the food chain, with enormous brains and opposable thumbs?"

His gaze challenged me to argue. I couldn't, since I shared his view. But I could explain, and he looked willing to listen. This might be my only chance.

"Being the dominant species is precisely the reason." I tried to sound casual, not pedantic. "Humans might have reached a physical plateau, but like all life we're compelled to recycle and evolve. To balance our ability to create and destroy, we have to develop a higher mental and spiritual capacity. Religions provide a framework. If everybody didn't believe in something greater, then we'd all give up for lack of purpose. Doesn't matter how stupid as long as it works."

"But it doesn't. Look at the world!" He flung open his arms.

"Which one?"

Buck's mouth snapped closed and he scowled, his eyes glinting teal in the sunlight. "The human world. Out there. The natural one, like here, is ruled by gravity and photosynthesis, and it's perfect. The laws are fair and unbiased. All we have to do is learn to live by them and everything will be fine."

"But you've just described the premise of reincarnation. It works just like your perfect natural world. Matter breaks down then recombines, perpetually. Energy transfers but never dies. Why can't the spirit do likewise? Nobody can define it, yet everything's got some form of driving life force that comes from somewhere then passes to somewhere, within a biochemical machine. In higher mammals, the spirit is self-conscious. It must have some practical purpose, since Nature lets her faulty experiments die out rather than evolve. Humans, despite their faults, continue to develop. They don't teach their children well, unless they follow certain religions. The reincarnationists believe in 'as above, so below,' and 'what goes around comes around.' So they check their negative impulses now so they won't have to pay for them later."

"Ah yes," Buck sneered, rolling his eyes skyward. Then he quoted in a fruity voice: "The cosmic accounting system. Moral debits and credits totted up over successive lives."

I sing-songed back, "And when the columns balance, your soul has reached a perfected state."

"Then what?"

I shrugged. "Then you don't have to come back any more."

"Who wants that? I like being incarnate."

"Wouldn't it be easier to face losing your body if you knew you could either live forever in another plane or take on a new body and another chance?"

He frowned. "I think I'd rather fertilize a tree."

After a pause he added, "Besides, we need perfected souls right here. It's selfish to act for your own future comfort instead of making a better world for the next generation. That's why I went militant for a while, spiking trees and shooting bulldozers. People are such assholes, refusing to realize that we can adapt to different work and environments but plants and animals are stuck in their biomes. We think we're God, free to fuck with nature and judge who gets to live and die. So don't talk to me about religion, Madeline, since it either reinforces the 'I'm God' attitude or makes people shirk responsibility for their actions."

Whew! I was glad to be on the ground. "Better watch it, Buck—you're living one of religion's oldest credos!"

He checked his next outburst to say, "What do you mean?"

"Adversity builds character. You used to be an apathetic white boy. Now you're an outraged environmentalist. Why don't you work for Greenpeace or something?"

"I probably will if I ever build up enough to get out of here. When you get room and board with a job, you don't get squat for pay."

"Didn't you get paid on the tour?"

"Just expenses. They were afraid I'd drink it or blow it up my nose."

"How long have you been straight?"

"Since I stepped onto their tour bus. Although lately I've been wondering what they put in the food!"

We grinned, then I dragged us back to the subject. "I'm not promoting God, I'm just trying to explain—"

"It can't be explained, Mad, that's the problem. Rationalized, yes. But not explained."

"You mean . . . religion? Or god with a capital G?"

"I mean sex."

"What?"

While I struggled with his non sequitur, he swung a leg over the horse's neck and slid down before me.

"When you think about sex," he said, grabbing my upper arms, "you realize there can't be a God."

He kissed me so hard it hurt, grinding his pelvis against mine. My body surged in response but I fought it, almost frightened by his change.

He pushed me away to arm's length, smiling at my confusion. Since he emanated no malice, I stood fast and let him lead to wherever he was going. I even helped him along by saying, "I'm not sure how sex and God cancel each other out."

He released me. "Because the plan makes no sense. Any god that sees all, knows all, cares about all—especially people—wouldn't make such a bad mistake."

I scowled down at his hands, which were sliding the front zipper of my dress up and down. "Look at men and women," he continued. "Basically, we don't get along. We're like two different species. We don't understand each other. On the whole, we don't like each other. We want different things. We live differently, think differently, feel differently . . . the only reason we get together is sex. But how many men and women in any couple want the same thing there? So to me that says, Animal Kingdom. Nature added pleasure to guarantee we'd reproduce."

I zipped up my dress and turned away from him, mind churning. He went on, as if voicing a well-practiced, long-stifled theory. "That setup fits the natural world. Most animals pair up to mate then go their separate ways. We would, too, except for that religion crap. Which is all about humans and nothing about God. What a joke! There's no deity up there keeping an eye on each person; giving a rat's ass what happens to any of us; weaving some grand design for our personal development. That's pure egotism! If some god really controlled nature, then it would make sense to make humans not spoil their own nests. To make them want to work together, to make them compatible by design, not force them through millennia of slow improvement. The speed we evolve is pathetic, especially in proportion to our minds. What a waste! We're the same greedy, insecure morons we've been since day one. All the cultures and religions we've dreamed up to justify ourselves don't change the facts we fuck, we eat, we fight for position, we die, just like every other creature. We just happen to have that big gray-matter machine upstairs plus those opposable thumbs."

He paused for breath, staring at my back, waiting for reaction. I wanted to tackle him then and there in the grass. But I restrained myself to a cool rotation to face him.

"There are two flaws to your logic."

He kept his mouth pressed shut while clenching and unclenching his fists. I spoke in as highbrow and neutral a tone as I could.

"First, most God systems presuppose a Devil, which you're failing to consider. That can account for the negatives you listed. Second . . ."

I inhaled, stilled all muscles, and compelled him to share my memory of the times we had lain together, truly joined. That sense of purpose and bonding—more real than body parts and breathing. It took no special vision to see the memory reflected in his eyes.

I released my breath. "If there's no god of any sort, Buck, how can you account for that?"

He rushed an answer. "Sensory overload."

I put my hands on my hips. He tried again. "Part of the pleasure system. Makes lovers want to stay together, gives them a reason to keep company, so that females have the long-term benefit of a male's strength and fidelity, and he has the benefit of her nurturing and knowing which are his own children. The ego-need that created religion makes people crave something special to help them make choices, like, who will be their mate. So they rationalize any intense physical feeling into meaning." He ended with a satisfied smirk.

"Jeezus, you sound like a textbook! You just pass Psych 101 or something?"

"No, I've been attending the school of life!"

"And it's taught you how to rationalize pretty well, yourself!"

"Yeah, well, I gotta figure out what the hell is going on around here, since no one sees fit to tell me. I'm just Pete's loser cousin, hanging around."

"And whose fault is that?"

He strode off to collect Nova. Oh-oh. I had a long hike ahead if he rode away.

No, he slid aboard with a strength and grace I could only envy, then rode back to me. Pulling up, he extended an arm. I clutched his hand, hooked my toe on his boot, then swung up behind him. Nova, startled, jogged a few steps while Buck gathered reins.

"This is all very interesting, Madeline," he said as we backtracked across the field, "but it doesn't tell me anything. Like how or why you can violate my privacy, or where Raoul fits in."

"Simple. He can do it, too."

Buck swore. "So you guys have been having some sort of mental fencing match while the rest of us run around fixing tractors?"

I laughed. "More or less"—thinking, He's taking this awfully well.

"Be careful, Madeline." He shook his head. "You can get hurt fooling around with invisible energies. Remember, the guys who harnessed electricity and atomic power and X-rays got pretty toasted before they got it right!"

"Now tell me something I don't know!" I snapped, reminded of my fears. For all I knew, Raoul had eavesdropped on the entire conversation. Telepathy, once mastered, knew no distance limits. And if consciousness did survive death, then Raoul might haunt us for the rest of time!

I hoped he was one of those lost souls who devolve out of existence, so degenerate they can't sustain the spark of life. I also hoped that Buck's mind, opening and shuttering spastically, wouldn't appear to such an entity as easy prey. Was I obliged to warn him, to make him listen, or would the anxiety thus generated weaken his defense?

I needed an Etiquette Guide to Psychic Awakening. Surely it was unethical to lean my cheek against Buck's back and spy on his efforts to reconcile the form pressing against him with the robed figure he kept meeting in dreams on the temple stairs! My flashing that image, earlier, had frightened him witless. I withdrew from his mind, recalling my objections to Dru's and Allanna's probing. "It was necessary," Allanna had said. Was it truly necessary for me to shock Buck this way, or was I indulging in mind games, too?

As we drew near the abandoned saddle, he grew tense within my embrace. I sat back and rested my hands on my thighs until he drew up near the boulder, then we slipped to the ground. He busied himself with saddling the stallion. I hovered, weighing my desire to complete the tale and ensure his understanding against the likelihood that he had absorbed his fill. His darting glances warned me to keep my distance. I decided to heed him, and trust that his recovering curiosity would bring him back for more.

"I'm heading back," I announced, starting down the trail toward the valley. He said nothing, having fallen into the sulk I knew so well. Minutes later, I heard Nova's hooves striking pebbles behind me. Buck caught up, passed, then wheeled the horse to block my path.

I braced myself for a cutting last word. He couldn't manage one; instead, settled for a Kit-like glare. Then he reversed Nova and proceeded downward. *Touché!* I sent after him, looking forward to the next round.

16
Backlash

After the morning's exertions, followed by hours of scrubbing porcelain and tile, then the usual dusty sorting and stacking in the library, I was ready for a parboil in the hot tub. The best time to get it alone was during supper, so I skipped that meal as I had the others, donned a full-length terry robe, and sneaked down to the basement after a snack in my rooms.

Someone else had the same idea, two chambers away, grunting and banging through a workout. Despite the staff's hygienic efforts, the basement smelled of sweat and chlorine. I tuned it out and sank into the steaming water. Only the clanking from the weight room kept me from sinking into sleep.

The metallic rhythm sounded like a pickax chipping against bedrock, which evoked an image of prisoners on a chain gang. This transformed as I watched into a movie of slavery and torture in the fiery pits of Hell.

Up from the flames came Raoul's gargoyle mask, to hang in space and leer at me while fire fingers reached out through eye sockets and ears—suddenly a dwelling's windows. People and horses ran screaming across its lawns, trampling twisted and charred bodies while I watched, paralyzed—deafened by the uproar, breathless from the heat.

Then the clanging stopped and I sat alone in a vat of steaming water. Not for long: A nicely muscled young man appeared in the doorway buffing his hair with a towel. He stood bare and dripping from a fast-rinse shower. He stopped buffing upon registering my presence.

"Hello, again," I said, pretending not to notice the activity below his waist.

Buck suppressed it with a snarl. "Are you following me around or something?"

"No, we just seem to be on intersecting paths today."

Buck growled but didn't walk out. He ditched his towel then settled into the tub with a flinch followed by a long sigh. My eyes feasted on his body as the diners feasted upstairs.

"Not hungry tonight?" He gestured upstairs toward their muffled activity.

"Too tired," I answered, not daring to add, Besides, I'm too nauseous. A minute ago I was knee deep in blackened bodies. Oh Buck, if you only knew!

He sensed my enervation and didn't push, merely closed his eyes and eased deeper into the water.

We simmered in awkward silence for a while. I suspected he was waiting for me to project something onto his mental canvas. Heh-heh . . . how about some burning horses, Buck?

I refrained, so the silence continued. He filled it by activating the massage jets for a few minutes. About the time I concluded he would ignore me until I left, he shut off the jets and said into the sudden quiet, "If the weather is good tomorrow, why not take your ride with me."

I opened my eyes. "A fence run?"

His eyes remained closed. "Yeah. My turn again. I'm tired of riding alone."

Hmm. An opening to broach another hot topic. "Doesn't Julia go with you?"

He lifted a pink and glistening shoulder. "Sometimes. But I need a break from her. I talk to the same three people all the time, or nobody. 'Bout time I got to know the rest!"

I stifled my retort: After ten years and today's scene, you consider us strangers?

Well, it was true, in a way. I should be pleased with this gesture of reconciliation. Dru would be satisfied, and Kit could hardly complain.

But I preferred the condensed method of getting reacquainted. Buck sprawled before me, naked; I had a hunger that dinner couldn't sate. He was arm's length away and probably willing. But people were stomping down the stairs.

My invitation slid under the water with me. Upon surfacing, I heard the chatter of men with iron digestion partaking of sport for dessert. By their voices I recognized Seth and Greg, down for their weekly handball game. Lighter footsteps trailed them down the stairs. Buck opened his eyes halfway and looked at me. Anything we said would be overheard until the game got underway.

Seth and Greg moved straight to the court without cruising the cubicles. The third party, however, padded along the aisles.

My warning prickle activated a second before Kit swung into the spa room. His thunderclap presence sat us up so fast we slopped water onto the floor.

Kit's eyes, at first sparkling, skipped over me to Buck, narrowed, then returned and sharpened into knife points. He stabbed me with them, then gave the blade a verbal twist.

"I should have known."

I expected him to spin on his heel and lope back up the staircase. No point in stopping him, for what could I say?

Kit gave me hope by remaining planted. Buck startled both of us by saying, "Welcome back."

Kit's glare swung to him. "Actually, you're the one I'm looking for."

Smack! Why not just backhand me across the cheek?

I retaliated, "Why don't you join us?"

Kit's feet shifted but he neither approached nor retreated. Buck spread his arms along the tub rim. "So what do you want?"

"I was hoping to get the truth, since she wouldn't tell me."

"What makes you think I will?"

"At this point, I don't."

Buck and I sighed and struggled not to look at each other. Kit's face colored and his gaze darted between us. I sat with thudding heart, holding my breath.

Buck said, "Listen, if you two got problems, work it out between you. I just came in to relax and found Mad already here."

He pushed himself upright, cascading water. The effect was like Poseidon emerging from the sea. The elevated tub floor allowed him to tower above Kit magnificently. In stepping out, disdaining towels and handrails, he dripped on the challenger and stalked to the dressing room.

Seth and Greg, watching from the doorway, parted before him. They stepped together again, stifling snickers, to wink at me before withdrawing. Kit, whose back remained to the door, stood clenched so tight he quivered. Neither of us spoke until feet started pounding and squeaking in the ball court.

"Goddamn you!" he burst.

I struggled to keep my voice even. "It's just as he said. I was here, and he walked in."

"I wish I could believe you."

"Then don't. Turn right around and go back where you ran away to. Or take off your clothes and get in here, and I'll tell you the truth."

He glared, then pivoted, took one step toward the doorway, then hesitated. From the red burn flooding his neck, I knew that war raged within.

Oh please, please, please! I sent with all my heart.

Slowly, he reversed. After another glare, he dropped his gaze and yanked off his ratty sweatshirt, unzipped and kicked away his dirty jeans.

I held my breath as he climbed into the hot tub. His hair drifted to the sides as he slid down, stopping at his lower lip, still not looking at me, his brows low and straight.

My turn for a big gesture. I floated across the space between us and straddled his lap.

You want the truth, boy?

I pressed my mouth to his and clasped my hands around his head to keep him there, flattening my breasts against his chest. It took him a few heartbeats to recover, then hands, tongue, and groin engaged. We added more steam and bubbles to the tub before our bracing feet slipped and we jerked off the seat. The resulting nose full of water broke us apart. We sputtered and laughed, then righted ourselves, looking around. No one else had entered the basement, and the other men remained occupied. Their thump-whack-wheeze-gasp from the ball court masked our words.

"Start talking," he demanded, leaning back to put space back between us. I didn't know where to begin. The truth.

"I only found out he was here the night of the concert. And he was supposed to leave the next day. Dru kept him here because of the Raoul business. I got both of them—and you—thrown at me in the same hour! I couldn't escape 'cause I wrecked my car on top of it all. And if I'd had you take me home, all those pictures were on the walls."

Kit's unflinching gaze flinched. The silence between us filled with thundering from the ball court. Kit said only, "We'd better go upstairs."

So he could see for himself what hung on my walls now. I nodded and we climbed out, dried off, slipped into clothing, ascended from the basement, traversed the hallways, climbed the grand staircase, trudged the length of the south wing. New Atlanteans we passed looked quizzically at Kit and said "Hi!" or "Welcome back!" I wouldn't need to call Blanche for her to get the news.

When we entered my now-stuffed suite, Kit kept his back to me by scanning the paintings. I wondered how I would have felt if his walls had displayed photos of women instead of cars. In hopeful deference, I had put up everything not containing Buck images. Newer pieces awaiting frames stood propped against anything available. On my drawing table lay a nude portrait of Kit, derived from the sketch session. I covered it with a sweatshirt while he studied the other works.

"Is this a vision?" He squinted at a canvas atop a bookcase.

"More or less." More, a compilation of them all. In the foreground, a bowman shot at the lone survivor of dead horses: a white stallion rearing above a prince in golden trappings limp on the ground. Fangs dripped within a fog swirling around them, which blurred into screaming faces engulfed in fire. A horned moon rose behind the skeleton of a burned-out building, laughing at the devastation while watching through vertical-slitted eyes.

Kit rotated to face me. "I guess it's true that a picture's worth a thousand words. This tells me more than your words ever did. That's why, when I found a stack of them in my hands, I had to look."

"Which is why I didn't want you to see some of them." I turned away.

"Like that portrait. That fucking exhibit! How long were you guys together to warrant that?"

I plunked into a chair and stared at my knees. "Officially, never. But it lasted on and off from senior year until Blanche and Dru moved here."

"So he's the guy who glowed at you."

"Yes."

"I'm nothing like him, Madeline. Why the hell did you see in him what you saw in me?"

"I didn't ask to see anything, Kit. You both flared at me on your own."

"Well, I didn't do it on purpose!"

"Neither did he. He didn't even know I was there."

"Jeez!" He shook his hair and his fists. "I hate this shit. It only happens here, too. That's what I needed to know."

I doubted it only happened here but didn't say so. Now that I had grasped the first step of conscious projection . . .

He returned his back to me and resumed scanning the paintings. I stood and demanded, "Where did you go for so long? Damn it, I was worried sick about you!"

He turned. "Drove across the country and back, then camped for a while in the Adirondacks. Did some cleanup work in California—an old racing buddy of mine got creamed by that last quake. It did me good to see the outside world—a therapy I'd recommend for you."

"No need—it's piped in constantly. Keeps confirming my desire to never go back out."

"What about the visions?"

I shook my head. "Nothing, except . . ."

I chilled so fast my skin broke into goosebumps. No visions during Kit's absence, yet a new one minutes before his return. Oh no. It couldn't be!

"Except what?" Kit said sharply.

I had to decide in that instant whether to take a blind-faith plunge or play it safe and dodge him. Already I had lost him once for hedging; now he was standing in my quarters, despite all odds. His timing relative to Raoul had to be another one of those unnerving coincidences. Please, let it be so, powers-that-be! I had seen this man's soul. I had to believe him. I had to trust him now to make him trust me.

After a big gulp I said, "I had a ghoulish vision in the hot tub seconds before Buck arrived and minutes before you did. No visions at all since Raoul left and never returned, or when you left and did return. But Buck's been here all along."

"What the hell does that mean!"

"I'd sure like to know!"

His brows lowered and nostrils flared. "So you think it's been me all along, not Raoul?"

"No. I'm thinking it's the combinations that matter."

He stood silent, eyes blank but sparking, fists clenching and releasing. I grew weary and turned to sit down. No, I wanted him next to me. I went to the bedroom and lay down. Colin had shipped me a new waterbed rather than drain, disassemble, haul, reassemble, and fill my bed from the cottage. John Powers had eagerly installed the new one.

Kit followed me a moment later. After glaring down at me, he eased onto the mattress and laid his head upon my breast. I snugged my arms around him. We lay quiet for a while, waiting for the other to stiffen, to reject. The longer nothing happened, the more we unwound.

Presently Kit said, "But it's not the same combinations every time."

I released a silent sigh of relief. "No. I had trouble with that, too. But it might be a floating pattern. Like, this place offers one energy boost. Combining it with Blanche and Dru ramps it up a notch. Add in me, or me and you, or you, me, and Buck, and things get really lively. Something like that."

I didn't want to talk about this now, or ever. Just wanted to kiss him, enfold him, make everything else go away. Unfortunately, reality persisted regardless of what I wanted.

Kit accepted a kiss but kept talking. "So who can tap this energy, and do what with it, for how long?"

"I wish I knew. More, I wish I knew why. Do certain of us have links to each other, which generate the energy in the first place? Or maybe Raoul isn't connected with any of us but can parasite off what we create."

"How would he do something like that?"

I shrugged, feeling the old frustration anew. "I don't know. But I'm starting to learn in spite of myself. I can't describe the feeling. It sneaks up on me. The raw force seems to come with our plumbing, but using it deliberately requires technique. There are thousands of books on the subject but none actually teach you how to do it."

"Raoul must've found one."

"Or else he's one of those lucky people who figure it out. Maybe it comes naturally. Dru can just . . . do it. I've asked but he can't explain how. So I'm thinking it's like your mechanical ability, or my art talent. No trick to have it—an intuitive skill that comes without effort but can be refined with training. Like some people are born athletes. Why can't others be telepaths?"

"I suppose. What is telepathy, really?"

"Thought transference. One direction or two. It works best if the receiver is consciously willing or unconsciously open, but a strong telepath can butt into someone's head at will. And if you're really good and have a lot of power on tap, you can even attack someone by sending thought-forms through an astral tube."

"Huh?" Kit's lip curled.

"An astral tube. That's a channel through the—well, start with the astral plane. That's the next one up from here in . . . I guess it would be frequency. You know how we can't hear or see certain sound or light waves but other animals can? So it is with a 'higher plane,' which is called the astral. It parallels reality but has its own laws. We can perceive it with our higher senses when they're developed—or shocked awake, as in my case. More often, we go there passively during hypnosis, meditation, coma, or sleep. It's accessible to the mind but never the body. Most people only enter after they've left their bodies for good."

"Yeah, right."

Kit gazed at the ceiling. I could almost hear the open road calling to him, just as a clairaudient siren song had lured me onto New Atlantis rocks.

"Agreed. There is zero, zippo, nada proof for any of this. But in theory, an accomplished psychic could move through this plane in his astral body, or open a channel using psychometry and send forth images, creatures, emotions—or just plain watch, never leaving his house."

"I've never heard of psychometry."

I chewed my lip while forming a cogent description. "It's getting psychic impressions from an object, the way that smelling something can trigger a memory. Those impressions tell you the object's history or something about its owner, or give you an imprint to target from."

Kit turned. "Is that why you tried to stop Raoul from touching Dru at the press conference?"

"Yes. And he's already touched Blanche a dozen times."

"Yet she doesn't get visions. Has he ever touched you?"

"No. What about you?"

"Well, I shake hands with everybody on first meeting. Can't say any guy has touched me otherwise, and Blanche didn't notice I exist until you did."

He rolled and lay on his side next to me, head propped on his fist. "So can you do any of this stuff, or are you just quoting from books?"

"Mostly quoting. I've started getting clear exchanges with Dru, I've always had a nonverbal link with Blanche, and earlier I experimented on Buck and almost got punched."

Kit worked to keep expression from his face. "What did you do?"

I sighed. "Projected an image from our past that only he would recognize. And I did it on demand. Scared the crap out of him."

This time Kit's face registered something. Esteem, perhaps. Mistrust again. He confirmed the mix by saying, "Wanna try it with me?"

"Maybe later. Right now I'm too tense. Then, it was spontaneous —these things seem to work best that way, at least for me. I did try psychometry after you left, handling your stuff in the gatehouse, but nothing happened. Even if I could do it, it wouldn't work with Raoul because I don't have anything he's touched."

"What about that envelope?"

I shook my head. "Allanna tried to read from it, failed, then burned it. Besides, we all saw how I reacted just by looking! I'd be afraid to go near it!"

"I don't blame you." Kit chuckled grimly. "But this thought-form business would explain your hallucinations."

"I don't think so. They're just my mind knee-jerk-reacting to things I can't otherwise sense. And it doesn't really matter. All we need to know is that Raoul can project, and perceive through remote entities, now has us imprinted, and . . ."

I couldn't complete the thought.

Kit completed it his own way. "Do you really know all that for fact?"

"No. It's deduction. But no other explanation fits."

"Except the one you haven't thought of yet."

He smiled and trailed a finger up the thin, soft skin of my inner forearm. My loins tingled. I stroked him in kind for a while, as we both thought.

He broke the silence. "Someone once told me that astral projection is what you're doing when you dream you're flying. Or sometimes when people die they flash their images to loved ones far away. It's like we have a shell, some kind of see-through overlay, that's separate but connected. Like a human is a sort of onion, with layers and layers between body and soul."

He grinned at the image. My emotions added a half-twist to their flip. Unaware, he continued, "I mean, it kinda makes sense. But all the junk people attach to it makes me want to puke. Why do they insist there's one true path to find or follow? I can blow holes in any belief system in five minutes. It makes no difference what flavor you prefer. In the great machine, you don't matter at all! All that matters in our little subsystems is how we treat each other. It's what you do, not what you think, that counts."

"Hah! I can't decide whether you sound more like Blanche, Dru, or Buck. I think you've been living here too long!"

"I'm more than ready to live somewhere else. Wanna go?"

"Ask me again when this is over."

"It looks pretty over to me."

"I thought so too until that vision just before you got back."

"Shit. Well, why don't we go somewhere together so you can rule out whether I'm the one causing your visions?"

"Because my sister's in the middle of this, and she's not gonna leave. Remember, she's the one who started it, she and Dru, feeling a presence they wanted me to verify. It followed them on tour while Raoul was with them and you were here. It's only when we all got here that anything became visible. You might be an amplifier, allowing me to perceive Raoul."

"In that case, things might start getting interesting."

"In that case, I'll wish you didn't come back!"

"But for now . . ." He rolled and pinned me with a playful snarl. My bathrobe gave way without a fight.

17
Black Bolts from the Blue

The next morning, with Kit trimmed and shaven, we went down to breakfast holding hands. Everyone present noticed and came to the correct conclusion. Tactfully, they made no comment, leaving us to refuel in peace.

Kit galloped off after a quick bite to recover ground he had lost, leaving me to nurse coffees with Blanche and Dru. We weren't the only ones loitering that morning. Jim and Mark, Maxine and Cassandra, Alexis and Jessie chatted at separate tables, while Cornelius sat in the corner with a book. Troy and Adam, in sweatsuits, sat on the terrace, watched by a cat from a sunny spot on the wall.

"Has anyone told Kit," Blanche asked, "that Buck has usurped his position?"

"Sort of." I wondered who would prevail.

Dru turned to me. "I hear the Deadly Duo had a close encounter in the tub last evening."

I groaned. "Please, don't ask!"

"We've already heard a colorful version." His face twitched as he suppressed a laugh. Blanche got a face ache trying to do same.

"It was more stupid than funny," I said, "not to mention embarrassing!"

"Madeline the pea hen," Dru quipped, "with two cocks vying for her favor, strutting around in full display!"

He and Blanche laughed out loud, at the same time releasing images that made me guffaw. In turn, I projected a more substantive competition that would really impress me—causing Blanche to clap a hand over her mouth and Dru to cry, "For shame!" He retaliated with a stream of racy images involving my two triangles. I lost the contact when giggles turned my stomach into knots.

In the ensuing silence, I identified what had been missing from his transmission. The first one, jumbled and colorful, had been buoyant with Blanche's wit; the second had been focused, potent, and wholly male. Blanche had made no equivalent solo contribution, yet she had followed our volley.

I drew a tighter veil around my consciousness and averted my eyes. Then, in experiment, I fast-balled a silent inquiry to both: *Where is Kit this moment?*

Unpacking his gear, Dru flashed back.

"In the gatehouse," Blanche answered aloud. She cocked her head and looked at me.

"Just wondering," I replied, studying my nails.

She transferred her attention to Dru, who explained with facial expression. I followed without tuning in, having again lost contact when emotion swept me back to the physical plane. There I would stay until the tide receded. No loss, as those thoughts were best kept to myself.

Dru and Blanche, still open, spoke through their eyes above up-tipped mugs. Suddenly Dru's eyes bulged and the mug fell from his fingers to bounce off the table and spew coffee for yards. Blanche and I leaped back; Dru crumpled forward with a thin wail and curled his arms around his head.

The wail swelled to a scream broken by gasping as he slipped to the floor. Blanche dove after him, while I stood numb. Everyone else dropped what they were doing to rush across the dining hall.

"Dru! What's wrong!"

"My god—what's happening?"

"Dru! Dru! Are you all right?"

"What, is he choking?"

I stepped back as a circle knelt around him. Mark rose from it to sprint to the intercom and shout. For a second I felt woozy, as Dru's pain dragged down my spinal cord like a desperate hand; abruptly, vision cleared and I saw a black filament spiraling in through the French doors to penetrate Dru's head.

While I stood there thinking, Gee, that looks like an electrical cord gone wild!—*HOW DARE YOU ATTACK HIM YOU HORRIBLE THING!*—heat scorched through my body. My vision blanked for an instant, skull nearly split from pressure, then sight cleared to show the invading coil retracting to leave Dru limp on the floor.

I remained paralyzed for a few seconds but didn't keel over like Allanna had when she expulsed the raven. Once control returned, I swiveled my head to see Blanche weeping into her hands as Dru, now sitting, patted her back and murmured reassurance. Aside from an ashen face, he appeared unaffected. He waved away the crowd fluttering around him, which backed off only when Brian arrived to take charge.

I slipped unnoticed onto the terrace to gulp air. The back panorama always soothed me: today, sky more uniformly, vivid blue than any paint could make it; leaves flashing amber, copper, scarlet, and tangerine. The lawn remained emerald, although the wild grass beyond it had faded to beige stalks. In the distance, fields were variegated shades of ocher, divided into puzzle shapes by the meandering silver creek. Not a hint of anything unnatural or evil.

Then where had it come from? Where had it gone? Were there fissures in the heavens as in the earth which sometimes slipped and scrambled reality? Was the mansion some kind of inverse lightning rod drawing black bolts from the blue?

I returned to the dining room. Adam and Troy had escorted Dru and Blanche to the carriage house. A larger group than we had started with remained, buzzing.

"He said it was like the ultimate migraine."

"Looked more like a seizure to me!"

"I thought he was having a stroke."

"I didn't know he gets migraines."

"Neither did I. But he's had weird visions and passed out before . . . I wonder if that was another one?"

"He didn't say anything about seeing anything."

"Did you see anything?"

"Goddess, no!"

"Just—"

"He looked all right when it was over. I wonder . . ."

"Hey Madeline! What happened?"

"Did anything happen to you?"

I paused then decided the time for secrecy had passed. "I saw some sort of malevolent energy form that looked like a black snake zapping him in the head."

"What do you mean?" asked Cassandra.

"Exactly what I said. I don't know what it was. Did any of you experience anything?"

They all shook their heads. Damn. I was tired of being alone in this!

"If any of you, or anyone you talk to, has any kind of weird moment, let us know immediately! I'll be at the carriage house."

Cries of "What's going on?" followed me out the door, but no one had the nerve to pursue and ask directly. I met the same question halfway to the carriage house, where I encountered Adam and Troy returning.

"Madeline!" Adam hailed. "What the heck is going on? Dru just kicked us out, said he's fine, we'll talk later."

"Then that's probably the best plan. But so you know, there's a negative psychic energy buzzing around and it took a swipe at him. Keep your eyes and ears open for anything deviant and tell us right away."

They saluted and kept walking. I was impressed by how easy human power was to wield. I had noticed over the years that the first person to act with authority in an emergency usually received instant obedience. By snapping out a few instructions, I had become a leader.

Blanche opened the door before I knocked, her face streaked with mascara and eyes swollen but clear.

"Are you okay?" I asked her. She nodded and led me inside.

Dru lay on the couch staring at the ceiling. He didn't acknowledge my approach.

"It was a black lightning bolt," I stated.

He took a long time to reply. "I guess our friend has been a busy boy. If he could've done that before, he wouldn't have bothered sending packages!"

"Where can he be getting such power!" Blanche wrung her hands.

"Drawing circles in his basement and chanting spells," Dru snapped. "Eye of newt, tongue of frog—how the hell should I know! Maybe he finally found himself a coven. Lord knows some of those heavy-metal freaks get pretty sick, and what better target practice than yours truly, the White King of Rock and Roll?"

He moaned and rolled over.

"Did you get any visuals?" I persisted.

He shook his head and mumbled, "Just pain. Just meat cleaver, dentist drill pain. My god, I couldn't believe it! Thought I'd had an aneurysm or something. Or someone came up behind me with an ax." He shuddered.

After a pause, during which Blanche and I exchanged looks, he added in a broken voice, "You know, I always thought I was a nice guy. How can he hate me so much? I always did him good!" Followed by a muffled sob.

Blanche knelt to draw a blanket over his shoulders and kiss his nape. To our astonishment, he swatted her away.

We retreated to the bedroom, mixing stiff drinks en route.

"Did you see it?" I said, shoving clothes and magazines aside to sit on a loveseat.

Blanche reclined across her mattress. "No. But I felt it. A cold so intense it froze me in my chair!"

She closed her eyes, drew a deep breath, then opened her lids to stare unfocused. "But I didn't see any cause for it . . . then I couldn't see anything at all. I thought someone had popped a bag over my head! Then that I'd died—such sudden cold and darkness. Then agony, followed by a slow-motion movie of people running across the floor."

A lone tear tracked down her cheek. She knocked back half her drink. I drained mine then described my view of the scene. Blanche listened without blinking, reminding me of a wilted daffodil as she slouched in a pale-yellow jumpsuit with orange and green drizzling down from the collar. I looked like a pagan priestess with wild hair and a white turtleneck beneath a black belted robe.

We both sat up at the sound of downstairs knocking. Dru did not call out in response. Blanche scurried off and returned moments later with Mark after Dru snarled them away. I stood as Mark followed Blanche into the bedroom, looking so normal he seemed freaky in his plaid shirt and tan corduroys and knobby boots. "What happened," he demanded with neither greeting nor smile.

I explained, ending with, "So despite what your computer and your contacts say, Raoul hasn't simply moved on to other pastures. He's holed up somewhere with a lot of books or a good teacher, taking a crash course in the black arts."

Mark snorted. "Why bother with spells and sacrifices when a weapon would do the job?"

"Depends on what job you want to do, I guess."

Blanche broke in. "Some people need those rituals for discipline or atmosphere. It's like church—you can worship God anywhere and in any form, but most people like the structure and trappings to focus their mood and make the whole thing seem mystical and important."

I nodded. "And regular terrorism is too easy, too impersonal, too—final. Nasties like to toy with their victims, not just erase them. Where's the power rush when your target is dead? Much more fun to keep them frightened and squirming. Pop out of nowhere and goose them, give yourself ten points if they have a heart attack."

"No finesse in shooting a machine gun or setting a detonator," Blanche said.

Mark retorted, "Whereas creating attack tongs with your mind offers a challenge, I suppose."

Sport, Kit had said. He might be right. I thought of cats and orcas, two predators that toyed with their prey before devouring it. These were inherently neutral beings, driven by their nature. If you added evil intent to that nature . . .

Aloud I said, "The control part, yes, is mighty challenging. But the process itself is simple. It's like sticking pins in a voodoo doll. All you need is an intense desire and a linked object to focus on. Then the hate will go wherever it's sent."

"Works with love, too," Blanche said.

Mark ignored her. "In that case, I ought to be able to nail the bastard where he stands!"

"He could be anywhere," I said, "though it would be easier to send that thing from nearby."

"The twins are already out looking, and Allanna's on her way over."

"Is everyone else accounted for?" I worried about a pair of blue-eyed boys.

"Not yet. Jeezus, what if that thing strikes again?"

I wondered same but doubted the likelihood. "It takes a lot of energy to manifest something remotely. Whoever—or whatever—will need to recover for a while." But power is like a muscle, I didn't add. It gets stronger when exercised.

I looked at Blanche. "We ought to sit with him whether he likes it or not."

"No," said Mark. "You keep away from him!"

We looked up with open mouths. Mark's glare rested on me. As I returned it, he softened. "Ah, look, uh, I'm sorry. But you're as much a target as Dru." His gaze swung to Blanche. "And you too. I want you all to keep apart as much as possible until this is over."

"It won't be over until we destroy him," Blanche the Peace Princess declared.

We gaped at her. Mark recovered first. "We'll find him, and kill him if we have to. But I'm not gonna let him get you first!"

He left with a door slam that rattled the paintings. More than that was rattled, judging by our bugged eyes and trembling hands.

18
The Plan

Blanche flopped back on her bed. "This is all my fault."

I sat up on the loveseat. "Where'd you get that idea?"

"Simple. I'm the straw that broke the camel's back!"

"Blanche, that's garbage!"

She flipped a hand. "I'm not being conceited. It's just the only explanation. I'm what turned Raoul's jealousy of Dru personal. Otherwise he'd have tried to leech off him indefinitely, not be trying to hurt him."

"You don't know that. All we've got is speculation. We could be wrong."

"Then where is he? Why no word? Even if he was dead, someone would contact us."

"I don't know. But if you're the reason for him turning, I would expect him to want to hurt you directly, for spurning him, and indirectly by tormenting Dru."

"And you. But that's how he can hurt me most."

"You mean, slowly destroying your lover, and driving your sister mad, thus breaking you but leaving your perfect body intact?"

"Something like that. And New Atlantis makes the whole thing more gratifying. Just think what it would mean if he took us down by himself!"

"Did you ever reject him, face to face and unmistakable?"

"No. He never did anything blatant enough to justify that."

"Then he's probably just after Dru. You were a late addition to the program. Raoul had a long time to build up resentment. Dru winning you was—you're right, probably the last straw. But that's not the same as being your fault!"

"Whether I'm the cause or effect doesn't matter. I'm still the trigger."

"Do you know anything else about his life to account for it? Was he an abused child? Always second-best and walked on? Big personal failures somewhere?"

"Well, like Dru, he came from a busted-up home and mean streets. Or so he said. But why would someone who's made good harp on an ugly origin? Look at Dru! He left it all behind and grew from it."

"Maybe that's the problem. You've spent too much time among the beautiful people, Blanche. There are folks out there who smolder for decades over early pains. Most just rot into bad health and worse finances. Some go the other way and overachieve, blotting out all emotion. Others become ordinary joes who abuse their own children. Others inflict their pain on themselves; still others become mass murderers. And some get their kicks from transferring their pain to people who 'deserve' it then relishing their misery from a safe place."

"Raoul," Blanche said to herself.

"That's my bet. But sometimes people come out of the womb that way. What bothers me about Raoul is what he's not doing. If he has in fact crossed a line and is out to bring down Dru or New Atlantis, why isn't he creating scandals you can't disprove, or lobbing grenades over the wall, or kidnapping or raping you, or murdering Dru or stealing his money? Instead, he's invoking power. The legendary stuff that only gods are supposed to control. That science has never been able to prove. And he's doing it without retreating to a mountaintop for twenty years and studying with masters. In fact, he's pulled it together in a short life of indulgence—wholly counter to the way it's supposed to happen. What's so special about Raoul Lamont that he can have the power that's eluded everyone else?"

Blanche paled. "Could he be the Antichrist?"

"I hope not! That would make Dru the Second Coming and the rest of us a lot more important than the facts suggest!"

"But that's just what the facts are suggesting. Maybe New Atlantis is more important than we thought."

"I dunno. Colin and Kit say there's plenty of talk about us out there, most of it exaggerated, but we've got nowhere near the clout of, say, the President or the Pope."

"Are you sure? Madeline, Dru's songs have sold in every country, in more languages than I can count. Some people will buy his music before buying food. He's not only a household name, but a global name. We get letters from Timbuktu, for heaven's sake! That makes him bigger than the Pope and President put together, in my book. Next time you talk to Colin, ask him to recite figures for you."

"I've already tried. He gives me all this guff about confidentiality."

Blanche sighed. "Yeah, I suppose he would. Dru gets vague with me, too. But his influence is enormous, Mad. Don't you get it? We have to live inside a fortress and go outside with bodyguards. Too many people think he is a god!"

I gnawed a knuckle before saying, "My question stands. People as big as Dru always have detractors, sometimes hostile. You've investigated them all by now, I'm sure. So why's Raoul the one to become dangerous? Was he hired by people who want to stop Dru and chose Raoul because he was bitter and inside?"

"The investigators have been working that angle for a long time. It's not clear that any one group feels Dru is a threat. Nor can they tie Raoul to anyone beyond what Colin already reported. They can't tie him to anything, period! Most of the history and credentials he gave proved false as soon as they were probed to the next level. We didn't do that first time around. Why should we?"

"But now?

"Nothing new."

"Not even a car?"

"Abandoned in JFK's long-term parking lot. But no one of his name on any flight lists, no credit card activity since the finale."

"That reeks of alternate ID."

"Yep. So how do you find out what name he might be using when he doesn't have a record? That takes a long time. And if we can't charge anything criminal, then none of our guys can get into his house or stuff like that."

"Colin's guys might, when no one's looking."

Same guys who had created phony ID for me and Blanche the year after my poster was released and we had been harassed daily. Nothing had gotten hot enough to need escaping from, but it helped psychologically to have the means.

Our fake licenses were due to expire next year; time to chat with Colin. Credit cards, not requiring photos, we kept alive on our own by paying annual fees.

I was tempted to use these documents now and run to safety. As if that were possible with a telepathic foe!

"So what are we supposed to do, sit here while he torments us? We have to stop him, Blanche, before he gets out of hand."

"Not much we can do except beat him at his own game."

"What, hate him to death?"

She grinned. "No, by loving."

"That's the trick Christ used. Look what they did to him!"

"That's because he forgave everything. But forgiveness is a lousy defense."

"I would say the same for love!"

Blanche lifted her chin. "Love is the most powerful force in the universe. But nobody puts it to productive use! They think it has to be all sweetness and sacrifice and compassion. Which is why hate overpowers it every time."

"But if it's vicious, it's not love any more."

"Doesn't have to be vicious, only strong. To stand up for itself, the way one lion will roar at another, protecting its territory. Or a lioness will protect her cubs. Or the way you go hard on people to pull them out of downhill slides."

"Tough love," I recalled aloud.

"Hurting to heal," Blanche agreed. "Which is what medicine does half the time. But I mean just creating strong boundaries, using love to keep harm at bay. On a big scale, think of how global war has been avoided for decades because of arsenals counterbalancing each other, or economic blackmail. Equal, opposite forces of some type. What are love and hate? Flip sides of the same coin, equivalent powers. I think if we face Raoul with the same energy he's concentrating on us, we can cancel him out, maybe even overpower him!"

"Er, Blanche, that's great, except for one detail. How do we focus what kind of energy on a target we can't see?"

She rose regally, much as Buck had emerged from the hot tub. "First thing is to consolidate our psychic energy. No more private meditations or telepathic chat."

She flicked her eyes at me. I stared her down. "We can't suppress people like that!"

"But we can't have them running around with open heads, either. Why do you think Dru got zapped and you didn't? No one has to stop meditating, just do it in controlled conditions. Like monitored teams, or all together in a group. Then instead of everyone focusing inward, on themselves, all focus outward, exclusively on Raoul."

I envisioned sunbeams through a magnifying lens, igniting tinder. Yes, the idea was worth exploring. We returned to the living room to run it by Dru.

"Forget it," he said, sniffing. "You're free to do whatever you want. But don't ask me to expose my mind again to that sadist. Or be anywhere near someone sitting there as bait."

"But Dru—"

"For any reason! If you want to play with dynamite, go ahead. But don't come crying to me when you get sucker-punched and brain-fried like I just did!"

"But Dru," Blanche appealed, "we've got to fight fire with fire. How else are we going to solve this problem?"

"We'll find a solution. If you'll go away, I might even be able to think of one!"

We backed out of the room. Blanche had tears in the corners of her eyes. We both wondered if Dru was acting normally for someone who had been traumatized by a psychic attack, or if we were seeing the start of a personality change resulting from it.

Another knock downstairs preceded Kit's entrance. He sprang up the steps two at a time, swept the room with his glance, then approached Blanche, wiped a tear from her cheek, and took both of her hands.

"Fill me in."

We withdrew to the kitchen. No door to shut but Blanche and I decided tacitly that we wanted Dru to hear. Blanche started with her version, I followed with mine. Kit listened, wearing his hawk mask. At the end he said, "Was it one of those thought-form things through an astral tube like you were telling me about?"

"That's my best guess."

"In that case, you guys need to get out of here. Go stay with Colin or at a secure hotel. There's nothing yet to show that Raoul can get you out in the real world."

"No, Kit, it doesn't work that way," Blanche said.

"Then all of you disband. It's harder to hit a moving target!"

"But our energy massed together makes it harder to draw a bead on any one mind. Besides, we don't want his attention now."

I described our plan. Allanna arrived in the middle of it, but held back to listen. Kit shook his head. "Don't risk it. You don't know enough about it."

"Got any better ideas?"

"Yeah—find him and beat the crap out of him!"

I was tempted to laugh but kept stern. "If you know something that a team of professionals doesn't, and can pull him out of thin air, be my guest!"

"I know enough to hire more professionals if mine don't get results!"

"Fine. Do that. I, meanwhile, will help Blanche, who's the only one to suggest something we can do directly. I think we should try it, since we're fighting an invisible enemy. I would rather do that in a group than anything alone!"

Kit cursed to himself. "All right. What do you want me to do?"

Blanche took over, joined by Allanna. By day's end they had organized two meditation groups, which they called "power circles," to visualize a forcefield around New Atlantis that would repel any form of invading entity. They performed the ritual twice a day thereafter.

By the end of a week, most of New Atlantis had joined the practice, making four sets of seven people boosting the forcefield. Dru, Kit, Buck, Julia, Cassandra, Mark, Gene, and Cornelius abstained. I worried that we abetted Raoul by creating a house divided. However, evidence suggested that our plan would work.

Rather, lack of evidence convinced us. Nobody, self included, reported so much as a bad dream for weeks. The community's energy level jumped several notches. New Atlantis lived up to expectations at an accelerated pace. So many requests came in for interviews and visits that the band began hinting they might do another concert months earlier than planned, or start offering compound tours.

"No, no, no!" counseled Colin during his weekly phone-in. "With Raoul still unaccounted for, and no medical explanation for the visions or Dru's collapse, you're asking for trouble by inviting publicity. It's a miracle that nothing has leaked out!"

The band agreed, so they devised a compromise: a Halloween party for extended family and friends. Full costumes and masks required, with an unveiling at the end.

"So are you coming?" I asked Colin on the telephone.

A rustle came through the line as he fanned his datebook. After a grunt he said, "Believe it or not, I've got nothing scheduled!"

That did test my credulity, since he had some sport booked every weekend, client meetings every weekday, and a dozen business or vacation trips every year. Despite this, he managed to keep on top of Dru's finances, stay in touch with us, and write Cassandra letters.

A week before the Halloween party, Dru joined a power circle. The following morning he and Blanche came to breakfast together, all smiles. I dared drop my shield for a quick peek into their minds and met visions of tangled bedclothes. *Shut your windows!* I yelled at them.

They responded with startled glances, then concentrated on their food. Minutes later, I saw them playing footsie under the table. Dru looked up and quirked his lips at me, then turned away.

Within a day he was leading one of the circles. Soon after he combined two into one. The abstainers, one at a time, sampled the process, until only Cornelius and Buck remained detached. Kit sat in without comment, offering solidarity. And body guarding, since John Powers seemed to have abdicated once it became known that Kit and I were a pair. I felt more secure with Kit on hand but not enough to lead any circles. Nonetheless, I contributed my energy every day.

It became difficult to share doubts in the face of such enthusiasm. The plan, on one hand, seemed to work, so I didn't want to undermine confidence. On the other hand, too many elements of the premise that inspired it failed to make sense.

For example, if Raoul was the source of our psychic troubles, and jealousy drove him, then how did the two connect? Could jealousy alone really take one beyond normal physical limitations? I had long been jealous of Blanche; and Julia—among many—had long been jealous of me. Yet none of us had gone off the deep end. How ferocious did one's feeling have to be?

And was love the right counter to it? For hate and fear, yes. But jealousy was a different emotion. Its opposite would be what, compassion? Generosity? Altruism? Indifference?

Meanwhile, an essential element of jealousy was desire. Desire was a component of lust, not love. Love could exist without a need for sexual expression. But lust compelled possession, penetration. Nonsexual desire also involved possession, as well as power.

It came down to power. "Absolute power corrupts absolutely," said Lord Acton, a British historian, long ago. Others considered lust a corruption of love. Could I love Kit or Buck without desiring them? No. Love and lust were integral there. Yet with Dru, once my curiosity had been satisfied, my lust for him vanished, although I still craved interaction. But I could dismiss him from my thoughts, which I couldn't do with Kit or Buck. One or the other was always percolating in the background if not the foreground of my concerns. How great a step was it from that to obsession?

Raoul had been denied possession—intimacy—even attention from Blanche. I had been rejected by Buck but had never felt the need to capture and punish him in retaliation (aside from some petty spite of the "Ha ha, serves you right!" variety). Raoul needed to punish and control. The difference was, I had experienced acknowledgment from and intimacy with Buck, knew his love existed even if he had rejected my sharing of it. Raoul had experienced only unrelieved lust. And now he appeared to be absolutely corrupted by absolute power. So, were certain fanatics right and sex truly was sinful—the work of the devil? I had always believed it to be a bridge between souls.

These thoughts took me into dreamless slumber. In the morning, when Dru failed to appear for breakfast, my guts boiled in near panic. According to Blanche, however, he claimed a sore throat and was taking the day off. Yet he didn't answer the door when I stopped by with soup at lunchtime. I intended to try later, but ended up sweeping the grounds.

A wall alarm had tripped without its camera catching anything. Everyone dropped their duties and joined a fruitless search. We couldn't call between buildings because the phones, intercoms, and radios kept quitting then coming back randomly around the compound. Computers spit strange graphics onto their screens. That night, something disturbed the livestock in their byres. In the morning, each residence found dead rats or skunks on the front stoop—all incised neatly down the middle and the eyes plucked out.

"That's it, Mad—time to go home!" Kit grabbed my arm in both hands and dragged me away from breakfast. I skidded after him until the newel post came into reach. "But Kit, when he's active we have a chance to catch him!"

Kit detached my hand from the newel post and twisted my arm up behind me. "Ow! Ow! Ow!" I cried as he propelled me toward the front door.

"Sorry, Mad, any hunting and catching will be done by security. You, Blanche, and Dru are going out of harm's way!"

I stomped his instep and jabbed with my free elbow. His grip loosened a fraction. I escaped. "Kit, he can find us anywhere! If we run, he'll just follow."

Kit checked his pursuit and glowered, breathing hard through his nostrils. I half expected him to paw the ground and charge. "Madeline, I can't protect you from something invisible. We have to assume it's here until something suggests not. John and Jake are already out looking."

He lunged for me. I jumped backward. "He's only trying to unnerve us into dropping our shields. And if we panic, he'll succeed."

At that moment Mark popped out of his office, swearing. "Irene just told me that Hill House's lights went on and doors flew open by themselves at three-thirty this morning."

"And did Lawrence tell you," Kit sneered, "that he woke up in his locked room to find his furniture moved?"

Mark and I cursed at the sheer meanness of messing with a blind person like that. This topper made me see Kit's point. To generate so much poltergeist-type activity in such a brief time begged for proximity to a power source. In that case, distance from same was a good idea. But it might also mean Raoul had acquired so much power that he could become dangerous on a wider scale. In that case, we baby psychics were the only thing in his way. I dared not unshield and scan for him properly—that's what he was waiting for. Better to grope than give him advantage.

"Where's Dru?" I flung at Mark and Kit.

They looked at each other. Mark answered, "I was just looking for him. Blanche buzzed me wondering if I'd seen him. Nobody in the studio, so she's calling around."

"Where's Blanche?" Kit asked.

"Carriage house."

Kit turned to me. "C'mon, Mad, I want you all off the compound."

"I think I know where Dru is hiding. You go sit on Blanche, I'll bring him in."

Kit barred the door with his arm. "You tell me and I go get him."

"It's not as simple as 'he's in the men's room.' He'll need to be talked into leaving. I might be able to do it, but I promise you won't."

Kit sputtered but relented. I deemed him a fool for trusting me but took advantage nonetheless. Dru would surely agree this was the wrong time to leave New Atlantis and would help me mount a good argument. If only I had gone when I had the chance!

Too late now, I thought, heading for the door.

When danger had been theory, I had wanted to abandon ship; now that danger was real, I would go down with the ship like a captain. In a way I was, as part of the triumvirate. And I would never find out if I was a cause or an effect unless I weathered the storm.

19
Mayday

Outside, the wind chased and bit like a nasty dog, blowing dried foliage into confetti. It flapped my denim skirt around my ankles, swirled my hair into a Medusa style, and sliced through the sweater I had put on against the house's chill.

I sprinted to the studio. No lights on within, but the outside lamp had been fooled by the overcast into turning on and caught an ATV's rump protruding from shadow. I aimed for the door closest to it, slowing my pace.

From the basement doorway, I heard the hum of electrical devices on standby but no animal movements. A certain prickle, however, hinted I was not alone. Dru or Raoul? I couldn't dismiss that wall alarm and empty camera. Maybe Dru and Raoul stalked each other somewhere in this labyrinth. I squelched the urge to call Dru's name and tiptoed into the video studio.

Leaving the lights off, I wove between lighting poles and wooden frames, which threw confusing shadows. Dully gleaming dials and screens, snarled together with cable, watched me in the wan light seeping through window slits just above ground. Around the perimeter, a dozen sets littered with props and miniatures, storyboards and diagrams, preserved a moment of animation. They reminded me of Mount Vesuvius victims entombed midstride by poisonous fumes and a scalding ash cloud, or mammoths trapped in ice blocks, frozen instantly when the Earth's gravitational field turned upside down.

The recording studio on midlevel offered easier hunting. I could see straight through interconnected glass rooms. No masses or motion among the folding chairs and microphone stands, headsets and sheet music. Some instruments still lay around, umbilically connected to walls. The control room door stood open, offering a glimpse of the mixing board and banks of switches, indicator lights, players and recorders, and computers. I peeked behind the door and scanned the notes and schedules tacked everywhere, looking for anything new or disturbed. No such clues, so I moved upstairs to the lounge.

Here, despite the stale air, I caught a fresh scent. My nerves prickled as they had at the concert when I had come aware of the spook. This sensation lacked the chill of the first, although it still felt negative. An odd contrast to the bright wood and posters on the walls and closed office door. Light came through trapezoidal windows and canted skylights. Beyond them branches swayed across an ashen sky.

I paused to decide that the office door hid Dru, not Raoul or the two together. Then I entered without knocking, knowing I wouldn't receive a "Come in."

Dru slumped in a tilt-back swivel chair with his foot propped against his desk. The hand resting on his upraised knee twiddled a pencil as he stared, unseeing. Concave cheeks, shadowed eyes, hair unwashed—and uncut for months now, he looked as haunted as I had in September, when he had confronted me on the balcony.

The parallel ended there. "What do you want," he snapped without turning.

I wanted to hug him. "We need to talk."

"So talk."

I leaned against his desk and crossed my arms and ankles. "It would help if you listened."

"I doubt you'll say anything I haven't already thought or heard."

I gaped at him, awed by the chasm I had to cross. He held his aura close, as if clutching a cloak against a blizzard. He also kept his face averted, until I hit hard enough to hurt.

"You wimp—you're making it easy for him!"

"Fuck off, Madeline, you don't know shit about it."

"Fuck yourself—I know about your headache."

"I don't have any headache."

"Which you've had since you combined the circles, I'll bet."

Long pause. "I don't know when it started. All I know is, it won't stop."

"You might as well have fired a signal flare. He was waiting and zeroed in."

Dru rubbed his temples. "Why didn't he zap you while he was at it?"

"I've no idea. Maybe he just wants you."

He whipped me with a glare that made me glad the black karate coat he wore over jeans was ornamental. He augmented the effect by narrowing his eyes and showing his teeth. "I don't need you to tell me the obvious."

"It's not obvious. He might not know about me yet."

"How could he not? You broadcast like a—"

"But he might not be able to tell me from Blanche."

"Your similarity is only skin deep. He's too powerful not to miss you."

"Power does not equal discernment. He might not be able to tell people apart! Except you, who he's known and studied for years, and gotten an imprint from."

"He's also touched Blanche—pawed her up a few times, actually. Why doesn't she get a drill bit through the brain?"

"He took his imprint from you when he was in a supernatural mode at the press conference. So maybe he never got her under those conditions. Or her positive vibes are too strong. Or if our patterns are similar, he might not risk toasting her in an effort to get me."

"Hell, I could tell your vibes apart before I even met you!"

"That doesn't mean Raoul can. Just because he can do things you can't doesn't mean you can't be one up on him another way. Obviously, you're not good at shielding. You never had to. But I bet you could give him a taste of his own medicine. He doesn't have to shield, because nobody's after him."

Dru sagged. "I couldn't even if I wanted to."

"Come on, Dru. All your work for New Atlantis is down the drain if you crap out now!"

"You don't understand." He swung his head, then pressed both hands against the desk to push himself upright and walk away from me. He missed the door by several feet so stood facing the wall. A framed gold record gave him an ironic halo.

I said, "If it helps, we can leave the compound. Kit's waiting to take us—we can at least draw Raoul's attention away from New Atlantis. He'll have to let up in order to track you. Or let up on you to keep the compound under control."

Dru pivoted to face me with bloodshot eyes. "It doesn't matter—it's too late. He's stronger, Madeline. He's pinned me through the brain like a goddamn bug! No, like a fish—he hooked me the first day I opened, and plays me like a salmon. The more I fight, the deeper his barb sinks. As long as I do what he wants, I'm fine. But the minute I—"

He gasped and shuddered, squeezing his eyes shut. His face became cadaverous—I rushed forward to steer him into a chair. He crumpled into it and buried his face in his hands, wheezing. I stroked his back until the seizure passed. I could neither see nor sense anything attacking him. Had Raoul somehow implanted a metastasizing self-doubt?

As Dru recovered, panting, I fast-shuffled my priorities. New number one: Get him away from New Atlantis. Where was the intercom in this place? I glanced around. Did a double take at the filing cabinet. Yes, a coffee mug was floating four inches above the surface. I turned away then looked back. It still hovered. Oh dear.

I stared at the mug, so cold inside I wasn't sure I could move if I decided what to do. My rigidity caught Dru's attention. Before he could ask the trouble, it illustrated itself.

The mug sailed chest high across the office. Dru and I tracked it with bulging eyes. Thankfully, the door didn't open for it. The two smacked together then the mug followed its coffee dregs to the floor.

At the crash, Dru bolted. I froze. Rerun of Buck and me in the marble circle. This time I recovered fast and started to follow. Dru galloped across the lounge, skidded on a throw rug, then plunged down the stairs with coattail flapping. I couldn't catch up with him so stopped trying. I found the intercom, sent a Mayday message to the mansion and carriage house, then ran outside, vaulted aboard Dru's abandoned ATV, and motocrossed to Hill House.

Only Allanna knew more about occult manifestations than I did. I found her mixing batter at the kitchen counter, while Troy read at the table and their son Pip sat on the floor between them mauling toys. Upstairs, someone sang; downstairs, someone yammered. Daniel split logs into kindling out back. I clattered into their peace, gasping, "Allanna, come quickly! Dru—"

The ceramic mixing bowl in Allanna's hands exploded. She staggered back screaming and clawing at her face. I ducked against pelting shards and batter. Troy took a gash in his neck along with a back and head full of slivers, not enough to prevent him from scooping up Allanna and rushing her to the sofa, shouting, "Get Brian!" as he left the room.

I headed the other way, toward the ATV, but nearly fell over Pip, who was batter-caked but otherwise unharmed. His head-numbing wail delayed my departure. I hoisted him onto my hip as feet pounded upstairs, downstairs, and across the porch.

When Daniel, Irene, and Karla arrived, I waved them into the living room, handing Pip to Irene as she passed. By the time Karla came back for supplies, I had gathered towels, water, and ointments. She hustled them away while I scraped up debris then jumped aboard the ATV and tore back to the main house.

I could hear excited chatter from the dining room, but the entry hall was abandoned. I nipped into the parlor to page Brian and Kit, instructing them to fetch Allanna in Kit's ready vehicle for a fast trip to the emergency room, then ran for cover before crossing anyone's path. What else might happen when I startled somebody open? What would rush in if I opened my own mind?

Safe (hah!) in the main hall water closet, I fussed with my appearance. The person in the mirror looked alien, although nothing external had changed. Yet somehow I had become a lightning rod for negative power. Raoul had rendered me harmless to himself by making me dangerous to my world!

At least Kit and Allanna would be off-compound for a while. The hospital was well over twenty miles away. We were nearly as remote from other help. But how could public servants help us against Raoul?

With Dru and Allanna out of order, it came down to me against an elemental power. How had Raoul harnessed it? Surrendered unconditionally, I supposed. But how did one signal surrender, to what power? How could I graduate to vessel from sieve? Meditation wasn't the trick—Dru and Allanna pressed a mental button and popped into higher consciousness. Surely Raoul didn't sit cross-legged in his living room chanting "om"!

More crucial, what guaranteed the inflowing energy would be positive? A gamble could prove fatal—no second chance if I goofed. New Atlantis would fall if I became a tool for Evil. Why, I could subjugate the populace then fling open the door! A good hunk of the world would be contaminated by our contact. Blanche had been right—he wanted us all!

I understood, then, as if someone had mapped it out on a blackboard. To gain what he wanted, Raoul had tried the shortcut of Satanism. But he had found the rituals hollow, the powers available to a human too constrained. Satanism required a belief system: God and the Devil, within a Christian or pagan framework. Dru and New Atlantis propounded neither of these. It preached individual faith in personalized trappings, caring only about responsibility—integrity—love—peace as means to enable humankind's evolution. A do-it-yourself style of spirituality. In the process, a few of us, aided by energy from place and community, developed extrasensory powers. Raoul needed same in order to take revenge, to dominate, to control.

Failing at the original plan of twisting Dru into self-sabotage, Raoul could still take him out in a more gratifying way. His studies must have taught him he could bypass human limits by offering himself as an instrument. The dark powers had found him and flooded in.

Nothing else could account for the speed of his development. Nothing else explained why he targeted New Atlantis.

Having submitted to the dark powers, Raoul shared their insatiability. By nature, Evil can't rest until it has conquered every soul. Good has spent millennia trying to maintain a stalemate. Either force needs fifty-one percent to establish the trend for the next age.

During the current transition between millennia, both powers had their elbows on the table and hands clasped for an arm wrestle. I should have realized that positive and negative were evenly matched. Sure, there was massive strife and poverty, but this had led to equally massive construction and social and environmental projects. Likewise, crippling national debts had triggered novel trade-offs between countries, whose borders were dissolving because of communications and crises, which in turn eroded excuses for global war. The pollution and terrorism threatening everyone inspired brilliant scientific work and created a common enemy. On it went in seesaw balance, with recovery or destruction at even odds.

New Atlantis doubled as portal and pivot point in the balance. The powers had surely marked its genesis long before it arose. While the positive lured us on, the negative worked to disrupt us. Once it found a willing instrument, it had a crowbar to wedge into our cracks.

That made us pawns in a game we hadn't imagined. Good maneuvered us this way; Evil counter-moved and said, "Check." Destiny resulted when individuals rose to their potential and triumphed, or faltered and failed, or froze in confusion and got run over. In fate's trajectory equation, free will was the variable X.

Which meant we could outfox the powers by running zigzags. I began one by moving with no idea where I would go. Out of the water closet, through the hall, out the main door, across the front behind the rhododendrons. Must keep away from anyone vulnerable. The people I needed most, I had to shun.

Then again, that thing might materialize on its own now that it had me running. Or zap me where I crouched, to die alone and in vain.

I must find a way to anticipate its next action! Why did it toy with us, what was it trying to prove?

As I chewed my nails, peering through the shrivelled foliage, I began to feel stupid. Anyone passing close could see me—hiding from something that only I could see! Except for the floating coffee mug . . . which I recognized now as stage dressing, the climax of cliché occult horrors. The bogeyman said "Boo!" and the people cowered or scattered. Reflex fear, predictable behavior . . . time to exercise free will again and buck the trend.

Speak of the devil—

Buck's head bobbed into view up the driveway then veered across the lawn toward the carriage house. I went still as he slowed, glancing around. The wind alternately masked noise or carried it to our ears. I heard him knock on the carriage house door, watched him stare at the ankh doorknocker, then go inside without an answer. Not liking that, I gave up my den and crossed the lawn.

On the carriage house stoop I paused to strain my ears—heard nothing but wind sough. Paused a little longer to suppress the tremor in my limbs. Then, following Buck's lead, I let myself inside.

The carriage house hummed as the studio had, as if abandoned. I stood in the stairwell outside the utility room until I picked up mumbling from the bedroom, plus a slight heat and blur where Buck had just passed. By now, Blanche should have sensed my presence, yet she didn't investigate. So I crept up the stairs and along the hall to the closed bedroom door, where I squatted and eavesdropped.

The voices stopped. I sucked in my breath. The door swung open and Dru's shadow fell upon me. "Come in, Madeline," he said coldly, stepping aside.

Buck stared as I entered. His aura, of dark colors spiked with orange and red, hung close to his outline. Dru's aura had blots in it and flared then faded like a pulsating bruise. For a long minute he stood dumb, forgetting our presence. Blanche stood within arm's reach in a quivering rose nimbus, afraid to touch him. Buck and I faced them from farther apart.

Dru snapped to and demanded, "What do you want this time?"

"We need to talk. Right now. I've worked out some of the pattern."

The room's atmospheric charge suddenly jumped. I recognized the same electric buzz through my body that I had experienced in science class when our teacher had demonstrated conductivity. We had closed a circuit by holding hands while the teacher and a student touched poles on a mild battery. I would never forget the metallic jangle along my nerves.

I felt it now as a haze gathered in the window corner. Watching it peripherally, I collected my muscles for who knew what. Dru assembled his wits, blinked, and opened his mouth to say something. It came out a strangled yelp as the haze congealed into a black lightning bolt and stabbed him in the head.

His eyes bulged and hands flew to his face before he buckled forward, screaming. Blanche lunged to direct his fall toward the mattress, but he hit the floor anyway and locked into a fetal curl. The jagged coil followed, growing and darkening as it fed on his agony. Blanche rocked him, crying, as his howls became brays. I couldn't move to aid them, for my feet had welded to the carpet. Internal pressure rose until I feared my bowels would burst and scalp blow open. I saw the invading presence as a red zigzag across a blackening screen.

Intellect divorced itself from my body. I became molten and liberated, reaching deep within while extending through dimensions to draw energy into a spear then throw. When my expulsion hit the attack tong, cold fire zinged through my tooth roots. The thing shattered then coalesced and returned a stab. I never felt it hit; someone must have dropped a match into a gas tank. Explosion erased the room with deafening light.

20
The Blast

For an instant I thought I had vaporized—all sensation ceased and only a fragment of my mind remained cognizant. A second later I found my feet on the floor and head upright, skin hot but unburned. My body hair stood until the charge dissipated. Only then did my senses recover and I dared blink or move.

I was the only one standing. Incredibly, no scorch damage or overturned furniture marred the room. Dru pushed himself to his feet and scuffed across the carpet to touch me. For a moment his face hung slack and eyes searched mine, then he smiled.

"Well done, Aurora!" He clapped me on the shoulder. Blanche came up behind him, a crooked grin breaking through the shock on her face. Buck jumped up but kept his back pressed to the wall, watching me with his eye whites showing all the way around.

I shared his feelings. "I don't believe—what did I—"

My head spun and diaphragm stuck. Before anyone could comment, I passed out.

When consciousness returned, I found five people standing around me. Three looked down at me on Blanche and Dru's mattress; one was talking; the fifth stared at the nude Blanches on the wall behind my head. I stayed silent until Dru finished explaining to Brian and Adam. While they listened, I returned Adam's gaze.

"Incredible," he breathed at the end. "Madeline, are you all right?"

All other eyes swung toward me.

"Yes. I feel fine." I sat up. No dizziness, and heartbeat held steady.

Nonetheless, Brian checked my vitals. When he finished, I took and slurped the drink Blanche offered, then asked Dru, "How about you?"

He shook his head, with eyes round and arms extended. "Perfectly fine. You blasted me clean. Thanks!"

"Nothing to it!" I quipped, and everyone but Buck chortled.

"Do you think you could do that again?" Adam queried.

"I doubt it."

"Nonsense." Dru snorted. "You can do it any time you want! But you'll have to learn to restrain yourself! That—blast—was overcompensation for what's been jamming up inside you for years. Next time it won't be so violent."

"But what did I do?"

"From what I can figure, you were so petrified and outraged that everything went BOOM before you could think to hold back. The power manifested as, well, like a white-light tidal wave, knocking us ass over tea kettle and neutralizing that—thing. Maybe even destroying it."

"New frontiers of physics . . ." Adam mumbled as my jaw wagged. Brian rolled his eyes and looked away.

Blanche clasped my hand. "Do you feel any different?"

"Yes—no—yes. No tension. Not much strength, either, but that knot that always restricted me is gone." I touched my breast in wonderment. "I feel—lubricated. All parts moving freely at last!"

"Makes primal scream therapy look pretty pale," Brian said, reminding us that the media would die for such a story, which reminded us in turn that lips must stay zipped.

Dru said to Blanche and Brian, "If Madeline alone and spastic can throw fireballs, think of what the group can do linked and controlled!"

His eyes gleamed. Blanche leaned away from me to take his hand. "Then let's get on with it! Make a forcefield so strong he can never penetrate."

"Yeah, but what about when we go outside?" Adam said, frowning. "And what about people already out there? Not fair if we're the only ones immune to this thing. If it can't get us, won't it bother somebody else?"

My chest caved in, as if fear and responsibility had acquired mass and sat upon me. "Where's Kit?"

Silence.

"How long have I been out?"

Dru shrugged. "Maybe an hour."

"They're not back yet from the clinic," Blanche explained. Brian added, "But Troy called—he and Allanna are both fine, they'll be back after she's had her splinters pulled out."

"How did they account for the bowl exploding?"

Smirks and chuckles circulated until Adam said, "Something stupid but plausible, like it fell off a shelf onto the counter edge."

"You wouldn't call that plausible if you saw the splinters! Ceramic should break into chunks. This thing flew into daggers and needles, like fine glass."

Dru sighed. "Hopefully, the hospital is discreet. Otherwise we'll have the press on us by tomorrow."

"Worry about that later," Blanche said. "What are we going to tell our people tonight?"

"The truth," Brian stated.

"Yes, but—" Adam began then looked at Buck. A mushroom cloud must have appeared on his internal horizon. He saw nothing outside himself, just stood aghast.

"Most everyone already knows something's happening," Blanche said, "and will demand an explanation. We can't leave them frightened or confused, especially since they've been meditating together to keep Raoul at bay."

"Didn't work so hot!" Adam sneered.

We squirmed in silent agreement. I returned attention to Buck, whom I hadn't yet seen blink. His catatonia pulled me; I wanted to reassure him. More than that, I wanted to follow him to where I suspected he had gone, get enfolded into his arms, and hear the words "There, there, everything will be all right" spoken with conviction.

No such comfort to be had, so I concentrated on restoring focus to his eyes. That was easier than understanding what I had done to kill it!

I felt split, as though I jointly occupied two selves. One watched the other; one operated behind the other's back. At least the right power had come through when I needed it! But I couldn't tell whether it had come from within or without.

Dru, following my attention, stepped close to Buck and spoke his name. No response. Blanche touched him. "Hey, Buck . . . you okay?"

He blinked and muttered. His gaze remained fixed on me, out of focus.

"Nobody home," Adam muttered to Dru behind his hand. Dru narrowed his eyes and lifted his hands, palms outward. Seconds later, the air began tingling and auras sprang into view. Buck's was ragged, the others were vibrant. I couldn't see what I emitted but knew it was there.

Brian said, "Lie him down, keep him warm, put his feet up."

"I'll drive him down the hill," Adam offered.

"I think walking would do him better," Blanche said, reading my mind. I finished the thought verbally: "Get him back into reality, give him hot food. I'll walk him back to The Glen and fix us something."

Although Brian inhaled, he didn't argue. Dru shared his concern. "He's in shock, Mad, we ought to treat him for it."

I pursed my lips and pushed away the covers. "But it's been an hour and he isn't pale or sweating. Look, I'm the one who shocked him, let me calm him down."

Brian settled the matter by producing his gear again and examining Buck by conventional method. "He's all right mechanically, just shorted out upstairs. Bring him around by whatever works." He stepped back to let us fight about it. Buck continued his Pet Rock imitation while Dru and I stared each other down.

"Whoa!" Adam backed away. "Don't get her excited again!"

Dru blinked and turned his eyes. "Of course not. Madeline, you get him back in order, we'll set up a power circle." His tone reminded us who was running the show.

Brian offered, "Give them ten minutes to get down the hill, then we can follow in the car and pick up anyone who's passed out."

He had noticed the blood draining from my face as I raised myself to standing. Dizziness cleared within seconds, and a blip of confidence followed. Telling myself, If I can still see auras, I've still got the power, I shuffled around the bed to touch Buck's arm.

He recoiled like a sea anemone brushed by a passing fish. When my hand failed to sting through his sweater, he balanced himself, blinked a few times, then accepted my arm in linkage. We exited the scene at an arthritic shuffle.

The sharp air revived me enough to walk unaided. Buck snatched up my wrist when I detached. "No. I—"

His rusty voice startled both of us. He swallowed and looked away, then threw glances up, down, sideways, as if amazed to discover the world as he had left it, midafternoon. We had missed lunch—that is, assuming anyone had been composed enough to prepare it. The grounds looked barren; all windows shut, and blank with gray reflected light. The wind still sent leaves scratching across the driveways and limbs clacking together. I shivered and leaned closer to Buck, who this time didn't flinch.

He tightened hold on my hand then pulled me after him off the driveway. We descended the wooded path between arms of the dirt drive, faster at each stride. Slope and gravity might account for it, but if so Buck should have put on the brakes and steadied me. Instead he kept pulling as resurging emotion propelled him. It telegraphed up my arm, shook my daze away, and provoked my adrenaline. I half expected him to throw me down and rip off my clothes.

Not a bad idea. Terror was the ultimate aphrodisiac! Earthquakes, tornadoes, and bombings sent people diving together all the time. The compulsion grew by the second, until I lusted for Buck, Kit, or anyone. Then it died, like a punctured balloon, as we popped out of the woods and into view of The Glen.

Once inside, Buck unreeled a new personality: Mister Hyper. Zoom! He blurred through the kitchen assembling steaks, potatoes, peppers, and onions, answering Rob's casual, "How ya doin'?" with the chipmunklike gabble of a fast-forwarded tape. Rob watched over his glasses from the lounger where he sat reading. When meat sizzling under the broiler cloaked Buck's ears, Rob beckoned me over and asked behind his hand, "What's with him?"

"He's, er, reacting." At Rob's cocked brows I added, "We had a bizarre experience earlier—the wildest one yet. You'll hear about it tonight if you haven't already—there's going to be a giant power circle. Buck isn't taking it too well."

"So I see . . ."

We resumed watching. Buck's torso, visible above the counter dividing common room from kitchen, zipped back and forth between refrigerator, countertops, and stove. Whack whack whack! Diced vegetables and potatoes. Sssssssssst! Into the frying pan they went. Clink, clunk, pop—foosh—a beer was retrieved and opened. "Want one?" he yelled over his shoulder as he opened the broiler and flipped the steaks.

"Sure," Rob said as I replied, "No thank you." We exchanged wary looks as Buck dashed over with dripping bottle in one hand and long-tined fork in the other. His apron read, "Old Musicians Never Die, They Just Decompose."

"How do you want yours?" he chirped.

"Rare," I sighed. He scurried away.

I grabbed the moment to use the intercom: first Dru, then the gatehouse. No, Kit and company still hadn't returned. I inhaled a curse then exhaled relief. I was about to dial Colin when Buck battered a fork inside a pot.

"Chow time!"

He dropped the kettle to scoop up napkins and utensils, loading everything onto a tray and heading for the staircase. He was halfway up before I had crossed the common room. I followed with lifted skirt. The stairs, like The Glen's communal telephone and bathrooms, made me grateful I lived in the main house. Although carpeted for traction, they were steep, open slats without railing—almost as treacherous as Valhalla's iron spiral. The two lodges otherwise shared a layout symmetrical around the plumbing, with identical doors and windows. Valhalla divided into four suites instead of bedrooms, whereas The Glen slept four upstairs and two down.

Buck's room on the north corner contained a platform bed, a dresser, and a stool at a worktable. A lone bookcase held titles alphabetically arranged. Nothing on it I recognized, nor any sound system beyond a portable radio/tape/CD player. Two bedside tables supported generic lamps, and a shelf over the workbench held discs and sheet music. The windows bore no curtains; the wood floor carried no carpet. He left no clothes draped around or shoes to trip on, used no bed covering beyond an army blanket and mismatched sheets. His guitar cases were propped in a corner. He owned no calendar, no photographs, no mementos, no clock.

Also missing were the artworks I had given him. The wood-panel walls displayed one poster of an alpine scene plus a magazine glossy of a white horse. I would have liked it better if he had wallpapered with puppy dogs or centerfolds. Even black-velvet paintings would be better than this.

He ignored my scan to shovel down nourishment. A flush signaling restoration crept into his cheeks. Beyond his shoulder, books on witchcraft, psi, quantum theory, and reincarnation were stacked on the side table, all titles from the library I had not noticed were gone.

This discovery brought prickles to my stomach, which recalled me to eating. The steak was so delicious I had to stare at it for a while. Chewing flesh brought a primal satisfaction I had once taken for granted. Now I understood where savages had gotten the idea that one could gain strength by eating something's body. I also suspected that Eve had been booted from Eden for eating meat, not an apple. After months of enforced vegetarianism, I relished a sense of sin.

Buck, when finished, put his plate aside and sagged into a wedge of pillows against the headboard. I felt his satiation without looking up. I also felt his gaze land on me and linger with rising interest. Suddenly shy—suddenly seventeen!—I concentrated on my plate.

Silence lasted until he licked his lips and remarked, "That was good."

I agreed. When no comment followed, I placed my dishes on the side table then asked, "What happened to all your stuff?"

I remembered an apartment in New Hampshire with overflowing shelves, killer stereo, battered furniture. He had covered peeling paint with prints and my paintings framed by his own hand. Those hands had also built models and had been learning to craft dulcimers. Everything else had been stuffed into treacherous closets. The Glen closets combined couldn't hold all that!

He shrugged. "Left it behind or dropped it along the way, I guess. I lived out of a pack for the last part. And here you don't need much, so it doesn't matter."

His gaze drifted away.

Doesn't matter? I wanted to scream. You threw away my paintings?

Through tightened lips I replied, "Makes it easy to move on short notice, I suppose."

"I don't plan on going anywhere," he snapped.

"Even after today?"

"Especially after today! Jeezus, I got blown across a room by a fireball. How can I dismiss that?"

"Most people would try. In fact, I'm still trying! I don't understand what I did or how it happened and I'm terrified it'll happen again."

I spoke in a flat voice, afraid to release emotion. A tingle crept up from my abdomen, between my shoulder blades, and out through my arms. If Buck touched me, a giant spark might arc between us. What was I, radioactive? How could I make it go away?

"Am I glowing?" I asked.

"Not that I can see."

He continued looking with a baffled yet contemptuous expression. I felt six inches tall, eight-armed, with green skin.

Buck shook his head and stood to move tray and dishes to the work bench. On return he uncased a guitar and carried it by the neck, then slung it across his thighs upon settling back on the mattress.

I cringed: Serenading had been his standard technique for changing the subject. When he began twiddling idly, atonally, I recognized his older habit of occupying his fingers while he thought.

Once his hands settled into a pattern, he looked up. "I suppose you'd better tell me the rest of it."

The remark prompted yellow warning lights in my head. I didn't heed them. Buck's book pile and recovery made it clear he was ready to learn.

"It started on the fire road," I opened, looking down at my hands and noticing gnawed fingernails. Repetition had polished my vision story to a smooth narrative. I omitted only the satin sheets part and kissing Buck on the temple stairs.

His fingers stopped fiddling as his attention deepened. When I finished, he said, "So you mean that time in the tub—I caught you in the middle of a vision?"

"No, you arrived just as it ended."

"No wonder you looked so green!"

I looked away, distracted by a new stab of dread in my innards. Once again, I had failed to consider Kit.

Buck, lost in memory, didn't notice my scowl. "You know, Dru looked like that when I got to the carriage house. And that must be what he and Blanche were fighting about."

He paused to drain his beer bottle. "I went over to sign the contract —had no idea anything was happening. Just thought that, with all the junk that had happened already, they needed somebody uninvolved, unaffected, more than ever."

I choked back laughter. He didn't notice. "Then my radio went nuts with emergency calls. Brian and Mark caught Dru at the carriage house but he chucked them out. Brian told Kit to take Allanna to ER without them. He flew by me on the road. I went on to Dru's, knowing I could take him down if I had to. When I got there, he and Blanche were shouting at each other. Dru took one look at me and stormed into the bedroom and slammed the door. Blanche and I plowed in after him. He suddenly went quiet—tired and gray, almost green. Blanche was trying to explain what was up when Dru opened the door and there you were!"

His eyes swung around to regard me. I could see straight through them to where his thoughts lay unvoiced: *That alone was enough to knock me over. But what came next! You're a demon in your own right, Miss Aurora Borealis. No man—and never any woman—should have power like that!*

I was tempted to push him off the bed with it. Instead, I returned his gaze. "Go on."

He sighed and laid the guitar across his lap. "Well, the whole time I was there, Dru's head and shoulders looked hazy. Like a cloud of gnats was swarming him, that he kept swatting away. It moved into the corner when you came in. The last thing I remember is it coming alive."

"Nothing else?"

His jaw flexed as he struggled to extract pictures from a blurred memory. "Not really. Just people suddenly lunging and falling down. The room got so cold I couldn't think or move or say anything. Then this white wave washed over and—I guess I passed out."

"Shorted out is more like it! Don't worry, everyone does when they get proof."

"Proof, all right!" Buck flung up his hands. "But of what? Okay, so the universe contains forces some humans can manipulate. But why are they messing up our affairs? We're not involved in anything earth-shaking. And Raoul—he makes no sense, somebody wicked falling for Blanche. She brings out just the opposite: Every man within a mile of her tries to out-good Dru. She's an anti-Medusa, turning everyone into puddles instead of stone!"

I laughed, then sobered. "But this guy has given up on goodness. Hell, he's given up himself. The dark powers are rewarding him for service by giving him more power! The original point was to demoralize if not cripple us. Or else take over and turn our intentions inside out. We have the potential to sway a critical mass, even reveal a mystery of the universe. If we show that supernatural power is real, then political power will be devastated and the world will have to create new social orders. This can only be for the better, unless Evil gains control. I think it already has—Raoul seems to be trying to take Dru down directly. And sooner or later he will, unless we can figure out how to take him out first."

Buck shook his head. "I can't believe this whole stupid thing is orchestrated by some cosmic intelligence. Not to mention focusing on us! And how did I get dragged into it? And you? Sorry, Mad, you might be gorgeous and talented, but why did you get picked to wear the white hat? If anyone at New Atlantis, it should go to Dru or your sister. And for the black hat? Of all the psychopaths running around, why Raoul?"

I turned my palms out. "We're still not sure it's Raoul. But who else? The black hat had to be someone who could get to us, yet not blow in shooting like Rambo. Someone decaying, not born rotten. He probably started warping during his teens, since puberty is when people are most open to psionic forces. But it could be something as dumb as a bad reaction to peer pressure—like, while all his classmates were giggling over astrology, a sick, abused loner got the idea to study the black arts."

Buck laughed then mocked in falsetto, "Hey baby, what's your sign?" then answered himself in basso profundo: "An inverted pentacle, sweetie, what's yours?"

How bright his grin could be when spontaneous! It extended all the way into his eyes. I rarely saw that simple beauty; never expected it at such a time.

With effort, I returned to sobriety. "Maybe he was spurned by his first love and has been obsessed with beautiful blondes ever since. Whatever reason, I'm sure he invited the dark powers to join him. If he were simply damaged, like a broken window, power would just breeze through and drive him differently. Like stalking any beautiful blonde and raping her at knife point then peeling off her skin."

Buck nodded. "You mean, the reverse of idiot savants or saintly cripples."

"Yeah, or intact people like Dru and Allanna who work to attract power. These are rare in positive or negative—and it's a testament to nature's balance that both exist in the same place and time."

Buck grunted agreement and placed his guitar beside him with its neck resting on a pillow. The gesture refreshed my awareness of how little space separated us on the bed. Has Julia slept here? I wondered in a spurt of bitterness. Will he run to her now for comfort in her normalcy? Would any man want a woman who can conjure powerballs out of air?

The questions flooded my eyes when I lifted my head to look at him. He awaited my gaze with a wary squint. The jolt I felt when our eyes met proclaimed that our minds and moods had also synchronized. Our bodies wanted to join in. We sat in a deadlock, wondering who would break it. The answer came as a muted thundering downstairs.

21
Shrapnel

Running footsteps jarred the floorboards then the staircase. Seconds later, Buck's door began to shake.

"Madeline! Hey, Madeline!" Kit's fists pounded the panels. "Damn it, I know you're in there—open up!"

Blood plummeted to our feet. The doorknob rattled. "Get out of there, you slut! Unlock this goddamn door!"

Fists again—boom, boom, boom.

I shot a look at Buck before leaping for the handle. Although I hadn't noticed him lock the door I was grateful he had.

"Hold on, I'm coming. And jeezus, Kit—shut up!"

The yanked-open door revealed Kit with purple face and fist raised for a final hammering. "How dare you," he hissed through bared teeth as his arm fell.

Buck loomed behind me. "Cool down, man," he said in a menacing tone.

Kit ignored him. "Get out here right now!"

He grabbed for my arm. I jerked it away. "Good god, Kit—what's the matter with you!"

I almost said, Who are you? Kit's eyes, normally a vivid, transparent blue like diamonds or tropical seas, now seemed opaque, the soul within masked or dormant. Or replaced by another. Or else I had misjudged him beyond measure and was seeing his true self for the first time.

"Nothing wrong except my woman in another guy's bed behind a locked door!"

I flapped my arms. "Kit, I am fully clothed and standing!"

"Yeah? So why the lock? Listen, Mad—just get outa here. I don't want you with him!"

Buck stepped forward. "You don't own her, Douglas. The lady is free to go wherever she wants!"

"Not any more!" Kit pulled me into the hall. I stumbled; recovered my balance; then slammed him across the face with open palm. I couldn't have stopped him better if I had kneed him in the testicles. Kit's eyes popped and jaw fell open, hands dropped to his sides. Then he burst into tears and fled.

"Kit! Kit!" I crouched to run but stopped there, sure I couldn't catch him. So I spun to face Buck, whose face twisted in shock and dismay. "God, Buck—I'm sorry—I don't know—"

Buck smeared a hand across his face. "What the hell?"

No time to answer. I headed for the stairs.

Buck followed at a staggering shuffle, a pied piper for the household. I disregarded them to attack the intercom.

"Blanche? Red alert! Kit just showed up raving and has taken off—I think on his dirt bike. I don't have a vehicle to follow. Could—"

Dru came on. "What's happened?"

"Kit just barged in and—forget it, I'll explain later. But it might be that whatever I chased off the compound snagged him on its way out!"

Blanche's voice jumped in from the background. "I got the gate."

"Thanks." The four points from which we could control the front gate included the carriage house. Normally, people operated it from the office or gatehouse or remote units in certain vehicles, including Kit's. "Lock it. I'll be up there quick unless I find him first."

Behind me, someone cleared his throat the moment I closed the channel. I spun to see Rob standing in the kitchen, Pete and Jim peeking around doorways, and both twins crouched on the stairs behind Buck at the foot.

"Need help, Mad?" Rob ventured, hoping I would say no.

"A car would be good."

"There's one out back."

Buck stepped forward. "I'll drive you."

"No—don't come unless I call." *I'm not losing both of you in one night!* Dismissing the car, I pulled the door open then slammed it behind me and ran outside.

Clutching my sweater close, I sprinted up the road as though a swarm of bats was after me. More likely, an evil spirit, who seemed to be shooting at me through my clan. Dru and Allanna I could half understand, but how did it get into Kit? And what would it drive him to do? I heard his dirt bike shut off abruptly up near the house.

I found it lying in the circle at the end of a skid gouge in the crushed stone. Blanche met me on the front stairs wearing a sweatsuit under a parka. Without speaking, she led me to my suite where Kit lay belly-up on the bed, his torso blocked by Dru's hunched back.

"How did you subdue him?"

"Shhh!" Blanche held a finger to her pursed lips. "He subdued himself. Rode up as we went out to look for him and swung the bike into a stop so hard it went out from under him. He conked his head on the way down. We carried him in."

I nodded and, still shivering, took my place beside Dru and watched his palms skim the length of Kit's body. Blanche breathed over my shoulder. We felt heat emanating from Dru's hands, heard his whispered incantations. After he relaxed his arms and straightened, Kit slept deeply with flushed cheeks.

We stepped into the sitting room. I demanded, "What did you do to him, Dru? When did you start healing? How do you do it?"

He stared. "You gave me the power with that blast."

"Me!"

"You're a conduit, Mad," Blanche said, "just as Dru's a conduit for healing power."

"And Kit just became a conduit for destructive power. But Dru, you did it on purpose. What button did you push?"

He shrugged. "Same one I use to visit the glittery void, or talk to you telepathically. I don't know how to describe it. Can you say how you tell your heart to beat or hand to move?"

"Shit!" I punched the air with both fists, stomped in a circle, then collected myself and looked at him. "You work on that description. We need to know!"

In the subsequent silence, Blanche buzzed The Glen with an update, then raided my snack cabinet and mini fridge. Dru dragged his hands through his hair.

"If he was possessed before, it's left him now. I've called Brian and sent a messenger to Hill House. And locked the gate against remotes."

I nodded while watching Kit from the doorway, unable to see his aura. Did he still have one? I had seen it while Dru channeled the healing force. Did I need that booster, or did I have enough power on my own until emotion shut it down?

Brian knocked once and entered, frowning and windblown. "Now what?" He swept past us to Kit.

"You tell me!" Dru exclaimed. "This kid showed up at The Glen frothing and didn't quit until first Mad hit him then he knocked himself out dropping his bike. Did Troy or Allanna say anything was wrong with him while they were traveling?"

Brian didn't answer for a moment. Then he rose from bedside and plucked stethoscope hooks from his ears. "No. They said he was fine. Calm and capable, but angry. Didn't buy the story about the bowl and was worried about being delayed. Thought Madeline had tricked him. And thought for sure New Atlantis would be a heap of rubble when we got back."

"What about Allanna?"

"She was either in pain or doped up—I doubt her sensors are working well."

"Did they feel any atmosphere or presence when they entered the compound?"

Brian shook his head. "Didn't mention anything. Kit drove in, dropped them off at Hill House, then came back here."

His ginger eyebrows puckered. "I take it something happened in that interval?"

More knocks brought Troy, whose mustache drooped and hair hung in haphazard, gray-streaked coils. "What the hell is going on?"

"How's Allanna?" Dru returned.

"She's okay. Resting." He looked past us to Kit and stiffened. "What happened to him?"

"We think he got backhanded by the thing that got me and Allanna."

Dru synopsized the day's events, ending with, "So did you notice anything that might account for this?"

Troy ruminated then said, "No, but I did find it curious that no people were outside the gate." He raised his eyes and looked at us in sequence. "You get so used to seeing them—and ignoring them—it's like they're part of the forest."

"Well, it's getting colder . . ." Blanche suggested.

"But they usually don't go away until it's ten below," Dru finished.

We looked at each other. Dru sucked in his gut and concluded, "So I'd guess the entity's hanging around our perimeter. We're going to try an all-group power circle to cancel it out."

"The sooner the better!" Troy agreed.

Dru's eyes smoldered from the effort of self-control. Blanche, hugging her parka closed across her chest, looked like a frightened doe. They exchanged glances, then Dru slid an arm around her shoulders before instructing, "Brian, you make sure everyone at the lodges comes up for supper. Troy, you round up Hill House and Julia, and find your brothers. I want one to watch Allanna and the other to stay with Kit while we hold the circle."

I stepped forward. "It's my place to sit with him."

"No, Mad, we need you in the circle."

I opened my mouth to argue just as "Uhnnn . . . !" came from behind us. We knelt over my bed in one motion.

"Uhnnnh," Kit groaned again, twisting his head from side to side. I sat on the padded side rail and took his hand, stroking his forehead.

"Uhnnnh, ooooah, waitaminnit, what happened? Whas goinon?"

His eyes popped open, seeming violet in the meager light. They drifted for a moment then focused on my face. "Mad? Why'd you do that to me?" He tried to sit up but floundered on the mattress. Dru and Blanche pressed him back. His grip tightened on my hand.

"I'm not the guilty party, Kit. You—"

His face skewed. "You love him more than me! You lied to me again! I can tell!" He pushed my hand away and sat up. "Get out of my bedroom!" he shouted at the onlookers.

Dru said quietly, "Kit, you've been ill, and it's important that you sleep again. We can talk when you wake up."

He touched Kit between the eyebrows. Kit sagged back into the bed.

The rest of us stepped back and resumed arguing strategy. After Troy left to carry out his assignment, the intercom buzzed.

I stepped into the anteroom and touched the panel. "Yes?"

"Mad? It's me. Everything okay up there?"

A thrill cascaded through my body. I couldn't remember the last time Buck had called me, or spoken in such a warm tone. "For the moment," I replied. "It seems that Kit had a passing encounter with the enemy. He appears to be sleeping it off." I crossed my fingers.

"There?"

"Yes."

"Well . . . call me if you need me."

If interested parties hadn't been listening, I would have said more than "Thank you. Please come up for dinner and help in the power circle. I'll see you then."

Or would he be next?

Turning back to Dru, Blanche, and Brian, I said, "Leave me with Kit for now, I'll come down when John shows up."

They nodded and departed after hugging and kissing me. I closed the door behind them then slid the bolt.

After leaning my forehead against the panel for a long moment, I returned to the bedroom. Kit lay stretched out with covers up to his chin, his face seeming ancient in the angled glare of the nightstand lamp. I flicked it off and considered lying beside him. That would rock the waterbed, which might disturb the healing sleep Dru had imposed. Could I augment it with my own power? No, that might incinerate him. And if the lightning rod effect was still active, I might channel another demon!

What had happened to the demon I'd blasted? Had I injured it, or had it retreated? Had it come back through Kit, or were we dealing with plural entities? If just one, had it been so weakened that a blow could jar it loose? How did these things work!

Regardless, I didn't know whether my power—or luck—had limits. "When in doubt, don't" seemed prudent; better to keep my one advantage in reserve. But if I ever got a chance, ever found a way, then I would blast my enemy into oblivion.

After kissing Kit's forehead, I drew the curtains. Fastened the windows and closed the vents while at it, and avoided the mirror. Remembering certain movies, I thought twice about entering the bathroom. No blood ran from the taps; no ax murderer lurked in the shower. Nonetheless, I looked over my shoulder while changing, and nearly ricocheted off the ceiling when Kit released a slurping snore.

I settled into the anteroom, studying my paintings. Through their symbols, my life passed before my eyes. I closed my eyes, shuddering, and focused on barriers. Added another wall, barbed wire, and a forcefield to my mental picture. Envisioned Kit awake and laughing at fear. Then I imagined myself a porpoise and dove to Atlantis. But there I saw myself as a scientist, peering through a microscope to an aberrant world beneath the skin.

Anyone looking at me would believe I had everything. While I couldn't argue the fact and was grateful for my privileges, I longed to shriek, It's not what it seems! Welcome to New Atlantis, the funhouse. No way back, and nothing but a booby-trapped maze going forward; no way to predict what might pop up where and when.

I gasped and spun when something behind me moved, to find Kit leaning against the door frame in a T-shirt and blue bikini briefs.

He had crossed one ankle over the other and both arms across his diaphragm. His eyes looked normal; the guy I knew was back in place behind them. I exhaled and steadied myself with the back of a chair.

"Are you all right?" I whispered.

He pushed himself upright. "I think so. What happened?"

At my inhalation, his eyes hardened. "Or don't I want to know?"

"You'd probably rather not." Nevertheless, I told him, reciting the fusillade of events since we had parted in the entry hall. Kit maintained a deadpan until I reached the part about the blast. Then his eyes briefly widened before his whole face tightened into a scowl. It held there until I described his overdramatic entrance. At that he opened and closed his mouth then averted his eyes.

I crossed the distance between us to hug him. He clenched me so tight he almost cracked my ribs. Then he released me and turned away, saying with a hollow laugh, "I'm damn glad we're in a locked community!"

"Is it time to call in someone? We've got to have help!"

"Why? We've got you—the prophesied savior! Seems to me you're the right weapon in the right place at the right time!"

"Oh god, Kit, please—I've no idea what I'm doing!"

"But you've obviously got all the right stuff. Besides, getting outside help will mean instant scandal, no matter how much hush money they pay."

His eyes flickered, making me wonder what scornful family he hoped to keep in the dark. Which in turn recalled my mother living in Paris. Unaware I had gone near New Atlantis, she might have a coronary if her entire brood showed up in the headlines! She had already endured near-fatal shock when her test-pilot husband had died, leaving her with infant twins and a toddler. We had been raised by relatives while Mother weathered grief. Its depth and duration first wakened me to the idea of soulmates. Looking at Kit, I wondered how I would feel if he died.

No! I shook the thought away and refocused on the present. "It doesn't have to be a scandal, if we choose the right professionals.

I mean, we've had investigators for months now and they haven't made a peep."

"They also haven't found Raoul. You think a parapsychologist or exorcist will do any better?"

"I don't know. But I'm willing to try. I can't carry this whole thing alone! Especially working blind. So damn it—tell me what happened to you!"

He lifted a shoulder, almost a twitch, then paced the anteroom after pulling on a sweatshirt. "Not much to tell. It's all in pieces, like a fading dream."

"Try. I need to know. Start when I last saw you."

He stopped. "Well, I was pissed. And suspicious. I thought you were jerking my chain. Knew something was real wrong when Dru came screaming up the hill, freaking about a coffee mug. I ran down to the studio, didn't see anything but an upside-down one in the office, thought you'd thrown it at him. Then Brian grabbed me for ambulance driver, and Troy and Allanna gave me some crap about shattering glass. I thought you'd gone nuts and were running around attacking people. But with Allanna bleeding all over the place, swearing up and down you were sane, I didn't have much choice but to keep driving."

He sighed and shook his head, eyes on the floor. "I dunno, it started to eat at me. All your deceits, all that everyone wouldn't tell me. Then I started counting the ways I'd ever been used and screwed. I thought of Julia with Buck and all the fights I had with my family, getting disowned when I refused to enlist, then every race I lost, the weeks in the hospital . . ."

His face blanked then contorted as he relived his transformation. "Then, while driving, I started to feel kinda strange. Empty, on one hand, but really strong. Nothing mattered. I wasn't going to take it any more. I couldn't stop thinking about you and Buck. I saw you in an X-rated movie playing on the windshield. I was gonna get you back good and punish Dru and New Atlantis while at it. So when I learned you were at The Glen, that was like waving a red flag in front of toro! I actually saw red. Which is the last thing I remember until I woke up here."

I closed my eyes and sagged into an armchair. Kit crossed the floor to squat beside me. At first he kept his face turned, then reached up to finger my hair. I tipped my head against his shoulder to hide an escaping teardrop. He sensed it anyway; stood and brought me up with him to kiss deeply. His ardor made my muscles slacken, and a moan eased from my throat.

I should have predicted the door knock. Kit stiffened, swore, then retreated to the bedroom while I answered the summons.

22
Escape

Expecting Blanche, Dru, or John, I unlocked and opened without query. Finding Buck there, I almost shrieked and slammed the door in his face.

"How's Kit?" He pressed his hand against the panel to keep the door open.

Kit swung into view with narrowed eyes and flared nostrils. "What do you want."

Half undressed, he managed to look bigger and meaner. I stepped back as Buck walked in. Both men refused to look at me.

"I came to see if you've recovered," Buck declared.

Kit moved forward. "What's it to you?"

"Plenty! That was a bad scene back there, and I want to make sure everything is cool."

Kit's expression upgraded from venomous to doubtful. Buck switched his gaze to me. "Also, to tell you they're waiting for you in the dining hall."

"I thought they were sending John to relieve me."

Buck jutted his chin at Kit. "Dru knows he's awake."

Kit retreated to the bedroom for pants. Buck looked at me. I asked the question he was waiting for. "Are you going to sit in the circle?"

"I kinda think I oughta."

"Don't do it unless you mean it."

"I mean to understand what's going on, and do whatever I can to fix it."

We held eye contact until I looked away, saying, "It wouldn't hurt to have one of us not connected, in case something goes wrong."

"Cornelius is still a circle virgin. I doubt he'll join in."

"I'll be happy to miss it," Kit said upon return.

"You've got an excuse. And no one's expecting you."

I liked that idea.

Kit shook his head and moved past us. "If all of us together have a chance of frying this guy, I'm willing to give it a shot."

Buck and I exchanged glances then followed. The three of us went downstairs, entering the dining hall with the men flanking me. Everyone observed us like one big eye.

To keep them guessing, we dispersed to nonadjacent seats. The tables were already shoved back with chairs arranged in a circle. I cringed upon sitting, unwilling to face all those eyes when I wanted to curl into a ball under the bed. A cone of fear was thrusting up through my diaphragm like a submarine volcano on a fault line. I needed to cram it back down into a pellet buried in my guts where it normally lived. But to walk out now would undermine my cohorts. So I distracted myself by flipping the New Atlantis medallion between my fingers and decoding it, no longer caring who saw me with it.

One token: self and unity. Two sides: balance—yin/yang. The pyramid on the obverse side expressed mathematical formulas; its four faces represented the seasons and the base elements of the physical realm: earth, air, fire, water. Each pyramid face formed a triangle, the universal symbol of trinity. On the two faces showing, an infinity sign—a Möbius strip—and an ankh, the Egyptian symbol of life, had been engraved.

Seven rays emanated from behind the pyramid. These could be the color spectrum, the musical scale, the seven seas and continents, seven races of man, seven wonders of the world, seven-year itch, or any other collection. Whatever one wanted to see, one could find.

Same held true with the picture on the flip side, where a unicorn pranced before a mountain beneath a sun and moon. Some thought the unicorn represented Christ; others considered it the symbol of purity or elusive idealism. The mountain and sky offered many interpretations, but to me the significance lay in where they met. Earth and sky; science and spirituality. New Atlantis rising from the old. Ancient knowledge combined with modern technology. All these related to the zodiac, the twelve signs of which, in four triads, formed the border design on both sides of the disk.

I slipped it back inside my top and turned to incoming traffic. Dru swept in; caught sight of me in his scan of the room; moved to Troy, Mark, and—surprise—Allanna.

Blanche veered toward the chair I had saved for her, while all eyes tracked her passage across the room. She sat like a deflating parachute in her crimson caftan with gold piping. Dru had chosen an ascetic look: white wrap-front tunic, white pants and slippers, and a red triangle drawn between his brows.

Dru took the twins' entrance as a cue to start the program. All chatter subsided the moment he stood.

"Friends, there's something new and wonderful we have to do. Maybe not so new, since most of you have been helping already. But all of you are aware of abnormal goings-on. On the surface, they seem like poltergeist activity: objects moving of their own volition, mysterious events, people experiencing psychic traumas. This is because we've got not a poltergeist but a demon—a negative entity targeting us, and stealing New Atlantis's energy to enhance its power. We've discovered that we need to merge our strengths in order to fight it. I'm hoping that, when you understand, you'll volunteer your personal power."

He went on to relate the tale of Blanche, Madeline, and Raoul, cribbing information from my head as if it were written on his sleeve. I vowed to invade his mind sometime when he was in the bathroom, or photograph him there and tack the pictures on the bulletin board. I could feel him shielding against the embarrassment and resentment I projected across the room.

"When she fainted at the cookout . . ." he was saying. Julia rolled her eyes toward me, as did half the circle. Only John Powers and a puffy, bandaged Allanna watched me steadily. Buck and Kit, several chairs away from me in opposite directions, slouched and scowled at their fingernails. Neither noticed auras rising, blurring people together in a subtle glimmer. Some folks blinked and looked around with curious gazes; the rest didn't pull their attention from Dru.

"Raven . . . envelope . . . ceramic bowl . . ." he continued.

Kit and Buck reminded me of two shirts on a revolving rack in a department store. Same style and price tag; different color and size. Someone would ultimately bear them off to separate destinies. Until then, I was the rod from which they hung.

"Scorchless fireball . . ." Dru said, moving many in the audience to swivel and stare at me.

I ignored them, lost in private mysteries. Why two of them? Was either of them my soulmate? How could I tell? Whose place was it to decide? Both played lover, student, tormentor, and savior. Both dismissed Blanche but liked Julia and loved me. Had this crazy combo been forced by an Atlantean mass reincarnation? Would we otherwise have cycled separately through each other's lives?

"So you see," Dru concluded, "this creature has become a conduit for the dark powers. Successful because at first he offered no resistance, and now they've bored him so smooth that he can't. Their potency comes from focusing through his senses. His mobility makes it hard for us to aim in return. What we must do, then, is become a mirror—catching that pinpoint wherever it hits to bounce it back before the source relocates. Combat focus by being unfocused; fuse our energies into a greater strength. In other words, do as one community what you've been doing in groups. The first step in creating this reflective forcefield is to close the circle by joining hands."

He stepped forward with both arms extended. Irene and Allanna, seated, draped their fingers across his upturned palms. He curled his hands around them and lowered his voice. "Rearrange yourselves into a more potent sequence. Sit with your spouse or best friend, or any special someone. Conversely, if you're uncomfortable participating, feel free to leave the room."

A shuffle ensued but no one departed. I remained seated in indecision, concerned about the linked hands. In previous circles, no one had touched each other. Also, Cornelius was present and showed no signs of leaving.

Blanche removed herself to Dru's side while Kit occupied the chair she had vacated. I expected John to sit on my left side, but that place was taken by Buck. A new triumvirate!—which didn't go unnoticed. Blanche led Dru across the floor to us and sat beside Kit. Dru linked with Allanna on his far side, who linked in turn to her husband through her child. Troy held hands with Leslee, who connected him to Adam, who sat with Alexis and Brian, who surprised me by linking with Jessie, followed by Lawrence and Lu. Lu led into the twins; Brenda and Jim Casey; Irene and Jeff; Daniel and Karla. Their two daughters sat between Pete and Cornelius, who began an all-men block including Seth and Greg. Then came Cassandra, Mark, and finally Julia. She closed the loop at Buck, at which I felt a different tingling through my left arm.

As we settled, power burgeoned in my arms and belly. While it flowed out and in through my lovers, it manifested visibly as an aura embracing the group. For the first time I saw us as a unit. We comprised a magical 36.

The same groupings I had noted on the pendant now danced before me as numbers: $36 = 3 + 6 = 9 = 3 \times 3$; $3 + 3 = 6$; $6 \times 6 = 36$; $3 \times 6 = 18$; $1 + 8 = 9$; $9 \times 2 = 18$; $18 \times 2 = 36$ . . .

Digits telescoped before my eyes, swirling into geometric patterns overlaying the ring of faces. These faces were blank, anxious, or serene, and represented the races and sexual preferences of humankind. As many different body types and clothing styles, colors and patterns were present. I ranked among the boring in zip-front sweatshirt over jeans.

When the room vibrated in silence, Dru inhaled then sent out his voice. His clear, cool tone, holding pitch with no accompaniment, absorbed our attention as would a candle in a dark room. By the time he trailed off on the final note, the group was profoundly entranced.

A soundless buzzing in our heads drowned out background noises. A current swelled up one arm, across the shoulders, and out the other arm of everyone in the ring. Sparkling patterns swirled on the insides of eyelids—or in the atmosphere, for those compelled to peek. Dru's aura engulfed him and stung the eyes of any watcher. I dropped my lids and let his image fill my mind . . . falling into his radiance and adding mine to it, uniting to push darkness away.

After a time, the current changed from sizzle to pulsation as heart-beats fell into sync with each other. I came to feel like a membrane sac filled with warm fluid. My face smiled of its own accord, matched by thirty-five identical expressions I could see without opening my eyes. Even Buck and Kit experienced thrill, communicated by heat surges through their hands as they discovered the true altered state of consciousness. Buck greeted it so ecstatically I had to crush his knuckles to prevent his spirit from shooting out of his body. The pain stab he received whizzed through the circle, shattering unity. One by one, lolling heads straightened, eyes blinked open, and feet shifted on the floor. The tingling faded and with it the group's aura, until everyone became alert.

Dru signaled the end by dropping his hands, at which people began coughing and shuffling like a theater audience when the house lights return. Dru inspected the now-ragged circle. Seventy eyes stared back, awaiting his cue. With a sigh then a smile, he stood and said, "Thank you." We grinned and babbled in response. Many craned their heads, still seeing a glimmer. Cornelius, ever the skeptic, challenged, "Will this work?"

Shouts of, "Of course!" and "How can it not?" accompanied shrugs and tolerant laughter. I sneaked a glance at Kit, who sat limp and bemused. Buck, on the other hand, stood tall and looked around like an eagle. Julia hung on his arm while they avoided my eye. Dru, meanwhile, waited to catch it. When I faced him, he talked on.

"The force is only as powerful as we make it. We got a great start this evening, but it will need continual boost. Try to hold this state of mind until our next joining, which we'll perform daily. We've got people coming in soon and need to guarantee their safety as well as our own, and show them a good time while at it. In fact, the Halloween party might make a great circle! Now, if you'll all help push the chairs and tables back, we can enjoy our meal."

He gave us a last look then whisked Blanche from the dining hall. Group mumble became a clamor as people rearranged. The kitchen door swung as the crew scurried in and out with vats of rich vegetable stew and bread steaming in baskets. We dove in while jabbering and laughing, between hugs and kisses. Over dessert and coffee, we broke into song.

Singing sustained group euphoria between dinnertime power circles. While people worked, they sang, and the more creative among us wrote new pieces. I held back on singing at first, suspicious of the speed with which the climate had changed. But the evidence of my senses showed nothing to worry about, and sustaining fear when I could have been happy took too much effort. Once I joined in the first songfest, the rest became easier. When tempted to falter, I reminded myself that pillars of triumvirates should support solidarity. Soon enough, I stopped looking over my shoulder.

The band worked marathon hours on their new album, *Atlantean Dream,* including a feature video of Blanche dancing, entitled "Thing of Beauty." I sat in on several sessions to absorb the mood and sketch layouts for the cover. I also filled a sketchbook with portraits and local landscapes blended with expansions of the medallion imagery as illustrations for Cornelius's book, *The New Atlantis Story.* This included drawings of Blanche and me in our Atlantean princess costumes. Once word of that got around, people asked to see the real thing.

So we held an open photo shoot, for which people brought cameras and we posed with props and sets. Full regalia put us in tiaras and armbands, plunge necklines, slit skirts, snug bodices. Our gowns had begun life as leotards, to which we had added gauze and jewels. Blanche's dress, in willow green, featured an over-the-shoulder train and gold-link hip girdle; I had omitted the train in favor of a layered skirt with handkerchief hemline that swirled when I moved. My gown was the color of Kit's eyes and accented with blue gemstones and silver. At the sight of us, women sighed in envy and men drooled.

All except Kit, who attended neither session. In fact, he seemed to be avoiding me, even though he showed up for each power circle and slept in my bed.

When I inquired about his activities, he gave polite but evasive answers. According to his words and the fresh wounds on his hands, there was much to be done to accommodate the party guests. Since he otherwise acted normally and went off grounds without incident, I wasted no time worrying and only a few minutes wondering. Our success in vanquishing evil, plus the thrill of belonging, discouraged me from seeking trouble.

My trust was rewarded late afternoon before the Halloween party. While teetering on a ladder held by Cassandra, hanging decorations in the entry hall, I heard a sound outside I didn't believe. Like an echo from another life came the growl of a V8 engine. It started faintly, revving and falling through upshifts, then dropped to a loping, familiar idle as it pulled into the circle.

I cried out, leaped off the ladder, and pushed through the front entry. When the heavy outer door gave way, I galloped down the steps with arms flung open, squealing like a groupie. Kit deserved nothing less, having become my idol by resurrecting the Tiger.

He sat grinning with one elbow over the door, the top down and wearing sunglasses despite overcast skies and forty-degree temperature.

"Hey, baby, going my way?"

"Anywhere you want to take me!"

I hopped over the door into the passenger seat to kiss him breathless. On surfacing, he gunned the motor, punched the car into gear, and shot down the drive. The gate swung open as we approached and scraped shut after us. Kit cleared a path through the campers, who had returned after the first power circle, by accelerating toward them. I laughed and clapped as they dove clear and the car took off like a land-bound jet.

Roaring horsepower and buffeting wind made it impossible to thank him. For the half-hour we tore along the mountain roads, I sat pasted against the seat with three O's for mouth and eyes. Kit drove faster than I had ever dared, as casually as a Sunday tourist. My mind reeled from the shock of entering reality and heart resonated like a gong from the force of his gift.

New possibilities opened, as broad and deep as the vista that stretched before us when he finally pulled into a ridgeline siding. Despite the fading variegated foliage, the world could have been newly born and we the only people alive. My chest heaved as I struggled to master emotion. Kit reached across the stick to take my hand.

"Are you ready to think about leaving?"

I snapped my head around to look at him, knowing what he asked yet needing it spelled out. "What do you mean?"

He shifted to face me. "It's over. New Atlantis is thriving. You figured out your psychic problem and won the day. You've been inside the walls for three months now, forgetting who you used to be. It's safe to go home. Can I take you?" He paused. "And stay?"

I gaped at him. "You mean—I mean, what would you do?"

"I can work anywhere. You can paint anywhere. Between us we can make a decent living, get our own place. Go back to racing. Have a life."

I heard what he didn't say: Leave the psychic world behind. Forget about darkness. Let New Atlantis fend for itself. And get Buck Williams out of the picture.

"Are you asking me to marry you?"

He flushed and faced forward. "I guess so."

"I would feel better if you knew so!"

He turned, in full hawk mask. Then he lunged across the transmission tunnel and kissed me fiercely. My head spun and body liquefied, but my mind shot back to memories of parked cars and Buck.

Damn!

Kit felt me stiffen and pulled away. "Does that mean no?"

I looked out the windshield. A rock settled into my stomach. "It means that I can't. I'm just . . . not ready."

He squelched a sigh and settled back in driver's position. "What will it take?"

I didn't want to answer. But I owed him honesty, even if it hurt. "Magic."

He looked back at me with narrowed eyes beneath a cocked brow.

"Some sign," I elaborated. "Something outside myself I can't possibly misconstrue, to tell me you and I are meant to be. Or some sureness deep in my heart I've not yet known. And something to convince me we're safe from dark powers, so it's not all for nothing."

Kit exhaled through pursed lips. "That's a tall order!" He started the engine.

"Maybe I'm a fool, but I believe it's possible. That might be the only thing I do believe!"

"Glad to know I'm not the only fool."

He tossed me a sad one-cornered smile then snicked the Tiger into gear and took off. Retracing our route, he drove at terrifying speed. I welcomed the rush of air—noise—freedom—and the old-fashioned power made by exploding fossil fuel in metal chambers, conceived and designed and forged by man. Buck's line, "I like being incarnate" flashed through my mind.

Realizing that I was where I had often longed to be, I reeled in my attention back to the present. Kit's hands and feet danced across wheel, shifter, and pedals, his eyes far down the roadscape or darting across the mirrors. The speedometer climbed. The curves tightened and hillsides closed in. We hurtled along thirty percent faster than I had ever driven, since I reached my limits long before the Tiger did. Kit showed me how to bridge the difference.

Sensing my focus, he began to narrate, answering each question as it entered my mind but before it reached my tongue. Our awarenesses merged and I lost the distinction between our limbs and nerve endings, at the same time felt every nuance in the car's handling and saw, heard, and smelled the environment streak by. Kit became that person I had seen and known at our first encounter, this time without the rippling atmosphere. As before, the moment I recognized him, the portal between realities snapped shut and plopped me outside on the doorstep.

Somewhere in that microsecond Kit had decided on a course change. He double-clutch downshifted, braked, turned ninety degrees, and accelerated from state road onto dirt byway. It paralleled a stream then ascended a two-track, deeper into the forest. Earlier vehicles had squashed the leaf fall into a smooth path. After a few hundred yards, the woods opened into a glade beside a staircase waterfall into a swimming hole. Rounded boulders testified to violent spring runoff.

Kit parked, got out, pulled a blanket from behind the seat, slung it over his shoulder, then opened my door for me. I stared in defiance. He did not respond in words. While I couldn't hear him telepathically, everything in his stance said, *I dare you.* Dare to make love with me outside New Atlantis. Here with the rushing, indifferent water, the clear, tart air, the damp earth, the birds and critters, no people, no magic, no help, no escape, no deception. Just me and thee in the real world.

I gulped. There was no going back from that level of intimacy. How could I participate if my heart wasn't sure?

He held out his hand in ultimatum. All or nothing, it seemed to say. I couldn't bear living with his hurt and contempt if I refused the commitment he was offering. I would probably never be any more ready than I was now.

So I placed my fingers across his palm, limp and trembling. He closed his hand around them, warm and firm. The shame of submission made me avert my eyes. He hoisted me into his arms and dared me again, to look at him and hold the gaze, so long that I squirmed and looked away. He crooked my chin with a finger and drew my face back until I met his gaze again, then rewarded me with a kiss. Sweet and gentle until I tried to break contact, at which he cupped a hand behind my head and pressed our mouths together. My rogue body started to percolate. As soon as he felt it, Kit pulled back.

Air rushed between us. I almost gasped. But this time I held his eye. He smiled. I gave him a shaky one back. He raised a hand to hold my face, raised the other one to unclip my hair. It tumbled like the waterfall around my shoulders and breasts. He lifted it, let it slide through his fingers, pulled it into a clump behind my head, let it cascade again. Still looking into my eyes, daring me to look away.

One by one, my knees, heart, and spine melted. I closed my eyes and stood pliant as he ran his hands around my face, down my neck and arms, then back up my torso. He paused until my eyes reopened, to dare me again, to kiss me again, first lightly, then roughly, then pressed close and ran his hands up my back, down my thighs, between my legs.

By then I could no longer stand there passive. My melting became a meltdown, while my skin threatened to break out singing. Kit snuffed in a chuckle then slipped his hands beneath my sweatsuit. His scratchy palms added an extra tingle to his touch. I opened my eyes, met his, and we both laughed.

"I love you," I couldn't help saying.

Kit buried his face into my neck with a jubilant growl and crushed me to him. I gurgled in half laughter, half tears, then struggled free and dove for his zipper, wanting to hear him shout. Moments later he did, a clear, boy cry to the treetops. Instead of then falling slack, he scooped me up and spread us across the blanket on a patch of dried grass and leaves nearer the falls. Accompanied by water music, we peeled off each other's clothes and explored what they had covered, rendered golden in the filtered daylight, unhassled by bugs.

Still no words passed between us. Nor could I read his thoughts or his eyes, although we met gazes every few minutes to make sure the other was okay. Then we closed our eyes and cycled between ferocity and tenderness, with time out for play or panting. At intervals I went deaf, dumb, and blind for long, dreamy seconds; when I subsided he brought me up again, adding his release to mine.

Once spent, we curled together, breathing and throbbing in harmony. I stroked and kissed him and held him tightly, unwilling to let him go.

Apparently I didn't. An unknown time later, I awoke to find us in the same position. Muscles and joints had stiffened to achiness. Light had faded to dusk, bringing the temperature down with it. I snugged the blanket closer and fingered his hair like bronze fibers, skating my lips over his textures. He stirred and murmured as these touches penetrated his doze, then his muscles regained tension. With eyes still closed, he captured my fingers and kissed them, uncurled them and kissed my palm.

From there it was a short step to another clinch, although we elongated the process. This time my mind occasionally drifted, wondering if Dru or Raoul hovered in the ether, a disembodied voyeur. Kit erased such thoughts by switching from sensualist to satyr. We coupled again, fast and wild, until he stiffened then relaxed with a gasp.

Still silent, we rested, recovered, then staggered to waterside. After splashing ourselves into goosebumps from the stream that tumbled by, we dried and dressed and returned to the car. I hadn't yet thanked him for its repair but couldn't push the words out. My thoughts looped on one concept: Next time he asks, I'll say yes.

We made it back to New Atlantis in time for him to shower before reporting to duty. He had drawn first gate watch for the party. I was late for my rendezvous with Blanche. She and I had planned to dress together, meeting at the carriage house. I knocked on its door, too cotton-kneed to realize nobody was answering. A stab of anxiety woke me up. Maybe some guests had arrived early, or she was socializing in another building. But why had she left no lights on for her or Dru's return?

Blanche, where are you?

No response, but no surprise, either. Only Dru could telepathically speak with her at will. Otherwise Blanche received thoughts and emotions like voices jumping out of a cocktail party, in snatches akin to my visions. Mostly she perceived a background muttering with peaks and valleys, and the occasional sentence penetrating when she was in a relaxed state of mind.

I need not have bothered trying. Upon entering my suite, I found her waiting at the front window. She stood with back to me and hands clasped behind her, legs locked into an X.

"Ah, there you are," I greeted.

She pivoted on her toes then plunked down to face me. At the sight of her face, I backed a step. "Blanche, what's wrong?"

She stared into me. "I was afraid of that."

"What?"

"You can't feel it, can you?"

"Feel what? God, I feel terrific!"

"I'm sure you do. The circles backfired, Madeline. You just proved it. The Thing is back."

I groped behind me for my vanity bench and sat with a thump. "W-what do you mean?"

She punched her fists against her hips. "Damn it, you're just like the rest of them—jacklit by your own brilliance! You can't see, much less imagine, what's about to run you down!"

"So tell me! What's happened?"

"I told you. It's back. It never left."

A tendril of fear began to climb through my abdomen. I banished it with a defiant, "Nonsense!" and picked up a brush to untangle my hair. "No Thing can lurk around without me knowing. Same with Dru, and half the rest."

"Not any more! You've all been blinded. You can't see it, but everyone's eyes are glazed."

"Hah! Wouldn't yours be if you'd just been ravished in the great outdoors by the man of your dreams?"

Her scowl didn't crack.

"Blanche, didn't you hear me?"

"No dreams coming true if you don't survive tonight!"

"Why wouldn't I?" I smacked down my brush.

Blanche seethed and paced behind me in the mirror. Glancing at my reflection, I noted that my eyes were their usual gray-green.

Blanche stopped. "You can't tell they're glazed when you're looking through them!"

I spun to face her. "Are you accusing—"

She answered with a ringing slap across my face.

I shrieked; pressed one hand against my cheek and lashed out with the other; launched myself into a stagger; fell on the floor. When the pain daggers subsided, I stared up Blanche's black-clad body between her breasts and into her eyes. They bulged with emotion but held steady as she controlled her breathing. I understood all as I lay and looked at her. The weight of it—the magnitude of our self-deception—kept me voiceless and flattened for minutes.

23
All Hallows Eve

We had been wrong. Fatally mistaken. The energy we had believed was creating a reflective forcefield had in fact been attracting minus to plus. For a while, at the boundary, the forces had been balanced enough to repel like same magnetic poles. But in the time between our power circles, negative energy had seeped in through our relaxed, distracted minds. While we looked outward for it, it lurked behind us and swelled inside us. Yet we received no bad visions, for it was using our energy and images. We had simply given it, while trying to fight it, exactly what it needed to corrupt New Atlantis.

"Oh Blanche!" I wailed, wiping my nose on my sleeve. "Blanche, you're right!"

"Of course I am! Would I hit you for anything else?"

She extended a hand that shocked me on contact. When I sat again at my vanity, she proffered a tissue and I blew my nose.

"It's been developing since the first power circle," she said. "I recovered after a night's sleep, but when no one else did, I got worried. Especially since I stopped hearing anybody. No stray thoughts, no fluctuation in group mood or individual feelings—even in Dru, even in you! You were all stuck in high gear, in a nonstop creativity orgasm. Like lab mice that can't stop pressing the lever because the electroshock to their pleasure centers feels so good!"

I recalled the feeling wistfully, knowing I'd never again experience it: invincible optimism and enjoyment in the greatest and smallest things. Freedom from doubt—which had returned outside then vanished upon reentering the compound.

"It was better than any drug, Blanche. And impossible to think that anything so wonderful could be bad!"

"Worse than any drug, 'cause there's no side effect except bursting good health. Then the main effect of us media darlings leading millions the wrong way."

"The ultimate costume—white hat on the outside, black hole within."

"He's even got perfect timing: a full moon and Halloween!"

"Oh god!" I moaned, wishing there were one to save us. Upon twisting to face the mirror, I jolted alert at the sight of me. "Blanche, the gate. We can't let anyone else get sucked into this!"

"Too late. But if you snapped out of it, so might the rest."

"Wait a minute, why aren't you affected?"

"Can't you guess?" She pointed at her chest and jeered, "Why not li'l ole me? Because I'm the prize!" She flung open her arms. "The precious china doll locked into the cabinet! Madeline, you're expecting this thing to be rational. It may be intelligent and logical, but it never believed I had a brain. Raoul wanted the perfect woman—which to him was tits and ass, a beautiful face, an empty cranium—a body whose proper place was on its back or hanging on his arm. Remember, the powers are channeling through this particular man, not reanimating a dead body. He put me on a pedestal the moment he saw me. And all the trouble he's had since then has come from anyone but me."

"I thought he wanted to get back at you for rejecting him."

"And so he has, especially if he fouls up New Atlantis. He never believed I had hurt him on purpose. No, it was Dru and New Atlantis polluting my thoughts!"

I plopped my face into my hands and shook it. "This is too bizarre!"

"Get a grip, Mad. We've got to fix it—tonight!"

"I think I'd rather leave." This time, I had a car.

Blanche handed me a jacket. I pulled on more substantial shoes than the slippers Kit had caught me in. Kit. Oh Kit. I went for the intercom. Blanche called after me, "Try if you want, but it's no good."

I looked back at her then punched the gatehouse numbers. "Kit?"

Too many seconds passed without reply. I slapped the intercom panel. "Kit, are you there? C'mon, Kit, answer me!"

Silence. Not even the faint crackle that signaled an open line. I licked my lips and swallowed a few times but could not restore moisture to my mouth. Blanche, her own voice raspy, said, "Try the carriage house."

Same empty air. Then I tried all the buildings and Mark's mobile unit. No answer, no static. At that, I wrenched open the door and ran down the hall to the gallery phone. Blanche followed at half tiptoe, half crab scuttle, glancing at the doors muffling music and laughter. I ignored them to jiggle the phone button, trying to coax a dial tone into the dead line.

"It was like that when I tried you earlier," Blanche said from behind me. I placed down the hand set, listening to gears spinning but not engaging in my mind.

She towed me back to the anteroom. "I told you, it's too late. I think it's domed over the compound, lobotomizing everyone who comes in!"

"I didn't feel a change when we came in, and the gate opened and closed okay for us."

"Since you didn't feel a change when it first happened, why would you now?"

"I think Kit felt something but couldn't recognize it."

"And he's more vulnerable than you—c'mon, we'd better check."

Remembering the night something else had looked out at me through his eyes, I leaped for the door.

Blanche grabbed her cloak on the way out. I followed her down the hallway.

"I figured that if I couldn't shake you awake," she said, "I'd hoist a set of keys and get out of here. Go get Colin—and the cavalry—and pull out whoever we could."

"Why didn't you try me first?"

"I did, but couldn't find you. Somebody told me you and Kit had gone off grounds. I couldn't be sure what state you were in or if you'd be back, so I started looking for anybody who'd take me seriously. Total failure, so I came here to wait. You proved my theory by waking up when I slapped you. We've got to smack the rest and hope it works."

"It should. Remember when Kit barged in on me and Buck?"

"That's what gave me the idea."

We cantered down the stairs to the entry hall, which stood ready to receive. Archways were framed by cornstalks, and wall fixtures streamed orange and black crepe paper. Jack-o'-lanterns marched down the stair curve in ascending size. A straw-stuffed scarecrow hung by a noose from the chandelier, which held electric candles. More of them, in floor-standing candelabras, illuminated the halls. Dried cornstalks and vines had been twisted into wreaths and mounted on doors and in niches. We passed them without pause, hastening to Mark's office, where the remote lock failed to work. Rolling our eyes at each other, we backtracked and opened the front door to trees rattling in the wind below an orange hunter's moon.

We passed through the porte cochère, scanning the shadows and sniffing for enemy. No scents met our nostrils except wood smoke and crushed leaves, and cleansing cold. All windows in sight were sealed and illuminated. No sight or sound of pedestrians, and no new vehicles parked in the loop.

No one in the carriage house, either. "It was like this when I stopped for you earlier. Where's Dru?"

"Last I knew, laughing me out the door."

She tried and failed to lock the gate from here, too. Then spat a string of words I hadn't heard her use in years. We slumped for a moment, thinking and dreading. Blanche's eyes turned to the clock. "We've still got time. Since the gate closed behind you, it should be okay for now. Dru's probably at Valhalla—they're planning a warm-up circle. I'm supposed to join them and bring you. If we start with him, it might be easier to disconnect the others."

I nodded and we headed out again. Valhalla would take me farther from Kit but closer to Buck, who might be easiest to break free.

Unless the circle was in progress, and he was in it.

"Blanche, busting in on them in a trance state might be dangerous."

"More dangerous letting them sit open while we twiddle our thumbs. C'mon, I can't think of anything better. Unless you want to start blasting people?"

"Hell no!"

I spotted a pair of mountain bikes parked against a tree. "Let's take those. Why don't I go get Kit and the Tiger and meet you at Valhalla."

"The Tiger?" Blanche stopped. I pushed her forward.

"Yeah, Kit fixed it. That's where we were. I'll—"

"No, Mad, we better not separate. If we can't wake up anyone else, or if some of them turn nasty—"

I sighed, swung my leg over the bicycle, and pushed off behind Blanche. We careened down the hill in the moonlit dark, contriving excuses in case we found everyone normal. I was glad for the breather when we pushed into Valhalla without knocking, to find a foursome resting their elbows on a card table, each holding a fan of spades-hearts-clubs-diamonds in hand.

The wind slammed the door behind us, scattering leaves and papers.

"Hey!"

Adam, Leslee, Mark, and Dru looked up as one, their faces blank canvases upon which firelight cast a dancing, scarlet glow. Top-Forty music babbled from the sound system.

"Hey!" Mark repeated, voice angry but eyes leaden. "Whaddaya doing?"

Blanche and I stared. "We're, uh, looking for Dru . . ."

They regarded us blankly while I scanned the table. Amid ashtray and tumblers, discard piles, notepads and pens, I saw a roach clip and rolling papers, plus a razor blade and mirror coated with white dust. Ingredients of the old-fashioned kind of party. Maybe that's why they all had glassy eyes.

Dru grinned. "We've been waiting for you. Pull up a chair, girls, have a seat!"

When neither of us moved, Adam patted his lap. "Come on, Madeline, I could use some coaching!"

Blanche stammered, "Er, what are you playing?"

Mark beamed. "Why, Canasta, of course!"

"What'd you think it was, tarot?" Leslee sneered.

"I, uh—"

Dru winked at Blanche. "I bet they thought it was poker. She likes to think I'm a rambling, gambling man!"

Blanche choked and clawed her hands. Oblivious, Adam said, "We need someone to help keep score."

Mark indicated the chair beside him. "You're welcome to spectate 'til everyone's here for the circle. Meanwhile . . ." He grinned and withdrew a vial of cocaine from his breast pocket. "A little something to warm you up?"

"Choose your poison." Leslee slapped a bulging baggy of pot onto the table. Adam flourished a labeled bottle. From behind him, upstairs, music blared as someone opened a door and closed it again, releasing smoke and laughter. I half expected a panty raid or a fire-extinguisher fight next. We needed only a beer keg to complete the frat party ambiance. No trace of Halloween, except a chill preventing the fire from warming the room. My belly and breasts began to tingle. Behind me, beyond the walls, the wind erratically thundered and slashed. The Canasta teams resumed their game as if never interrupted, babbling and hooting, flicking cards, while we stood and gawked.

I looked at Blanche, who nodded. Then I stepped forward, grabbed Dru by the collar, and flung him backward onto the floor.

His head hit with a crack that knocked him senseless.

"Hey!" Mark and Adam jumped up. Blanche blocked them by yanking Leslee from her chair and hurling her over the sofa-back onto the cushions. Adam spun, distracted, but Mark roared and dove for my waist. I jumped clear, backing into Adam, who pinned my arms and lifted me. I flung my weight downward and flipped him over my head. Blanche kicked then punched Mark, who fell on top of Adam. By then Leslee had crawled over the sofa-back with bared teeth and taloned hands, hissing, "What the hell are you doing! Who do you think you are!"

Blanche stepped forward and gave her a one-two slap across the face. Leslee tumbled backward with a screech that drew the upstairs people at a run. We dashed for the door, but Brian snared Blanche's arm and Alexis my jacket. I escaped Alexis by ducking out of the sleeves, then spun to wrestle Brian away from Blanche—jumping over Cassandra who had fallen over Adam. Two blurred forms leaped at me. I dispatched one with a kick to the knee, the other with an elbow slam to the side of the head, then freed Blanche from Brian by kicking him in the balls.

He fell away, howling, while Alexis and comrades ran outside to raise help from The Glen. Panting, Blanche and I stooped to check the bodies. Dru remained out cold with a lump on his noggin, Adam twitched with his wind knocked out, and Leslee crouched on the far side of the sofa, whimpering as she daubed her bleeding nose with her hem. Brian rolled and whined with hands clamped over his crotch, while Mark climbed upright aided by a chair.

We froze back to back in a wrestler's ready position. Mark swayed in place with drifting eyes. Then a glint appeared within them and he scanned the debris in comprehension. His lips drew back in a slow smile as he said, "So that's what it takes to break a spell, huh?"

"Mark . . . ?" Blanche's voice rose. We straightened, uncurling our fists. I stepped toward him. "Are you all right?"

He shook his head, as if to free it from cobwebs, and ran a hand through his hair. "Yeah, I guess so. Thanks."

Thanks! Blanche and I whirled to hug each other. Turning back to Mark, I noticed a weak but colorful aura glowing around him. "Blanche—" I pointed. "Do you see it?"

"Yes. That's what happened when I hit you. Look—we got her, too."

Leslee peered through her mauled hair, sucking a knuckle, from within a nimbus. Mark started when he saw her. "Wow!" He faced us. "It really works!"

"Come on," Blanche commanded. "Help with the others. We've got to pop as many as we can before the guests arrive!"

Mark staggered across the room to fetch his jacket. Leslee tipped her head at the forms gasping or mute on the floor.

"Shouldn't I stay with them?"

"Yes." Blanche frowned. "Make sure they're okay, then hit them again and patch them up for the party." Turning to Mark: "Let's go."

We went back out into the night, only to confront The Glen's war party. Alexis, in the lead, shouted, "There they are!"

Rob, Pete, Buck, and three others ran at us as a wall. Mark dumped Rob, Blanche kicked Pete, I parried Alexis and bashed the next guy in the stomach, Blanche rabbit-punched his shadow, Mark flipped the next one, leaving us a three-headed gorgon facing Buck. He didn't pause to think about it, simply spun and fled.

I shot after him. Blanche and Mark ran back to find vehicles. I ignored their departure, intent on flashing white soles leading me into the forest. The trees grew closer and thicker, tripping and scraping. Buck's greater strength, impelled by panic and guided by wood lore, allowed him to gain ground. I would have lost him if he hadn't glanced back and stumbled. A helpful root pitched him onto his face.

Adrenaline pushed me the remaining distance. Buck crouched on elbows and knees, head down and spitting dirt, until I fell onto his back. His breath whooshed out in a startled grunt as my weight flattened him. We panted for a minute while the wind wheezed over our heads.

By the time my heartbeat stabilized, Buck was glowing and cursing. I eased off him to permit rolling over, then repinioned him with chest and arms.

"Jeezus, LaRue—is it so bad you've got to tackle people to convince them?"

I nodded, still breathless. "Jeezus," he said again. I would have happily frozen to death with him on the forest floor rather than get up and run again. But shrill voices were crashing in our direction, accompanied by bobbing lights.

Buck heaved me up by the hand and dragged me along a stream bed. Our pursuers soon bogged down in the woods. I lapsed into silent staggering, grateful to follow another's lead for a while. This jousting with invisible menace had to go! I preferred being a zombie;

how pleasant life was when free of anxiety! And how fragile that state: It could be shattered by a blow. I had feared that a round of blasting would be required. It seemed now that normalcy might return before the party, since anyone could swing a fist.

As we cleared the trees and scurried along the driveway, an engine roar broke through the wind. Headlights pierced the leaves in a swinging arc; seconds later, the Tiger appeared around the last uphill turn, grinding gears and squalling tires, catching us in its beams.

Instead of slowing and swerving, the car aimed and accelerated. Buck cuffed me across the back to send me sprawling onto the crispy grass. The Tiger whipped by, spraying gravel. As I lifted my head, its taillights winked out of sight over the hill.

Buck jumped up, swearing, and ran across the drive to pull me upright. "You okay? Let's get him before he kills somebody." He didn't say, *That guy's lethal even when he ain't possessed!* but I heard the thought.

Buck headed for the mansion. I had to jog to keep him in sight.

Blanche and Mark had passed through, evidenced by strewn bodies in the entry hall. The conscious crawled to their feet and bellowed, their eyes still hazy; if any had snapped free, they had followed Mark and Blanche. Buck and Kit had disappeared, leaving me with bruised zombies. Why didn't everyone wake up when hit?

I backed into the south corridor, wondering if we should punch them somewhere specific. Didn't matter with the former bar fighter who emerged from the parlor, spinning his keys around one finger. By the time I got close enough, he would have me on the floor.

"Hey, Mad, where's your boyfriend?" Kit taunted.

Buck answered by springing into the hall behind him in a dive for Kit's legs. Both men slammed to the marble with a sickening bone crack. I screamed as Kit shriveled, then gasped as an aura flared around him when Buck backed away.

He signaled me to come forward and grab some limbs, but I had been stalled by a revelation. "Buck—I see the pattern!"

"Goody for you, Madeline. Give me a hand!"

"It's only the doubters," I puffed as we hauled Kit up the staircase. "The believers won't wake up if we hit them with bombs!"

"Then we'll just have to nuke 'em. Or you'll have to blast 'em. We can't have a party with everyone like this!"

Around us, the house revived. We expected a raving horde to stampede around a corner brandishing knives and torches. The victims astounded us afresh by merely cleaning up and resuming party preparations. I gave up trying to fathom, choosing to conserve my energy for what promised to be the longest of nights.

24
Masquerade

Buck slammed and locked my suite's outer door. We bundled Kit onto the waterbed then parted, for me to lift Kit's eyelid and peer at his pupil while Buck slouched against the wall muttering and rubbing his face.

Once I had finished checking Kit for damages, I looked at Buck with upturned palms and shook my head. He pushed himself across the floor to sit beside me on the padded bed rail.

"I didn't hurt him, did I?" He slid an arm around my back.

"I don't think so. But you thoroughly knocked him out. It'll be a while."

Buck nodded then kissed me. I responded hungrily, needing the strength of pumping hormones and hot blood. The long, twisting kiss refreshed us both as if we had been rugs shaken out a window. Buck broke it when the downstairs noise suddenly rose.

"Jeezus, we forgot to block the gate!" He jumped upright.

I raked back my hair. "Go get the Wagoneer and do it the hard way, though there's probably so many people here it doesn't matter. While you're at it, see who's salvageable. If we knock enough of them back to their senses, we might squeak through."

"Unless that thing gets pissed off and changes tactics."

"It shouldn't—anything too violent will blow our credibility. The thing wants to possess Dru or break him, so to rule New Atlantis, which'll work as long as the world believes Dru is Dru, leading or collapsing under his own power. We can't influence enough people if all our press is hysterical."

Buck shook his head. "You can't know its reasoning. We still ought to get you, Blanche, and Dru outa here, just in case."

"Same problem. When the hosts don't show up for their own party, people ask questions. Just as bad as if we stop them at the door and send them home. While creating a scandal might stop this thing tonight, it won't be permanent. And with nothing to lose, it might get mean. I think we should try to keep the mess contained 'til we figure a way out."

"Then I'll find Dru and tie him to a chair and slap him 'til he comes around."

"Um, he might need a little more muscle. Maybe I should go."

"I'll come get you if it comes to that."

"Get somebody onto the phone system while you're at it!"

He nodded and moved away. I checked him with a hand on his thigh. "Be careful, Buck. Just because they're passive doesn't mean they're safe."

He lifted his hands and snorted, looking at the ceiling. Then he bent, kissed me hard, started for the door, then hesitated. "See you at the party, I guess. Will I recognize you?"

I smiled. "You won't be able to miss me!"

He raised his eyebrows, then left.

I remained seated, hands limp between my thighs. Kit's aura had faded but still flared at each breath before ebbing to a multicolored haze. Was I glowing, too? If so, it must be green, from envy. A check in the mirror showed only my tattered façade. Some Atlantean princess! I looked like a corpse risen from the dead by way of a sewer!

I felt half dead, too, with chest pains and throbbing joints and bruises. My hands trembled, one knee bled. Time to visit the bathroom and start repairs.

Between each task, I stepped out to check Kit. How cruel: the toughest kid in town flattened again by a spirit! An hour ago he had been a masterpiece of virility. Looking at him so helpless churned my stomach and loosened my knees.

"Come on, boy, wake up! Don't die from a brain hemorrhage now!"

I lifted his lids and shone a penlight into his pupils. They contracted normally. He twitched when I pinched him. His pulse blipped slowly but strong.

I filled a plastic bag with ice cubes to place on the lump that had blossomed on his skull. A scrape around it was clotted with hair and blood, so I daubed that clean before returning to the bath. When scrubbed pink and clad in a robe, I pulled my vanity bench to bedside, laid pillows around my feet, sat straight, placed my hands in my lap, and closed my eyes.

Relaxation came easily, aided by exhaustion. I was busy coaxing energy up from belly out to fingertips when Blanche barged in the door.

"Holy mother of god!" She slung a garment bag onto the bed in one smooth arc. "What an outrageous night! Look at this!"

She hiked up her leggings to expose gashed shins, socks bunched around her ankles, a swollen knee, a missing shoe. I left my bench to inspect the hurts, straightening to ask her, "What about Dru?"

"I have no idea. But his costume was gone when I went to get mine, so I'm sure he'll be at the party. I wish my hands weren't broken, I'd love to belt him! But no time for that—the guests are rolling in."

"Did you meet any?"

"No, I snuck up the back stairs."

I nodded and turned back to Kit. Blanche followed the motion. "He's not sleeping, is he."

I shook my head then explained as she knelt at bedside.

"Have you tried smelling salts? Or ammonia?"

I again shook my head. "Don't have any."

Blanche rose with a slight gasp—of pain or inspiration, I couldn't tell. "Madeline, have you tried . . ." Her eyebrows bobbed. ". . . your bionic woman trick?"

"I was about to when you burst in."

"Oh, well—don't let me interrupt you!" She skittered backward with a sweep of her arms. I returned to my bench then shot a warning glance over my shoulder. Blanche swished into the bathroom, thumping the door shut behind.

I turned to Kit and stroked back his hair. After skimming his lips with mine, I settled into balanced posture. Closed my eyes, drew the charge back to the surface, held my hands above his body, then visualized Kit alive and well . . .

. . . Kit pulling his dirt bike into a wheelie . . .

. . . his truculent pout fading into a wary scowl then melting into a smile as we talked . . .

. . . his jaw rigid and eyes unblinking under lowered brows, arms jutting out and turning as he steered the Tiger through a mountain maze . . .

. . . the arc of his cheekbone over which I traced my finger as he leaned above me, eyes hooded by hair and shadow . . .

. . . my pounding heart as he pressed against me, then an expanding color sphere and heat rush as I dragged my hands along his skin—

My vision went white then black, and all muscles locked in spasm. A moment later, conscious but minus motor control, I crumpled to the floor.

Blanche must have been peeking, for she arrived right away with a glass of water. Her flutterings ceased when I blinked away stars and contrails to focus on her face.

"Madeline!" she whispered.

I sat up despite her resistance. "Kit?"

He sat on the edge of the bed, elbows on knees with chin in his hand, regarding me from inside a cool blue glow. "Guess that thing got me again, huh?"

He smiled. Relief caused my vision to recede into a pinpoint of light through a gray screen. I clawed back to clarity as Blanche said, "It got everybody except me."

Kit started to question her but got interrupted by me climbing onto him from the floor. "Are you sure you're all right?" I asked between kisses.

"No, my head is killing me. What'd you do, clobber me with a board?"

"No, we tackled you in the hallway."

Kit scowled and rubbed his sore spot. "I've had enough of this shit. Where's my bow and arrow? I'm ready to kill this guy!"

"I'll help you," Blanche and I chorused.

Kit laughed then sobered. "I'd rather you both get out of here." He dug in his pocket and pulled out the Tiger key.

"You know we can't," I declared.

"Then somebody's gonna die tonight and it ain't gonna be us." He stood and repocketed the key.

"How will you identify him with everyone running around in disguise?" Blanche queried.

"That's your job. You're the bait. And you—" He turned to me. "—will point the finger. Then duck, 'cause I'm gonna take him out."

"Kit—"

"Madeline, either get dressed and see this through or get off the compound."

Anger surged—and with it, power. I could have kicked him with it. The hot tingle soothed me. Between the two of us, we would end this farce before the night was over.

"All right." I turned to the closet to fetch my Aurora Borealis costume. Blanche, unbagging her Lady Azilde outfit, briefed Kit on everything that had transpired since he and I had returned from the forest.

He responded, "My costume's in the car. I'll scope what's going on while I get it. You get down to the party and find Raoul. I'm gonna block the gate with the biggest thing we got to keep any more from coming in."

"Any hope Raoul will be fashionably late?" Blanche asked the room. Nobody bothered to answer, certain he was either already here or so powerful that he didn't need to be.

Kit, steel-faced, popped me a kiss then departed on his mission. I fought the urge to whimper, wanting a grander expression in case I never saw him again. The clothes he would return in weren't the green archer getup but a pirate costume. The antique sword and scabbard he had borrowed for the occasion were the only weapons on the compound.

. . . except for the petite Saturday Night Special Blanche tucked into the thigh pocket of her skirt, and the stiletto I tucked into mine. Colin had not allowed his sisters to model in the City without protection.

Those careers had also trained us to bathe, dress, paint, adorn, and finally mask ourselves inside twenty minutes. Downstairs, the muted roar of voices grew; outside, more car doors slammed. Blanche and I steadied each other through our twin link, unwilling to believe anything bad would really happen but fearing it down to our gilded toenails.

After a last mirror check and careful hug, we took deep breaths and entered the corridor. Conversation, suddenly loud, carried up from the entry hall. It dwindled when we appeared at the head of the staircase, and faces tilted upward. Blanche began her descent, tracing her fingers along the handrail. Her train oozed along the steps behind. A murmur broke out as she reached the middle landing, which I took as cue to make my own entrance.

Quaking knees and three-inch heels undermined my elegance. I clutched the handrail to keep from stumbling. The crew below blurred together in an aura that seemed smeared, like gods' finger-painting. Nothing more complex than gender showed beneath animal heads, drapery, paint, and masks.

Someone in a clown suit hovered near the front doorway. The rest filled the hall in clusters, their torsos facing each other but necks twisted around to watch us. When I reached the floor, a man clothed in green except for the feather in his cap moved forward to greet me. I recognized the archer of my vision, and fought back faintness while placing my fingers across his palm.

"Aurora, my darling!" Colin's rich voice said. "You look exquisite—a true princess. I'm so pleased to see you again!"

After choking and clearing my throat, I responded, "Ah, Sir Robin Hood! The pleasure is mine." I gestured beyond him to a leering Dracula. "Is this one of your Merry Men?"

Colin looked over his shoulder. "I have no idea."

Before I could determine whether Colin's eyes were glazed, the vampire swooped forward to envelop me in his cape and stifle my gasp with a kiss. When we came up for air, onlookers cheered and applauded. Dracula stepped away to give Blanche the swooping kiss treatment, then moved on to another astonished lass. Kit popped up behind to slip his hand under my skirt and tweak me before getting sucked away by the mass bumbling toward the ballroom, cleaving around me and Colin like a river bypassing rock. I slapped Kit's retreating hand then turned back to my brother.

His eyes were clear, so I took my relief out on him.

"Not funny, wearing that costume! What happened to Sherlock Holmes?"

We stepped over smashed pumpkins and torn streamers. Colin observed them with casual disdain. "I thought it was time to force the issue. And this happens to be loaded, if anything goes wrong." He patted a quiver slung over his shoulder then glanced around. "But where's my target?"

I shoved past a laughing dawdler. "I'm hoping Kit blocked the gate before your target gets here."

"I was last one in, unless someone brings a tank."

Colin clutched my skirt to keep us attached through the swarming beasts, aliens, monsters, historical figures, animate objects—at least twice as many as had been invited, along with uncostumed fans who had capitalized on their lucky break. Their numbers would overtax our food, drink, and seating. Worse, Raoul could be anything, anywhere, among the flashing cameras and laughter. At least no one could organize a power circle! That thought, however, did not bring me cheer.

In the ballroom, Colin and I stood in the bar line, scanning for Dru, Blanche, Kit, Buck, Cassandra. After a few minutes he bent his head close to yell over the thumping rock music, "This reminds me of the pub scene in *Star Wars*."

As I nodded, he added, "I was expecting something a bit more sedate!"

"So were we all. Oh Colin—"

"Mad, what's going on? Has the issue already forced itself?"

"Yes, but I can't explain here."

The scarecrow and legged cigarette pack before us collected their drinks and moved away. We stepped up to order, served by a bartender who looked through his ski mask with glazed eyes. His height and shape suggested Jim dressed as a cat burglar. I watched his hands while he mixed my drink. Hoping he hadn't spiked any bottles, I let my glass slop as we jostled across the room to a clear space near the hors d'oeuvres table. To observers, we were Robin Hood and an overdressed Maid Marian leaning against a tapestry while surveying the ball.

We couldn't differentiate between minglers and dancers. Everyone moved in every direction; we were an oddity, standing still. I spotted Kit in line at the beer keg, swiveling and laughing. Blanche wove through the crowd, charming and seducing with little effect beyond a clown who guarded her tail. He should have been Jake, but the clown was too tall. I later pegged the twins watching from opposite corners, one wearing camouflage combat gear, and the other berobed as an Arab sheik.

I didn't need a closer look to know that their eyes were unfocused. Indeed, a score of the gypsies, mummies, superheroes, et cetera, shuffled without direction, stuck within the spell. Half the rest bounced on their toes and looked through their masks with sparkling gazes. The remainder staggered, eyes blurred from intoxicants. The differences were so marked that even Colin could sort them out.

"Madeline, what's with those guys?" He pointed to a foursome who faced each other swaying with open mouths.

"Same as with them." I nodded sideways at two ladies in tavern-wench dress doing the zombie dance for Kit. He gawked at their bulging, upward-trussed breasts and laughed uncertainly at their giggles. He must have felt my gaze across the room, for he unsheathed his sword at the wenches and scattered them, then resheathed it and snaked across the floor to us.

"Mad—" Kit began, although I could not hear the word above the racket. He stepped closer and hollered, "Do you see them? Can you feel—"

I cut him off with a chopping hand motion. "Yeah, they're all over the place. But look there." I gestured with my chin at the doorway, where a gypsy and the scarecrow conferred so cozily that their auras merged. "Jeff and Leslee," I guessed, adding, "Can you see their glow?"

"Yes, I can." Kit whipped his head around. "There's another." He pointed at a Cat Woman built like Julia. "And Blanche, too." He pivoted back to face me. "And you! Are these the people you—"

"What are you talking about!" snarled Colin.

I sighed, cursed, and ignored him. "Kit, I don't care if Raoul's here—let's finish this up. Start luring people outside as discreetly as possible then slug them as hard as you can without breaking bones."

"What!" Colin squawked.

"Only the ones who aren't glowing, and only people who live here if you can tell. No injuries, just a resounding stun. Tie them up if you have to and keep going 'til they wake up."

Kit grinned, all teeth. "Anyone in particular?"

"Avoid the band, I'll take care of them. Once you've got a few snapped out, send them back in to mingle and focus all their energy on the people of their choice. Try to recover the rest that way, no more hitting unless you catch Raoul. Then do what you want. But go far enough away that you won't be witnessed!"

"I hear and will obey, Mistress!" He bowed away backward.

I turned to Colin. "Did you hear everything I just said?"

"Yes, but—"

"Then go find Blanche. Cut her away from that clown—and find out who he is, while you're at it—then tell her what I've done. She'll pick up from there. And tell her I'm starting with the band."

"Madeline, wait! This is nuts! Don't you—"

"Colin, it's out of control! Get moving!"

He scuttled away.

I stood for a moment, hyperventilating. My blood felt like magma, my body a full bladder trying not to burst. I had no clear vision of what to accomplish; instinct had taken over. It might be too late to stop the falling dominos, but there was still time to prevent whatever would be triggered when the last one flopped. Yet I hesitated; nobody was hurting anyone, should I have another drink to calm me?

While I vacillated, music blasted through eight speakers. I stood on tiptoe to survey the shifting heads. A purple cone hat with white stars, marking Dru, had moved across the ballroom. Nearby I noticed a second cone: shorter, blunter, bright yellow with an orange pompom in a nest of red, insanely curly hair. Dru and that clown—but no Blanche. Dropping my head and pointing my elbows, I bulldozed across the floor.

25
True Colors

Hands groped as I passed; laughter, like cawing crows, pierced the solid atmosphere of music, sweat, and perfume. My stomach knotted, almost upchucking its contents when I broke free of dancers to an open view. Dru, as Merlin, stood with half the Round Table in attendance: Troy as Sir Lancelot; Allanna as Morgan le Fay; Pete as Mordred, with his hand up under his companion's skirt. I recognized her as Alexis, normally Brian's possessive wife but tonight a belly dancer rubbing her breasts and buttocks against Pete's hands.

Adam performed likewise with Lady Godiva. He wore black studded leathers and a greased pompadour, and leered beneath mirror sunglasses; she wore a blonde knee-length wig and a mask. No wonder Leslee huddled with Jeff in the doorway! I wanted to join them after witnessing Dru. He stood at the head of the group, laughing and boasting, while Irene as Morticia Addams wormed her hand under his white-starred purple robe. This inspired an onlooking couple to start necking, looked upon in turn by the grinning clown. I drew deep breaths to keep from exploding. When a hand clamped down on my hip from behind, I almost did.

Somehow I kept it to a yelp and a spinning leap.

"Easy, Mad—whoa!"

It was Buck, disguised as Wild Bill Hickok in a handlebar mustache, wearing a fringed jacket and ten-gallon hat. I collapsed against him between a pair of pistols.

He held me, saying, "I was going to ask you to dance, but guess not!"

"Maybe in the next life," I mumbled into his chest, stealing a moment to hide in his arms and swoop far from New Atlantis. Then I pushed us apart.

Before turning away, I met his eyes and saw the unmasked soul behind them. My heart swelled and I touched his face before I could check the urge. "Just catch me if I fall, okay?"

His cheek twitched in a smile attempt that he abandoned for a nod. I wrenched my gaze back to the chaos. His support propelled me through the body maze until I stood chest to chest with Dru. By then I believed I could double-slap our leader across the face with no hands.

As I relaxed my muscles to gather power, Casanova cleared a swath across the buffet table and spread Godiva upon it. Falling crockery, groaning planks, and the resulting hoots and hollers destroyed my focus. Dru—no, not Dru any more—watched it all through Merlin's empty irises. I tried again to calm my heartbeat and control my breathing . . . reach for that mental trigger . . . then Troy grabbed my arm and tugged me off balance.

"Hey, wow—this is a night for royalty! Princess Aurora, how kind of you to grace Camelot with your presence!"

He smooched me right in front of his wife. Allanna didn't notice, having turned away to intercept Buck's swing. Troy lifted his head to watch her twine around and kiss the cowboy. I raised my arm to take advantage of a clear shot—to hell with blasting! Troy saw the motion and snatched my wrist, twisting it, braying in delight as I squirmed to escape his now two-armed hold, in which position he tried for another kiss.

"Now, now, children!" Dru pulled away from Irene to separate us. Hope surged then died as Dru, pinning both my wrists behind my back with one hand, shook a finger before Troy's face. "All offerings must be sampled and approved by the wizard first, remember?"

Troy looked at his feet. "So sorry, stupid of me to forget!"

He then smiled and plucked up Irene, who clamped herself to his hip and rib cage. I tried to slip Dru when he released my wrists, but he caught me back by the shoulders.

"No you don't, little princess! The wizard must inspect and approve you, first!"

His blank gaze darkened and slithered down my neckline. Buck escaped Allanna and pushed forward. Dru flicked him backward as casually as I would finger-flick an insect, except that he used no fingers. Or arms or hands or feet. Barely a sidelong glance, and whap! Buck went staggering. Which told me that the stalemate had been broken and power was gonna fly.

My own power, mixed with terror, spiraled up my backbone. Dru slid his hands down my neckline to my cleavage, flipped his wrists, and ripped my dress open as if it were paper. I shrieked—backpedaled—flung my arms—and immolated.

Uprushing heat and light expulsed to take down everyone before me in a scramble of arms, legs, and jewelry. As before, body and mind coalesced after that instant of disintegration; this time I found myself hanging by the armpits from Buck's hands. The ballroom was stunned to muteness beneath the bellowing speakers. Talk and motion resumed abruptly when some woman began to wail.

"What the hell!" sputtered Troy, pivoting between me sagging in Buck's arms and Pete being hoisted by Irene and Allanna. Adam grinned with sunglasses dangling from one ear, his eyes flaring then misting over. I tried in vain to collect my wits and give him a final zap.

Pete shook off the women to stand before me with clear eyes and splayed fingers. "Aurora—I'm sorry. My god—" He looked around, comprehending. "Please forgive us! And let me help."

His glow swelled like a sunrise. Buck propped me up with one hand and reached with the other to pull Pete from the clique. Blanche broke through the spectators, trailed by Colin. When she and I locked gazes, I tipped my head toward Adam; she riveted her gaze to him, frowned, and discharged a strobelike flash. Adam's hands flew to his face as he staggered backward. But he remained vertical with wobbling head, while Blanche took a second shot at Troy and restored him to himself.

I didn't know or care how my twin had harnessed the power. It seemed we all had, for zapping caught on like a teenage fad. The ballroom became a giant firefly jar as some New Atlanteans shot and others toppled; the gatecrashers screamed and bolted, while the rest shuffled or sprinted in circles, bleating questions that drew no response.

Blanche locked Allanna in a brilliant beam that twitched her like an animal hurled against a high-voltage fence until she collapsed then recovered. Buck and Kit, Pete, Adam, and others giddily punched or blasted, while Colin and a Tin Man aided those who fell. Their ricocheting energies boosted fields already present, making auras psychedelic, exposing black holes.

I recovered control of my head and appendages. My direct path of exit was barred by Dru. He swayed in place with eyeballs wandering in and out of phase, almost spinning, as cosmic forces played tug-of-war with his mind. A black radiance arched above us, terminating at Dru's hairline. I traced it backward to a yellow cone with orange pompom over gumball nose, and met with gun-barrel eyes.

At once my mind blanked and skin constricted. Just as fast, heat geysered from my abdomen and gushed toward Dru. It bowled over nearby people, while the clown observed with folded arms and tapping shoe. When my surge died and I could meet his eyes again, he gave a slow, hideous smile—then blinked.

The floor thrust upward into jagged pieces as an earthquake shuddered through the foundation, tossing bodies, platters, and furniture, snapping pillars and wires. Screams mixed with wails and gurgles as the music cut and speakers tumbled; windows and lights exploded. Then, with the same abruptness, the room went dark and still.

I remained splayed but standing on a tilted slab of parquetry. Reflexively, I straightened my tiara; all I could think was, Thank god he didn't aim!

The hunks of stone, the shattered glass and hissing wires—a mere display. My god! That power! And I had nothing left to return. My body felt detached and hollow. Mouth dry; knees rattling; synapses fried. I had perhaps two seconds before Raoul finished admiring his handiwork and turned to destroy me. Nothing to lose, then, by playing the game by his rules.

Kissing my life and soul goodbye, I flung open my neural network and commanded all powers to rush in.

White oblivion followed, broken only by pain and ending in blackness. I floated down to nowhere and stayed there for an age.

More like thirty seconds. I woke up on a bucking floor facing a battle of titans. Dru and Raoul had each other locked in a sizzling field so bright it silhouetted them, in which they strained as if moving in triple-g. At first I whined at my failure—Raoul continued at full power, untouched by my last, best try. Then it registered that Dru was giving back as good as he got. I had managed after all to free and recharge him! Relief flowed through my useless limbs.

Raoul ripped clear of the flashing stasis before both men vaporized, which sent Dru backpedaling with flailing arms. My mouth fell open and throat convulsed but no sound escaped. No muscles answered, either. I couldn't even track Raoul as he ran outside my field of vision. Dru regained his feet and pursued, leaving a glowing contrail. In the frame they vacated, shouting people zapped and scrambled while light beams from torches and vidicams jumped like hyper frogs. Overhead, metal shrieked as the chandelier lurched on its damaged chains and sprinkled shards onto the rubble.

The stinging rain informed me that I was lying smack beneath it. I tried to lift my head, jack onto my elbows and scramble, but still couldn't move. Oh no, was I going to die by chandelier, skewered into the ground by a thousand glass needles? Help! Where were my people? How about those body-guarding twins? Everyone else ran over or around me. About the time I realized I might be invisible among a debris pile, camouflage arms bored under my back and knees, wrestled me clear, then deposited me behind a pillar. Seconds later, a rush of air ended in explosion.

Shrieks! Crystal darts puncturing skin! Stampeding bodies! When the reverberation faded, dust sparkled in flashes while die-hards shot energy beams at anyone not doing same. My vision blurred then cleared then doubled. During the clear moment, I saw Buck climbing toward me over bent metal and chunks of stone. He scooped me up like a forklift at the same moment I heard Kit bellow after him, "Get her outa here!"

I must have passed out again, for I next came aware of lying on a springy, silken mattress. It stretched out for acres, into a yellowish glow like distant firelight that held back gloom. Inside a cave? No, not dank enough. And the firelight didn't flicker, must be a lamp. As my senses roused, I felt a twinge of familiarity. The flannel sheet across my chest looked and smelled like . . . mine.

Adrenaline shocked me fully conscious. My sheet, my bed, my room, behind the crystal doorknob, accessible only by gold key. I touched the flat between my breasts and found it empty. No necklace or bodice, and my shoes missing, also, leaving me half nude on a fur bed.

A silhouette, sitting in the classic *Thinker* position, looked up at my rustle.

"Mad?" he whispered.

"Buck? Thank god! What am I doing here?"

"You don't remember?" He moved from chair to mattress.

"No. Last I remember is the ballroom collapsing. Raoul—oh! What happened! How much time has passed? Where are—"

I sat up, relief gone as fast as it had come. Buck embraced me. "Ssssh, sssh, take it easy. You're safe here."

"Safe! If he can take out the ballroom, he can level the mansion. Where is he? Did Dru get him? What about Blanche, Kit, Colin—"

Buck placed a finger across my lips. "Blanche finally burned out after zapping a hundred people with light spears. She pretty much knocked the whole party clear of the spell. Raoul got away, last seen running into the forest with a lynch mob after him, including your brother. Dru carried Blanche back to the carriage house while everyone else broke into search parties and stomped around the grounds. I guess they're still out there. I've been here for the last hour or so, hoping you'd wake up."

"Have they searched this house?"

"Don't think so. Raoul ran outside, and Mark locked all the doors and windows before the party."

I snorted. "That won't stop him!" But I felt a smidgen better. In fact, I could feel again, as well as move all parts.

"What about Kit? Is he all right?"

Buck rolled onto an elbow. "Better than that—he's the hero. Someone falls over rubble, Kit picks 'em up. Someone gashed by flying glass, Kit cleans 'em up. He stopped Irene from gibbering and made her set up a nursing station in the dining hall. Then pulled a spotlight out of somewhere, plugged it into the Jeep's cigarette lighter, and took off into the woods. Last I heard, he was back helping Jim and Greg get the generator going. Guess it worked, since we got light."

He grinned, at which point I finally noticed he'd shed his costume mustache.

"What a bitch getting you up those stairs in total darkness! Later I got a flashlight and set up some candles. The power came on, I dunno, twenty minutes ago. But the phones are still out, and sooner or later the cops are going to show up. A lot of freaked-out people ran off before we could stop them."

I snuggled the bedspread closer and looked around the room. I had been in it once during daytime, to acquaint myself with the amenities and stock the closet. Now the blue paint and black cabinets seemed shrouded and strange. The hooded lamplight glinted off frames and fittings. I recognized one of my paintings over Buck's shoulder. I had left it here to stamp the room Mine.

He tipped me back while stretching out beside me. "You've been here a few hours. Since the chandelier fell."

"How did you learn about these rooms? You're not a member."

He scoffed. "You really think something this juicy could stay a secret?"

"Who told you?"

"You mean, who showed me?"

I turned my head away. "I don't care."

"Let's say that when I saw a gold key hanging out the front of your dress with your tits and medallion, I knew a safe place to go."

"Thank you, I guess."

"You're welcome. So are you okay or not?"

I turned my head back to face him. "Okay. Just sore. Empty. Scared. We can't stay here while Raoul's still loose. Are those loaded?" I gestured my chin at Buck's gunbelt hanging from the chair he'd been using.

"Real but not loaded. Though you'd be shocked by how many peaceful New Atlanteans popped up with guns!"

"Not really. Colin showed up with deer arrows, and I've—" I groped my thigh pocket. "Never mind, it's gone."

"Your boyfriend's out there with a sawed-off shotgun!"

I sat up. "We should be out there with him! We can't stop until Raoul is captured or killed."

"Jeez, what ever happened to 'make love, not war'?"

"Love didn't work. It never has."

Buck tipped me back to horizontal. "Maybe it can't stop violence, but it can shore people up to face it."

I slid my eyes sideways at him, coming aware of our position. He added, "And just think: If somebody had loved Raoul, all this shit would never have happened. Or he'd be walking beside Dru, trying to turn the world into utopia."

"We can't know that."

"Nope. But it's possible, and shows you the power love does have."

He traced a finger down my bruised cheekbone. I shivered, all nerves as alive as they had been dead before.

"If we ever get out of this," he continued, "I was kinda hoping we could . . ."

"Let's get through tonight, first."

Though I spoke solemnly, I wanted to hoot—after all the battling between Good and Evil, Murphy's Law was going to triumph. What worse time could Buck and I choose to make peace?

He lay slack and extended, his head propped up by the heel of his hand as the other idly stroked my hip. He still wore fringed denims but had shed the accessories. His hair, grown out from a summer cut, had been scrambled by the mayhem. His gaze shifted from dazed to focused as shock, fatigue, and thrill cycled inside him. At each change he smiled, frowned, or drooped while we held our private debates, until, wordlessly, we agreed.

At that, his palm slid up the curve of my body. Then he peeled down the flannel, rolled half atop me, kissed my forehead, nose, and eyelids, and placed his mouth across my waiting lips. I signaled willingness with a throat moan. He responded with a deeper kiss and searching hands. We twined together, our breathing accompanied by a hint of music from adjacent rooms. We ignored it to set our own tempo . . . sometimes frantic, sometimes slow . . . easing him out of his filthy clothes. His skin was hot and smooth up and down the length of me. I welcomed its taste, scent, and texture as I would my long-lost home.

Our bodies parted only once in the ensuing hours, for Buck to mount a disc in a conveniently sited player. He chose a sampler of Dru's love songs while I squirmed childlike on the slithery bed. He crawled back to me with a grin on the verge of giggles and thumped down onto my chest. I gasped then squeaked as he rolled us across the mattress. We didn't stop laughing until we stopped at the edge.

Once nose to nose again, our smiles faded. After a few tentative kisses, Buck settled to the serious business of loving me until I cried. At first we fought for dominance, refusing to drop the barriers we had sustained for so long. But we both needed reassurance at the most primal level, and I surrendered to his strength at the same moment he gave in to his lonely soul.

At that point sight and hearing fell away and we entered the plane where lights flow like water, submerging us until we became spiraling and weightless, void of form. Our battle became a dance, our thoughts and feelings fused together. We created the perfect power circle: yin and yang balanced in a perpetual loop.

Dream veils parted to reveal us standing halfway up the stairs of a familiar temple. Buck kissed me there, clothed, with the same passion we kissed naked now. I recognized both moments as preludes to final partings. If the cycle repeated, I would not have him in my arms again for a thousand years.

"No!" I cried, though in this life it came out "Yes!" as our union reached its peak. For me it passed quickly, dragged down by consciousness. I used the secret parts of my body to sustain his climax until he sobbed.

The music grew louder as our panting subsided. Buck's breath steamed against my chest, where he had collapsed and I held him captive in my arms. We lay silent through the remaining songs, our hands following the rhythms. I memorized Buck's details while kissing his neck, face, and shoulders, vowing to recall every nuance in the desolate nights to come.

We jerked when the player snapped off into silence. Yet we stayed entwined, knowing all would change when we rolled apart. We fought to stay awake, finding sleep a new enemy. Our depleted bodies, however, finally sabotaged us. For the first and last time I fell asleep in his arms.

26
Fireworks

Just before dawn the gong went off, resounding through the forest. I sat up, wide-eyed; Buck roused on the third deep boom. The lamp still glowed, cutting a yellow cone through a gray curtain. I realized from the odor that it was smoke, not misty dawn.

"Oh my god!"

"What?" Buck jerked upright. I coughed, extending my arm to block him. "No! Stay down!"

He batted my hand away. "Are you nuts? That's the fire alarm! The house must be burning!"

"This house is made of stone."

"And loaded with flammables. That bastard is burning us out!"

Buck stood and groped for his jeans. I groped likewise for words that would arrest him.

"Buck, wait. The house is all right. We're not the ones he's after."

The fire gong ebbed into a quiet that filled with shouts and door slams. Buck looked toward the hallway then down at me on the bed. "I'm not gonna find out the hard way that you're wrong, Madeline. So c'mon, get some clothes on!"

He stomped into his pants legs. "Hurry up—you wanna get roasted?"

His eyes bulged, and he yanked his arm away when I gripped it. "Please don't go!" was all I could say.

He threw a robe at me then bent to find his cowboy boots. Either smoke or desperation brought tears to my eyes.

"Buck—I beg you—don't go out there!"

He got the message and froze with his hand on the knob. After hesitating, he swung to lock gazes, his face made brutal by shadow and fear. "What do you mean—what did you see!"

I crossed the floor and clutched him. "Just—don't go."

His eyes bored into mine, seeking the hidden pictures. A rap sounded on the door before I could reveal.

"Hey! Hey!" the knocker insisted. "Anybody in there?"

Buck wrenched open the door to find a half-dressed Seth shivering in the hallway. Behind him, with bugged eyes, stood a dressed and shivering Greg. Both were blinded to our faces and my nakedness by their urgency. "C'mon—the carriage house is on fire! All hands on deck!"

They moved on to the next room and raised Kit and Julia. How did they get a key? I futilely thought. Colin and Cassandra, still in costume, headed for the staircase, followed by Cornelius and Maxine. Buck shoved me back inside and slammed the door. "Listen, I want to know why I can't go down there and help with the fire!"

"A falling, flaming beam has your name on it."

He flinched as if I had slapped him, and his hands, gripping my shoulders, tightened as his jaw muscles worked.

"Are you sure?"

I tried not to bleat. "Yes. It's part of the vision—I dreamed it last night, I can't help it, but I haven't been wrong yet!"

Buck dropped his arms and walked to the window. "Do these things always come true?"

"No. They're warnings. They give you a chance to choose."

"So if I don't go out there I won't get hurt?"

"I can't promise that. But if you go near that fire, you're playing poker with your life as stake!"

"Jeezus!" Buck turned to face me. "We should at least go down and help the others—there's plenty I can do without—"

He strode to the door. "Get dressed. I'll meet you downstairs."

"Buck—"

The door closed behind him. I scooted across the floor and pulled it open. "Buck, wait, please!"

My cries hung in the empty corridor. The door at the head of the staircase slipped shut.

"Damn!" I rotated in half steps, jerking my hands, hating every second I hesitated. Finally I pulled on the robe then descended the paneled staircase to the second floor.

The gallery was unoccupied yet lit from end to end. I dashed along the carpet and down the south wing to my suite. Every bedroom door stood open, and the windows on the courtyard side glowed scarlet and yellow with not dawn but flames.

As fast as I could move I donned outdoor clothes and headed for the front stairway. Each stride brought me closer to brightness and noise. Black smoke roiled in the entry hall, choking people. They sprawled or staggered in the porte cochère, attended by others ducking beneath the smoke with hands or cloths pressed over their mouths.

I dodged between them to the driveway circle, for a view of flames stretching out the carriage house's windows. Our fire truck and two volunteer units hosed vainly, gawked at by a crowd. Some cold heart recorded everything on vidicam, while a few brave New Atlanteans shot fire extinguishers at burning cars and vegetation. Sirens wailed closer from the road. I spotted Kit among the firemen, but no Buck, Blanche, Dru, or Colin. Skirting the fire and scanning sooty faces, I worked my way around the house.

Blanche, plus Dru and Adam, huddled on the side lawn beside rescued treasures. We sighted each other at the same moment and broke into a run.

"Blanche!"

"Madeline!"

We collided at the flagstone walkway. Her hug buried me in red-fox fur. The coat told me more about her escape than I could have learned from several sentences. Dru and Adam came forward and sheltered us with heavy arms. Dru confirmed my thoughts while we watched the fire. Yes, he had seen a threat coming. No, he had not known in what form. So he had sat vigil until Blanche recovered, taking breaks to pack their valuables in case they had to run.

However, exhaustion triumphed over anxiety. In the darkest hour, they had nodded off. Raoul, somehow knowing, had torched the carriage house and everything in the vicinity. Cars too far away to be ignited by the house, and too far apart to spark each other, burned ferociously. Isolated trees were flaming skeletons. The house had gone up on all sides.

Blanche and Dru had wakened at once and made two trips before the exits were blocked. Everything they couldn't carry they had flung out into the yard. Raoul was long gone; the carriage house beyond salvaging. The watchers turned away when a Jeep roared up the drive.

Gene leaped out. "Hill House has gone up! Hurry—get those trucks up there!"

Confusion erupted as people rearranged into teams, filling all vehicles, which raced out the drive. A dozen people—including Buck—ran for the escarpment trail. Blanche and Dru tried to pull me after them into the Wagoneer, but I broke away to grab the remaining ATV. My Tiger, in the circle, resembled a fallen meteorite still smoking. I recognized it only from remembering where Kit parked.

Troy beat me to the ATV, which made footwork my only option. So I ran: around the house, across the back lawn, down the tiers to the cliff path. Balked at the edge, seeing no passage between black and gray. I couldn't worry about broken bones so launched down the scree, pinballing between tree trunks and boulders, until I overbalanced. Arms flailing, I tumbled down frozen dirt, broken rocks, and jagged grasses; too surprised to yell, then too stunned to even whimper after I skidded to a stop. Yet I had to gather my wits and my muscles, and get up and get to Hill House—find Buck—no, get to the stables—no—

The stables! My god, the stables were next! The vision leaped up before me, clear as a movie: burning buildings, strewn bodies, screaming horses galloping across a yard. Raoul was torching the outbuildings to exhaust us with running. When we were lame and huddled in the surviving mansion, he would bring it down on our heads.

Until then we would chase him to the stables, The Glen and Valhalla, and the studio—

Ignoring blood and bruises, I got up and ran.

Grass lashed my knees as I cut across the pasture. Atop the hill on my right, Hill House glowed violent orange; dead ahead, the first forked fire-tongues ate through the stable's roof. People and headlights raced toward both conflagrations, while shouts and bobbing lights carried over the field. I sprinted through a monochrome picture until my lungs locked and knees buckled, and I slammed forward onto my chin.

Miraculously, my jawbone didn't shatter. The blow, however, knocked me halfway out. When the chirping birds and spinning planets abated so that I could crawl on hands and knees, I peered over the grass to see the stable now engulfed plus Nova's barn combusting and Julia's trailer puffing smoke; people running helter skelter, screaming. Rescued horses careened across paddocks or threw sparks from their shoes on the access road. A horse with rider took off across the valley toward the forest.

I staggered to my feet and pressed onward. Blanche and Dru stood with hands linked and legs braced, focusing power on the main stable. Since my own psychic batteries had run dry, I joined the crowd hurling dirt, water, and dry chemical at hot spots while county volunteers hooked up pumps and hoses, and fought us back from the fires. Kit defied them to drop an empty extinguisher and run toward the bellowing and hammering from Nova's barn. Buck released a blindfolded horse and streaked across the yard after him. I screamed protests that neither man heard.

Buck and two firemen chased Kit into Nova's inferno. I ran after them but was snatched and flung backward, followed by curses. When I righted myself and wiped my eyes clear, I saw Nova burst through his door with mane and tail glowing behind. Kit dragged alongside, clinging to Nova's neck, his feet bumping and skidding until they tangled with the horse's legs and pitched both into a tumble. Nova scrabbled upright across Kit then thundered past me. A fireman turned his hose on the horse, taking him down again but dousing the flames.

I sprinted to Kit, who writhed and hollered on the ground clutching his thigh. As I fell to his side, Dru's legs jumped over my back.

"Get out of here!" he yelled, dragging Kit away. As I scrambled, a roar of heat and pressure blew us apart—pelting us with sparks and splinters as the hayloft of one barn and roof of the other collapsed. Crashing timbers cut off some screams and triggered others more awful; the smoke grew thicker and putrid. With the ground rumbling beneath hooves, feet, tires, and timbers, I thought the earth had split open and would suck us under. I got up to run again but stopped at the sight of Nova's barn.

In seconds, it had become a skeleton fleshed with fire. Two firemen dragging Buck sought escape between the uprights, but a dangling beam toppled down to chop Buck from their arms. They sprang clear with shouts—one dashed back for Buck behind a screen of flames. More timbers buckled. The fireman emerged empty-handed, charred and smoking. I ran forward again but iron arms caught me and dragged me back.

"Stay clear, you stupid bitch!" demanded a voice that threw me to hands which tossed me into a three-truck cul-de-sac. It would have qualified as rescue had I not become boxed in with a frenzied horse. Suliemann banged against the trucks, whinnying shrilly. He could not perceive the gap as an escape route, since the space glowed orange and smelled of smoke and death.

The need to calm him and save us both restored some order to my madness. I could do nothing further for my loved ones, who were either productively helping or in others' capable hands. Rather than keep getting in the way, I could serve by getting this horse out of the way and—better yet—get back to work on the bigger problem. Raoul remained unvanquished, and I was still standing.

I swung toward a fresh racket. Suliemann had slammed both heels into a fender then lunged over a side panel half into a pickup's bed. I couldn't soothe him over the noise, so I squashed my urges and sauntered toward him, facing him sideways, from where he could see me. Stayed clear while he extricated himself from the pickup, scraping his belly, then I closed while he fretted. On getting near enough to grab his mane, I tried to swing on bareback. He skittered and spun but didn't shake my grip, even after bashing me against a truck. I ignored the blow and hopped onto a bumper, still clutching him. From there I was able to flop onto his back.

I landed with one leg astride and hung on as he leaped through the opening I had been blocking. My pounce either broke his panic or made it so much worse that he ran blind. He galloped a quarter-mile before I could scramble upright. Just in time—we flew over a fence then crossed the valley until meeting its stream.

Suliemann followed the silver ribbon uphill toward the reservoir. I crouched jockey style, half unconscious, until he slowed and sputtered through his nostrils. The change jarred me alert; I realized that trees shielded us from fire glow. Dawn now suffused the sky.

Suliemann's jog eased into a walk. I straightened and inhaled, dropped my legs, flexed my ankles. We were enveloped in dark silence tangy with pines. I unclenched my hands from his charred mane and sought my bearings. Had the other rider come this way?

Answer came as a nearby shout and crashing in the underbrush. Suliemann shied, almost dumping me, and gathered for flight. I contained him by yanking on his mane and bearing down on his kidneys. He spiked his ears forward when I craned over his neck to identify the sounds.

Somewhere between us and the reservoir the other rider pursued a runner—hunter hurling threats as he flushed his quarry from the woods. Without understanding the words, I grasped their significance, and pummeled Suliemann into a canter after the receding noise.

The Morab understood the need to follow but did so at his own pace. We jogged downhill and uphill between whiplashing branches. The cries subsided but the footfalls became louder as the forest thinned and ground became rocky; then, abruptly, voices and footsteps stopped.

We burst into open space where the ground plunged away into the amphitheater. Suliemann locked his knees with a startled snort and skidded across the gravel to the rim. We jerked to a halt that flung me half up his neck. On regaining my seat, I looked down into the terraced bowl to see a black streak leaping from terrace to terrace with a green blur a few yards behind. Opposite us on the rim walkway, a four-legged ghost trailing a rope threw up its head and whinnied. Raoul and Colin looked up reflexively. Both stumbled and fell.

Colin recovered first and gained on Raoul, who had bounced down two tiers and rattled his senses. I would have pinned him there with an energy ray but nothing rose to my command. Instead I kicked Suliemann down the slanted aisle and cheered on my brother. His green leggings and boots flashed beneath a parka and hatless head, one arm pumping as the other clamped the quiver against his back. His free fist held a longbow, and three broadheads rattled in his quiver. I went slack in mesmerization, waiting for the speeding image to reach the pose freeze-branded into my mind all those months ago—terrified that the picture wouldn't match in the end. Already they differed: My green archer had not been wearing a parka, and he had been frozen in daylight with bow at full draw.

Suliemann veered then rabbit-hopped down to the level on which Raoul sprinted. My lurching for balance pushed the horse into a canter, directly toward Raoul along the curved footwell between tiers. Blocked, Raoul had no choice but to jump downward. An uphill scramble would destroy what was left of his lead.

Colin leaped after him but skidded on a frost-coated bench, spilling his arrows. Swearing and flailing, he recovered one while Raoul ran flat-out across the amphitheater floor. I tried to pivot my horse and go after him—with both of our powers gone, I finally held the advantage. But Suliemann would only circle. In passing flashes I saw Colin straighten, brace his legs, draw his bow, nock the arrow. Just as I wrestled Suliemann to a halt, the arrow flew.

My mind grabbed and held the instant, so that Colin's stretch was connected by a line through the air to the bull's-eye beneath Raoul's flexed shoulder blade. The arrow skewered him with a crack-squish I heard from yards away. Raoul's howl, as he pitched forward and skidded to limpness, echoed around the bowl and faded into the sky.

27
The Morning After

After seconds filled with bird twitterings, the remnants of my control shattered and I emptied my lungs in a scream. Suliemann neighed and leaped from beneath me. For a moment I hung in space, then crashed to the front-row bench, nose at Colin's kneecaps. I heard him cry my name through a spinning red fog.

Then he eased me onto my back, loosened my clothing at neck and waist, and daubed my streaming face while tucking his parka around me. "It's all right, Mad, it's over, everything's gonna be all right . . . it's okay, Madeline—please don't cry!"

I didn't realize I had started. Once aware, I couldn't stop. Huge, ugly, snorting sobs, like a two-year-old overdue for her nap after falling off a swing backward. Colin endured, once again serving as daddy, ignoring business in order to take care of his little girl.

Eventually my adult mind surfaced. I gave a final sniff, gagged on blood, then spat before releasing Colin from duty with a feeble smile. "Good shot, Robin!"

He patted my unscraped cheek, relieved by my attempted humor. "I'll tell you something, Miss LaRue. I'd never have hit him if I hadn't assumed I would, which is a trait you scornfully call overconfidence."

"No more scorn," I mumbled, dribbling at the mouth. Just how badly was I hurt? I still couldn't feel my appendages. Was I paralyzed? Or merely in shock?

Directing my forearm by sight, I clutched Colin's sleeve and croaked, "Gotta—get back—the house."

He shook his head. "I'm not picking you up in that condition!"

"Don't leave me alone in the woods with a corpse!"

"Then sit up. Or move your legs. You have to prove you're not hurt. Better yet, lie still while I get help."

He looked over at Raoul's shell then up the terraces. "Where's that goddamn horse?"

"Don't worry, either one'll come at a whistle."

While Colin tried different whistles, I curled fingers, wriggled toes, swiveled my head, bent my elbows. Shooting pains told me that everything worked. Nonetheless, I couldn't face being carried. Colin had abandoned that idea as soon as he registered what it would entail.

He also abandoned me, turning away to splay his hands over his face. "Jeezus. Fuck. Damn. I just killed a guy."

"He stopped being a guy a long time ago. You might have just saved the world. Think about that!" Then I whimpered. "Are you sure he's dead?"

I couldn't bear to look for myself, lest the corpse wink at me. Raoul was gone so suddenly, so simply, it couldn't be true. And truly, would the ordeal ever be over? Where did his soul go, if he'd ever had one? Would it reincarnate through some other weak-willed victim? This life or next? Or would Raoul's demise trigger another body into action—tomorrow? Or would Evil now stay disembodied until the next millennium wheeled around?

Colin crunched across the dirt. "He's dead, all right." He kicked the body. "At least I don't have to carry him!"

Colin's knees crackled as he bent to double check for life signs. "Yuck. Now I know why I never took up hunting. What should I do about this arrow?"

When I didn't answer, he walked back to check me. Frosty plumes escaped his nostrils at every breath. I glared up through a similar cloud and begged, "Get me outa here!"

"If you can climb that aisle on your own power, I'll get you onto a horse. Really, Mad, it'll hurt more if I carry you."

"I know. I mean, help me up." We heaved and grunted together until I was balanced on gimpy legs. As he half pushed, half dragged me up the aisle, I couldn't resist a backward look. "Are you sure he's dead? Maybe we should bury him."

"No way, José. Without him we can't explain the carnage to the cops. Not when every fire department in the county watched the complex go up and a hundred people caught it on video!"

"But—"

"Look, it's my ass in the hot seat. My arrow in a dead guy's back, who I chased down on horseback while he was on foot. Kinda hard to claim self-defense without explaining why!"

He broke off to catch his breath. Then panted, "Be a lot worse, to mess with evidence, at a crime scene. Maybe, if there weren't so many witnesses, I'd try to bury everything—Raoul's got no people, that we could find, it'd be easy. But we've got an inquiry logged, which may be the only thing that saves my hide. That and the witnesses. God knows how many saw so much weird shit, lots of scary puzzles. It'll take months, to piece together attendance alone. And by now, it'll be all over the news."

This took us to the amphitheater rim, where we paused to rest and convince Riyadh that I was not the bogeyman. Suliemann watched from a cautious distance, swiveling his ears. I marveled that Colin had already thought so far ahead, when all I could embrace were the simple, jumbo problems of getting my battered body onto a four-legged pogo stick then getting through the rest of my days in a world turned upside down.

Colin secured Suliemann with his belt around the horse's throat, then held Riyadh's halter rope while giving me a leg up. Riyadh jigged but otherwise cooperated. I patted him gratefully, knowing how much easier steering would be with a rope. Suliemann would follow Riyadh, making Colin's ride easier than mine had been. Before he mounted, however, I suggested, "Why don't you stay here, make sure that bastard doesn't walk away on you."

Colin sighed. "He's very dead, Mad." He held up fingers stained by blood.

I shuddered. "You saw what he did. Can you really trust him?"

Colin frowned down into the bowl. "I guess I should wait. You send help pronto."

I nodded, shrugging out of his parka, which he shrugged back into. My own blood stained its shoulder and sleeve. The lip from which that blood had spilled was clotted and swollen. I must have bitten through it when I fell.

"As fast as I can," I promised, squeezing Riyadh into a canter. Thank the gods for smooth-gaited, intelligent horses! My bruises barely got jostled, and I directed with legs and the single rein down the track to the loop road then up it, across the lawns, to the manse.

Or as close to it as I could get. What with the smoldering carriage house, bedraggled onlookers, and unfamiliar men waving and shouting or muttering into radios, and a barricade of vehicles with flashing lights, I couldn't get near without challenge. Fortunately, the onlookers included Mark, who jogged over to me as I drew my mount to a bouncing halt inside the marble circle. "Where—" he started.

I slashed my hand through the air to cut him off. "Raoul's dead. Colin's got him in the amphitheater. Get help down there now!"

He ran off, yelling back over his shoulder, "Your people are down below. Better go."

I spurred Riyadh around the north wing before anyone official could nab me and again I descended the escarpment trail—much slower this time, and much dicier on horseback. As we loped across the plain toward ruins smoking in the sunrise, I saw horses and people wandering between cars and trucks and every form of compound vehicle. A Jeep lay upside down, its top crushed. Firemen still hosed the gutted buildings. Near Nova's ex-barn, a group huddled near the stallion, held by Julia. They rotated as one toward Riyadh's hoofbeats. Stray horses whinnied at us; Riyadh whinnied back.

Blanche broke from the cluster to meet me, still cocooned in her fur coat, now soggy and soiled. Her face lived up to her name beneath soot smudged across her cheekbones like macabre blusher.

"You all right?" I called to her.

She nodded.

"Where's Kit, Buck, and Dru?" I continued as she took Riyadh's head and I slid off. My knees buckled upon landing. She gasped while reaching to catch me; Troy and Cornelius ran over to help. Back on my feet, I told them the one piece of good news to come out of the night. They barely paused to express relief before hitting me with the bad news.

"You just missed the helicopter and ambulance," Troy said grimly. "They took Buck and Gene—bad shape, both of them. Dru's riding with Buck."

Blanche added, "Kit's still here—broke his leg bad, Madeline. They've called another ambulance but it won't get here for half an hour, so we're taking him in the Wagoneer as soon as it comes back from the house."

She towed me while she talked, ending as we reached the group, which had gathered in that spot to shelter Kit. He lay on a stretcher, buried in blankets, with Brian crouching at his shoulder keeping tabs. Kit's splinted leg formed lumps beneath the blankets. All that showed above them was his ashen face.

"Oh Kit!" I knelt beside him and cupped his filthy cheek in my filthy hand.

"Hey Mad." He attempted a smile rubberized by painkillers. "I'm okay, really. Nova just stepped on me a couple times."

Brian snorted. "Kicked the shit outa ya is more like it." Kit started to shrug then winced and paled further. The Wagoneer arrived, driven by Adam and overseen by the county sheriff. Kit moaned as they hoisted him into the vehicle, then passed out. I rode inside with him and Brian, holding Kit's hand and touching his face, kissing him at least once a minute. A deputy rode up front with Adam. Blanche followed in a car with Troy, John, and Jake. Pete and Allanna had already followed Buck and Gene to the hospital. Everyone else stayed behind to mop up.

We left one team of county and state police questioning guests, firemen, and whatever New Atlanteans they could intercept, while another team followed Mark, Seth, and Greg to the amphitheater.

Once outside the gate, we had to push our fenders against fans and reporters, who formed a convoy behind us all the way to the hospital.

Upon arrival, we were engulfed by the usual emergency-room frenzy. Unfazed staff wrenched me away from Kit to stitch my lip while wheeling him upstairs for surgery on his broken femur and tibia and crushed ankle. They dispatched our companions to private waiting rooms while security staff and our official escorts dealt with demands and cameras. I pressed everyone for information about Buck, but learned nothing more than "intensive care unit." Meanwhile, Gene had been pronounced dead on arrival, having broken his neck when he rolled the Jeep.

So much disaster—I didn't know on whom or what to focus. Emotions coursed through me faster than I could feel them, while my mind lagged behind. My body was more than challenged by holding a cup with a twisted hand I had not noticed, and sipping liquid through a straw around a lip that felt the size of a Frisbee. Not permitted to recuperate alone, I slouched in my own private waiting cell with my own private shadow, John, whose twin trailed mine through hospital corridors looking for Dru, Pete, or Allanna.

A television muttered in the background. I ignored it, along with the muffled noises in the halls as the staff continued its somber business—except for one burst of shouting and running footsteps followed by cryptic calls on the PA. Another poor soul must have gone into cardiac arrest. Hopefully not Buck or Kit. I pondered anew how to coerce information about them from anyone. Wondered how long I would have to wait, to what end.

The years since I had smoked cigarettes evaporated. I needed nicotine, chased by undiluted liquor, to endure what I had still to face. Possessed by this new, old need, I sat up to scan the room. John came alert at my first move. I saw no ashtrays, no vending machines, and various No Smoking signs. How compassionate. In that case, I would go wherever the smokers went outside. Or else get my own pack and pace off my stress.

Turning to John, I asked, "Who ended up with car keys?"

Ow—it hurt to talk with half a mouth. At least I could talk! John answered by pulling a key ring from his pocket.

I reached for the purse that wasn't there, saying, "Will you get me some cigarettes?"

He shook his head.

I looked away, cursing, then tried again. "Will you either escort me to the smoking section or take me out to get some?"

He nodded and stood.

I started for the door but stepped back as it opened into me. A near miss on being clouted in the face again. Dru entered, pulled up short in surprise, then eased the door shut behind him. He smiled. "Ah, there you are. I see you survived. Congratulations!"

I looked at him sharply—a hug and commiserating words would have been more appropriate. But he was back in his leader mode, eyes clear, self under extreme control. Going along, I replied, "Blanche has been looking for you."

"I know. We connected. She's on her way home with everyone else. I'm rounding up the stragglers."

"I'm not going until assured that Kit and Buck are stabilized and I can see them."

"That's what I figured. Wanted to see how you're holding up before the shit hits the fan."

I laughed bitterly. "Hasn't it already?"

He half smiled. "Yes, but I've got to talk to all those reporters waiting outside, then a thousand officials. It's going to get a lot worse before it gets better. But I want you to know: It will get better. Just hang in there."

I scowled, sensing a subtext. "I don't have much choice."

"Oh, you always have choices." He sat nonchalantly. I struggled to pay attention, having become obsessed with desire for a cigarette.

The moment I flopped back into my chair, John slipped out of the room. I dismissed thought of him to inspect Dru. Although grubby, he didn't look tired. Rather, he looked taut and shiny, as if all the power I had lost had been transferred to him. Could he have absorbed Raoul's, too? Did he even know that his enemy had expired?

"By the way, Dru, are you aware that Colin nailed Raoul?"

Dru blinked. "Is that who got him? All I know is that his presence disappeared. I felt reborn and recharged. I thought perhaps you had run him down."

I explained. Dru nodded, gazing at his steepled fingers. Then he dazzled me with an abrupt, fully open gaze. "Thank you."

"For what? You and Blanche and Colin did all the work. And Kit and Buck and everyone else fought the fires. All I did was run around and fall down!"

The thought made me smile. Ha ha to Allanna! She who predicted I would vanquish Evil!

"But it was you who wouldn't let me succumb to him," Dru persisted. "You who made him reveal his true self. You who kept all of us strong enough to fulfill our roles. Your refusal to totally believe in anything kept you immune from his full effect, while faith or fear handicapped the rest of us. No, Mad, we wouldn't have won without you. That's why you were chosen."

For a moment, I warmed. Then anger took over. "Are you sure we won? Look what it gained us!" I swung my arm to include both hospital and smoldering ruins at home.

"Absolutely," Dru declared. "You think you're seeing an end but it's actually a beginning. Don't forget, you can't have birth without blood and pain. If Evil had won, we'd have lost everything, or else been left a population unable to raise an argument. But Good has kept everyone outside us intact, plus provided evidence to prove the point."

"What point?"

I found no point in the waste we had just experienced. War was always pointless hell, regardless of who won. There had to be a better way!

Dru inhaled. "The point is, there really is something out there that's mightier than we are, and watching. This truth no longer needs to be concealed."

"It can't be. The whole debacle got witnessed!"

"Which is the very point. And that's what will lead to a new world."

Dru stood and paced, unable to contain his fervor. "That's what the powers wanted. That's why the revelation is happening now. We've gone global and micro and techno enough to capture and measure cosmic secrets. So it's time to roll them out. The upheaval you're worried about will be the new common enemy that unifies the planet. Next time it will be aliens landing, but first we have to learn a few things so we won't destroy them, or worship them as gods. Now we have to face our own gods and rename them. Only sure knowledge they exist will change our destructive nature."

"Jeezus, you're as bad as Blanche—fight hate with love, create by destroying. It seems to have escaped your notice that simple, human violence stopped Raoul!"

"That's because psychic and physical forces can't operate fully in each other's plane. I'm ashamed we didn't figure that out earlier—it might have kept things from going this far. But at least we learned it and now can move on."

"To what? Do you have any idea what legal problems we just incurred? Especially if anyone believes you!"

"They'll believe me, all right. Believe us. Which will take care of the legal problems, as long as we stay calm and cooperate. So tell the truth when you're asked, Mad, and when it comes to it, let them test you. I'll do everything possible to protect our privacy. But we must share our story with everyone on the planet. Then let the rest take care of itself."

"You're crazed!"

"No, I'm right. Clichés are clichés because they're true. Knowledge is power. Darkness is followed by dawn. You now know firsthand that Good is stronger than Evil. And life evolves on an upward spiral."

"Pah. Don't forget that the spiral is the concept behind the screw!"

That broke his mania. As he stared at me, I sneered, "You know, the screw? Basic mechanical unit of the world? Screw is what karma does to individuals who serve the many. Sure, everything might even out in the end, but so far in human history, all the gods—powers—whatever we should call them—have always screwed their instruments. You'll get your turn someday!"

"It's already started. I'm just going to wring it for all it's worth!"

So there. He shut me right up.

John chose that moment to return with my cigarettes, allowing Dru to slip out with a snide, "See you back at the ranch" before we could discuss who would pay Buck's and Kit's medical bills, who would call and comfort the affected families. How we would commemorate the dead. Who to hire to represent Colin. And who besides Dru had any power left, and why, and how much, and what we were going to do about it.

John tossed me the cigarette pack. I ripped it open and lit a coffin nail, vowing to cart Dru to the loony bin if I didn't find him shuddering in delayed reaction inside a week.

For the interim, I worked on composing myself. Chain smoking made me reel in dizziness, spiked with nausea. While it passed, I made, discarded, and reformulated plans. John waited like a stone, keeping his eye occupied with the television. I continued ignoring it until he stiffened and touched my arm.

The screen filled with Rosalind Burke from TV 16 News, hunched into the collar of her red coat, clutching her microphone in a red-gloved hand. Her spotlit face was so white beneath lipstick and eye-shadow that she looked like a vampire. Her breath formed staccato puffs. Behind her, a crowd wearing similar expressions herded close.

John turned up the volume to catch her in the middle of a news flash:

"—hospital, where injured New Atlanteans were taken after half their compound burned to the ground last night during a costume ball. But this was no Halloween prank or accident—allegedly it's arson, and some witnesses claim the fires were set by paranormal means. Pyrokinesis, they call it—after a wild night of telekinesis, also known as moving objects using mental power. Many reports have come out describing psychic powers of all kinds. Police and fire crews remain skeptical, but here at the hospital we may have proof positive. Just minutes ago a badly burned New Atlantean, whom doctors had doomed to death or permanent disfigurement, walked out of intensive care, then apparently slugged a passerby in the hall, stole his clothes, keys, and wallet, and disappeared. Nurses swear the patient had been admitted with burns covering three-quarters of his body, yet witnesses and security cameras saw the same man, skin intact but hair missing, walking out as casual as you please. His bed is empty. No other patients are missing. Nurses swear they never left him unattended, but—"

I shrieked in belated understanding. John lunged to stop me as I dove for the door and ran out.

He chased me down the hall, almost caught me at an intersection where I turned the wrong way, but I beat him to a staircase. He finally tackled me at the bottom landing just before I burst into the lobby.

For seconds he squashed me against the wall, one hand over my mouth, the other twisting my arm up behind me. I struggled, whimpering and steaming through my nostrils, until his patience wore me down. The instant he felt my surrender, he released me. My lip resumed throbbing and seeping blood.

We glared at each other from arm's length, me wishing that he would speak or I could read his mind. Perhaps he could touch mine, for I came to understand that he wanted me to stop and look first. At that, I heard a ruckus beyond the door, in the lobby. We looked at each other; he nodded; I eased the door open a crack and peered out.

The lobby contained a mob around TV-camera lights. Between jostling shoulders I spotted Rosalind Burke's red coat and the top of Dru's head poking up in the eye of the maelstrom. John and I slipped into the lobby and moved between people who ignored us to gape at the interview in progress. I understood their fascination upon hearing Dru's words:

"That's right, I healed him."

"But how?" Rosalind asked for us all.

"I'm not sure. But I had the power. By whatever means, it came to me. And he needed it. So I let him choose."

"Choose what, life or death?"

"Not exactly. You see, I had more power than I need, so I gave him some of the extra to help choose between futures. He opted to heal himself so he could finish his work healing the planet. Unfortunately, that work lies outside New Atlantis, so he had to get away before your lot ran him down."

A babble drowned out further comments. I seized the moment to jump up—yes, Blanche was beside him—then duck down beside John and mouthed, "Where's the car?"

He tipped his head sideways and led me away from the still-growing crowd, around a wing to the emergency entrance. The interview faded in volume as we retreated but grew louder inside my head. Tonight it would be all over the news; tomorrow, the headlines on every paper. Dru Montclair, mega-superstar-turned-god, had just pulled a stunt nobody could ignore.

I had to escape before he got cocky and demonstrated on live telecast. Had to get back to New Atlantis and retrieve my papers and money before people recovered from shock and factored me into the equation. And I had to find Buck before the cops did—or before he plugged back into the underground that had concealed him once before from professional diggers—or before Dru's healing powers proved temporary, and Buck collapsed and died. And just like Buck, I had to cover as much ground as possible with a narrow lead time. To salvage what I could before life as we knew it crashed to an end.

Part Three

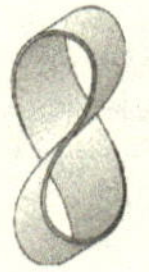

28
Ashes

Now what?

That had been the question for four months. Answers that had rolled in like waves had only led to the same question, renewed with more options. No answer satisfied anyone. The version in progress had started an electrical fire inside me that refused to go out.

It drove me to the tor overlooking New Atlantis on a frigid February afternoon. From there I contemplated the scree below my feet, wondering if a fall down there would be enough to kill me, or whether I would bounce from ledge to boulder to tree to scrabble, breaking every bone but coming to rest alive. The thought of such pain no longer disturbed me. Death had become the only way out of a no-win nightmare.

I visualized the chaotic hours that would pass before anyone found me, hunting through subzero darkness beyond range of search lamps. From the ether I would point and whoop in laughter, watching the Watchers panic in fear that I had escaped, paying them back with the hassle of hauling my carcass up a cliff and having to explain it.

That reverie was shattered by bootsteps crunching the trail behind me. I whirled to look—which shot my own feet out in opposite directions, into a scramble that launched me into a belly-flop rotating toward the cliff edge. Too terrified to shriek, I clawed through my mittens, dug in my toes, with as much grab as I would get on oil-coated marble. Yet I stopped with a jerk as my parka belt snagged a stone pimple in the ice.

For seconds? minutes? I sprawled there, gasping. When adrenaline subsided and cold seeped in, I lay shivering and limp. Didn't dare move lest I start the process over again. My toes, I knew without looking, had stopped millimeters from the lip.

Well, that answered one question! If I really wanted to die I wouldn't have struggled, and would now unhook my belt to slip into oblivion instead of creeping my hand under my stomach until I gripped the protuberance and regained control.

The boots crunched closer. I wriggled to gain a hold against the pimple before whoever it was caught me in this predicament. Once upon a time, Buck had watched me from that trail across the chasm, astride Nova. I would give anything to look up and see him again. But I couldn't raise my head until I had shoved myself onto textured surface, which took several muscle-straining, belly-crawling minutes. When I at last looked up, surprise almost jolted me off the cliff again. There stood Buck after all.

Then he was gone.

I stared; blinked; stared; then spat curses and turned away, thinking, Here we go again. Visions would not be ending with Raoul. At least this one appeared benevolent! But was it the beginning of another sequence of events that would come true, or the classic flash of a loved one "crossing over"? Oh please no—not that, please let him be surviving somewhere, trying to reach me through the only available channel. Please give me back enough power to connect with him. Oh please, you cursed god-devils, please do me one favor!

Glancing around, I saw only arctic landscape under a leaden sky, until I looked back across the chasm to see Dru Montclair standing where Buck should have been. He looked like a sun-bleached stick poked through a blue marshmallow in his down parka and pointy ski hat. My own winter gear made me a keg supported by sausages, with Frankenstein feet, boxing-mitt hands, and a surprised cat on my head.

I was tempted again to jump, to make him watch me fall and splatter. Maybe then he would recognize the error of his ways.

But the memory-vision of Buck had restored my control, so I chose simple retreating from the precipice. It would take Dru a few minutes to catch me at the trail junction; if I got a good lead I could stay ahead and loop back through the forest. The slick footing should discourage him from sprinting after me.

Alas, I should have known. Dru could sail over ice as well as he could fly through dimensions. He overtook me at the trail junction.

"Madeline," he panted. "Please stop running away!"

I kept walking. "Fuck you, Dru!"

That's all I had been able to think toward him since the night he gave a four-hour exclusive interview to Rosalind Burke and company. He had told absolutely everything on network TV. They had cut a deal: He would tell all if they censored nothing. It would be his only statement outside of court, assuming Colin went to trial. A host of attorneys was still debating that question. Meanwhile, every scientist with clout was waiting in line to test his claims.

"It isn't fair to blame me for everything," he entreated.

"None of it would have happened if not for you!"

"That's not true—I'm only the trigger."

"The lightning rod!"

"No, the hinge pin. It's bigger than both of us. And would happen somewhere else if it couldn't happen here."

"If you'd kept your mouth shut, maybe it wouldn't have happened here!"

His tone turned nasty to match mine. "My mouth had nothing to do with it. Your body is the bigger culprit."

I halted and slapped him with a look. "What does—"

"Your 'accident' of birth. Who are you a twin to? The perfect person to attract both the good and the evil eye. That eye will always see you, too."

I chilled. He had made a point I couldn't argue. Lord, he was good at that. I hated him anew. "That doesn't mean you had to blab everything to the masses! We're prisoners in our own home now! Irate mobs outside, goddamn bugs in our bedrooms! And me being persecuted because they think I'm sandbagging. If I still could, I would level this place and walk away!"

Our boots scraped in the ensuing silence. I regretted leaving the precipice, where I could have shoved him over the edge.

Knowing him, though, he would levitate instead of fall. These days Dru had whatever power he wanted on tap, filtered through his utopian dream. Repair a terminally burned body? No problem. Just give him five minutes. Yet he wouldn't restore Gene to life or repair Kit's leg. Need a psi demonstration to run tests on? No problem. He—and Blanche—merrily aced all standard ESP tests (while I flunked them all) and demonstrated half the known psychic skills. Yet he wouldn't use them to protect us. Wouldn't use anyone's ethics but his own in deciding limits. Kept forgetting he was a man who could make mistakes.

"Blowing out won't solve anything," he continued. "Only make it worse. House arrest is better than federal prison."

"Maybe the food's better. But the Feds are already here."

"That only makes sense. You've got a dead person with no background, no identity, and several investigations going on. You have an alien force with weapons potential. You've got a missing witness who's also a living miracle. Of course Big Brother will send in his special teams! And the international guys are right behind. Especially since you've got family in Europe."

Who, fortunately, had the wit to stay there. Mother had chimed in to offer sanctuary if we needed it, plus legal support if Colin needed it, but otherwise kept her distance and bore the digs into her background with gritted teeth. She didn't have to fake a fear of flying given how her husband had died, so no one dragged her across the Atlantic when she proved uninteresting. But as mother to such appalling children, she remained suspect, and her husband's death was twisted by some into a conspiracy. Clearly, if we ever escaped New Atlantis, her chateau was not a place where we could hide.

"So how long will this go on?" I demanded. "How long will you allow your private property to be invaded?"

"Until Colin is cleared."

"That won't satisfy them."

"No, but there's your answer, Madeline. The only way to discourage them is to satisfy them. And that won't happen until they believe we are under their power. Resist them, and they'll press harder. They won't relax until they're convinced we're harmless. Which—"

"But—"

"—which is why we've got to overwhelm them with information. If we remain mysterious and frightening, they won't stop probing. But if we're fascinating and willing, then they'll settle back into a lower-level steady state, with fewer specialists here for longer term. The aggressive types will refocus on protecting what they have which nobody else has—us aliens. It's better to be safe in a zoo than facing extinction in a hostile environment."

"I don't recall getting to vote on that one!"

"None of us did. It's the only course."

We walked in stride as the trail widened and roughened. I purposely broke step while keeping pace.

"What you fail to see, Dru, is that the zoo is the hostile environment. Ever since that Dave guy showed up. You all but sent him an engraved invitation by passing the skeptic society's million-dollar test! Before that, it was just frustrating and humiliating. Now it's invasive and threatening. By staying oh-so-submissive and cooperative, you're letting them back us into a corner. But they've gotten out of line. We got rid of one enemy only to gain another. Sometimes I wonder if it's the same force in a different form."

"I'll talk to him."

"Not good enough."

"What do you want me to do, throw them out?" He stopped and glared. "Any act of aggression will make it worse. How would you like to be surrounded by guns, Madeline?"

I stood shaking, unable to argue that point. He rushed on. "If we kick them out, then we'll have to run for it. All in different directions, the rest of our lives on the lam. At least now we still have each other, in our safe and comfortable home. We can still access our money. We're a huge, positive influence just sitting here getting news coverage and being studied. No one would dare harm us. But if we fight?"

He shook his head and exhaled through pursed lips. "Then the same pattern will just repeat itself. We'll have accomplished nothing. The one thing I will not do is endure all this for nothing!"

"Oh, so you mean I have to and you don't?"

He stood rigid, steaming through his nostrils. "Look, Madeline. My job is to prove it can be done—period. It's up to everyone else to decide what to do with it. I make no claim to have the answers—I'm a model, like New Atlantis. And now my job is to stay as benign as possible so people can sort it out. You already did your job—for which I'm eternally grateful—but if you're still miserable, don't blame me. I didn't make you stay here. I bought you hours that night in which to get away. I even healed your goddamn lover to give you both a chance!"

"Yeah, a chance for him to run away from me again!"

"Jeez, is that what this is about? Do you really think that's what he's doing?"

"Do you know any different?"

Dru threw back his head and rolled his eyes, then looked at me. "No. I'm not chatting with him in the astral plane, and I didn't give him instructions. I asked if he wanted another chance and if he understood the consequences. He said yes."

"Who wouldn't, if the choice was deformity from massive burns, or death—when you don't believe in an afterlife?"

"It would have been much easier and less painful to die. But being on the brink of death can make life's meaning much clearer. Buck knew he still had work to do."

"And it was supposed to include me!"

"How do you know that?"

"I—"

I clamped my mouth shut. Dru couldn't know or understand my perfect union with Buck that last night, unless I let him inside my head. Words wouldn't do the job.

Maybe because my bond with Buck hadn't, really, been unbreakable? After all, he had thrown away my paintings and abandoned me twice! I harbored a secret relief that I wouldn't have to choose between him and Kit, along with a secret fear that he would turn up at the gate one day and force me to make that choice.

John and I had searched for him all night after the Debacle. Then returned to New Atlantis to find the place besieged. We had about-faced and camped at the hospital until authorities cornered us for questioning. After that, back to New Atlantis under escort. I had planned to stuff vitals in a backpack and escape during my next hospital visit, but since then had not been allowed off-compound without official company. Couldn't pass through the mob without it, anyway.

Unlike Buck, nobody had bequeathed me extra power I could use for cloaking. If Dru—or the gods—had any such power left to bestow, they refused to oblige.

Which made me wonder, for the millionth time: Why were psychic abilities so unreliable, and unevenly distributed? Was the reason as simple as individuality: Just as everyone had different physical-mental-emotional characteristics, did everyone possess different psychic powers to different degrees at different times?

If so, cloaking must be an extra-special skill, granted only to masters or lucky recipients with desperate need. In Buck's case, how long would it last? It made sense to buy him the time needed to recover and make decisions. If or when it wore off, what would he do?

Given the difficulty of coming back undetected, I had to assume he either no longer could shield himself and didn't dare come near us, or he did not want to come back, cloaking or not. I couldn't decide which option hurt more. The first time I had lost him, he was running from fear of me, his feelings unacknowledged. This time, he was hiding from larger consequences, with his feelings for me revealed. Which translated into: First he rejected me as a person in one life; now he rejected me as a soulmate through the ages. Unless he couldn't get back to New Atlantis. For all I knew, he was signaling like mad in the astral plane and I couldn't perceive him.

I probably could if I dared. Constant reflection had taught me that power came through when I was off-guard or terrified. After the Debacle, my guard had locked on; and, although my mind admitted fear, my body knew only rage. If I channeled power through that filter . . . I closed my eyes against the thought.

Dru followed my facial expressions, if not my internal dialogue, then resumed his defense. "That healing cost me, Madeline, in ways you can't understand. And if Buck chose to walk away and you chose to come back here, that's not my problem. I just opened the door. And while I may have the power to get you out of here now, I don't have the power to repair the damages. So don't ask me to destroy everything for you. And don't hate me for it, either."

"Why not?" My voice cracked. "I lost everything for you!"

"For me, not because of. You did what you felt you had to, of your own free will."

"Yeah, jerked around like a marionette. Ever heard of emotional blackmail?"

"Yeah, it's something like what you're pulling on me!"

He spun and stomped back up the trail.

I bolted after him, grabbing his sleeve to jerk him to a halt. "Goddamn it, Dru, listen to me! You may be right about me, but you're wrong about the bigger picture. Passivity is the course that really will make it all for nothing!"

His fixed gaze and clamped mouth encouraged me to go on.

"Remember what Blanche said. Fight with love. But fight we must, waving any banner, in order to validate our victory. It's not enough to prove there's a grand intelligence running the universe. What it's taught us is that intelligence guides energies which link with matter, positive and negative, to keep things slightly off balance, like a camshaft, resulting in your upward spiral. When something threatens to disrupt that trend, something opposite manifests to counter it. In our case, Evil built up too much in one man so we were activated to give Good direct access to the problem. Luckily, Good prevailed. Which leads to the point you keep misinterpreting. Your job isn't to prove it can be done technically. You have to show how to integrate it into life."

"Which I'm doing by allowing open access and testing. That has to come first."

"Correct, but not this way! Good hasn't won if Evil remains in the driver's seat. Showcasing your power isn't enough. Without demonstrating what good it can do, we'll just turn another cycle instead triggering a spiral. Another Raoul will develop because nothing's in place to stop him. So when the next cosmic battle comes, his side will win. Then you truly will have gone through all this for nothing!"

Dru stood red-faced with blue lips.

I pressed on. "And it isn't about just you. You might be the figurehead, but you wouldn't have inherited all the power without Blanche and me and all of New Atlantis doing our parts. We have to contribute something now, too. Like putting the brakes on these guys so they don't go crazy. They're already violating our agreements—not to mention our civil rights—by spying on us, and classifying their info. They're treating us like plutonium and secret formulas because they're afraid. Don't you see them twitching when we walk by? And mentally signing the evil eye?"

He turned away as my words kept hammering. "You're right in one thing: They know we have the power to control them and can't trust that we won't use it. Their only protection is to control us. Not just you and Blanche, whose power is active, but anyone else whose power could come back. They never saw Raoul in action, can only imagine his impact. Nor can they imagine anyone mature enough to restrain that kind of strength. So it's only a matter of time before they start drugging our food or water. Because every day it's a little likelier that one of us will reach the end of our rope and lash out."

Dru pulled back his lips and sucked air through his teeth—the most overt effort at self-control I had seen him display. It was the first clue that he might indeed be yielding. I yearned for the telepathy that would have told me what seethed behind his façade.

"You're giving me mixed signals, Madeline," he said in a flat voice, his eyes half-lidded. "Do you want my blessing for an escape, or to do something to change the situation?"

"You can do both with one act. Just short them out. Not hurt them, just . . . make them forget us. Lose interest. Turn their attention toward something else. Make them feel guilty. Or take the fear away. Just—something—to reduce our importance enough to regain our privacy and freedom of movement."

Dru stamped his foot. "That is so goddamn unethical I won't even consider it. I didn't bother fighting Raoul only to be just like him!"

"But you're not! We all know it. And you know it in your heart. The end justifies the means sometimes."

"No, Madeline, it never does. You are what you do as well as what you believe. And you have to be consistent to have harmony inside and out."

He was morally right so I didn't argue. Rather, I didn't argue out loud. Yet Dru leaned away from me, as if my emotions generated a wind or an odor. In a way they did both, emitting a field to which he was sensitive. I may have gone head-blind as a receiver but I could still transmit a tidal wave. It gave the same effect as bellowing into his ear.

"Besides," he said after a long rumination, "the energy draw would probably kill me. I may have the ability, Mad, but I don't have the raw, sustained power."

My heart skipped. I said carefully, "But you do in a power circle."

I didn't need to say more. His tiny shrug, a dip of the head toward lifted shoulder, told me that the idea had crossed his mind. Then he walked away.

29
Healing

I stood until cold set in then followed, taking a different trail when they split for the long way around. That downhill skid through the woods calmed me enough to think.

Our vent-and-dent session had freed me from the emotional hamster wheel I'd been spinning within ever since the Debacle. Now, though I had no new ideas, I did feel a lightening and expanding that comes with hope. I could start gnawing on my cage instead of shaking the bars and wailing. If no better solution arrived, I could at least chew until my teeth gave out.

So I finally conceded that Dru's point was valid. However, mine was, too. He didn't have the right to make decisions for us. I would swallow it with less indigestion if he would take a vote. We had never held a meeting to discuss position and strategy. Our model community had fractured like any other, relying on its leader to run the show. Such passivity always led to tyranny. And if anyone doubted that we were being tyrannized, ask them why Dru and I had been shouting at each other on top of an icy ridge.

Following the trampled path across the flat, I passed rubble from the two barns and Julia's trailer, outlined by a foot of snow. Below it lay a pit grave for seven horses. The survivors pawed in their paddocks for any edible bits in the snowpack. At night or during storms they withdrew into the sheds we had slapped together for the season. Above and beyond them, Hill House poked charred timbers through the icing, reminding me of shipwrecks lodged in sandbars. The carriage house gave a different air, as did the closed-off ballroom. Their tumbled stones looked more like ruins after a bombing blitz.

Only the studio, the lodges, the gatehouse and garage, and the mansion remained standing. Investigators had taken over the gatehouse and lodges, adding a few trailers of their own, forcing all New Atlanteans into the manse. Outside the front gate, fanatics rotated shifts, accompanied by journalists. The back gate had been discovered and now fended off its own protesters, media, and fans. Several times a week the security system reported attempted wall breaches. We regularly chased off helicopters, even hang gliders and a parachutist. Our mail had to be screened for toxic powders and ticking packages. One bomb had blown through a remote section of wall. The culprits had been nabbed and the wall repaired within twenty-four hours. That was one nice thing about live-in cops.

I puffed up the final slope to the mansion, pausing at the top to gaze across the front lawn and driveway circle, admiring the bleakly beautiful house rising from the snow. Its marble blocks carried a hue halfway between the white blanket around it and the gunmetal sky behind it. My heartstrings twanged each time I admitted it was my home.

My home. Invaded.

Anger returned. I sucked it in and carried on, wondering how long I could last before exploding.

Inside, the entry hall stood empty, although puddled from earlier traffic. The house crew had laid out plastic and rubber sheets to protect the floor. There was nobody in sight, but voices drifted down both corridors. Dinner would not be served for at least two hours, so if I shed outerwear fast and stowed it in the coatroom, I could run upstairs and hide out a little longer.

Oops—bad assumption. Kit lay in wait for me in the tower suite. Having been evicted from the gatehouse, he now shared my quarters. For the first six weeks after the Debacle, however, he had lain hospitalized in traction.

"Where have you been?" he demanded as I entered the suite.

I sighed. "Up on the promontory, debating whether to jump."

That earned me a snort. "Typical: Me sitting here working up a plan to get us both out, and you taking the easy way out on your own."

I stared, not sure which half of his sting to respond to, or whether to try. Since the Debacle, his life had comprised pain and painkillers, screws and pins, casts and braces of decreasing size, crutches and canes and physical therapy. Bad enough, until his family had butted in. Like many other New Atlantis relatives, they had tried to extract their "loved ones" from "that twisted cult" or whatever they labeled us. Lawsuits flapped around New Atlantis like vultures circling a dying beast. Kit for once went with the majority and opted to remain behind walls until the ballyhoo subsided. Then shared our surprise when doors stopped opening to let us out.

I bit back what I wanted to say, dropped into a chair, and asked instead, "What's your plan? I could use some inspiration!"

He shrugged, avoiding my eye as he had since the hospital. "Jake got out. I think I know how he did it."

I sat up. He shook his head, flicking his eyes toward the wall. "What you don't know, you can't tell."

I sagged. Though we owned detecting devices now, nobody quite trusted any rooms since finding two electronic bugs in the mansion. Kit flopped his head back, scowled with his eyes shut, and rubbed his forehead. He still looked gray and gaunt, nowhere near fit enough to get out and get away with it. He grunted as he hoisted himself with his arms and hobbled into the bedroom. I debated whether to follow, hungry for comfort but dreading another rebuff.

Simmering beneath our external miseries, unforgotten and unspoken, was the glimpse we had caught of each other in the hallway after the fire gong had sounded. Him emerging from a gold-key room with Julia; me emerging with Buck. I had vowed to never raise the subject. He surely had, too. We had lain together every night since his release like two fallen tree trunks. One more night of that would send me swan-diving off the tor.

I entered the bedroom and changed into loungewear while he stretched out on the bed pretending to read a paperback. Even without special power I could feel him tracking my moves. When swaddled in fleece and woollies, I eased down onto the bed beside him. His eyes flashed blue sparks at me. Ignoring them, I snuggled against his side and whispered, "Tell me your plan."

He lay silent so long I thought he would refuse. Finally he let the book drop and looked at me. Having won his gaze I held it, hoping to see truth in his eyes.

"You really wanted to jump?" he said after a moment.

"Yes, but not enough to do it."

"Don't."

My heart unclenched. "I learned today that I can't."

He nodded. "There's a better way."

"I'm all ears!" It almost came out, I'm all yours! but I held my dignity.

So that no electronic ears could hear us, or electronic eyes could read our lips, he shifted covers and clothing, until we were ensconced in an infrared-confusing cocoon. "There's one way out that won't trip an alarm or is covered by a camera," he whispered. "I heard about it from John and Jake."

"They talk?"

"To some of us. How do you think I learned about their twin goddess thing?"

"I thought you had gotten it from Troy or Allanna. I didn't think John and Jake communicated with anyone else."

"No, the twins are guys like anyone else. They'll talk about work and women."

Significant pause. "Anyway, I learned from what they sorta didn't say that there's a blind spot in the wall for anyone who wants to get dirty. Don't have to fiddle with electronics or anything, just crawl out."

"Then what? No place to go but the village—pretty vulnerable on foot and conspicuous as hell!"

"That's where my checkups come in."

"You mean . . . you can get to a phone?"

"Sorta. There's one in the exam room, and plenty in the office. The guards stay in the waiting area, and I sometimes get left in the exam room for a few minutes. Or I could just ask to use a phone—they don't know any different."

"But your call could be traced."

"Yeah, but we'd be long gone by then. All I have to do is set up a vehicle drop-off. Even if the guy who does it gets nabbed, all he knows is what he left us and when. Stick a different plate on it then leave it at an airport. Or run it through a paint job then trade it in for something else. That'll buy us a lot of time."

"Then what? It can all be traced. You'd have to get fake ID."

"That, too, can be arranged."

I felt his smirk and sniffed a giggle. "It's clear you spent some time on the wrong side of the tracks!"

Kit shrugged. "The tricky part will be getting money. I'm sure our accounts are tagged."

"Not all."

He lay still, waiting. I finished, "It helps to have a worrywart financial wizard for a brother, who's been protecting you all your life."

Kit didn't speak but his chest heaved in a sigh and he relaxed a notch. After many minutes of silence, I confessed, "I wish I could go with you to the clinic."

"If they wouldn't let you go when I was crippled, they sure won't when I'm cleared to work and drive again!"

Which would occur in two days. Two more days . . . helicoptered to the specialist who had reconstructed his ankle, for final X-rays and screw removal.

"So . . . how long do we wait, until spring?" I slipped my fingers under his shirt. Encountered another layer. Worked beneath it until I reached hot skin.

Kit suppressed a quiver and his voice tightened. "Things might blow up before then. Or just end, as if nothing happened. Depends a lot on Dru, plus all those behind-the-sceners we don't know about."

"But in winter we'd leave so many tracks."

"Mud season's the best bet. Lotsa tracks, but real confusing, and not so many people willing to slog around."

More silence. I let it stand, tracing my fingers across the landscape beneath his clothes. His muscles remained firm despite months of inactivity. And despite his mind's resistance, one particular body part firmed up as well. I teased him lightly but persistently until his hormones began to boil and his emotions boiled over. He kicked off the covers, yanked clothing out of the way, and pumped himself dry into my body. Then dragged me back into the dark, steamy blanket-womb, where we started over. Much more personal this time; fast first, then slow. Same pattern but always different, and beyond my ability to predict.

As we lay together afterward, first just breathing on each other then brainstorming escape plans, I felt something settle inside me. Kit had answered a question my heart had asked but my mind hadn't yet formed: A soulmate and a lifemate did not have to be the same person. That combination was probably the rarest in human affairs, hence most valued. Although I still couldn't tell which person Kit was, I would embrace him and move forward. I might miss Buck with every other breath, but I could live without him; whereas without Kit, I would have jumped off the cliff today.

Perhaps Dru sensed this acceptance in me. Or he had psychically eavesdropped on our schemings, or been swayed by my arguments. For whatever reason he chose that moment to put the intercom on public address and startle me and Kit a foot off the mattress.

"Power circle tomorrow afternoon at two o'clock," he announced, then clicked off.

30
Fire and Ice

Everyone whispered about it all day and started gathering well before the slated hour. When Kit and I entered the dining hall, tables had already been pushed aside and chairs set into a circle. Outside, sun glittered on the snow, and icicles stretched three feet down from the eaves. Cassandra drew the curtains against the glare, enclosing us in twilight. It took me a moment to register that thirty-six people filled the room.

My god, Dru had invited the Watchers! How could he? First refusing to hold any circles, now inviting the research team to our post-Debacle debut! Had he drafted them in order to reach our magic number, or was this a demo to be followed by electrodes and monitors?

I looked at Blanche who, waiting to receive my gaze, shrugged in her place across the circle. I sat with Kit on my left hand, John Powers on my right. John's palms were damp although he sat apparently unfocused, unblinking. I wondered what he observed and thought. Someday I ought to ask.

Three dozen people in the room and no one even muttered. Instead, most stared at Dru. I was not alone in shooting bullets at him through my eyes. He must have briefed the research team, for they demurely took the seats he pointed out, which were staggered at intervals between New Atlanteans. For each new face, I remembered one missing: Gene, deceased. Rob, judged harmless and released at his request, now lying low in New Jersey with his family. Brian and Alexis, leading a cult of neopagans and promoting energy healing. The escapees, Buck and Jake

Powers. Nobody believed I didn't know where Buck had gone, and nobody could get a syllable out of John about his twin.

We had also lost Brenda, who had lost her paradise and gone back to office towers; as well as the innocents Lu, Jessie, Seth, and Greg. These had suddenly recalled that they belonged to persecuted minorities and fled as soon as they were cleared. Maxine had left as enigmatically as she had arrived and resided. The one real shocker had been Pete quitting the band.

Pete's walkout proved I was not the only one upset by Buck's vanishing act. His entire family was on the rampage, giving the legal squad even more to do.

The million dollars Dru had earned by passing the skeptic society's tests had been escrowed to cover legal fees and lost revenues. This supported Colin, who had been released into "protective custody" and was "cooperating with authorities" by staying with us. He sat now with Blanche on one hand and Cassandra on the other. Although he retained his starch, he no more looked like an investment banker than I looked like a model. Only Blanche remained visually untarnished.

Now hostile intruders contaminated the circle. Well, not all hostile. Clayton, for example, seemed thrilled to be attending. In a way he fit in, resembling Gene with his gawky frizziness, and shining with a physicist's glee at the mysteries we presented. And Lorene wasn't half bad, either. Her soft-focused blondeness was marred by frown lines. She held herself aloof but was always kind. The skeptic society team, conversely, had been harsh and snide during testing. We'd all cheered when Dru and Blanche stumped them—then cried when their reluctant acceptance, confirmed by that big check, had drawn the acute interest that now entrapped us.

Most of the investigators reminded me of apathetic doctors or cops hiding behind their badges. All performed their duties or served their callings. Most allowed curiosity or fear into their eyes. Each struggled to stay detached, polite, and professional. Except for the one bad apple in every bunch, Dave.

He sat ten people away, assessing everyone. I could envision Raoul occupying his chair. They looked nothing alike—Dave, a sandy brunet, had hazel eyes that nonetheless recalled Raoul's bullet holes. Looking into them I saw a soulless calculator hungry for power. Apparently the muscles of a champion, legal authority, and a license to carry didn't satisfy him. Thank goodness black contrails didn't follow him around!

For all I knew, they did. My inability to perceive such things scared me more than seeing them would.

Once everyone had settled, hands connected, Dru looked at each of us in sequence then closed his eyes and opened his throat in song. Kit's grip on my hand slackened at once. I slid my eyes sideways in surprise and tightened my grip around his fingers. He kept his eyes closed and squeezed back. I nodded at the reassurance and closed my eyes as well.

A nerve jangle rose, popping my eyes back open. The energy had not come through so fast before. I almost withdrew my hands but the group seemed calm, all eyes closed or half-lidded. I had to force my foot to stop jiggling so I didn't disrupt the flow.

Dru let his voice meld with the background music. This in turn rose in a soft crescendo of electronic bass emulating a pulse. Faces and shoulders slackened as I watched, despite an underlying tension. In previous circles, our fears had been mental and consequences imagined; now, consequences set every emotion raging in our guts. Suppression made them more potent, and our physical contact gave them a channel. The Watchers did not disrupt the flow because they felt the same.

How ironic, I thought, that unity would come from shared anxiety. Maybe Dru was right after all, and he would win our freedom by seducing the antagonists over to our side.

His voice faded below the music. My heartbeat fell into sync with it, matching the group's. The shrill tingle of their contact changed to a thrum that pulled down my eyelids. Soon the links in our chain dissolved into a continuum of colors, images, and sounds.

Without feeling the shift, I lost my physical boundaries and extended in all directions. Minds twinkled in the dark and silent voices composed a babble; a pleasant, formless company, with whom I floated for a while. My muscles unkinked cell by sinew until stress and thought and ego dissipated. I recognized the state I had hoped to reach by dying.

No, came a voice inside my cranium. *Your work here is not done.*

What? I shrieked back, to emptiness. It bulged with pressure, kissing me like a wind-stirred frond, carrying a chuckle. The presence left an aftertaste of knowledge: I had been chosen because my pigheaded conceit would not let me die.

I flailed internally, pulling my body in around me. On regaining some cohesion, I opened my eyes and turned to Dru. His face sagged in trance. If he were aware of me at any level, he refused to engage. Blanche too remained closed and slouched, unaware of the intrusion or incurious about it. Kit and John seemed lost in their own worlds.

The music had risen to a steady, hypnotic pattern too lyrical to be a chant yet too monotonous for a song. It worked like gravity against open eyelids, like weights against muscles. Despite myself, I sank back into mesmerization.

The music accompanied me to this plane but remained in the background. Occasionally a crackle from the fireplace poked through. The group's energy rose and flowed through the circle—welcoming, embracing, fortifying while it calmed. Spirits mingled and merged, emotions transferred. I couldn't tell where I began and someone else ended.

Within this effervescence, individuals appeared and retreated, trying out their astral wings. Kit spiraled up my arm and wrapped himself around me; from the other side, Dru penetrated Kit's and John's protection to illuminate my mind.

Well, well. Fancy meeting you here!

Long time no see, I replied.

Blanche signed on with a flare piggy-backed to Dru's essence. I flared myself, in thrill, wanting to whoop and celebrate—then went cold upon realizing that the earlier voice hadn't come from Blanche or Dru.

Mad, what's going on? You're seesawing like Jekyll and Hyde!

Oh Dru, I can't—I don't—the voice—

My agitation went nonverbal. Dru psychically reached out to take my hand.

Easy, it's all right, what are you talking about?

You couldn't feel it? I couldn't describe it. Distress eroded buoyancy, to send me falling back inside myself. I landed as if on pavement, with a jolt up the spine, ringing ears, and visual starbursts. When the effects cleared, I tried to relax and regain contact, but I had broken the ring's concentration as well as my own.

My ego shriveled into a kernel as feet shuffled, chins lifted, eyes fluttered open. The minutes I expected for recovery were cut to seconds by Dru jerking upright in his chair. His eyes sprang open in the same motion; spun into focus; then tightened on Dave across the circle. Dave returned the stare in a deadpan, then dropped his hands and kicked back his chair.

Standing with fists clenched, he flung a final, arrogant look at Dru, sniffed at the group, then stomped from the dining hall. Dru's gaze followed like poisoned arrows while the rest of us sat rigid, as if lightning had just retracted from the center of the floor.

Kit leaned close to my ear. "What happened?"

"I'm not sure, I missed it too."

Damn! So brief a connection, returning so fast to brick-headedness. I hated being ignorant instead of in the know. If I didn't move fast, then I would be the last to learn what had happened. Dru and Blanche had already left the room.

Six of us followed, almost overtaking them in the hallway. No Dave in sight, but that didn't stop the king and queen of New Atlantis. They paused only to grab coats then marched outside into the brittle afternoon. I snatched a cloak off a peg and immediately regretted not taking a parka. The way my nostrils crystallized and eyeballs smarted marked the air temp at less than ten degrees.

Our knot stretched into a knotted line across the front lawn. Dru and Blanche strode on a beaten snow path toward the amphitheater trail, short-cutting to the lower dirt drive. Mark followed in hiking boots, jeans, and a sweater. I half-trotted in his footsteps, panting clouds as I twined the cloak around me and skidded on the crust. Troy and Allanna trailed behind me, trailed further by Clayton and Lorene.

Dru skittered down a slope onto the plowed lower drive and wheeled to face us. When Troy and Allanna caught up, we New Atlanteans formed a line before the approaching outsiders, who slowed. Dru straightened to full height and declared in his coldest voice, "Go back to the house."

Lorene stepped forward, hand out and mouth open. Dru set his face so that all ridges and lines tautened over their bones, and dropped his eyelids to half mast over a glare. Air steamed through his nostrils; otherwise, he didn't move. But the snow beneath Lorene's feet liquefied so fast she jerked downward two inches.

She backed a step with a squeal then gawked between Clayton, Dru, and the puddle. Clayton did same, his jaw hanging open like everyone's except Dru's. Lorene turned, slowly and stiffly, watching him over her shoulder until her neck wouldn't take it. Then she poked Clayton and herded him back toward the house. Her gesture equated the snap of a stopwatch. I wasn't sure how much time remained but knew it would run out fast.

Dru's face and shoulders sagged and he looked down at his shivering companions. With a sideways head nod, he gestured for us to follow.

We stomped single file along a white road striated by blue shadows. My feet had gone numb and ears ached. No one spoke, either because their faces were too stiff or minds were too stunned. For a few minutes I feared that Dru planned an exodus through the back wall into the forest. Then he diverted up the amphitheater track, to a spot where we could congregate and see anyone approaching before they saw us. But they could hear us first if we talked too loud.

Children had been sledding in the amphitheater earlier, providing a smooth channel down and rough steps back up. Otherwise, we would have needed ice axes, crampons, and ropes to descend into the bowl. Dru, after a chuckle, sat on the rim then launched himself down the chute formed by an unstepped aisle. A few seconds later he spun to a stop on his back on the floor. At his grin and wave, Blanche settled into the slide and flew, followed by Troy, Mark, and Allanna. Their descending giggles and safe landings moved me to wrap my cloak tighter and let gravity suck me away.

The whoosh!—recalling my earlier whoops! on the cliff—scared a scream out of me. Hands waited at the bottom to break my speed and scoop me up. Adrenaline kept me warm for several minutes. By the time we settled down to business, however, I had joined my cronies in tucking hands under armpits and stamping feet.

Mark, blue-lipped, demanded, "So what's going on, Dru? What happened in the circle?"

"Dave," Allanna responded, as Dru said, "The Feds are going to pull something after all."

"That cocky little weasel," Blanche inserted, "thought his attitude served as a mind shield. Thought he could sit in a circle and get without giving."

"And when Madeline's distress shot around," Dru said, "it spiked everyone—and, in Dave's case, startled him open, giving me a full view of his thoughts."

"I take it you didn't get a pretty picture," Troy prompted, rubbing melt off his mustache.

Dru sighed. "They've decided they can't ever let us loose. We're too dangerous. And they're really worried that it's heritable—they want to control our kids. They can only contain all variables by removing us from the spotlight. And the only way to do that is against our will."

A motion above made us catch our breath and pivot. On recognizing John Powers, who lifted a hand, we pivoted back. John settled into sentry position.

"So what are we going to do?" asked Mark.

"That depends on what they're gonna do," answered Troy.

We looked at Dru. He shook his head. "I didn't learn much. It was just a wave of hatred—and satisfaction that soon they'd be calling the shots instead of us. I guess they've been debating plans for a while and only just decided. Or got clearance. I caught them off guard by inviting them into a circle. But either their curiosity got the better of them, or they thought bowing out would be too obvious."

"You weren't too subtle back there yourself!" chided Troy.

We jiggled in place until Mark broke the quiet. "I wish I knew if you scared them enough to back off or goaded them into action."

"Enough to step back and recalculate, I would guess," Allanna replied.

Troy said, "But now they know we're planning something and will double their guard."

Dru nodded. "So we act fast. They might try pulling us out one by one to avoid a media spectacle. Maybe fabricate an incident to justify it. Or declare us insane, crippled by our powers, and put away for everyone's good."

"Hell, they'll probably combine it all tomorrow by torching the place and telling the media we died in the inferno," Mark sneered. "Meanwhile, we're all stashed in some top-secret laboratory for the rest of our lives."

"Not all," Troy reminded us.

Mark steamed then erupted. "We've got rights. Can't we just stage an uprising and drive the bastards out?"

"And risk a retaliation?" Blanche countered. "Do you really want the military to butt in?"

"Makes no difference, they'll come after us anyway. I'd rather be under siege in my own castle than on the run the rest of my life."

"You underestimate the opposing mentality," said Allanna. "Nobody pushes governments around. They've all bankrupted their countries making sure we know it. And absolutely none will let a superior weapon out of their hands."

Troy agreed. "They'd kill us before they'd give us up. Regardless of what we consider ourselves, they have to consider us loose cannons with unlimited potential for disruption. If they leave us alive, they must keep our wings clipped. Dru's way doesn't serve that."

"Which leaves the unacceptable choice of cooperating or taking control," Dru concluded. "You folks, individually and together, have convinced me it's my duty to take over."

We gazed at him, frostbite forgotten. He closed his eyes, sighed, composed himself, and went on.

"I'm not sure how or when, but when the right moment presents itself I'll blank them out. For as long as I can, and if possible plant an opposite prerogative so when they wake up they'll go away and write us off as another fraud. Or at least harmless. Even if that succeeds, there's no telling how long it will hold, so we'll have to run anyway and use that time to cover our tracks. The only thing I can guarantee is a head start."

The pain in his eyes broke the pieces of my heart into smaller fragments. Blanche pressed against him. Dru hugged her while dropping his head and stubbing the ice with his sneaker.

"We've been siphoning money out of our accounts into cash for months and adding it to reserves we originally stockpiled. This will be distributed at odd times and places. We'll work out escape routes with you one on one, but plan your own in case we don't get a chance. Absolutely nothing is to go into writing and you're not to discuss your destination with anyone. The largest unit to travel together is a couple. Parents have to split their children. The psychics will do all the tracking, and when the coast is clear we'll arrange a rendezvous. Until then, concentrate on burying yourselves as deep as possible. So when my signal comes—you won't be able to misconstrue it—move as fast as you can and don't look back."

The chill in my heart completed the cold's permeation of my body. For the moment, nothing seemed more vital than cuddling before a fireplace with Kit, sipping hot cocoa and soup. Until attaining those comforts I could not think coherently. Thus I broke up the powwow by starting up the track cut into the amphitheater tiers.

John met me at the top, offering an arm for stability. I shook my head and stumbled onward, ignoring the surprise he triggered by meeting my eye. I wished someone had brought a snowmobile so I could travel as fast as my fear compelled me. It had just struck me that Kit would be the first and easiest person to abduct.

31
Breakout

Our group entered the house by different doors and dispersed to our quarters. My heart clogged my throat when I found Kit absent, then settled back into my chest when I found his note: "Stay here, I'm looking for you."

I waited in the shower. He returned while I was rinsing my hair; the only warning came when the curtain rings rattled, then an urgent man embraced me inside the spray. My squeak relaxed into hums then moans then gasps until the hot water ran out. Then, in a confusion of towels and bath mats, we finished on the floor.

We lay there until discomfort invaded. I untangled my limbs from his and planted a kiss on his cheek, murmuring, "I look forward to running away with you."

Kit lifted his head. "So Dru's gonna do something?"

"Yep." I recounted the meeting as we dried and dressed.

Kit scowled. "That explains all the door slams and whispers after Clayton and Lorene came back. Jeez, I hope it doesn't blow apart for a couple more days—I want to get this last screw out of me and have a chance to plan!"

"They need time, too," I hoped aloud. "But you're helpless tomorrow if they decide to take you as hostage or something."

"Maybe," Kit said, his face in its iciest hawk mask. I wondered how many people he could take down if he tried.

A moment later he added, "But it'll make things worse if I refuse to go."

"Then I'll go with you."

Kit shook his head. "Even if you sweet-talk them into it, there's only four places in the chopper and there's always two bodyguards plus the pilot and me."

I rose and crossed to my jewelry box. From amid a jumble of necklaces I pulled out two car keys and dropped one into his hand.

"This is to my Jetta. It was in the shop when I got stuck here last summer. Colin moved it to the farm where he rides to stop racking up storage fees at the shop, and not clog up his own driveway, since there's only one garage and fussy neighbors, plus Raoul skulking around at the time."

"Where's the farm?"

"Across the line in New York." I gave him directions. "I'm sure the car is snowbound with flat tires and bad gas and a dead battery. But it's still registered. If you ever need wheels, it's something no one would think of for a while. Especially if I'm somewhere else."

Kit pocketed the key. "Thanks. I'll take the Tiger's plate tomorrow, just in case."

I winced at the memory of my beautiful roadster now charred black except for the rear quarter, tail pipe, and license plate, all perfect. "I think you need two plates for a Massachusetts registration."

"For this, I only need one and a valid sticker," Kit said with a wink.

I looked at him askance. "Dare I ask how many plate swaps and hot-wires you've got under your belt?"

"Ask all you want, but don't expect an answer." He grinned.

"Let me put it this way: You ever get caught?"

"Nope."

"Then let's hope they don't search you tomorrow before you leave."

He shrugged. "I doubt they'll expect me to try anything if I'm empty-handed. My parka's got one of those back pockets for field notebooks. I'm zipping the plate into that, it won't bulge."

"Well, there's a small blessing: Private chopper pickup, you don't have to go through an airport metal detector!"

We smiled, then I put the other Jetta key in my purse while Kit ruminated. "As long as we're doing just-in-case," he said when I looked up, "do you remember your VIN?"

"For the Jetta or the Tiger?"

"Tiger."

"Of course." Did any owner of a rare car not know its vehicle identification number?

Kit nodded. "Where it's marked on the car got melted down in the fire. So if you destroy your paper records too, then no one but us will know that number. If we get separated, leave a message with the Tiger Club. I know the president. Your VIN will be our code."

"Oh! Okay. So . . . where shall we go, or meet?"

"I dunno. Let's not talk about it here." He glanced into the room corners. "How about the shop—Mark left me a pump motor I need to fix today."

We bundled up and walked in hand down the sanded driveway toward the gatehouse. Kit still limped but ignored any pain.

"So what happened in the circle?" he opened once we cleared the mansion.

"Dave—"

"No, I mean you. I felt it. Before the Dave thing."

I balked before saying, "It was mostly a fuzzy jumble, but something . . . opened. I might be starting to get some power back."

Kit halted and dropped my hand. "Damn it, Mad, are you ever gonna be straight with me?"

I opened my mouth but he spoke first. "You're hedging again. If you can't trust me by now, then I can't trust you. I can put up with it here, but if we live outside then we need to trust each other all the way."

"I trust you with my life!"

"I'd be a dead man if I trusted you with mine!"

My face went hot. Kit, having uncorked, let the rest gush out. "Hell, I'd rely on Buck before I'd rely on you! He's either in your face or doesn't say anything. Either way, there's something real. But you always weasel, and hedge, and mislead, and have secret conversations. I'm sure you've got escape plans of your own that have nothing to do with me!"

I stopped and faced him. "You're right. I've got half a dozen scenarios. It's called 'survival instinct.' If you try to say you don't have it, I'll spit in your face!"

"Of course I have it, that's why I'm worried. You lie, Madeline."

"So do you, Kit!"

"Oh yeah? When?"

"Lying, hiding, they're the same thing. You've told me nothing about your history, which I doubt is lily white."

He hooked his thumbs in his pockets and cast a hip. "I guess I thought your soul-vision was thorough. My version of it told me enough about you that I didn't need to grill you!"

Kit sighed and went from clenched to slack. "Why can't you just tell me things straight? You panicked in the circle then ran away from me. I expect better from someone I've been sleeping with for six months! But you don't feel that sex and honesty go together. That combination is what makes it love, not fucking."

My eyes stung. "If I say 'I love you' will you believe me?"

"I don't know. That's the point." He limped away.

I followed. "The circle thing wasn't anything bad or secret. It just sounds stupid, and I don't trust it myself, so I didn't want to say."

Kit waited, eyes ahead as we scuffed down the drive.

"I heard a voice. It wasn't Dru's, or anyone I recognize. It told me my work here isn't done yet. Without giving me a clue what that work's supposed to be!"

"Hmmph."

We walked a few steps in thought. Then I offered, "Dru once called me a catalyst."

"What's left to catalyze?" Kit's voice dripped acid.

"I don't want to know! A breakout, I guess. At least we've catalyzed him into accepting other ideas. But I worry about what he might do. And talk about trust—relying on him, Blanche, and Allanna to track everyone, that's pure pie in the sky!"

"Then your job is probably to catalyze a resolution."

"Don't ask me how!"

"Why don't you sleep with Dave, that ought to do it."

"What!"

Kit laughed harshly. "You think sex has nothing to do with this?"

"I—"

"Look." He stopped and took up both my hands, hard. "I'm not the only one who doesn't trust you, but my reasons are personal. Most people don't because of your looks. Then add in all your talents and privileges—luck like that is so rare, it's considered an achievement. Or a reward. Or a sin. Or a crime."

"That's—"

"You know and I know you didn't choose your body. But other people believe we're involved in that choice. And people like Dave who are slaves to lust think anyone gorgeous has the same lusts. He hides his sex greed under power plays so assumes you do the same. I'm sure if you were ugly—if any of you psychics were ugly nobodies—we wouldn't have these problems."

He paused to think, releasing my hands. "But Dave knows you're a sleeper, and you influence Dru. Most everyone believes you screw him, too. So they're just waiting for you to pull something. And if you get out, the Feds'll go after you as much as him."

"Dear god."

"Even if you don't consciously use your body as a weapon, it's hard for anyone looking at you to believe that."

"But what about Blanche? She's the real power behind the throne but nobody's paranoid about her!"

We resumed walking. "That's because she hides in Dru's shadow, and pulls off that innocent act. But don't forget—Raoul went for her and tried to shut down you and Dru."

"Jeezus. I keep wondering how many more like him are out there."

Kit shrugged. "Not many, I think. But that's what this is all about—sex, and psychics coming out of the closet. At this point all Dru's trying to do is prevent witch hunts. If you blow him off and get out too early, Mad, you'll have to worry about getting burned at the stake."

"And if we went with his original plan, then we'd have to worry about collective burning at the stake to assure the public all witches have been destroyed and the world is safe again for nuclear war!"

My voice broke but tears didn't follow. By then we had reached the gatehouse yard so had to stop talking. Once inside the garage, Kit moved to his workbench to tinker with the pump motor, while I lifted the tarp off the back end of the Tiger. It still smelled of burned oil and metal. Kit handed me a wrench as he passed so I popped off the license plate. Kit tucked it inside his jacket. Then he gave me spare keys to all his running vehicles, finished his task, and rounded up a snowmobile. We puttered back to the house on it, dropped off Mark's motor, then zoomed around the grounds for a while just for fun.

Throughout dinner, which most people took to their rooms and the remainder ate in pairs at separate tables, I regarded my extended family with blinders removed. What did they truly think about me? If I could command psychic power, would I probe their minds to find out? I had felt no moral qualms when insight had come in flashes, unbidden. But what Kit had said . . . was there anyone who didn't assume I was a conniving slut? Did having multiple lovers make me one? Or did soul-connecting change the rules?

We retired early but stayed up late, scheming. Kit fell asleep before I did, secure in his sexuality if not about my love. How could I tell him I loved him, wanted him, needed him, so that he would believe me? What assurance did he require? He had once wanted a gold ring, but now we both knew that wouldn't do it. I exhausted myself into sleep trying to think of the right words or gesture.

In the morning, he underplayed our goodbyes while his escort waited. Restraining myself from clinging to him and keening nearly ruptured my seams. I played my part like a good girl: sleepy, affectionate, and unworried. As they flew away, I retreated to the dining hall, filling my plate from the buffet and joining my sister at her table by the terrace window.

Blanche sat alone. As Dru often slept late, his absence meant nothing, although the Feds nursing coffees and the paper at a corner table might have other ideas. They didn't look at us, and we didn't look at them, but everyone courted headaches from peripheral spying. Residents chatted too brightly of New Atlantis concerns and the fickle Vermont weather. Today offered watery sunlight through high clouds presaging snow. The wind had turned and temperature hovered near freezing. In a few weeks we would find crocuses poking through melting snow, with flocks of robins following. For now we had a good day for a trail ride. I suggested that activity to Blanche.

"Sounds divine. I've got cabin fever." She looked at me significantly.

"In that case, shall we meet in your room or mine?"

We opted for mine, which lay on a lower level. Blanche and Dru, since losing their carriage house, had transferred to the converted attic rooms, which they split with Troy's family. Despite being closer neighbors, my twin and I saw even less of each other. We relied on empathy to provide comfort at a distance, while she hibernated with Dru and I kept an equally low profile. This day, twinged by a fear I could no longer call premonition, I grasped my chance to see and confide in her. For all I knew, it would be our last chance.

"Don't make it worse," she muttered sideways as we approached the door guard to smile and announce our destination.

"Looks like they're taking us seriously," I remarked after passing through and walking out of range. The Watchers had not stationed themselves in doorways before, only at compound exits.

"Ten to one we get tailed," Blanche replied.

We complicated our route by taking the escarpment trail to the valley. Yesterday's ice had softened to collapse beneath our weight, allowing slow but sure footing. We didn't talk until reaching the bottom, needing our breath and wits for trail negotiation. I marveled at the memory of myself careening down the steep zigzag in the predawn after Halloween.

Too little, too late—I couldn't help remembering. Though I had traversed this route many times since, that night's horror and heartbreak still haunted every step.

Blanche, for once, was not following my thoughts. "I'm going to miss it," she said, scanning the hill-bordered valley.

I looked at the face so like my own, even more so with a hat concealing her hair. "Me too, though I can't fully believe we're leaving."

"We might not get out if they step things up any further."

"What, exactly, does Dru plan to do to them?"

She took several strides along the road before replying. "Probably put them to sleep."

"You mean . . . knock them out for a day to wake up in an empty, old house wondering why they're there?"

"Something like that. But more like six hours—I doubt he can handle a day, even with me and Allanna boosting him. That's why he wants to do it real early some morning, catching them already asleep then prolonging it."

"Why not tie them up while you're at it?"

"Maybe we will, though that could get nasty. What if nobody finds them for a week?"

"Call Channel 16 on your way out."

We entered range of the barn so suspended conversation. The barn was actually a prefab shed inside a paddock to protect the feed and equipment we had salvaged. Several of the Morabs loitered within grabbing range, snuffling the tramped snow or dozing. All wore their fuzzy winter coats, requiring a good grooming plus a slow warm up and cool down for each ride.

We selected our favorites, curried and brushed them clean, slipped on bridles, then mounted bareback. The animals' bodies offered greater warmth and comfort than cold-stiffened saddles, and our winter clothes padded us against their spines.

A head count showed John Powers' pinto and Allanna's buckskin already out. Nova watched us from his paddock across the road. He trotted along the rail, mud-smudged but still magnificent.

I averted my eyes from the stable ruins as we passed, aware that human and animal parts still lay among them. The flowers I had strewn there were now crystallized shreds. Here in the silent whiteness tinged with violet and gray, I found it hard to believe a black night had been shattered by screams and orange. I longed for spring to cover the remains with yellow and green.

Once out of hearing range in all directions, and alone save for someone on a snowmobile across the plain, Blanche resumed talking.

"At any rate, that's what he's going to try. Not sure yet if, after getting out, we'll dive for cover or go public. No matter what, it's a cage for the rest of our lives."

"Are you sure you'll be able to trace and contact me? What if Dru burns out?"

"He won't. Don't worry, we'll know where you are. Wouldn't do it if there was doubt."

She looked away from the trail to smile at me. My heart twanged. I had gone through so much to join lives with her; now we had to separate again. Back to life with a throbbing phantom limb.

"How long before we can reunite?"

"Depends on the aftermath. But we figure five, maybe ten years."

"Yikes! When you think what happened in five months, I can't imagine five years!"

"But when you get your power back, we can stay in touch with no problem. Maybe even sneak visits."

I sighed. "I wish I had your faith. The power teases me but I can't call it up and practice until I'm somewhere absolutely safe. No telling when that will be! And whether I have it at all when I'm no longer living on a power point and being augmented by you and Dru."

"There are many power points across the planet. Head for one if you think it will help."

"Leaving behind a fleet of experts in the paranormal who know where all those points are? I don't think so!"

She shrugged. "Well, Dru's and my power aren't dependent on a physical source any more. And I'm sure yours isn't—you've just shut it out."

"For good reason!"

"It's just a faith issue, Mad. You don't want to believe what you know, and you're afraid to believe your dreams can come true. I can't help you with that. But I hope you'll believe in me enough to know I can find you when we're apart."

My eyes stung. "I don't have much choice, do I?"

She didn't reply.

After riding in silence for a few minutes, I asked, "If you and Dru are so on top of things, why can't you find Jake and Buck?"

"We know where Jake is—we're just not telling. But neither of us can find Buck because we're not linked to him, and he's probably so traumatized that he's shut down worse than you."

"Or dead." There, I said it.

She darted a glance at me. "I doubt that, but it's possible. You'll be free to look for him once you're out."

She didn't ask, What will you do if you find him? I couldn't answer that.

"What worries me more," I said, "is the message I got during the power circle."

She turned to me. I described the psychic command, followed by the sense of purpose attached to my stubbornness. "It's almost as if . . . something . . . doesn't want me to believe. But like before, I can't tell if the voice came from my subconscious or from outside myself. Or even from someone in the group."

"I felt you experience something but couldn't tell what. No words, though."

"It's a first for me, too, except for when Dru tunes in. Which he did shortly after. But the voice, the essence, wasn't the same."

"Hmm." Blanche's eyes sparked in mischief. "You get direct messages from the afterlife and you still don't believe?"

"Arrgggghh! Why do messages have to come from the afterlife? Can't there be other planes and other entities in present tense, without there being a place we go after death? Psychic power doesn't prove reincarnation."

"Makes it more likely, though. And at this point, I need the afterlife to look forward to!"

I glanced over and saw her face unmasked, revealing agony and exhaustion. The heart-twang I had felt earlier returned with pain. Blanche played the heroic queen so well that I sometimes forgot that her beauty, gaiety, fortitude, and loyalty took effort. Any flagging of her strength inspired mine.

As I groped for appropriate words, the horses churned through the snow and jingled their bits, rattled their nostrils. Another pain seared me as I realized that these, too, would have to be abandoned—unless we pressed our heels to their flanks and headed for the nearest wall. If I had brought wire cutters, a pack, and a gun, a breakout attempt might be worth it. As it was, we could merely appreciate equine nobility and the damp promise of snow in the air.

To revive us both, I nudged Riyadh into a jog, which Suliemann followed. We crunched across the valley to the river, now a rimed trickle, then hopped across it and cantered toward the uphill trail. There we slowed to follow Dru's and my boot tracks from two days earlier. These had been overmarked by other feet and hooves. A fresh spread of droppings indicated the pinto's or buckskin's passage. Behind us, maintaining an even distance, the snowmobile droned like a lazy beetle.

Halfway up the incline we turned off the promontory trail to move deeper into woodland. This led us to the reservoir bordered on one side by pines and the other by a snowfield edged with birches. New Atlantis's favorite picnic spot was presently unoccupied. Even the snowmobile had gone quiet, perhaps bogged down on the steep trail. As we traversed the meadow, another mechanical noise rose to replace it: whup-whup-whup-whup—the unmistakable beat of a helicopter. Blanche and I reined in upon recognizing the sound.

We panned the sky until a white-and-red helicopter swept into sight above the trees.

"Kit back already?"

I shook my head. "Wrong chopper. Wrong direction."

When Blanche didn't respond, I pulled my gaze from the clouds to check her. Caught the glint in her eye a half-second before she flung up both arms and waved.

"Blanche! What are you doing!" I grabbed her wrist and yanked it down. Our horses skittered apart, forcing me to let go.

She turned vivid eyes at me. "Mad—this is it—a perfect chance!"

She waved again. I shrieked upon grasping her intent. "But we can't leave now! Kit's at the doctor's! And Dru will croak if we disappear!"

"No he won't—it'll make everything easier." She kicked Suliemann forward. The helicopter swung around and hovered. Underneath its drumming I heard the snowmobile wind up behind the trees. Both noises pressed closer, grew louder and more urgent, quaking the atmosphere. I released Riyadh after Suliemann crying, "No Blanche, don't!" at her back.

She grinned over her shoulder and shouted, "Not you, Mad—just me."

The chopper descended, showing TV 16's logo on its door. Suliemann stretched into a gallop. The snowmobile broke into the field behind.

Riyadh caught up as Suliemann shied from the rotor whirlwind. Blanche jumped off and ran, ducked over. I saw three faces and a vidicam jostling in the cabin as its door slid open.

"Blanche! Please! Don't!" I screamed, jerking my horse back and forth. Though my heart raced after her, my body refused to follow. I could almost hear the shredding as my spirit was ripped in two. My chance to act was killed by the snowmobile charging onto the scene, nearly mowing down Suliemann just as the chopper lifted off with Blanche's leg dangling out the door.

The Fed sprang off his machine, unbundled a pistol, and shot at the helicopter. It continued ascending without a wobble. Through a blur of tears I saw Blanche waving frantically before the helicopter pivoted and departed, ever upward. After its thunder faded I still sat there, staring upward in shock.

32
Whiteout

The agent, red-faced and panting, waited until I looked at him. I recognized him as the young one, name forgotten, usually assigned to outdoor surveillance.

"Nice work," he said across the stillness.

"We didn't plan it," I replied in an equally cold tone.

"I can tell. But I doubt that anyone else will believe it."

I nodded and gathered the reins, feeling my face drag into a frown. A hollowness inside precluded any more tears. Suliemann, back by the birches, gave me something to aim for. He watched my approach with back-and-forth flicking ear.

The baby agent pulled out a radio and reported his failure. By the time I caught Suliemann and started leading him back to the stable, the snowmobile had puttered up to our heels.

"Sorry, but I'm going to have to escort you."

"Go fuck yourself," I said without fire.

"Look, if you both get away my job is history."

"You really expect me to care about your job?"

"No, but we're both in deep shit now and it might be easier if we cooperate."

I looked down at the black-suited youth cruising alongside me. His bullet-shaped machine provoked both horses into a sideways jig. "In that case, either ditch the sled and take this horse or go back to your masters. Stairways only come down from the sky for Blanche."

Glowering at me, the Fed gunned his engine. Riyadh half reared and whinnied while Suliemann plunged. I lost the lead rein so let the horse run back to the stable. Between the Fed activity and the riderless horse, everyone would know something had gone afoul.

Which left me a little time to regain my balance. I had so many problems now I didn't know which one to tackle first.

The crucial question was how much time remained before everything else went haywire. Probably before Kit came back—assuming they let him—in which case I should have run for the chopper.

The decision of whom to inform first was settled for me. Colin was waiting at the stable astride a snowmobile. As soon as Riyadh skidded down the trail onto the level plain, Colin buzzed across it to meet us. "Where's Blanche?" he yelled upon entering range.

I waited until we drew together before answering. "TV 16 caught us up by the reservoir. Blanche got the bright idea to jump ship."

"That's what they said but I couldn't believe it."

"Me neither. But she said, 'It'll make everything easier.' For her, I suppose."

Colin cursed and looked across the plain at nothing. His dark hair stood out against the snowy backdrop, though his complexion nearly matched it. In that moment I saw Blanche in his face—the features we all shared that were normally obscured by our mannerisms. A fresh pain stabbed my innards.

"I don't know." Colin turned back to me. "Maybe it will be easier. At least she's out. Maybe she'll expose this fiasco, hoping public outcry will make these goons let up on us. It's hard to whip up that kind of pressure from inside."

"Does Dru know yet?"

"He probably knew before she did it. But yeah, Mark paged him when the Fed called in, and he didn't sound too rattled over the intercom. Maybe they planned it."

"Don't see how they could have, though Dru did say we won't be able to misconstrue his signal. Blanche may have perceived the chopper as her signal—or, if she was linked with him when it happened, he might have told her to go ahead. I'm sure they've got a meet arranged."

"Tricky for the rest of us, unless the Feds give up and open the gate."

We exchanged glances. Then I cursed and rode on to the stable. Colin followed and gave me a lift back to the house. We left the horses with John and Julia, who demanded explanation: Julia loudly and John with one of his stares. We related the facts and moved on.

During the drive between buildings, Colin and I hashed over possibilities. We had only a few clear minutes, even puttering over the long route. I regretted not taking the time to conspire when I'd had it, to fill in blanks and explore options with my brother. Having lost my twin so abruptly, I couldn't bear losing my other sibling—or Kit, or anyone. Colin agreed that enduring whatever followed beat splitting up.

A decision we rued upon returning to the mansion. As I dismounted the snowmobile, Dave stepped outside and said, "Come with me please, Miss LaRue."

I planted my feet. "Where."

"The boss wants to see you in the parlor. You too, Mister LaRue."

Colin and I exchanged glances and conceded. But when Dave took my elbow to escort me, I yanked my arm free.

He rapped the parlor door before entering. Inside we found Dru, Adam, Troy, and Mark under interrogation. Mark broke off his bluster and whipped around, thrusting a forefinger at me. "Ask her! And yank her hair while you're at it—for all we know, they pulled a switch!"

I pressed a hand to my hair. "This is not a wig. And Blanche's move was not premeditated. But it was desperate, and we've got no one to thank but you."

I flung the last at Dave, the boss, and Lorene. They glared back, Dave with a menace that curled my toes. The others looked back and forth between us.

Colin stepped up beside me and counterattacked. "Regardless why she left, you can bet she's already talking, and lots of people will be happy to listen. You guys have overstepped your limits, and that's going to end right now. I'm calling in a new legal team—and you can follow every word on the extension—to tell them exactly what's been going on here. Between that and TV news, you'll have trouble explaining the difference between protecting and imprisoning."

He spun on his heel and left. Lorene shot after him. We heard a scuffle in the hall as the door closed.

Dru said to the Feds, "I suggest you start packing and leave quietly before dinner. Otherwise we'll take more drastic measures to help you along."

He spoke from a casual slouch in an armchair, his eyes half-lidded and voice indifferent. No one believed his tone; all stood or sat for a moment waiting for someone to respond.

Dave stood so rigid he almost shook and his face turned hypertension red while we watched.

"It doesn't work that way, Montclair. You stopped being master of this little universe the minute you revealed your true colors. We own you now, and are extending great courtesy in allowing you to remain here. All you've done is given us reason to cut back on the courtesy."

Dru shook his head. "You're the threat to national security, Dave, but it's clear you can't see that. Just be aware that I'm a man of peace so only fight in self-defense. You corner me, you'll find a Ninja wildcat."

In the silence that followed, we held our breath, braced for a showdown. How could he resist flexing his mental muscle, and how could Dave—clearly ready to burst a blood vessel—not assert his authority? If the power had been within me, I would have upended the parlor. However, both men just glared and withheld their weapons.

I almost screamed as minutes ticked by and nothing changed. No one could act without violence or reinforcements. We could only wait and see what Blanche triggered and act accordingly. Or else somehow take the other party by surprise.

Both sides retreated to strategize in private. Dru remained in the parlor with Adam, Troy, and Mark, then joined me, Colin, and Cassandra later in my suite.

He entered like a ghost and knelt on the floor in front of my armchair. My face dripped tears but my weeping had stopped.

Placing his hands on my knees, Dru looked long and deep into my eyes to convey his anguish. I knew how ardently he wished I could "hear" him, just as he knew how it hurt that I could not.

Colin jumped to his feet and resumed pacing. "Damn, I wish she didn't do it. C'mon, Dru—you know more than you're telling. What's she going to do, and how long do you think we can hold off these goons?"

Dru stood and faced him. "I really don't know." His voice still held that spooky calm. "She shut me off when she saw her opportunity. She's planning something but I don't know what or where. I trust it will help not hurt us. If she acts within twenty-four hours, we'll probably be able to stay."

"But what if they act first?" asked Cassandra, looking drawn.

Dru shrugged. "Then we react as necessary. Stay on alert to move at a moment's notice."

I bit my lips to keep my mouth shut. And crossed my fingers against anything happening before day's end. Kit and I had not settled on a meet point before he fell asleep last night.

Nobody mentioned him before they departed. I paced the suite, stopping at intervals to look out the windows. Clouds had closed in and started snowing. Part of me hoped for a two-foot dump, to slow things down for a while; another part wanted it to hold off a few more hours, to let Kit get home.

A third part, drained from stress, demanded I catch up on lost sleep. That, at least, would pass the time easier.

I lay down. I must have fallen right to sleep, for I came out of a deep, heavy void to a hyper-realistic dream.

In the dream, I slouched upright, with head hanging forward. My neck ached. I was vibrating. Hot air parched my nostrils and a familiar slap-scrape noise beat out the seconds. I opened one eye a crack, to behold diffuse amber light within overall darkness. Muffled rumbling suggested engines and car tires. Metal hovered near my front and right sides.

I opened the other eye and lifted my chin, then jerked as if electroshocked. Dear god, I was in a car in a blizzard in the middle of the night!

"What!"

I whipped around and was half garroted by a seat belt. Too real for a dream. I could remember nothing, imagine nothing, to account for this change.

The driver rolled an eye at me but otherwise didn't react. I shouldn't have been surprised to see John Powers, bundled up in a watch cap and fur-collared bomber jacket.

His jaw worked chewing gum as if it too were leather. He leaned his forearms against the wheel, letting it support him as we ground onward, following blurred red dots through a whiteout. Our vehicle's lights cut yellow cones through the pelting snow while the wipers streaked arcs across the windshield. The seat and cargo bay behind us were jammed with gear.

"This better be a dream," I said, not knowing whom I expected to answer. Though Kit had said John talked, I had never witnessed the act myself. Terrific: marooned in an inverse hell with no way to discover how I had gotten here. I slid a hand under the jacket and sweater I didn't remember donning and pinched myself hard. It hurt. I was awake.

I went cold with sweat. Syllables burst from my lips but I couldn't form them into words. My hands and feet groped for anything familiar and turned up my handbag. Whew! At least this necessity had come along! I must have blacked out for some reason but had not lost my mind. The bag contained articles I hadn't put there, such as a wallet-sized photo album, a pack of cigarettes, and a fat roll of fifties bound by rubber band.

Okay, someone had packed for me. This must be a kidnapping. Since I felt no head pain or lingering nausea, I had not been taken by force. That left an externally imposed blank-out, like Dru intended for the Feds. Had he tried it after all, and caught me too while sleeping? Or missed them and just conked out the psychics? Or was this personal and only I had been snatched?

No less than an afternoon and evening had passed since my last consciousness. The vehicle—Kit's ancient Land Rover—had empty dashboard sockets where radio, tape/CD, and clock should be. I wore no watch and could not see John's wrist. From the inches of snow on top of plowing, I deduced we were still in the same calendar day. Valentine's Day. Darkness made it after five p.m. White-spattered highway signs put us on a numbered byway in New Hampshire. A long way northeast of New Atlantis at thirty-five miles per hour!

"Jeezuscrist!" I turned to my abductor. "If you don't stop, I'm jumping out."

I unsnapped my seat belt. John scowled and shook his head but kept driving. I unlatched the door after an effort, only to have wet coldness suck in and splatter me. What would I do, assuming I survived the jump, with no supplies in the middle of nowhere?

I latched the door and tried another tactic. "Will you please stop somewhere and tell me what's happened, where we're going? If you treat me like a person instead of baggage, I'll be more amenable to coming along."

He glanced at me; back at the road; corrected the wheel; looked at me a little longer. I turned away to stare at his reflection in the window. When he stopped regarding me and concentrated forward again, I presumed we would proceed until the next way station and attempt to make a deal.

This gave me time to pull my wits together. John spoiled that chance by saying, "We can talk while we go."

I swiveled to look at him. A character had just turned into a human being.

"Then start talking, buddy. You owe me a big explanation!" And if I don't like it, I vowed silently, you forfeit the wheel.

33
The Wooden Indian

"Dru put you out," John stated.

"So I figured. But just me, or the Feds too?"

"He didn't wait 'til night. He couldn't. They were gonna move on us. Allanna helped him. It was harder than they expected."

His voice rasped after those simple sentences. He gestured at a teardrop backpack in my footwell. "Thermos."

I rummaged for it and poured him a cup of water. He drank three before continuing. "They knocked out all the Feds and scientists, you and Colin. Dru couldn't let you stay. I packed best I could and went out the back way. Only nonpsychic volunteers left behind."

"But there aren't enough cars for everybody."

A corner of his mouth twitched. "Some took the Feds' cars. Some pooled to stations."

"What about the people at the gate?"

"Don't know. Most all of us went out the back, only the Fed cars out the front. Tinted windows. And the blizzard sent most of the nutcases home."

"So what happened to Kit?"

John swallowed and kept his gaze forward. "He's already taken care of."

My voice sharpened. "What do you mean?"

"I mean, we got people inside the doc's office to give his guards some funny coffee."

I clutched his arm. "Where is he? I've got to contact him!"

John shook his head. “Sorry, we only arranged to get him out. Where he goes from there, only he knows. Or you.”

I let rip a string of obscenities and kicked the firewall. “All right, then where are we going?”

“We got a safe house set up.”

“Are you sure? They must have raised an alarm by now, the borders and airports—”

John shook his head again. “All bound and gagged until morning. Their memories blanked. It’ll take a while. And no one will spot us in this snow.”

Good point. I couldn’t make out detail of anything we passed. “Okay, then what?”

“We hide. If necessary, dump the car. Then we wait.”

I flopped back, needing to process the new info before resuming questions. So many unanswered, too many variables. Plus the small matter of being manipulated once more against my will.

A cold burn started in my stomach and spread until my head pounded. We droned on through the storm, which abated as we moved north. Perfect skiing powder filled our tracks. We were carrying skis, I discovered when we exited for food and restrooms. Two pairs and poles on a roof rack, adding verisimilitude to our story. According to John, we were sweethearts on a Valentine’s weekend trip to the Maine ski resorts. Without any east-west highways across northern New England, it made sense to be on secondary roads, our “plans” disrupted by foul weather. Conveniently, Kit’s Land Rover had four-wheel drive.

Before I got out of it, John checked me by the arm and said, “Please, Madeline—give it twenty-four hours.”

I stared him down then signaled acceptance by walking into the store.

We took our food to-go, which avoided drawing curiosity in the sparsely peopled outpost, and minimized my shell shock from facing the real world. Since landing at New Atlantis, I had left the compound only twice and both times had been preoccupied. Thus it had been six months—packed with surreal misadventures—since I had seen snack foods, neon signs, public bathrooms, parking lots, and strangers of all types.

Of course, I had seen all and more on television but without the smells and textures. Colors, too, different from what I remembered as real. I felt as though I had crash landed on another planet. Having reigned large in an enclosed world of beauty and talent, I now felt tiny and vulnerable in a huge world of ugliness and ignorance. Five minutes was all I could take.

We passed through unrecognized, aided by winter clothing. The store had no TV or radio, so we remained unaware of news left behind us. For now, making distance mattered more.

I sat in a mental whiteout as the miles passed. The snow stopped for a while, allowing speed-limit travel on plowed surface. I was surprised by the amount of traffic for the middle of a winter night.

More surprised by the being who chauffeured me through it. I turned to him and said, "You amaze me."

He glanced over with cocked eyebrow. I continued, "How many secret personalities you got hiding in that dumb Indian shell?" *Talk about weasels!* I sent to Kit.

John flashed a grin. It transformed his looks from sourpuss to enchanter, much like Kit. "As many as I need."

"Why have you faked it all this time?"

He hesitated before answering. "It was necessary."

"Pah! That should be the New Atlantis theme song. Necessary for what?"

"Your protection."

"From what"

"The wrong powers."

"Whereas I'm to trust that you're the right Powers. If that's your real surname. Or did your family adopt it for the symbolism?"

"It's real. Just a coincidence."

"Or karma."

He darted a glance at me. I smirked and winked. He looked back through the windshield with his jaw cords tensing and loosening.

My impatience mounted. "So when did you and Jake stop talking?"

He shrugged. "Around college."

"Then how did you get through classes?"

"Took all lecture or field courses. Read textbooks, passed tests, answered direct questions when required."

"What was your major? Where did you go? Did you graduate?"

"Anthropology. UVM. We did two years."

University of Vermont. In Burlington, Vermont's only true city. If he had in fact lived a normal life until New Atlantis, he must know people, understand how the world worked—two things I would not have expected of him just hours ago. At this rate, it would take days to extract his story. When he clammed up again to navigate a slippery hill, I swallowed my questions and clutched the door.

When the road leveled again, I announced, "After we get where we're going, you are to take no more actions that include me without my consent."

John snapped a glare at me. His black braid hung into his collar and a sheaf of bangs fell across one eye, bringing back the familiar Indian image. My silent, ubiquitous, devoted protector. However, the tension in his posture signaled threat.

"I won't force you to do anything," he said, slackening.

"But you have kidnapped me, which is a capital crime."

As he opened his mouth to rebut, I raised a hand and overrode him. "I know—it's all for my well-being. And Dru's the one who did the actual dirty work. For some reason, everyone treats me like a Ming vase to be kept from invading barbarians. I understand now why Blanche jumped into that chopper!"

I crossed my arms and tucked into myself. When he failed to speak, I pressed on. "So I want to know where you got the idea that you're fated to be my guardian and why it gives you the right to control me. And I want to know what you've planned with Dru and Allanna. And I want to hear it from the beginning, starting now!"

A flush crept up John's neck to his hairline. "It's a long story."

"Something tells me we've got plenty of time to kill."

He sighed. After a moment, he unreeled. "We were always telepathic. Never very friendly with other kids. But raised as normal as you could be in Jersey. Troy was a rebel with a knack for music so went on the road right after school and hooked up with Dru. Jake and I went the more academic route. You know, cultural anthropology, like, Native Americans. And botany, like, medicinal plants. And animals and ecology, more interested in fieldwork than getting in trouble. So we coasted through middle-class normalness, using it as camouflage when we realized how different we really were."

Nothing weird there; most people played along so to cover their idiosyncrasies and passions. We called it civilization: the behaviors constructed to make a tolerable norm.

Generations of psychopaths had proven how useful a front normality could be. John and Jake had taken it to invisibility.

"We both got the call when we were sixteen. Out camping, on a clear night in the mountains, we saw the aurora borealis. Then, going to sleep, we had the same dream and woke up knowing what we had to do. And that was to prepare in all ways to save twin princesses from Evil. We didn't know who, when, or where, but it was to be our life's work."

I shuddered. Even after living through premonition becoming real, I still curdled inside to think some intelligence moved us like chess pieces. We could exercise free will by running in zigzags, but once a course had been designed we stayed within its limits.

The powers appeared to work on a large and leisurely scale, first twisting strands of people's lives together then weaving those threads into tapestries and baskets. Once it had been "decided" that New Atlantis would be a pivot point, all its principals then had to be drawn in and provided with support.

Blanche and Madeline, as catalysts and magnets and vessels, required fail-safe backup. Their intimates were too entangled in the main design to be relied upon; only guardians, woven into the background fabric, would do.

Thus John and Jake: both naturally psionic and capable of prodigious learning and skill yet of no distinguished talent. Their brother provided access to New Atlantis; their sister-in-law nurtured and directed them. By their own inclination, the twins were secretive, loyal, and determined. It took a single vision, at the peak of their youthful ardor, to steer them onto the desired course.

"We spent a couple years with Allanna's Iroquois relatives, then we came to live with her and Troy at New Atlantis. She helped us develop our psi. Except for with each other, we're empaths like Blanche, so can feel you but not connect directly like you and Dru can."

"Could," I corrected.

He ignored me. "We learned a bunch of paying or self-sufficient crafts, and body and mind control. We knew only that we had to be ready for anything, and be in a position where no one knew about us or knew where we were, or cared."

He stopped talking to turn off the main road. We passed a sign with a name I recognized. A town waaaaaaaay up there by the Canadian border, renowned for low temperatures.

"Then Blanche arrived," he continued, "and everything started. Up 'til then, New Atlantis had been a clumsy construction project on a big estate. Dru's charisma factor shot up and both the compound and the world seemed to revolve around him. Jake was so blown away by Blanche he started walking into things."

John chuckled. "He was sure she was what we'd been waiting for, but it didn't feel right that she and Dru were to be our charges. 'Cause he had everybody looking after him and she, by extension, had them caring for her."

And now, I mused, who was there to look after the golden prince and princess? Yet I had a career bodyguard.

"Finally we learned that Blanche had a twin. Who would eventually find her way to us. It was clear from the start you were going to need protecting. With power and beauty like yours, and your lovers unreliable—well, the times you would need them most would be the times they couldn't or wouldn't help you. So here we are."

I looked at him hard and long. "So why here, of all places?"

"Connections. Jake and I spent time working off payroll, helping a lot of people, that the Feds will never trace."

"So where's Jake?"

"You'll see him soon."

"Do you know where Buck is?"

"No. You're the only one who might, and it looks like you don't."

I shook my head. "But it's possible he's up this way—when he disappeared before, he managed fine in Canada. When I realized we were heading north, I thought, well . . . maybe you were in touch with Jake and he left to set up a hiding place for Buck, and . . . you know . . ."

"No, Jake's set up a hiding place for us. And did the legwork to set up a group escape. Dru's not stupid—he saw something like this happening."

As did Colin, who had liquidated many of our holdings during the Raoul phase, just in case. I could access cash with my phony credit card, currently hidden in a wallet pocket. Along with Kit's spare Land Rover key. I tamped down that thought lest John catch it, covering with the remark, "I hope everybody who's out has adequate resources."

"Enough to get started. But we all had to travel light. Not just for speed, but to make sure we had clean baggage."

"Clean?" At first I thought he meant "laundered." Then I realized: "You mean, they might've bugged our stuff?"

He nodded. "Tracers. That's why we've got Kit's car. Since he couldn't use it, and I knew it was clean . . . he'd prepped it hoping you'd get away together."

I swallowed a lump, managing to nod in response.

John gave me a sideways look that conveyed his advantage in knowing more about me than I would ever know about him. Being transparent was a liability I could do without! Blanche and Dru and Colin and Allanna had all seen through me and anticipated my behavior, which was why they tended to act counter to my desires. They all served the good of the many, while I could be counted on to serve my needs, first.

My need now was to scream and throw things but I contained it. A tantrum would only make things harder, even though I might feel better for an hour.

34
Northern Lights

We passed through a darkened hamlet. Signs flashing by in our headlights identified a hunting/fishing/camping zone, amid dense conifer stands broken by lakes and rivers.

John turned at a sign I couldn't read and thumped over a plowed bank into a passage that had been driven on, unplowed, with the ruts refrozen and snowed over. We slithered along it to a shuttered lodge that rambled down a slope toward a white opening. Sheds and cabins, silhouetted by moonlight, studded the shore and lurked in the woods.

In one cabin, a light shone and smoke spiraled from the chimney. A pickup truck jutted its rear around the porch. As we disembarked, a form appeared in the only unshuttered window. He wiped the glass and peered at us, then vanished to the side and reappeared at the door just as we reached it.

Out stepped Jake Powers with a beard. The brothers embraced. I felt tears prick my eyes but held still until the twins separated. They stepped aside to let me enter.

As I passed Jake, our eyes met and held for the first time since my arrival at New Atlantis. We both shivered, me from seeing the man Blanche had chosen for her last fling; he from seeing her so close yet so far away. Since I still had hair tucked under hat, my unadorned and shadowed face could have been Blanche's. For an instant I too saw her face, like a transient film across Jake's.

We each shook the image away as John and I stomped inside. We left our boots on a rubber mat inside the door beside Jake's boots and snowshoes. Not knowing what else to do, I slopped into an armchair beside a radiating woodstove. Jake put a kettle on a range in the corner and cleared his dishes from the lone table.

We sat in the main room of a two-room cabin. Despite the fire, the air was chilly, although tropical compared to outside. A ticking travel clock advised me it was earlier than I expected.

"You made the news tonight," Jake opened.

I sat up straight. "What did you see?"

"A whole thing about the revolt at New Atlantis. Half the members disappeared. Feds claim they were drugged and hog-tied. Our people claim peaceful protest against oppression. Back and forth accusations. Half pathetic, half amusing."

"Anything about Blanche?" Again, our eyes met.

His expression remained stolid. "Only that she was the first one out."

"So who's left?" John inquired.

Jake shrugged. "Didn't say. But Colin and Mark were spouting off."

"Colin's there?" John's voice went high in surprise. I weakened with relief.

John and Jake switched to telecommunication. Both lounged with splayed limbs and half-closed eyes, their lips tweaked up in the corners—the look common to stoned collegians. I found it irritating and insulting but withheld protest. Fatigue had rendered emotion powerless to move me. I fell asleep before their silent dialogue ended.

Morning brought sunlight bouncing off snow cover. Only our tracks marked the blanket for acres around. Squinting through the unshuttered window, I observed a vacation camp closed for the season. Jake said to my back, "The owner opens up in April."

His voice was a notch lower than John's, his face a mirror image.

"Does the owner know we're here?"

"Yes and no. We have permission to use the place off season."

John, entering from outside, added, "We used to hunt and trap these parts."

I nodded to John then addressed Jake. "How long will we be here?"

"Until Blanche and Dru join us."

His expression flickered. My attention sharpened. He amended, "At least, they're supposed to. Dru sent me here to maintain a basein case, well, all this happened. He can communicate with me but I can't send back. Same with Blanche, at least, when they're together. None of us realized they amplify each other. I hope he can still reach her, because I've lost both of them."

I groaned. John said, "She's probably still in New York and Dru went to get her first. You know she'd never drive this far in winter alone."

She'd never drive this far in summer, either, I didn't say. Or come to a place like this at all if she had another choice. Now I understood why she'd opted for TV 16's helicopter.

"So this was to be the rendezvous point?" I prompted. "Plenty of cabins for us all, for a few weeks of rest?"

Jake nodded and moved to the window beside me, gesturing with his chin at another cabin across the way. "That one's yours."

Deep footprints between buildings told me one of the twins had slept there last night. I had been carried, asleep, to a squeaky bed in the second room of this cabin while John or Jake slept on a bedroll before the fire. Both had been up before I awoke.

Jake stepped away to pour coffee. We sat.

"How did you get here?" I asked him across the table while John cooked breakfast.

"I had a pickup stashed outside the compound and drove it here, borrowed the plates off the camp owner's plow truck."

"But how did you get out of New Atlantis?"

He stirred sugar into his coffee while deciding whether to tell me. After a quick upglance at his twin, he looked down again. "You know that river across our floodplain?"

I nodded. Memory of jumping it on Suliemann during the Debacle flashed in my mind.

"It exits the compound through a culvert under a boundary fence. Dumps you on the outskirts of Cold River Corners. Nine miles by road, but only a mile or so as the crow flies. There's an auto junkyard behind the old mill."

I contemplated access by culvert while we tucked into breakfast. The bacon, thick and chewy, was the first animal flesh I had eaten since sharing steaks with Buck in The Glen. Lordamercy, that day seemed years ago now. For a moment I placed my fork down as longing cramped my innards—longing for Buck, for Kit, for Blanche and Colin, for my power, for the luxury, space, and privacrustcy of our home. The twins paused to look up under their brows at me. When I resumed lifting eggs and toast to my mouth, they resumed eating.

"So what do we do if Blanche and Dru don't show up?" I asked. "John, did you actually see him leave?"

He shook his head. "He made us all go first."

"Then for all we know he's still there. Jake, you say you lost contact with him. Did it ever dawn on you that the power he used might have killed him?"

They plunked down their forks and paled identically. Then Jake shook his head. "They would have said so on the news."

"Maybe not. They might not know. If Colin's there, he probably wouldn't release the information. We ought to call."

"No land line here, and no cell reception. Anyway, the lines into New Atlantis might not be secure."

"So how will you get the coast-is-clear signal if you can't communicate with Dru or Blanche?"

"We wait," John stated. "I saw Troy and Allanna leave. They were in on this plan. So they'll either show up or contact us."

I pushed away my plate. "Dru said that plans were supposed to be private. Limited to a couple. Now you're telling me at least six people including him were in on this one. And you wonder why I'm not co-operative? Just think, if you'd told me, we could have skipped the whole kidnapping thing."

The twins looked at each other. I didn't need to hear their reason. I was considered unreliable, and incapable of a low profile. The group was much more secure with me ignorant, and me and Kit apart. I, however, was more secure with knowledge, and me and Kit together. Again, the good of the many was more important than the one.

Yet hadn't Dru said that my oneness had been the key to our victory?

"Never mind." I flapped my hand and left the table before either twin could respond.

Hunkering down into the same chair I'd flopped in last night, I understood what the voice in the circle had meant. My undone work was to show that faith must be open-eyed, not blind; trust must be earned, not given. And Blanche was right about love should be a lion, not a lamb. Free will, which led to destiny, versus blind faith, which led to fate, was what kept the universe evolving. All of which gave me a resolve to Do Something, without offering a clue what to do.

I started with the television. Satellite dish gave a hundred channels worth of information.

An hour's worth of channel surfing brought violence, betrayal, economic calamity, church blather, environmental disaster, celebrity scandal, the weather, commercials, and local news but nothing about escaped psychic lunatics, Dru Montclair, or Blanche LaRue.

John and Jake watched over my shoulder for a while then went outside to do something manly and twinly. I ached for my own twin, and the life we had lost; pondered how to recover it, and whether that was even possible.

I watched the box all day, smoking that pack of cigarettes John had provided and pacing the cabin. My private cabin, Jake informed me, had no TV. He and John came and went with wood and food but otherwise left me to simmer. Indeed, I felt like a bubbling cauldron.

It seemed a perfect time to exercise my psychic talents. But, as before, I couldn't generate anything special on my own. Though the twins carried an energy I could sense, it gave me the jitters rather than the familiar gut tingle that signified power. I would have thought that two twins plus one twin might form one of those combinations Kit and I had talked about.

Yet . . .

Jake could read Blanche and Dru when they were together but lost both when they were apart. Or one of them was out of order. Did that combination support my theory? And would a little power circle with John and Jake boost any of our powers?

The evening news came on before I could experiment with that question. I forgot it when the lead story filled the screen.

"This is Rosalind Burke with an exclusive from WXYZ news, TV 16. It seems the trouble never stops at New Atlantis. After last Halloween's encounter with an alleged demon that all but destroyed the compound, superstar songwriter Dru Montclair invited scientists and government agents to investigate his paranormal claims. According to Dan Francis of the American Skeptics Society, Dru and his fiancée, Blanche LaRue, passed stringent psi tests with flying colors, offering proof of telepathy and telekinesis. Allegedly, their demon known as Raoul Lamont, formerly the band's publicist, could perform pyrokinesis as well, but test results have not been released on the evidence supposedly left behind. For the past four months, scientists from federal and private agencies have been on site, investigating. Now an inside report reveals they have been investigating a little too closely."

Cut to aerial view of a snowy field. Wobbly at first, in sync with blatting helicopter blades; then zooming tight to tiny horsemen, copper and silver bugs on a white carpet.

I scooted onto the floor to crouch before the screen, watching the front view of Blanche and me waving arms and soundlessly arguing, then Blanche belting Suliemann and racing toward the chopper. Her features swelled into focus—a mix of fear and thrill. The camera lost her for a moment as the chopper dropped to intercept.

The voiceover continued: "Intense pressure drove Blanche LaRue to abandon New Atlantis when our team presented the opportunity. TV 16's crew had no previous contact with anyone inside the compound—in fact, our efforts to get the story had been met with prepared statements if not outright rebuffs—and in this case, gunshots!—which strongly suggest a cover-up. People have a right to know about research results on something so important as supernatural power!"

The picture reeled and jerked as crew and Blanche made contact. Her weight added to the full ship forced the pilot to overcompensate for a few seconds, during which I glimpsed her flushed cheeks, frantic eyes, and gold hair tufting out from beneath the cap half blown off her head.

Voices competed with straining rotors in an unintelligible racket. The cameraman, unable to maneuver, turned his lens back out the window to me on Riyadh staring after them, shrinking, as the snowmobile cut a black line across the snowfield. Then the picture switched back to a scowling Rosalind Burke at her news desk.

"Acting on a tip from a New Atlantis gate watcher, TV 16 sent a team to New Atlantis last night after the blizzard. There we found evidence of a revolt behind the walls."

A square behind her left shoulder came alive, showing the gate's unicorn/pyramid emblem in a spotlight. The camera panned down to focus on the entire investigating team in parkas and blankets, trussed to the gate's iron bars. Tarpaulins separated them from snow drifts and the trodden driveway apron. Civilians hovered around them, taunting as a mob would harass a chained bear. Of the half-dozen Feds and scientists awake, Dave bellowed the loudest, while Clayton cowered away from the headlights and camera spots, and Lorene stared like an angry eagle. Behind me, I heard John laugh.

He and Jake had clomped inside and stopped to watch the spectacle. It changed again, jumping time, to a close-up of Colin's lead attorney yelling through the gate bars into a microphone that a mittened hand jammed into his face.

"—clearly violating my clients' rights by holding them against their will. The teams have been evicted for trespassing and breach of contract and—"

"Is it true that Dru has fled for his life?"

"—all the psychics off the compound?"

Reporters peppered him with questions, while others, in a sequence of fast profiles, invited comments from the investigators.

"—psychotic freaks—"

"—hypothermia—"

"—obviously, an overreaction to pressure, an understandable reaction to scrutiny—"

"—used their evil power to knock us out and—"

Jake muttered, "Nobody's untying them."

And how long the Feds remained bound, we did not learn.

The picture reverted to the news desk, which promised an update on later broadcasts, then returned to sex and violence and consumer waste.

The three of us sat or stood for a moment, absorbing. Then Jake chuckled and resumed course to the woodstove. John remained sober. "The question is how will the agencies react."

"You think they'll come after you?" Jake asked over his shoulder.

I rose from my crouch. "They might. Depends on whether they're embarrassed and get in trouble with their higher-ups, or embarrassed and given free rein to get even."

"If they really believe us a threat, we'll be running forever," John said.

"But if you really are a threat," Jake countered, "you can fight back."

"But if we do, then we prove them right, and we're dead."

"That's why Dru evicted them that way," John said. "They can't prove he knocked 'em out, but everyone can see they weren't hurt. And no one can get in now unless they take the place by force. Since we got lawyers in first and film of someone escaping, there ought to be enough coverage and public support to keep the Feds from doing anything drastic."

"But that might encourage them to go after the rest of us. They can keep that covert."

"Yeah, but they don't know for sure who got out beyond Blanche and Kit."

I closed my eyes, rolled my lips under my teeth, and slumped. John placed a hand on my shoulder. Jake rose to make dinner. I escaped both for a moment in the bathroom.

Kit's had time to get my car, I calculated. And to hole up with one of those racing buddies I don't know. There was so much about him I didn't know, like where he was born, how old he was, whether he'd had other women besides Julia. We had lived only in the present, too distracted by New Atlantis affairs to have a proper one of our own. How different the present would be if I had run away and married him!

No second chance if I didn't cope with the latest New Atlantis debacle. "You said Dru blanked the Feds' memories," I flung at the twins. "But they all looked aware to me!"

John shrugged. "So maybe he's not as powerful as we hoped. But he got them out, didn't he?" The dark eyes glinted.

I shot back, "At what cost?"

Neither twin answered. We all moved to different corners of the cabin. I parked in front of the TV until the next cycle of stories came around. Nothing new, since the New Atlanteans would not let reporters inside. And all affected agencies refused to comment. So the channels covering the story replayed footage of Blanche's escape and the tied-up investigators, then interviewed people randomly on streets around the world.

An assembly line worker commented, "It all sounds pretty stupid to me." A white-haired lady said, "I'd rather they spent my tax dollars chasing down criminals." A hairdresser with a thick accent remarked, "All they're trying to do is spread enlightenment. Why can't the government leave them alone?"

A popular psychic predicted that Dru would surface in Sedona, Arizona; another put her money on Stonehenge; another on the pyramids. An irate religionist said that everyone associated with New Atlantis should burn in hell. Brian, our former doctor, declared, "They did the right thing." One of the gate groupies expressed faith that a new Atlantis would arise and the chosen would gravitate toward it, called by a psychic dog whistle, to begin a new era of peace and prosperity. A psychologist felt that all parties had responded naturally to the circumstances, and everyone would be wise to leave each other alone.

On it went, covering every possible opinion, until my eyes blurred and I switched off the set. This left me in near darkness. Jake had reclaimed his bed hours earlier and John snored lightly from the floor. Moonlight filled the forest and cabin with blue-white reflection. I twitched and hummed from too much caffeine, nicotine, and tension, so bundled up to try out my TV-less cabin and pace that floor.

Two feet from the porch, the night's magic embraced me. Here was all the luxury, space, and privacy that nature could offer. The woods stood silent and crystalline, in glowing silver, sharp black, indigo blue. Above the treetops, a million stars sparkled through the fog from my exhalations. A crust had formed atop the snow, allowing me to slide my boots down to the lakefront. Light bloomed as I emerged from beneath the tree canopy into acres of space rimmed by frosted hills. Out here the sky was nearly white with planet-spangled constellations. Below it the lake stretched away in an ice cream carpet.

I did not pause to question the ice's soundness before starting across it. Weeks would pass before it began to honeycomb apart. I walked far enough from shore to feel alone in the center. Then I halted and stood with neck craned upward, alternately sending my cares to the heavens and wishing they would send back some help.

My exertions and heavy clothing kept me warm for a few minutes. The night's stillness helped. So did dreamy visions of palm-lined beaches and turquoise ocean; for an instant I almost felt a tropical caress. It brought back memories of Blanche carping about winter weather and vowing to someday live on the equator. Which brought my chin down abruptly: I heard her call my name.

I looked around. The only sign of life was my shadow, thrown by a near-full moon. Blanche could only reach me if calling through the ether and my antenna had recovered to hear her. Yet I lacked the nerve tingle and molten solar plexus that signaled active power.

Before returning to the cabin, I looked again at the sky and picked out Polaris. The north star had guided so many before me to their destinations; why couldn't that work now? If my sleepwalking dream had any credence, Blanche had fled south. But the gods had proven themselves to be cruel, so more likely I was fated to finish my days in the arctic. Subsistence living as the twins' concubine, wearing furs year-round . . .

As I gazed upward, luminous veils rippled and flared like cosmic curtains in a breeze through an open window. I thought at first I was dreaming again, then recognized the northern lights—aurora borealis—from which I had taken my name.

Buck had called me Aurora the night I lost him. The memory still melted my legs. Until tonight, I had never seen the phenomenon. It shimmered above me, yellow-green streamers tinged with red, nearly filling the sky.

I stared until my eyes watered and neck cramped then lowered my chin, understanding why John and Jake had taken the aurora as a message. It left me feeling calm and chosen, filled with purpose. The chaos in my mind had fallen silent. At last, I knew what to do.

35
Twin Linkage

Time to head south.

For the moment, heading indoors would suffice. Cold had seeped through my layers and a warm cabin awaited me. Complete with warm-body option, who stood on the shoreline, arms at sides, as black and patient as a monolith.

Regret slashed through me like a winter wind. *Sorry,* I sent to John as I approached across the ice; *you cannot have me. I'm fond of you, I trust you, but my heart belongs to someone else.*

He did not turn away. Rather, he sent back a wave of love so strong it broke my step. He knew the truth and didn't care, wanting whatever he could have and mourning the rest. He loved me as tragically as I loved Buck, certain of the end before it started. I would play my role in his life then pass out of it, leaving him the bittersweetness of duty done, and a place in my heart as someone important. Buck, at least, had left me a memory to treasure. I decided to give the same to John.

So I walked directly into him. Despite the surprise, he did not flinch but folded me into his arms. His passion sprang free, like an embodied thing, diving through the open door into my heart and setting fires inside before I could react to its presence. By the time my mind caught up, his passion had captured my hungers and was feeding them all they needed. Which is how John and I came to be lip-locked and pelvic-melded on the lakeshore, our hands mining through each other's clothes.

Astonished awareness hit us at the same time. We broke apart with ragged breaths, looked at each other, then laughed aloud. His grin gleaming in the moonlight erased my hesitation. When he felt my psychic load lighten, he scooped me up and started toward the cabins. But the snow crust tangled his feet, so he let me slide down beside him. Still chuckling, we crunched and skittered up the incline, holding hands.

Inside the cabin, a fire already smoldered behind a grate. Its flicker provided the only light. I pulled off my hat and gloves, kicked off my boots, then stopped in invitation. John finished removing his own gear and moved in without pause.

I knew right away that he had either foreseen this event clairvoyantly or spent years planning all possible outcomes. The soul who had danced with mine on the lakeshore withdrew into some private temple and commenced some long-awaited ritual. He had read all the manuals, studied all the X-rated videos, practiced on god-knows-who, and compiled every bit of data on my mind, body, and soul he could acquire. Now he put it all into action.

I might as well have stepped out of my body and left it there for his gratification. What took place that night had nothing to do with me. Trouble was, his homework had taught him precisely how to enslave me inside my body, by taking it to states I had only read about in dirty books and only fantasized about with Kit. Thoughts could only half form between waves of screaming ecstasy that surely woke the hibernating animals. Whatever I did to him came from his direction—always tender, always voluntary, but never driven by my desire. I had expected to play the goddess but he had turned the tables. Somehow I lost my will when I gave myself to him.

That must be how Raoul fell to the dark powers, I thought when it was over. Dru had said, "At first he offered no resistance, and now they've bored him so smooth that he can't." The inverse happened to me in the act of love with a man who adored me. Like Kit and Dru had been driven by an invading spirit, I became everything John wanted and all that many people believed me to be. Unlike Kit and Dru, John had chosen to step over the threshold. As Raoul had. Dear gods, all that saved me from the same fate was John's soul!

He might have been obsessed, he might have been demented, and so starving for intimacy that he underestimated and misused his power, but still he loved me. True and simple. All he wanted was a pinnacle to remember for the rest of his life. Boy, did he succeed! I would never forget it, either. But I would always wish I'd had the experience with a different guy.

At last he passed out, smiling. I panted beside him until my sweat dried, too far past exhaustion to sleep. Despite the quivers that still rippled my body, I yearned for another lover—Kit or Buck—didn't matter—just someone who would ride me like a normal, randy male who didn't understand women. Someone willing to be bound by mysterious, special feelings, and willing to share his soul but not give it away, or hide it under a rock. My quest for a soulmate ended in that moment. What I really wanted was a balanced, sexy, mature, intelligent man.

The cabin chilled as the fire dwindled. I pulled the blanket around my shoulders and made sure it covered John. He roused and mumbled then fell into a light snore. I lay shell-shocked, wishing I had that book on psychic etiquette nobody had written. John had pulled knowledge of me, from me, without my awareness. But then, what was the difference between reading someone's words, deeds, and gestures, thereby getting to know them, and reading thought and emotion that leaked from their head? Having all that info let you know a person much better than usual. So if John or Dru or Blanche or Allanna had the ability to see into me, as I sometimes saw through others, whose fault was it that mental privacy got lost?

John stirred again, slipping a sinewy arm across my thigh and saying, "I know I'm not your soulmate."

My eyes popped open. He kept his closed but said clearly a minute later, "So I guess you can't be mine, either. It has to go both ways."

When I didn't answer, he opened his eyes. Although dark and flinty as Raoul's obsidian, they contained no evil, no madness. As I relaxed, a new thought spiked through the chaos in my mind. "It depends on how you define a soulmate."

He rolled onto an elbow, eyes intent.

I struggled to articulate. "I mean, if you think about it logistically, then you can have more than one soulmate. Look."

The ideas came in a rush. "If people really do pass through multiple lives, that covers a long period. Trying to match all soulmate pairs in the world lifetime after lifetime would surely tax the mightiest god! Even if there's more than one deity, or none at all, the numbers would be too complex to manage. So soulmates wouldn't catch each other in the flesh every time. Yet they'd still want and need partners when the soulmate wasn't around. Might we, then, have a revolving pool of candidates at different stages? Might you and I be just starting out, and Blanche and Dru at a peak, and me and Buck almost through, and me and Kit halfway?"

John rolled onto his back and stared upward. "That would explain a lot."

"Unless you look at it the way Buck does. Then the whole thing's a crock. He would say that finding meaning in life and love is just a conceit of the human animal. Therefore, lovers signify nothing more than a biological imperative to mate, with selection based on pheromones."

I wondered silently, Was there any way to determine the truth?

John worked at it. "You probably only know for sure when you're between lives, assessing what you did and what you still need to do. But when you're stuck down here, alone and ignorant, you can only follow your heart and hope it takes you to the right place."

At those words, my own heart cracked open and decades worth of angst spilled out. He flinched at its force then rolled me into a hard embrace as I caved in to tears, so exhausted by the schisms between my thoughts, feelings, and appearance; so frightened by all that had happened and the unknowns that lay ahead. As fast as I fell apart he strengthened, giving me the sheltering comfort a parent would give a child. Only then did I realize I had never known that security. It made me cry harder, aggravated by guilt that I had been so cold to someone so kind.

Eventually I sputtered into limpness, yet still he held me safe. We drowsed for a while, feeling each other's breath against our skin, until my heart calmed and mind reawoke. Then I reached for his lips and we began again, this time me melting into him to give back the best love and gratitude I could express. He answered by opening all of himself to me, no longer worshiping but just letting his coal-dark hair down to be the man he was that no one had truly seen before. We probably replayed Blanche and Jake's night in the gold-key love nest. But in this one-time splurge, we created a new unit of two half-twins, plugging the holes where the other's loneliness had leaked out and fortifying each other for the trials to come.

Spent, John fell into sleep again. I lay awake for a long while, wondering why I had never received a vision glow from him or Dru. I had foreseen sex with Dru, Buck, and Kit—three white guys with light eyes—yet had no clue that a dusky Indian would reroute my life and heal my psyche. A new variable X entering the equation. Which left me back where I had started: Why me? Why them? Why now? Why anything?

The questions stayed unanswered as light returned to the sky. John snored while I dipped in and out of sleep. The final time I came awake, my emotions congealed into a lump beneath my breastbone. I slid from beneath his arm and rose to dress.

The fired had burned down to a snapping ash pile so I moved as fast as I could without thumping. John's snores droned on. I didn't want to wake him but was done with deceiving. Lightly prodding him as I brushed my lips across his forehead, I whispered, "John, wake up."

His eyes snapped open and found me instantly. "You're going?"

"I have to."

His face turned to stone. "I know."

I gave him a final kiss then backed away, saying, "Fare thee well" as he sat up after me. He didn't rise, though, as I gathered my bags and reached for the door.

For a moment I became Dru, suddenly understanding how he had felt and why he'd said what he did after spending the night with me.

"Thank you, I love you," I repeated, giving my widest, most honest smile for his last view of me.

Then I escaped into the subzero morn.

36
The Wind and the Wave

The cold shocked me awake like a blow, also making the doors groan and snow shatter so loudly that Jake would have to investigate. I never learned if he even glanced through the window, for the Land Rover snapped to life at first turn of the key.

"Bless you, Kit!" I exhaled as it bore me southward. "South! South!" I chanted like a migrating bird that had left too late, until my head began to spin and eyeballs, too—not an oncoming vision but my body's mutiny against all that had occurred. Through a mist I saw a general store with gas pumps, its lights a yellow blur in the pastels of dawn. I hesitated before turning in—too close, they could overtake me, the only vehicle in sight—but both truck and I needed refueling before we could go on.

I leaned against the Land Rover during the eternity it sucked down its breakfast, then pulled my hat low and went inside. Ahh, hot coffee, sugared pastries, cases of energy drinks and snacks. I loaded up and took my change in coin from a woman-who's-seen-it-all at the register. Back in the truck, I sucked down my own breakfast while unfolding the withered map Kit kept in his glove box underneath tools.

It showed I was a long way from anywhere I might want to be. I had plenty of time to construct a plan while rolling. So I resumed rolling as the next yawning customer drove in.

At first I had to concentrate on managing the vehicle. I hadn't driven in months and never an aging four-wheel-drive SUV. By the time the cabin warmed so that I could remove hat and gloves, muscle memory had reawakened. I barreled down the two-lane a free woman and recovering race driver.

Still quivering inside from the night's intensity, I couldn't help but think of John. And Kit, Buck, Dru. What all of them meant, separately and together. A mystery I no longer had to solve.

It slammed me, then, that I was a one-hundred-percent free agent. All my troubles and obligations could be gone if I wanted to let go. I had the resources to travel anywhere and reinvent my life on all levels. The realization made blood surge into, then drain from, my head so abruptly that I had to pull over and park.

There, alone and woozy in somebody else's car along a two-lane in the middle of nowhere, I faced the ultimate crossroad. Which route I took today would drive the rest of my life—maybe lives. I needed to be really, really sure about who I was and what I wanted before I picked a direction. And I needed a secure bubble to make that decision within.

With a full tank of gas I had hours of undisturbed bubble time as long as I kept to the speed limit. So, once the dizziness passed, I put the Land Rover in gear and resumed rolling toward the only confluence of interstates in northern New England. That would give me the four points of the compass to choose from, as well as facilities for stocking up.

On the way, I asked myself the main question: *Madeline, what is your heart's desire?*

"To put the genie back in the bottle!" I replied aloud.

Sorry, not an option. Try again.

"Well, my desires haven't changed since I started: To live in a beautiful, safe place; to paint without inhibition; to share an interesting life with a perfectly matched partner; to have a purpose to fulfill."

Can you pick one?

"No."

Then you'll just have to put a plan together that allows all these things to happen. What do you need in order to succeed?

Many miles passed before I could answer that one. Then it came to me: "To become the wind or a wave, stop being a cork that bobs in whatever direction the forces choose."

What concrete fact or object do you possess that will allow you to start?

"The telephone number for the Tiger Club president in my wallet."

What concrete action can you perform with this?

"Find a private public telephone."

I waited to look for one until the Vermont–New Hampshire border, where the highway confluence provided restaurants and gas stations, restrooms and lodging. If any call I made was traced, pursuers would have to flip a coin to decide which way to follow me.

In a smelly plastic booth outside a strip mall, I dialed the Tiger guy. Nine rings passed before a groggy woman answered.

"I'm looking for Kit Douglas," I said without intro or apology.

"Who?"

"Kit Douglas. He gave me this number to relay messages."

"Who the hell are you?"

"His wife. Can you connect me to him?"

A man's voice rumbled in the background. The woman covered the phone with her hand but I heard, "Some girl looking for a Kit Douglas. What do I say?"

"Let me take it."

Then, louder: "This is Tony Martin. Can I help you?"

"I need to contact Kit Douglas. He left me this number. It's urgent."

"I can perhaps get him a message. Who's calling?"

I couldn't bear releasing my name, so snapped, "His wife. Please, it's urgent."

The voice dropped in suspicion. "I wasn't aware he had a wife."

"Oh don't split hairs—I'm his fiancée. He rebuilt my car as an engagement present. Sixty-seven Tiger, VIN eight nine four seven two oh two two."

"Ah. Now we're getting somewhere. He left you a message. He's headed for Hawaii and—"

"Hawaii!"

"—and would call in with flight data when he got it."

"Did he mean the island chain or the island actually named Hawaii?"

"Don't know."

"How long ago?"

"Last night."

"Jeez. He should know by now."

"I know. I'm not sure why we haven't heard from him—someone's been here all the time and we have an answering machine."

"Maybe he lucked into an empty seat on a plane heading out so can't call until he lands."

"Something like that, I hope."

"Did he say which airport?"

"No."

"What's he driving?"

"I think your Jetta."

"Did he tell you what happened?"

"No, but I gather it has something to do with that farce at New Atlantis. I hope none of those assholes have picked him up!"

"You and me both. They haven't found me yet but I'm not sure how long that'll last. Listen, I'm on the move without a cell phone, so can't leave a number. Can I call you later and see if he's checked in?"

"Sure."

"Thank you. What's your address there?"

Reluctantly, he told me. I thanked him again. "And please—if Kit calls, tell him to stay put until I catch up with him. Thank you very, very much!"

I disconnected before he could comment. Then, after a glance over both shoulders, I leaned against the wall and shook.

Hawaii. How tropical could you get! Had he hooked up with Blanche somehow and they were trying to call me in? A mere seven thousand miles between us . . . but . . . no passport required, no change of currency. Everybody spoke English. If I hauled butt to a big airport, I could be there for tomorrow's breakfast.

First I depleted my coin stash by dialing Colin's line at New Atlantis. He picked up on the first ring.

"It's me," I opened.

"About time. Which me?"

"I don't know if these calls are secure so I'm not going to say."

"Okay. I suppose you won't say where you are, either."

"No. I'm between points and trying to find out who's where."

"Everyone's here except you guys, Kit, Dru, Troy and Allanna, Cornelius, and the twins. You're alone, I take it?"

"Yes, but hopefully not for long. I'll contact you later."

I hung up. Then moved the Land Rover to a back corner of a parking lot, bundled under parkas and sweaters, and slouched down to either sleep or think. The sky helped conceal me by sending a snow squall that coated the windows. By dusk I had completed both a nap and a plan.

I timed my arrival at Cold River Corners to coincide with darkfall. Three times I missed the entrance to the correct field, which lay behind the defunct mill Jake had described, but once in it I followed tire and snow-machine tracks to an auto graveyard, aided by a three-quarter moon. A gutted panel truck and a burned camper shielded the Land Rover from casual observation. I had to cross open snow in order to reach the tree line, but once against it I was invisible if I stood still. Of course I had to move, scouting the perimeter until I spotted a passage. This led to the river, now a jagged trickle peeking between ledges of ice.

The snow had softened to deep sugar so it squished instead of crunched. I trudged upstream along a ragged shore until the channel disappeared into a four-foot-diameter culvert. Inside it, water ran under rotting ice disguised with mud, gravel, and litter. I stooped and straddled the effluvium, placing my feet along the crust where ice met culvert and balancing myself with hands probing along the curve above it. The air smelled of dirt and decay and cold.

At the far end, I encountered a grate. It didn't budge when I shook it. "Shit!" I spat, jumping when the word echoed back at me. Thanks, Jake, I added silently, for not mentioning this detail!

Preplanned revenge for dumping his brother, probably. Still swearing, I extracted a flashlight from my pack and examined the grate.

Four fresh bolts attached it to the culvert. No problem removing them if I had the right tools. Hopefully the Land Rover did.

I groped my way back to it, cursing the delay and wondering what I'd do if I couldn't dismount the grate or hold it once unbolted. Didn't have to find out thanks to Kit, who had stashed a box of wrenches in the back of the vehicle as well as in its glove box. This discovery gave me enough juice to crank icy nuts, tug the grate free, and balance it so that I could pass and remount it on the way back. I left the wrenches so I wouldn't have to tote their weight the remaining distance. Then scrambled up the rock-lined trench into New Atlantis.

Once free of the brush that concealed the trench, I stood in our valley looking up its length to the ridgetop mansion. My eyes teared up at the distant flicker of window lights.

In the right foreground, block shadows situated the horse sheds. No cover from there to the house. I would be a moving target against the white road and pastures so would have to stride in like I owned the place, trusting that no more infrared binoculars would be watching. More likely, a restless stargazer would spot me and think an undesirable had broken in. I would be okay as long as nobody panicked with a rifle.

But first . . . a minute to stop and simply stare. Nobody on the planet knew where I was; I could afford to absorb the moon-washed landscape, reminiscent of the lake I'd stood upon to watch the northern lights. No show tonight but still a flat-bottomed bowl embraced by hills and forest, as bright as midday but as if a blue filter hung over the sun. All the colors were there, just more intense and richer, nigh impossible to mix in paint to capture the eerie contrasts. Pondering how to do it carried me halfway down the road before I realized, brought back into the scene as an actor instead of a viewer by the scrape of my boots against the snow and swish and creak of my pants and coat and baggage.

Aside from those sounds, all was silent. Not even a dog to announce my progress or an owl to hoot from the trees. The journey brought to mind my forest drive into the compound via the back entrance. If only Kit would be here again to let me in!

Nope: I walked through the mansion's front door unchallenged. It could have been the foyer of a closed museum. Shiny stone exuded cold. Lights over the pictures had been turned off. No music or stirrings, only the creaks and groans of timbers and masonry, plus deep shadows broken by night-lights. Then a beacon from the parlor, spilling into the hall.

At the sound of my soles squeaking on stone, a head popped around the parlor door frame. "Who is it?" came Colin's voice.

"Me."

He stepped into the hall and pulled me into a bear hug. I hugged back, both of us resisting tears. He smelled of scotch and stale clothing. In response to my own scent, he exclaimed, "What did you do, come in through a sewer?"

I stepped away. "Close enough. A culvert where the creek exits."

"But that's barred."

I explained the twins' adjustments. Colin chuckled and shook his head, then returned to the parlor, flopped onto the sofa, and drained his tumbler. "Are you okay?"

"Other than strained shoulders and skinned knuckles, yes. Where is everybody?"

"Adam's having a shindig down at Valhalla to celebrate reclaiming it. Everyone who's not there is holed up in their room, depressed. It's been pretty strange around here."

"I'll bet. It's strange out there, too." I sat and gave him the short version of my adventure.

He processed the facts without asking for details. "You should have brought John and Jake with you. How are we going to contact them up there? We need everyone back so we can cut a deal with the Feds."

"Are they talking already?"

"Before the night was over. I've been on the phone with lawyers nonstop since. One is still here."

"So . . . what are they offering?"

Colin rose to pour drinks for both of us then sat beside me on the parlor loveseat. "It's not a bad deal. First, my murder charge thrown away. They've got enough now to prove self-defense. Second, all of us to lie as low as possible without hindering our careers. When we do go out, we must let the legal team know, and have reliable witnesses present. No solo junkets. We can have all the privacy we want inside our walls."

I nodded and shook my head as he talked.

"We're to make no statements to the press and release no stories pertaining to the, um, incident."

I said nothing about Cornelius, who had already smuggled out a manuscript.

Colin continued in his banker's voice, looking at the wall. "All psychics are to allow independent testing at reasonable intervals. They'll provide us with a list of which parties are to have uncensored access to all results. In return, they'll grant us protection from exploitation, harassment, and terrorism. No money is to change hands at any level."

"Protect us how? By moving in again?"

"No, security will be external. And based on our agreement that your powers will never be used to manipulate or harm—with those two words carefully defined. Pure scientific terms on both sides, no personal involvement."

"Hmph. Will any of us be allowed to live outside New Atlantis?"

"I doubt it. But I didn't ask, and they didn't offer."

I stood. "Then we're back to house arrest. And permanent shadows. That won't do it, Colin—we have to live normally if we're going to be any use to ourselves or the world."

"Since when have you lived normally? And what's the difference between being tailed by people who can protect you and people trying to take your picture or get your autograph?"

I pocketed my hands and turned my back. Colin resumed his brother guise. "You don't have to decide now. And nothing will happen 'til everyone's back. Do you think you can find Blanche or Dru or Kit?"

I shrugged then elaborated on the tropical theme that had emerged.

"Sounds pretty vague to me," Colin muttered.

"Sorry, but I'm grasping any straw I'm given until it proves to be a straw in the wind! So why are you here, anyway? I thought you were supposed to leave with the rest of us!"

Colin looked blankly at his tumbler, slack in his hands against his thighs. "Yeah, I was. But I knew Dru would try something stupid, so I blocked him."

"I didn't know you could do that."

"Why not? I've got two psychic sisters."

"You sandbagger! I've always wondered why you didn't get caught in the spell at the Halloween party. What else can you do?"

"Just that. I'm a professional bonehead."

I grinned then sobered. "Did you fight Dru or just block him?"

"Just blocked. I let him go. Let them all go. It was the only thing that would end it." He sighed. "I hope you're right about Blanche. We thought she was safe. Rosalind Burke had stashed her in her own apartment, started making arrangements . . . but when she went out to shoot another story—the one at the gate—Blanche skipped. She had promised to stay but apparently has her own agenda. I hope you didn't pass her on the road!"

"I doubt it. She wouldn't go there once she knew the Feds had been evicted. No, I'm pretty sure there's a problem and she's changed plan. That's why I'm heading back out as soon as I rest and bathe and repack."

"Are you officially here?"

"Only if I run into somebody in the hall. Otherwise, if anyone asks, you can say you heard from me but I wouldn't say where I was and will be back soon. I called you earlier to put an incoming on record so you won't get caught in a lie."

"Thanks." Colin saw me to the parlor door. The halls remained empty, although I heard voices in opposite directions. We exchanged hugs and kisses then I trotted upstairs to my suite.

37
Volcano

The rooms looked the same yet different. They had been abandoned in the middle of a day's events, then tidied by John after packing my bag with me slung over his shoulder. Nothing of Kit's appeared to be added or subtracted. But his scent lingered on the sheets and his voice vibrated subliminally in the walls.

After flopping on the bed to rest and remember, I rose to take the last hot, thorough shower I might have for days. Then, before repacking, I rooted through everything Kit had left in my suite. Typical of his kind, he didn't use an address-and-phone notebook; rather, kept such data on the backs of business cards stuffed in his wallet, which had gone out the door with him. Since he'd never told me the names or locations of any of his friends, and wouldn't run to his family, I had no leads without involving Mark or finding Dru.

Onward, then, to ransack Blanche and Dru's quarters. That required some tiptoeing and ducking but I gained the former gold-key room unseen. Dru had left it unlocked, as I'd suspected. Within, I found greater disarray than usual—sign of either a search by other parties or Dru's own haste and confusion in leaving. Blanche had had no chance to pack so everything she owned still lay amid the clutter. Except her wallet, which wasn't in her purse, or dresser, or jewelry box, or under the mattress, or in any of her drawers or pockets.

I sat on the bed. No wallet meant she had brought it with her on our trail ride. Absurd for an on-compound outing, unless she believed that anything might happen, any time. In that case, she would leave me a clue of her intent, knowing we might not get a chance to exchange plans.

I scanned the room. Half of what I saw belonged to Dru. Since I didn't know what of his should be there, I couldn't tell what was missing. Blanche would hide her message in plain sight. It would mean something only to me, just as my Tiger's VIN linked me and Kit.

I spotted it in seconds: her cosmetics case. Unlike every drawer and door, it did not stand open. Usually the case sprawled across her vanity in a marvel of unfolded compartments, overflowing with lipsticks and pencils, brushes and swabs and paints. I rose to lift the lid and began to tremble when I found the contents tidy. Looking first for an overall pattern, I was slow to find the aberration she had arranged. Amid jumbled lipsticks, two tubes lay with their labels pointing toward me: Bougainvillea and Coral. Another tropical theme.

I uncapped each stick. One was just an unused finger of vivid orange. The other had three letters carved into it with a fingernail: P.O.R.

Huh?

P.O.R. Press On Regardless. Point Of Reference. Peter Owen Randy. Peas, oatmeal, raisins. *Jeezus, Blanche, did you have to be that cryptic?*

I plunked back down on the bed. Now what?

Recalling that Kit was heading for Hawaii snapped my eyes into focus. Nothing about Hawaii on Blanche's bookshelf, but her wall calendar showed tropical beaches. She had often, during ordinary conversations before the Debacle, dreamed aloud about honeymooning in Hawaii. The calendar comprised shots of Hawaiian sites. I jumped up and flipped through the months, reading captions and photo credits, until reaching Pu'uhonoa O Honaunau. Its name in English after it in parentheses: Place of Refuge. A national park on the island of Hawaii.

Huzzah!

Dru's belongings revealed no corresponding message. I considered a side trip to the studio but didn't want to risk getting caught. I returned to my suite and finished packing. By midnight I was again slogging through mealy snow in darkness grayed by moonlight through clouds, shoulders bowed under the weight of luggage I should have carried in two trips.

As before, no one was abroad to notice my silhouette, so I covered the distance unharassed by anything beyond my fears. These I kept suppressed by portaging two bags through the culvert dry and undamaged. Then rehanging the grate, which tore my parka and further strained my muscles. Then slewing the Land Rover out of the graveyard and on to the correct highway. Then halting at a truck stop to call Tony Martin. "No message," he growled after being wakened in the middle of the night.

I kept myself from crying by dialing up airline reservations, testing my credit card for Sharlene MacRae. No hiccups. I had to stop once more to change into my business traveler's costume, but the closer I got to the City, the easier it was to be anonymous. I would have preferred flying out of Albany, which was smaller and closer, but I needed a major hub to get a direct flight to Honolulu on short notice. I didn't dare think about Kit, heading that way with god-knows-what ID and funds on him. If he had set off any flags, then a dozen Feds could be trailing him. Which meant they would be watching for any white, five-foot-seven, busty females aiming for the same place.

Owing to commuter traffic, I arrived at the airport after dawn. Wearing dark makeup under sunglasses with the lenses popped out, a curly black wig, and a pantsuit appropriate for first class, I strode into the terminal. Security staff eyed me but did no double takes. My documentation did its job, my luggage passed inspection. I had time to snatch up food and newspapers before the jumbo jet roared into the sky.

Unless a Fed happened to be sitting in the first-class cabin, I was safe (relatively speaking) once airborne. The corporate players and well-heeled vacationers traveling with me were less likely than the general populace to be following the New Atlantis story. My largest risk was that someone in the compartment happened to know Dru. But I recognized none of my fellow flyers; and, although most of them stole glances at me and wondered, none appeared to recognize me. This made me feel secure enough to finally sleep.

We were still above the continent when I awoke, stiff and crusty and hungry. The flight attendants catered to that need. Our food came decorated with orchids instead of parsley. The attendants wore Hawaiian-print shirts and dresses, and the in-flight magazine regaled the Hawaiian islands in articles and ads. I studied them for hotels, car rentals, and anything about Place of Refuge or other P.O.R. initials. Wondered how Blanche might have gotten there without benefit of her wigs and wardrobe for disguise. She had probably pilfered from Rosalind Burke, then done some fast shopping in the wonderfully indifferent City, taking cabs, looking different in each one.

She reminded me of the newspapers stuffed into my carry-on. Scrutiny of them passed more time. The articles I found repeated the TV coverage and expanded on opinions. None of it added up to any facts.

My confidence inched up a notch. Perhaps we weren't as important as we thought. While I didn't dare believe no one sought us, it looked like we might be able to move around for a while. The lead time Dru had bought us might be enough.

And I had catalyzed him into doing it.

As the jet soared over the world's largest ocean, I totted up what I had directly or indirectly caused other people to do. The list wasn't all good, but I could see a trend toward success. If I stopped doubting myself yet continued challenging others, I might prove more effective, more swiftly. That idea engrossed me for the remaining hours.

At last a decrease in the plane's whine marked our descent toward Honolulu. Everyone stirred in grateful anticipation, followed by unease as turbulence made us feel like were bumping down stairs on our collective behinds. We landed without event in dazzling sunshine. February's snow and ice lay half a day, thousands of miles, and twenty-odd degrees of latitude away.

I suffered a paralyzing moment while deplaning, as people braying "Aloha!" rushed forward flinging leis over our heads. They must have thought me part of the tour group I tagged behind. At first chance I cut clear and headed for the nearest telephone. I forgot about time zone differences until Tony Martin's answering machine picked up.

I left a message for Kit specifying my whereabouts. Then I browsed the airport shops for appropriate clothes. I sweltered in my suit, eager to slip into one of those splashy garments I kept seeing on women who wouldn't dare wear them on the mainland. These affirmed that Blanche would come here, for beautiful people abounded and she would not be conspicuous among every race and physiotype in outlandish dress. She would also be comfortable.

My interisland flight displayed a coastal highway encircling both Oahu, which I left behind, and Hawaii, where I landed. Both were formed of volcanic cones—still active on Hawaii, the Big Island—and flanked with serrated green mountains. Cliffs and beaches lined the shores. Everywhere in between, flowers burgeoned in neon colors. People walked, drove, bicycled, scootered, bused, or skated around in a range of undress that made Californians look inhibited. Above them clouds churned through white, slate, and violet, showing three rainbows between the airport and Kailua-Kona, where I came to rest.

Upon checking into my room, I tried Tony Martin again. Same result as before. Sighing, I retired to the balcony wearing the pareu I had bought in the airport gift shop, and read the guidebook I had bought at the same time.

Thus I learned that nothing in life is free and nowhere is truly safe. The intro pages of the guidebook, as well as the local phone book, contained Civil Defense instructions about what to do in earthquakes, hurricanes, volcanoes, and tsunamis. These flavored Hawaii the way seasons affected everywhere else in the U.S. I had thought California to be hazardous, with its quakes and mudslides and fires; the Hawaiian islands, a string of dots in a vast ocean, sat atop one of the most unstable spots in the Earth's crust.

Flying above those dots, I had recognized what a molecule I was in the universe. How could I expect to find the molecules I sought in such a huge world? I had to believe Blanche was sending me bread crumbs to follow. Believe it without understanding how or why. My only other choice was to skip to the nearest restaurant and start my life over from scratch. Or head back to New Atlantis and wait for whatever fate delivered. Instead, I ordered room service and stayed out of sight.

How pathetic, I thought after slipping my empty tray back into the corridor, to be alone in a hotel room in paradise. This was where lovers went for romantic getaways. After four lovers in six months I now had no one. Where, amid all that lust and passion, had I passed true love?

Did such a thing exist, or was I chasing a unicorn? Reflexively, my hand sought the pendant missing from between my breasts. It had been appropriated by Buck during the Debacle and I'd had no chance to reclaim it . . .

Memory drove me back into the room, where I tried Tony Martin again.

Still the answering machine. I squeezed back tears. Longing for Kit pulled me back into a memory as deep and real as a dream. I could feel the slack firmness of his muscles as he slept. Then the almost electric quickening in him as his interest was aroused. The metallic edge of his anger. The tenderness in his touch, so unexpected in his scarred hands.

My own hands cramped with the urge to draw him. My first portrait had not caught all that he was. If I was never to see him again, then I needed to get it right and carry his image with me. The best I could do was sketch him with a ballpoint pen on hotel stationery.

I didn't get far before jet lag took over. It took me deep into a dream of volcanoes. Spewing lava, steaming barrens, creeping black blobs edged in livid red—I even smelled sulfuric gases. Then I woke up to stale air conditioning in a sealed room, early morning, alone.

Volcanoes. Kiluea erupting continuously for years on Big Island. Whether I had received another message or my subconscious had made a connection after reading the guidebook didn't matter. I now knew for certain Blanche was here. What larger beacon could Dru have picked than an erupting volcano?

38
Place of Refuge

According to my guidebook, Volcanoes National Park was on the other side of the island. Place of Refuge, on this side, was likewise a national park. If I could find no clue of Blanche there, I would continue to Kiluea at Volcanoes. In either case, I had to wait until the park opened.

To celebrate having two options, I treated myself to breakfast in the hotel's lanai restaurant. Ahh, that was more like it: an open-air porch on the beach, roofed by trees and bounded by bougainvillea; a view of white sands, blinding blue sky and water, and bodies lined up like sausages to broil in the sun. They reminded me I needed to buy sunscreen. Fair-skinned from birth, and now New England winter fish-belly white, I would turn magenta within an hour if unprotected. A good reason to keep covered and thus harder to recognize.

Comfortable in the shade, I savored ordinary food prepared delectably (and garnished with orchids) chased with Kona coffee. And shared my juice with a tricolored cardinal, which perched on the glass.

On my way out, clad in a muumuu and an ash-blonde pageboy wig beneath floppy hat and sunglasses, I browsed through the hotel gift shop. It assured me that the world still made wonderful objects and carried on its business indifferent to my affairs. I had to keep both hands in my pockets to keep them out of my wallet. Almost succumbed to coral earrings and sunrise-colored pearls.

Beside them, displayed on a false bust, one necklace caught my attention. Since it offered nothing exciting—a knotted string of tiny white shells, some gold-spotted, separated at intervals by blue or yellow shells of the same type—I wondered what it was trying to tell me. The saleslady was engrossed with another customer, so I moved on to my rental car. However, I noted the shop's hours so to investigate when I returned.

If I came back with Blanche, I promised myself, I would buy the pearls and the earrings.

Place of Refuge, the guidebook said, was where "sinners and fugitives were guaranteed sanctuary no matter who or what they did." Ancient Hawaii had operated under a caste system driven by "kapu," a concept vaguely parallel to taboo in American culture. Kapu could be so severe that looking at the wrong person meant a death sentence. Conversely, the rigidity that led to such punishment allowed any refuge granted to remain secure. If you made it there, you could be absolved after the proper rituals. Exactly what psychic New Atlanteans needed.

By the time I arrived, tourists had already spread across the black lava peninsula examining its restored temples and gargoyle-esque idols carved from single logs like Amerindian totem poles. A forest of palms, planted to serve as beacons, canopied many acres, filtering the sun into a liquid gold-green light. Although ocean bordered three sides, the wind was silken across the skin while scattering voices so that people in sight could not hear each other. I drifted among them, wondering if anyone there besides me and the ghosts knew what it was like to break kapu and run for your life.

The thought drained me. I sat on a shady lava chunk protruding from the sand and gazed over the ocean, fighting back tears. In defiance, I pulled off my hat then my wig to let the wind run its fingers through my real hair, refusing to turn and check whether anyone noticed. For a few minutes, no one wandered close enough to recognize a face without using binoculars.

Then a tour bus disgorged its load at the Visitors' Center. Half those tourists found their way under the palms to discover the attractions in sight of my rock. I donned my hat but held my ground, listening to some senior ladies squawk over one of the gods' phallic symbols.

Sighing, I collected myself for departure. Silly of me to hope that following gut feeling would lead to a big clue. I had fantasized walking onto a beach and finding Dru and Blanche waiting. Hah! By now I should know better. Another intuition turned out to be wishful thinking.

While swinging my gaze across the peninsula, I tucked my wig into my tote and my hair under my hat. Everyone remained occupied with their own pursuits. I relaxed a bit then did a double take. One silhouette in green shadow wasn't moving. I stiffened. A female shape stood framed beneath crossing palm trees waiting for me to see and understand.

Blanche!

I managed to hold the shriek inside my head and restrain my rush to a saunter. She sauntered likewise, one thumb hooked under a shoulder bag strap, the other hand trailing a straw hat. She wore a flower-splashed dress that hid her figure, mirrored sunglasses, and calf-laced sandals. Her hair was a honey-brown ponytail wig.

As distance shrank between us we broke into identical smiles. We lunged the last two feet and grabbed each other into a hug that crackled joints. Only that armful of her warm, firm body and nostril blast of sunscreen convinced me she was real. When I released her, she grinned back at me. We both had tears dribbling down beneath our sunglasses.

"Oh Blanche, I thought I would never find you!"

"I knew you would, sooner or later."

"You and your crazy blind faith!"

"Nothing so lofty. I knew that if you didn't get my psychic signal, then you'd at least think like me because you can't help it. It might take a while but you'd figure it out."

"It helped that you left me a clue."

"Ah, but what led you to look for it?"

I gave her a dirty look. She grinned.

We commenced walking. "But why," I asked her, "did you come here if the rendezvous was set for New Hampshire? Jake expected you both at the camp."

Her eyes asked a question but she answered mine first. "That was Plan A—where to go if we got out together. I forced a switch to Plan B by leaving first."

"So this is where you'd meet if you got separated?"

"Yeah. We had to build in the chance that we might never connect. So if I had to be marooned, this was the best place."

She frowned. "I might be marooned. I've been here three days and no sign of him. I come by bus each day—we were supposed to meet under those palm trees. But . . . I can't feel him any more, haven't been able to since the eviction. I'm not sure if he can get here. Or remembers where to go."

She bit her lip and wiped her eyes. I squeezed her shoulder. "He might need time. Disguise will be tough for him, and that power drain probably forced him to lie low and recover for a while. I assume he has false ID?"

"Of course."

"Then you might need to wait a week for him."

"But Madeline, you don't get it. I can't feel him!"

I chewed on that for a moment. "You mean, you've never lost contact before?"

"Only when he was being hurt by Raoul."

I suddenly felt impaled. After swallowing I said, "I don't want to think it's happening again. My fear has been that as soon as we took out Raoul, someone else would be activated."

"Me too. I thought for a while it might be Dave, but he's just a normal asshole."

"How do we know if there's an abnormal one around? This ain't New Atlantis!"

"We'd know because we've both done it before. And don't give me that crap about losing your power—you can't be if you sensed anything I sent."

I wanted to tease her—Blanche, two obscenities in one minute!—but kept to the subject, recognizing her slips as signs of distress. "My power seems to be linked to New Atlantis. Or other people. I'm still not sure what the activating agent is, but I am sure I can't rev it up by myself."

"That's just your faith issue, Mad. You can do anything if you believe you can."

Power is like a muscle, I remembered thinking. It gets stronger when exercised. "Perhaps you're right. But there might be a mechanical limit, too. I think the reason psychic power has been so hard to nail down is that it's just like any other talent. Unmeasurable, and people have it to different degrees. And it blooms or fades under different conditions. Just like the weather—constantly changing, and unpredictable even though you can forecast it a little."

Blanche shrugged. "Maybe true. But look at it this way. It's still a talent. Or a skill. Do you remember learning to read? Or learning times tables? To draw and paint and drive? How hard was it in the beginning? Eventually your brain, and your body, learned what to do, and now you can do those so naturally that you don't even know how you do it. I think psychic power works the same way. You just proved it by finding me on the first try. Your reason and your intuition mixed so you can't tell me which came first, like the chicken and the egg."

"In that case, why are you worried about Dru? He'll find his way here eventually. And think about this: Kit is on his way to Hawaii as we speak. I sure didn't tell him to come here!"

Blanche halted. "How do you know?"

I told her the story while steering her toward the parking lot. We walked in silence while she thought.

"It fits," she said, nodding to herself. "He was susceptible to Raoul, no reason why he shouldn't be susceptible to Dru. I didn't project that volcano image!"

"Then either Dru did, or we've acquired a new psychic enemy."

Blanche shook her head. "I think we're done with that. Raoul was linked to a larger story. We've played our role and the story has moved on. A negative power like his might emerge somewhere else, trying to tip some other balance. I pity those poor souls! But we won this round, and now we need to take the inch we gained and turn it into a mile."

"Kinda hard without our leader."

"That's why you and I are here. We've got to find him so he can continue to lead."

And so you can sleep at night, I finished for her. Although, from the look in her tear-rimmed eyes, I knew she would step into Dru's role if need be and keep the torch burning.

We reached my rental car. I unlocked the doors and opened the windows to let heat whoosh out. We stood outside until it dissipated. "Where are you staying?" I asked.

"Up the road in Captain Cook. Sharing a bungalow, actually."

"With who?"

"A kapuna. Means 'grandmother' or 'wise old-timer.' She grows orchids."

We ducked into the car, wincing as we hit the seats. I turned the air conditioner on high as we drove away.

"How'd you hook up with her?"

Blanche smiled. "Years ago, she wrote me a fan letter. Nicest one I ever got, and the only one addressed to me, nothing about Dru. She invited me to visit her if I ever came to the islands. I never told anyone about it. So that gave me a safe place to go."

"Do you want to stay there or at my hotel? I've got to get back and see if there's a message from Kit."

"Hotel, but I've got to get my stuff and say goodbye."

She directed me to a vine-covered bungalow. Its grounds were overrun with greens and blooming colors and aflutter with birds. No person in sight, nor vehicles in the driveway. I hoped we had gotten lucky and Blanche could dash in, grab her bags, leave a note, and take off. Nope—a woman appeared in the open door on the lanai to watch our approach.

I had envisioned some squat and wizened white lady when I had been told to expect a grandmother. What greeted us was a Caucasian/

Polynesian mix about six feet tall, gaunt, with blue eyes, cafe-au-lait complexion, and white-streaked black mane. She wore a pareu tied low around her hips and a matching halter top, exposing an ungrand-motherly amount of weathered skin. When I recovered from surprise, I registered her necklace: the same tiny shells I had seen on display in my hotel gift shop.

"Aloha!" she greeted, descending the steps onto her shell walkway. "I see you found your friends."

"Not all of them," Blanche said, "although a good haul for one net casting. We're joining forces to catch the strays."

"You're welcome to stay here if you're willing to share one bed-room."

"Thanks," I broke in, "but I have a hotel room and we expect to be going off-island. We're just here to thank you and pick up her things."

"Help yourself," the grandma said with an arm sweep before van-ishing into her garden. Blanche and I exchanged glances, then Blanche collected her luggage. The kapuna peeked at us over a bougainvillea hedge. Then she disappeared during a moment I used to swig from a water bottle, only to reappear from the side of the house bearing two leis just as Blanche came down from the lanai.

"For your journey," she said, dunking the first lei over Blanche's head. "And for bringing a smile back to your sister's face," she said while placing mine. Both leis were made from tufted red blossoms I learned later were lehua, the official Hawaii lei flower. Each island had its own lei and color, worn for any occasion but especially for ar-riving and departing.

When I asked about the shell lei the kapuna wore, she answered, "Ah, these are pupu shells from Niihau, the Forbidden Island. My late husband gave it to me when we came here for our honeymoon. As you can see, the honeymoon never ended."

Blanche again went silent to suck back tears. The kapuna smiled and touched her cheek. "I'm sure you'll find him. He can't stay away for long! In a way I'm glad you misplaced him, for I enjoyed your company. If you can, stop by before you go home."

"Thank you." Blanche hugged the woman loosely so as not to squash her lei, then retreated to the car. We piled in with final waves then backed out the drive.

"I hope you paid her something," I said to Blanche, who frowned out the window.

"She wouldn't take money but she accepted groceries and a few cab rides."

"Does she understand what's going on? I couldn't tell by the way she talked."

"I'm not sure. She knows our music and our mission, but there's no TV in the house and I never saw her read a paper. I gave her a fuzzy story but she didn't ask questions. Mostly we talked about flowers and birds, and some Hawaiian legends."

"Did she say anything about Niihau?"

"About what?"

"Niihau. The Forbidden Island."

Blanche shrugged. "Only that it's privately owned. There are actually eight islands in the chain but only seven open to tourists. Niihau is some sort of reservation for native Hawaiians, though it's owned by whites. Last place on Earth where Hawaiian is the native language. Nobody can visit without an invitation. And—" She rushed in as I opened my mouth. "—we don't know anyone remotely connected with them."

"But it's a place of refuge. Maybe Dru got his wires crossed."

"But how could he have gotten there?" She pulled a guidebook from her bag and skimmed for facts. "The only way over is a supply run from Kauai using some 'vintage landing craft.' He couldn't hop that without sticking out like a sore thumb."

"No air service?"

"No. And no electricity or phone, either. Though . . ." She flipped pages. "The owners do run a helicopter tour from Kauai. To defray the cost of using the thing as a medevac. But it only touches down on two remote spots and they don't let you off unsupervised." She closed the book.

"How far apart are Niihau and Kauai?"

She reopened the book and trailed her finger down several pages. "About seventeen miles. We could get there if we rented a boat, I suppose. Do you know how to drive one?"

"No. Even if I did, we'd have to get charts to figure out what kind to rent. We'd be better off just hiring someone."

Blanche deflated. "That'll draw too much attention. So would any form of sneaking out there, or bribing someone. Same goes for Dru. He'd never pass as a Hawaiian. He can't possibly be there."

"I still think it's worth a look. I tried the obvious and found you."

"But if he really did short out, then he won't make obvious connections. You're probably right, he's just late getting here. I'd rather hang out a few days and keep trying Place of Refuge."

I would too, since parking upped the chances of catching Kit. At least I knew he was alive and well. I pined to stop all this running and just lie on some silver beach with him. My gut, however—or just logic—told me he could wait another day, whereas finding Dru was critical.

"Tell me more about that helicopter tour," I said.

Blanche flipped back and forth between index references to Niihau and the pages that mentioned it. Finally she said, "Everything launches from Kauai. Here's a safari tour. I guess Niihau is overrun with wild pigs and these guys have permission to hunt them. Yuck. Doesn't matter—reservations have to be made months in advance. Same for most of the scuba tours. We might be able to get this: One of the big hotels on Kauai offers a snorkeling and picnic adventure to Niihau for an afternoon. Nowhere near the settlement, but it'll get us over there."

"Perfect."

We returned to my hotel to pack and change disguises. I bought those earrings and necklace on the way in. After leaving another message for Kit, I heaved a big sigh, checked out, and drove to the airport. We boarded the next interisland flight to Kauai.

39
The Forbidden Island

Kauai, the Garden Island. "Where other Hawaiians go for the scenery," the guidebook said. Being the oldest of the main islands, it was the most eroded, thus had the most fertile soil, the roundest topography, the widest water courses—therefore, the lushest flora. Off its flank, in its rain shadow, lay the Forbidden Island: tiny, arid Niihau.

We arrived via Kauai's largest town and spent the rest of the day along the coast of the channel across from Niihau. Both islands had been blasted some years earlier by a hurricane, scars from which still showed between the rebuilt homes and businesses, regrown sugar cane fields and rainforest. We landed at a big-name resort that reluctantly admitted it had a room available. Had we presented our true identities, management would have rolled out the red carpet and trotted out the brass band. As it was, I waited in the car while Blanche transacted.

Upon winning the room key, she collected me and we ascended to our room with an ocean view. So innocent an action; so potentially big a mistake.

"That bellboy in the elevator recognized us," Blanche announced when we locked the hotel room door.

"How could he?" I assessed her camouflage. In safari shorts, fluorescent T-shirt, tennis shoes, straw hat over my pageboy wig, still wearing sunglasses, she looked like a sporty yuppie. I looked matronly in a muumuu, sun hat, and sandals plus her brown ponytail wig.

"I'm not sure what clued him in," she said. "But I felt his surprise and scrutiny until we got off."

My innards writhed. I had noticed the bellhop and his luggage, along with the couple that went with them plus two other guests wedged with us in the elevator. Out of habit I had kept my face averted and tuned them out. Another habit that closed my mind to useful stimuli. So much for being the wind or a wave!

"Keeping our glasses on inside might have done it," Blanche suggested, removing hers to show the beginnings of an inverse raccoon mask. "And we stood together—he could've seen that our profiles match."

I had never considered that giveaway. Yes, since I had not gained enough weight to blur my jawline, our identical profiles-hands-arms-throats-noses-postures could grab a discerning eye.

"Oh lord. I suppose it'd be worse to check back out." I plunked into a flowered chair. "We can just walk away, since you've already paid."

Blanche tugged off her hat and wig and strode to the window. Niihau floated on the horizon as a long, hazy hump. "Not yet—I didn't sense any hostility. Maybe he can help us. Let's see what happens."

I deferred to her will, grateful to be led after so much blind struggling. Nevertheless, we ordered dinner in.

While waiting for room service to arrive, I again called Tony Martin. His woman answered and read off a message. "Kit is on Big Island. He's booked under the name Mark Lester at a place outside Volcanoes Park—" She snarled the address and number.

Whee! My body flooded with joy, relief, adrenaline, hormones—I had to struggle to maintain a calm voice. "Thank you. In case I miss him, tell him I've hooked up with my sister and here's where we moved to." I made a point to add, "We're booked under her name: Sally MacRae."

An obscenity was followed by: "If you guys have enough bread to jet around Hawaii, why don't you just spring for cell phones and stop bothering people at night!"

She smacked down her handset.

I picked mine up again to dial Kit's hotel. As expected, "Mark Lester" wasn't there, surely out looking for us. This didn't prevent a wash of disappointment so strong it churned my stomach. I left a message to meet us tomorrow at our hotel. After hanging up I paced, hoping Kit had enough money to keep island hopping and no Feds were letting him run until he found us.

Dinner arrived. Blanche plowed through it while I poured out my escape story. At the end, she wiped her lips and smiled. "I told you those twins can make noise when aroused!"

I tried to smile back but couldn't. "You should've heard me! But I felt like two people. For the first round, my body didn't belong to me. My soul hid behind a wall and watched us. Then I fell apart and dumped all over him. He took it without blinking, like he always has. I don't know how he can stand it. I hated him and I needed him at the same time. I shouldn't feel that way over somebody I don't want, never wanted, have no interest in—don't want in my life! Yet he has so much strength he was able to restore mine when I lost it. And have enough left over to let me walk away!"

"Jake would do same for me. In fact, he did, then had to live with me and Dru under his nose every day! At least John watched you walk into the sunrise, to a future he may never know."

"What I keep wondering is what prevents them from turning into stalkers? For that matter, what's the real difference between them and Raoul? Unrequited love—knowledge of the psychic arts—violent lust—why didn't they turn like he did?"

"Two reasons. One is the quality of their souls versus Raoul. Not everyone will turn bad just because they have the chance. And two, we probably reduced that chance by giving what they asked for. Their whole lives were built on a fantasy. We validated it. Given how devoutly they clung to their purpose before either of us kissed them, I'm sure they cling to it more devoutly now. They will not rest in peace until you and I are reunited with our mates and safely back at New Atlantis. I'm surprised they haven't broken away to hunt us all down! But that's how strong their faith is. They'll keep our home—or hideaway—safe for us, trusting our mates to do protection duty while we're off site."

"Hah!" I said, extending my arms to express, "What mates?"

"At least we know Kit's here," Blanche countered. "And hopefully the three of us can find Dru."

"Let's see if we can dig up Buck while we're at it!"

Blanche rolled her eyes. "Do you really want him back? Isn't it clear you belong with Kit?"

I gazed out at the seascape. "Depends."

She waited while I gathered words. "The happiest moments of my life were with Buck."

"In bed."

"Yes. But we were just starting to get it right the rest of the time when . . ."

Blanche nodded. After a pause she asked, "What keeps you from going there with Kit?"

I didn't answer but I knew. Buck lay between us. And New Atlantis. On our own, in a normal world, Kit and I could be who and what we wanted to be, separately and together. Unfortunately, the world would never be normal again, especially if we didn't get Blanche and Dru back on track.

At that point I told her about my multi-stage soulmate theory. Her face puckered as she followed, then opened when she understood.

"Yes! That's it! You've just clarified the one thing about reincarnation I didn't understand!"

She feigned a swoon. I chuckled then chided, "There's still a lot to be explained. But there are times like this when as-above agrees with as-below. Meaning, you and I are attached to Dru and compelled to find him!"

"Do you think we should check out the volcano?"

"Next stop after Niihau if that comes up empty."

"My next stop is the shower then drinks at poolside," she decided. "To see what I can learn from people hanging around."

"I should go with you, but . . ."

"No, you go to bed. We'll be too conspicuous together. I won't stay long."

I couldn't argue, for jet lag was claiming me. "Just be sure you look different from when we checked in, and zap anyone who tries to pick you up!"

She obeyed, or so I presumed. I conked out before she finished showering. Despite the relief of having both her and Kit located, I still dreamed in fractured Hawaiian images. Strobe-fast scents and sounds and colors, many of which I had not yet experienced during this warped vacation . . . were they Blanche memories I picked up through our revived connection? Or Kit moments transmitted by his stress? Could they be cognizance bits from a damaged Dru?

In the morning Blanche reported a fruitful encounter during her pool mission. Over a second round of cocktails, a friendly couple had regaled her with stories about their snorkeling adventure on Niihau.

"The hotel flies them over in groups for a half or whole day, to beachcomb, picnic, and snorkel. They get a sightseeing buzz over the island, showing them the settlement but landing nowhere near it. Sometimes the natives come around to check out the strangers though usually they're reclusive. But—"

She dropped her voice. "Somebody's pitched a tent on a strip of beach below a cliff on the opposite side. It popped up a few days ago. According to the chopper pilot, the hermit living there is white."

I sat to attention. "How did he get there?"

"I can't imagine. They didn't see any boat."

"Maybe he broke kapu. Or is a friend of the owners."

"Maybe. Or maybe they don't know he's there."

"The Hawaiians must. The whole island's a ranch, they must range all over the place, especially the pig hunters. If it was a cinch for tourists to sneak out there, then there'd be an army camped along that beach!"

"It would be a cinch if you could make people not see you, or remember you."

I sat silent then said, "If Dru's still capable of masking himself, you should be able to feel him from this close. He wouldn't block you!"

"Unless he's broken."

I sighed. "Let's find out when the next snorkeling trip is going."

It turned out to be leaving for the day in twenty minutes, with two seats still open of the six on the chopper.

"You go," I said to Blanche. "I'll wait here for Kit."

"No, we're not splitting up for any reason. Either we all go together later, or you and I go now and leave a message for Kit. I vote for the latter in case he's being followed and we don't get another chance."

I sucked air through my teeth and conceded. While Blanche changed and packed, I left a message for Kit with the desk, making the clerk repeat it back to me twice along with a vow to pass it to her replacement at turn of shift. I also arranged, despite her protests, to leave Kit a key.

We bolted for the shuttle that took us and three other guests to a helipad. The relentless sun made hats and sunglasses imperative. To distract from our twinness, we wore differently cut shorts over different swimsuits under baggy versus snug tops, plus curly versus straight hair nailed on so as not to slide off in the water.

There had been no time to discuss strategy, and no privacy for it on the flight across the channel. While we schemed to ourselves, our cheery guide recited the guidebook on Niihau's primitive conditions. Our companions asked all the questions, about what fish we could expect to see—any sharks?—what were the chances we'd meet any natives, whether the helicopter would be staying or coming back to pick us up, and when.

Said helicopter skimmed low over the water. We could see depth changes by shifts from teal to periwinkle to azure, and count sails on the boats crisscrossing the sparkling surface beneath our shadow.

The island grew larger every second, resembling a whale breaching the surface. Like its sisters, Niihau possessed a central volcano, long ago weathered down to a ragged lump and skirted by flatland. We zoomed in from the north, swerving up to cross the pali, as Hawaiians called their prominences; then buzzed the empty southern dunes and beaches. On a narrow white strip where the pali plunged into seashore we saw a green, dome-style camper's tent. The guide ignored it; our companions were too scenery-struck to question it. No human anywhere near it.

Blanche and I tried to estimate distances as the chopper swung up the western side over the village, diagonally across the island to where Captain Cook had landed two centuries earlier. We overshot the northern tip to land on a torus-shaped islet and disembarked to a lecture about volcanic origins and bird habitats. Everyone marveled except Blanche, who shuffled and sighed and touched her face a lot, drawing concerned glances from our guide.

"Are you feeling all right?" Miss Cheer asked my sister.

Blanche flapped a hand. "I guess so . . . no, not really. I, uh, I'm feeling kind of faint."

"Oh god, you're not still sick, are you?" I griped, catching my cue.

"I, well, I feel kind of nauseous, but I don't think I'll throw up." She evaded my eye.

The guide cut short the tour and hustled us back into the chopper. We hopped across the passage to land on an isolated northern bay shore. Our companions, casting leery glances at Blanche, escaped and applied themselves to donning masks and flippers before she could spoil the outing. The guide hung back to determine whether she had a problem developing. Blanche confirmed it by slouching in her seat, removing her glasses to wipe her face, swallowing ominously. I fussed, popping in and out of the chopper in distressed indecision. The pilot fiddled with equipment. The guide ran down an options list hoping Blanche would choose.

As she dithered, the pilot said, "Why don't I just take her back with me."

Blanche sneaked a peek at me. The guide made token protests. I assured her, "Don't worry, we don't need a refund"—as if money were no object. Those were the days! All that mattered for the moment was convincing our leader that we were rich and therefore important and not angry at the hotel.

Blanche conceded to a return, caring more about relief than refunds. Keeping my lips clamped, I reentered the chopper beside the pilot. Blanche, moaning, curled up in the seat behind us. The guide and her charges waved us away in relief then ran clear of the rotors, which sandblasted everything in the vicinity. We lifted off tail first and angled out over the water.

About halfway across the channel, Blanche caught my eye and nodded. I waited while she wiped the cream off the open neck of a sunscreen bottle, then, as she pressed it against the pilot's neck, I yanked off his headset.

He jerked and cried out; the chopper dipped suddenly. He dismissed the "gun" at his head to level the aircraft, then yelled, "What the hell is going on?"

Blanche prodded him. "Just a little hijacking," she projected above the roar.

"You're kidding!"

"No joke. Turn the bird around."

"Jeezus lady, where can you hope to go out here? I don't have enough fuel to take you anywhere." Nonetheless, he banked the chopper into a turn.

"Back to Niihau. We have business with that camper on the beach. This is the only way we can get there. Put us down as close to him as you can."

"Jeezus, lady, you—"

She poked him. "Just do it. And don't worry. You won't get in trouble if you play along. In fact, you can earn some good pocket money if you're willing."

He hesitated. Blanche said, "Look, if you drop us off, then the guide thinks we're at the hotel and the hotel thinks we're with the guide. Nobody worries."

"Yeah, but then you can't get off the island."

"That's not your concern."

"Yes it is, if you're gonna pay me!"

"We'll pay you when we land. And double that if you come back for us later."

He glanced over his shoulder; Blanche pushed his face back forward with her free hand.

"Listen, lady, I don't own this thing. And I've got other runs today. Gotta fill in logs. Only so much fuel allotted to me. I can't throw away this job!"

"Then we'll pay you what you're earning until you get another one. Don't have it in my pocket this very minute, but my word is good."

He scoffed. "You expect me to believe you?"

She answered, "You ever heard of Dru Montclair?"

A silence filled with rotor noise followed. The pilot calculated his approach.

Niihau's south end loomed larger and clearer. We headed for a lake at the pali's foothills: the largest fresh-water lake in the Hawaiian islands, I remembered reading—ironic for the island with the lowest annual rainfall.

The pilot looked at me. I removed hat, wig, and glasses. He laughed. "I get it. You think that camper is your missing Dru. So that's not really a gun you're holding on me, is it?"

Blanche retracted her bottle. "Of course not. And we'd appreciate it if you'd just pretend you delivered us as promised and not make a stink unless that tour guide does. If you can't come back, contact this guy who should be waiting for us at the hotel, and he'll arrange for someone to get us. Here's where we're staying."

She rummaged in her tote bag and produced pen and paper. "If everything gets mucked up, here's a number where you can trace us, or at least hook into a good lawyer."

I added, "And please don't talk to the press. We've got people chasing us, and we're trying to round up our strays and get back to New Atlantis without getting caught. Other people have helped us but they volunteered, so we haven't paid them; but in your case, we'll pay you our combined fare for this drop-off, expenses if you can come back for us, and your salary if you get canned."

The pilot shook his head. "This is crazy. But you know, it might explain . . . last week, another pilot for this service told me he could've sworn he carried three passengers but came back with two. His logs reflected three and nobody contradicted him. But he could've sworn . . ."

Blanche and I exchanged victorious glances. She wrote down the pilot's address then belted back into her seat for the descent onto a pristine beach halfway between the south point and the pali. Again a sandstorm flattened all vegetation for yards before the rotors settled to a slow spin. We gathered our totes, emptied our wallets, shook the pilot's hand, and wished him well. He promised to deliver our message but otherwise keep his lips sealed. I prayed to every god in the universe that he would keep his word.

40
The Zombie

We hastened along the beach as fast as deep sand and midday sun permitted before he took off, resuming the sandstorm. Once he had cleared, we found ourselves still bending into a stiff breeze. On this side of the island, we caught channel winds but were protected from tempests and tsunamis by Kauai. Unless they approached from the other direction, which occasionally happened. Witness that hurricane, which had scored a direct hit on Niihau and Kauai. I had kept an ear tuned to weather reports since arriving, so knew that no storms were heading our way.

The hike shook loose my wits. Blanche labored on despite a colorless face below her visor. I scanned for people on the dunes to our left, the water to our right, the beach ahead of and behind us. All we saw during our trek was the dome tent with a mat and beach chair outside it, all set back from the water to lie in pali shade for part of the day.

Blanche marched up to the entrance flap and peered inside. Nobody home, as we had already guessed. But where could he have gone? We'd had two low-altitude sweeps and seen no one in the vicinity. Elsewhere on the island we had seen villagers and paniolos, the Hawaiian cowboys, all of whom had waved. The camper could only be in the village or out on a boat—the tent still contained personal belongings we didn't recognize, and unspoiled foodstuffs. If Dru was encamped here, he had taken disguise and retreat to extraordinary lengths.

Disappointment and dread immobilized us for minutes. Abruptly Blanche spun and dove into the tent to tear through the backpack, canvas and net bags, and bedroll. At her cry I ducked inside to find her holding a ukulele by the neck.

Hope spiked then collapsed. "Doesn't mean anything," I cautioned. "Half the population surely has one."

"But how many Niihauans own brand-new camping gear, and how many tourists travel without one scrap of paper, one camera, one dime?"

"He's probably carrying all that. Do you want to wait?"

"We must." She rocked back onto her heels from a kneeling position, then rose to a hunched-over stand. I had been crouching, both of us stained green by the nylon-filtered light.

We returned outside to debate action. I worried about Kit so favored hiking across the island to throw ourselves on the villagers' mercy, since we needed to get back regardless of the camper. Blanche, however, favored a vigil until the camper, the chopper, or angry islanders appeared. We couldn't go unnoticed long enough to starve, and no one would abduct us unless the pilot squealed—in which case we would likely see anyone coming. We compromised at waiting a few hours and scouting the immediate area.

We carried our bags along the shore until it narrowed and sprouted rocks that sheared up into cliffs. Some of the rocks jutted farther into the water than others, creating protected shallows. We could see marine creatures through the swelling and ebbing water, perfect for snorkeling. Apparently somebody else agreed, for we passed around one boulder to find a towel draped across the next. Beyond it lay a miniature cove in which an air pipe cruised like a shark fin above a blurry, human-sized form.

Blanche gasped. I grabbed her waistband to prevent her from jumping in. The Dru-fish paddled and splashed, unaware of us, plucking at shells and fending off curious fish. Then he spat his tube clear and lifted his head.

"Dru!" Blanche cried. He goggled at us through a mask half filled with water. Then the air shivered for an instant and he disappeared.

The pool remained, complete with fishes. Oh crap, I thought, understanding in a heartbeat. Just as Blanche started screaming, "Dru! It's me! Stop it! Stop it!" I shot out a thought-stream: *Friend, not foe!*

followed by every memory of love and happiness between us I could gather in two seconds. He shimmered into view for a fraction then blurred into the background. Still hurling thought at him—*friend, friend, friend, friend*—I hauled Blanche away from the water and clutched her in place, in view of the pool.

Friend, friend, friend . . .

We stared at the pool, willing it to reveal its occupant. I fought to suppress distracting thoughts in order to keep from scaring Dru away. This must be the power he gave to Buck—psychically convincing a viewer that they were seeing the background without the figure in the foreground. After a few minutes Dru reappeared, treading water as he looked back and forth between us. Finally he popped the breathing tube from his mouth and slid the mask back onto his head.

"Well, hi there, pretty ladies. Come on in!"

Blanche's face lost all muscle tone. No mistaking Dru's blankness. His eyes, as empty as they had been at the Debacle, showed either possession or nobody home.

I gambled on the latter and stepped into his reality. "Er, that's okay, we're just beachcombing. See you later!" then drew Blanche behind the boulder to give him bait and let him follow it. If need be, I would send her back naked and see if that worked. But she was shaking and so pale I feared she would faint, so I propelled her back toward the dome tent, pushed her rump down into the sand and head between her knees.

Dru didn't follow. Damn! And double damn—I heard an approaching chopper.

We sprinted to the tent and leaped inside it, Blanche running reflexively in response to my burst. We peeked out as the chopper rose into sight above the pali then sped by just feet above the water with faces peering through its windows.

I relaxed. A blue chopper, not our red-and-white one. Just tourist traffic, not pursuit. But the clock was ticking, and we had to secure Dru before anyone grabbed us first.

But how? I had projected him dead; wounded; vanished forever; but never not knowing his own soulmate! He must have exerted so much energy causing no one to see him that he lost the ability to recognize himself or anyone else. Now I knew how Buck had managed to stay uncaught, and prayed that he hadn't lost himself, too.

Blanche had recovered enough to whimper. I hugged her, saying, "We found him. Which means we can get him back physically. Then retrieve him mentally if he doesn't snap back by himself. He started to respond, but was so scared that he hid again."

Blanche took no comfort. "Oh Mad, he's toasted. I can't believe it. He took on too much. I shouldn't have left him. I should have buffered him. Oh god, I destroyed him. Or else the powers are punishing him for—"

I shook her. "Cut that right now!" Fire surged through my nerve channels. "Not another syllable. We've found him. We'll fix him. Now concentrate on getting off this damn island!"

When sure the coast was clear, we emerged from the tent and headed for the pali. Because it rose in stages from sand dunes to raw rock heights, we could gain altitude without shredding our hands and legs. We found a niche offering shade and shelter just before Dru came ashore naked, claimed his towel, and backtracked to his tent. If we hadn't already known, we could have deduced his condition from the vague way he walked, chatting to himself like a benign lunatic.

"I guess he really doesn't have a piece of paper to his name," I commented, since he carried no pouch or clothing.

"I think he's got a money belt," Blanche muttered. "I got distracted by the ukulele and forgot to look for it."

"He must. He couldn't have teleported here!"

I balked at that thought. Perhaps he could . . .

Shaking the thought away, I continued, "At least his self-preservation instinct is okay. I mean, he not only got here but had the wit to dye his hair and is running around bare-ass without getting sun poisoned."

"So how do we get him home? Just jiggle our boobs and promise whatever he desires so he'll tag along until we can get help?"

"If necessary. Maybe we'll get lucky and a few more contacts will wake him up."

Blanche didn't acknowledge, just sat with chin on updrawn knees and her arms looped around them. She stayed that way for hours while we watched and waited.

Dru entered his tent and did not reappear until it lay deep in shadow. Siesta time, I presumed, tempted to take a nap myself. But I refused my body's begging, recognizing this as another of those mind-over-matter occasions. Make that matter-over-mind, and back again. What were we caught in but a Möbius strip?

I reviewed each psychic event since I had arrived at New Atlantis. Evaluated each of my sexual encounters and stories I had heard. Compared relationships, factored Raoul in and out of the picture. Replayed conversations. And caught a glimpse of the solution to our dilemma.

Beside me, my twin shifted restlessly. I ventured, "Remember when we got the scare package from Raoul and I dove back through space and time to Atlantis to save myself?"

"Uh-huh." Her eyes started to flicker.

"I think that's where he is."

Blanche spit air through her lips. "He ain't gonna get there by swimming!"

"You know what I mean! Physically, he's found one of the safest places he can be. Mentally, he's gone where he believes nobody, but nobody, can get him. It'll take some mighty strong bait and powerful fishing line to pull him back."

Blanche sank into thought. I joined her, considering the illusion Dru had created in the pool. He couldn't be too toasted if he retained the power to make us not see him! Meanwhile, he was hiding from his own power, which had created misery instead of a golden future, and demolished his self-belief. I recalled the day I had felt like an inverse lightning rod and didn't dare go near my loved ones. Dru surely felt something similar and had put himself where he couldn't harm anyone again.

The day wore on as I worked out the puzzle. The pali prevented us from seeing if the red-and-white helicopter returned for its charges; we knew only that it never returned for us, although we heard two choppers out of sight. The only other craft we saw was a native-looking fishing boat cruising by beyond the surf. We also glimpsed tiny figures toward the south point, but our shore remained deserted. By dusk, when Dru lit his camp stove, we were eager to come out of hiding.

After shuffling clothes and hair so there was no mistaking our twinness, we picked our way down while Dru ate. Then he traded his bowl for the ukulele and hunched over it in his chair. Its tinny, twangy notes skipped to us on the breeze. Though the night was mild—Hawaii temperature rarely dipped below sixty—I shivered in my shorts and T-shirt. Dru wore only a pareu tied around his hips, plus a shell lei like the kapuna's. His hair, now black, skimmed his shoulders and hung in a veil shielding his face from our approach. I halted about fifteen feet away and let Blanche go on alone.

She swung into his range of vision and stood before him. He looked up, still playing. I was lanced by a memory of Buck twiddling guitar strings while he thought. Dru's hair slid back when he lifted his head, enabling me to see his expression. It didn't waver from serene blandness as he regarded Blanche.

"Why hello again, pretty lady. Or are you Madame Pele come to pitch me into the volcano?"

He giggled. Blanche glowered like the angry Hawaiian fire goddess he referred to. Her anguish surged to such a level that I half expected her to discharge a blast.

But she did nothing, so Dru played on. We held that tableau for long minutes.

I was tempted to try the proven remedy for zombie-ism but sensed that hitting him would only hurt him. There was no possessing power to be broken, no soul to be released. Dru's spirit had retreated so far that it left behind only his shell and essential nature: peaceful, friendly, lover of beauty, maker of music. And maleness. That usually functioned independently. I stepped forward and hissed to Blanche, "Take off your clothes!"

She glanced at me, stricken. Dru registered my arrival and exclaimed, "Ah, another one! I thought I saw two before. Oh joy, they match. What a lucky boy am I tonight!"

He put aside the ukulele. *C'mon, c'mon!* I drilled into his head. He stood, revealing the lump under his pareu I was hoping for. "Start stripping!" I whispered sideways to Blanche, twisting my arms to peel off my own T-shirt. But I had been so focused on luring Dru that I'd become insensitive to my sister. She'd held on too long without a breakdown and was crumbling into it now.

Blanche's eyes brimmed over and she spun away, running down the beach toward the water. I dashed after her until she flung herself into—whew!—the sand, not the waves. I backed off and let her lie there bawling, certain that her tears could not be stopped.

This left me standing on the beach halfway between her and Dru. To my dismay, he picked up his uke and resumed plucking tuneless notes. Damn, so close! Now he just brought to mind autistic children who croon to themselves during endless games that shut out reality. What on earth would we do if he could not be recovered? What a spectacle, dragging him home on an airplane! We would never get him past the press unless we enlisted the Feds' aid to transport him in secret. The thought made me sniff in sour laughter. Hey guys, now you know what power does. Dangerous, isn't he?

Curse those powers! No wonder cultures killed any citizen who possessed them. Even the most worthy could not bear the weight. Best intentions could not prevent them from destroying. They were like tornadoes—natural forces that cannot chart their own paths or avoid devastating whatever they touch. Blamelessly lethal. Beyond any puny human's control. Inevitable in the right conditions, impossible to undo once started. They might blow out of their own accord but will start up somewhere else another time.

I shook my head to stop the thought-stream. Though thinking my own thoughts, they came in another voice, overlaid and amplified, carrying emotion that wasn't mine. Startled, I looked back toward the water, to see Blanche still a prostrate lump in the sand, her back heaving. The ocean beyond her threw itself to shore and retreated, the emerging stars above her glinted in icy beauty, both as indifferent to our fates as any power could be.

The thought-stream deteriorated to a continuous pain, so strong it changed Blanche from empath into telepath. We needed to channel that into Dru's consciousness so he would emerge to help her. I tried to quiet myself and relay but knew in seconds it wouldn't work. There had to be a different, stronger connection. The strongest one, as shown me by John, Kit, Dru himself, and Buck.

I groaned, knowing the answer but not wanting to face it. Nevertheless, I dragged my feet across the beach and knelt beside Blanche. She pulled herself onto her elbows but kept her head down until her sobs ebbed. Presently she drew a wrist across her mouth and spat out sand.

"I'm all right," emerged as she pushed herself up onto one hip, braced by an arm.

"Listen." I whispered though no one could hear us. "I've got an idea. Can you focus?"

She nodded. I sat cross-legged beside her, feeling the sand's lingering warmth through my backside and bare feet. "It's time for a little power circle."

Her eyes snapped alert. "No way."

"Yes way. You were right—we've got to promise whatever he desires. And the biggest, most tempting forbidden fruit we can dangle is both of us together."

She looked away.

"It's all about triads, Blanche. Listen. First the combination of me, Buck, and Kit let me perceive Raoul. Then you, me, and Dru, boosted by me-Buck-Kit, allowed us to unbalance Raoul. All of us linked and out of control finally destroyed him. But then my power disappeared when Buck did and Kit got wounded. I continued to get glimmers because you, me, and Dru are still connected, but our estrangement and all the stress has kept it subdued. I've been feeling it more since I got you back and Kit approaching. But that's not good enough. We need you, me, and Dru physically linked to create the energy we need to pull him through."

Blanche moaned. "I could live with you two getting it on once, 'cause of what you needed to learn. But Mad, I don't want any ménage à trois with you!" She gulped back another sob.

"Me neither. But this is another case of needing to learn. Or rather, applying what we already know. Think of it in karmic terms. We're here because only our triad can put the right powers together and make them work. This is our chance to rectify mistakes made in both Atlantises. And though he needs us both, what he really needs right now is the best you can give him. Right here right now where nobody'll ever know."

It's simpler than that, I thought as Blanche cursed the gods she still believed in. Love and lust combined the right way, at the right time, between the right people, created the only conditions that allowed mind and body to jump their boundaries.

"If you can't accept the high road, then think about going home with a vegetable, and everyone else sticking their noses and fingers in," I summarized.

She shuddered. I left her to contemplate that alternative and walked back to the scrub beyond the beachhead where we had deposited our gear.

By the time I returned with it, Dru had retreated into his tent; the skies held moving lights but none headed near. We stood in a world of depth, shade, and texture. Under star- and moonlight reflected by pale sand, with the water's dim phosphorescence adding a surreal backdrop, we could see each other's expressions and identify items in our totes.

Blanche, still shaky, allowed me to direct. I extracted a pareu from my bag and let it banner in the airstream. "Put this on."

She obeyed, then stood like an ivory carving as I tied the oversized scarf around her. No hipslung skirt this time; rather, a one-shouldered dress drooping so low on the opposite side as to expose one breast. She practiced moving in it—tentative swirls and dance steps. I, meanwhile, stripped and donned a comparable wrap and pulled back my hair.

In the half light we were interchangeable. Anyone watching would have enjoyed the show. It'll get better, I promised the imaginary viewer. Then, stuffing our bags together and stashing them in their hollow, I led us toward Dru's tent.

41
Goddesses

We crouched at a safe distance and observed the landscape. No human light, sound, or motion anywhere that we could perceive. That left us no excuses. Blanche and I stood, clasped hands, and crossed the beach.

Outside the tent, I stepped aside to let Blanche go on solo. She inhaled and straightened then pushed aside the unsecured flap and ducked inside.

"Dru . . ." I heard her entice, my ear to the ripstop nylon. "Dru Montclair . . . remember me? I'm part of your dream."

"Oh wow . . . ! You mean I'm dreaming? But I feel awake."

"How can you tell? Are you a man dreaming you're a butterfly or a butterfly dreaming you're a man?"

Silence save for a rustle as Dru raised himself on his sleeping bag and regarded the apparition in bewilderment. I didn't need to see him to know.

He chuckled in this throat. "This is the best dream I've ever had!"

Another rustle as Blanche untied her garment and let it slide to the floor.

"If you're Madam Pele," he said, "I'll gladly jump into your volcano."

"But can you stand the heat?" Blanche replied in a tone that brought goosebumps to my skin. She remained on her knees, luring Dru forward. I felt her anxiety as if we were hardwired together through the wall.

When he touched her, I twitched at the voltage. She longed for and was repulsed by him in alternating waves. I peeked through the screened window to time my moment. Their shadows sat separate, connected by his hands sliding over her form.

Like her, I inhaled and straightened before entering. Unlike her, I held the flap open so he couldn't miss my silhouette.

"What's this?" he drawled, his hands disengaging.

"The rest of your dream," I answered, hoping my voice sounded as sultry as Blanche's.

He hummed. Blanche attached herself to one side while I slid into place on the other. We rubbed ourselves against him and entwined him with hands.

This interesting arrangement lasted for many minutes. I slipped my pareu off and around him in one sinuous motion before tossing it aside.

Since he had discarded his skirt before we got there, this left all three of us naked. Dru's body proved my theory that only his mind had been damaged. All male systems normal and ready to go.

At that cue, I pulled a maneuver Kit would have cheered had it been on a racetrack—downshifting and flooring it past the pacesetter to take the lead on the last lap. Physically, I slipped outside Dru's grasp but kept contact with him and Blanche with whatever finger, toe, or knee I could touch them with as they moved, in order to close the power circle and be free to close my eyes. Mentally, I reached back to the Debacle to remember the feeling I needed, then flung open my neural network and commanded healing power to rush in.

And it did!

The molten abdomen, electrified arms, pressurized head, pinpoint vision—I became supercharged again, though not overwhelmed and expulsing blasts willy-nilly. The power let me gather Dru and Blanche into a field wherein I visualized them ablaze in passion, drawing all that I knew from my night with him and life with her, and the images I'd stolen from John about his brother's wild night with Blanche and my own crazed fling with John, to make Blanche and Dru dig into each other with the voracity they feared to unleash.

I fueled them by reliving my uncorked lust for Kit and heartbreaking love for Buck; activating the sneakiest deceit I owned to fabricate my image in the tent and make it dance with them like the wanton that John had awakened, while I actually kneeled aside.

Then I battered my sister with all the jealousy I had stored and compelled her to exercise the erotica she had studied, and face the disgusting rape fantasies Raoul had imposed on her, to suck Dru's soul out of its hiding place, forcing him to respond to her craving in order to stanch the agony gushing from her like blood, to remember the joy and tenderness they had shared, to reclothe himself with his own image, visions, and longings; drawing, pulling, pushing, luring, punishing, forgiving, reassuring, harassing, seducing . . .

. . . which my twin enacted on the tent floor, driving Dru to the point I worried about burst blood vessels. He wouldn't release, just drowned in feeling. Blanche, possessed, wouldn't, couldn't stop.

I was about to pull her away when we both felt some cog slip in Dru's machinery and suddenly engage. All of our eyes popped open at the same time. Dru and Blanche saw only each other for the briefest moment before his eyes rolled back in his head as orgasm overtook him. Every nerve and muscle convulsed or expulsed and he even screamed, shocking us rigid. If the *Book of World Records* kept such statistics, he experienced the longest and most intense climax in history.

Then he fell unconscious, with Blanche's name formed on his lips but not uttered before his strength collapsed.

She crumpled atop him. I found myself standing with my head pressed against the tent fabric, my insides reverberating while sweat poured off my skin. When my limbs again moved and eyes resumed tracking, I shakily stooped to check the lovers' pulses. Dizziness thumped me down onto my naked rump, where I sat until recovered.

Once satisfied that Dru and Blanche were all right, I savored a moment of private triumph. I did it. I DID IT! Harnessed power all by myself and channeled it into something good, in spite of my doubts and fears, despite two damaged people for support. Nothing supernatural about it, though I still couldn't say where the power had come from. But it had been there when I needed it and obeyed my command.

So there, I sent to the silent, watching forces. *My work is done and you can't bully me any more!* The future belonged to me now, leaving the question: Could my integrity and imagination live up to it?

Regardless, when we got home I would buy a little checkered flag and stick the pole in a mini loving cup amid the trophies on top of my dresser. First, however, we had to get home!

I got up and dusted sand off my rear then peered around the tent flap. Good. No Feds surrounding us with leveled rifles. Nor natives speculating about exorcism. I would have given anything to find Kit standing outside, arms crossed over his chest and fuming. But we remained alone in the middle of the sea.

Blanche had partly wakened and stretched herself alongside Dru, stroking his face as she panted. I groped around for some liquid, found a water bag, then returned to the bed, dampened a pareu, and wiped the pair down. Blanche's awareness expanded to include me, and she watched, beneath almost closed eyelids, as I covered her and Dru with the dry pareu then daubed myself with the damp one. Eventually I sat back on my heels and met her gaze.

"Goddamn it," she murmured. "You were right. Thank you."

She fell back into sleep before I could respond.

Still shaky, warm and cold, unable to visualize beyond the next moment, I took another long drink then lay down on Dru's other side and tucked an edge of bedding around me. I must have passed out promptly, for something jostled me awake. It was Dru, his shadowed form stumbling upright and reaching for the tent flap, seeking Blanche, who was already gone.

Alarm shot me up and after. Outside, blackness had dimmed to grayness, heralding morning. For a moment I was back at New Atlantis in a predawn nightmare with buildings breaking into flame all around me, horses and people screaming, a fiery barn support crashing down on Buck. Then my mind caught up to my senses and returned me to an empty beach on the Forbidden Island. Ahead, Dru staggered toward Blanche's silhouette.

She stood in the undertow, scanning the heavens for her own Polaris. Stars winked out as we watched, replaced by a blush creeping across the sky. The pareu she had tossed around herself fluttered at one corner. Dru and I formed points on a line between her and the tent, each a dozen yards apart.

I halted close enough to intervene if necessary, far enough back to watch. Blanche ignored Dru until he sloshed into the water beside her. Then her head snapped around. They stared. He grabbed her. She resisted then buckled into his kiss.

I wasn't sure whether Dru was running on hormones alone or conscious of his actions. At least he had picked the right game to pursue! I ached seeing the intensity with which they embraced each other. Something more than glands had entered the picture.

It promised to go on for a while, so I collected our bags from the hollow and returned to the tent for some grooming. Then, in fresh shorts and T-shirt, my fanny pack containing our wallets cinched around my waist, I resumed position on the beachhead and watched the show. In any other situation, such voyeurism might have made me feel guilty or titillated. As it was, I studied symptoms and drew conclusions like a scientist, or wished that Kit and I could make love like that on the fringe of the sea.

Oh Kit. How could I explain this to him? I prayed to whomever, whatever, that I would not be forced to tell him about this experience. Or share a similar one with him, me, and Blanche.

Yet the knowledge gained was worth sharing. We had found the blend-point between psychic and physical power. Kit was right—it shifted along the continuum, wherever people and passion combined at a certain place to channel energies. But that place shifted, along with the people and passions that combined with it.

Passion, I realized, boosted the mind and heart the same way adrenaline boosted the body. Passion plus will equaled power, psychic or otherwise. In Dru, for example, when at low idle, his passion and will formed charisma. When he was ramped up, and fed by or merged with others, his passion and will led to telepathic exchange and healing. In desperate self-defense, he could generate psychokinesis. That's how he and I had fought Raoul, and how Allanna had expulsed the raven.

In my case, a wobbly will prevented consistent performance. Only when extreme emotion elbowed aside self-consciousness could I harness power. That accounted for my exchanges with Buck, as well. We had connected when our passions overwhelmed our inhibitions. Now, his drive to survive and to protect the planet allowed him to remain invisible. Continued success built up his confidence, in turn developing his will, in turn sustaining his power, in turn . . .

As with Dru. Extreme self-confidence let him harness power. When his ego had been shut down, his power had disappeared. For most of us, insecurity got in the way of organizing or sustaining passion to fuel psychic power. Then there was Raoul, whose insecurity had flipped to become extreme egotism, which gave him the will to channel jealousy, greed, and vengeance into a fire as potent as a laser.

John went the other way, opening wide to spirits by immersing himself in love. But while he had self-discipline, he lacked a mighty will. Thus he could receive but not harness, unlike classic mystics, who emptied themselves of all emotion and developed will into a gargantuan muscle—an unplugging of self that enabled them to control their bodies and minds to a degree that awed ordinary humans.

Blanche and Dru, extraordinary humans, could connect psychically because their mutual love was total. And Blanche's faith, similarly complete and indestructible, gave her the power to reach across distance and link with me during the random moments I could receive. I would be like her if I ever acquired the calm acceptance and confidence owned by successful psychics.

Regardless, these combinations occurred so erratically that their manifestations defied measurement. First, because the tools didn't exist to capture the energy; later, because no one understood what to measure, and so few people could command the right elements in the right time and place.

In theory, then, we could teleport off this island. Hah—tell that to my depleted bod! Same for Blanche and Dru, who had scudded down the sand into deeper, stronger current and were getting doused every few seconds by waves. I could see their smiles, see their lips form endearments. They might be working up some serious passion, but it wouldn't transport us through space today.

Dru finally stood, wobbled as a breaker spanked him, and pulled Blanche upright. Her pareu had drifted out of reach, to intrigue some fisherman some other day. Nude and glowing from within, their skin tinged by sunrise, they formed a picture I would paint someday. As they waded to shore, their smiles faded. Dry land represented reality, represented by me.

I stood to offer sweatshirts and towels, for it would be a while before the sun warmed one dry in seconds. Already Blanche's teeth chattered and Dru's lips had turned blue.

I looked into her eyes and saw gratitude, and in his saw lucidity. Oh hallelujah, I chanted internally. Then slid my arms around him and said, "Welcome back!"

"Glad to be here," he quipped, giving both of us a squeeze.

"How do you feel?" I inspected him as we shuffled up the beach, everyone's arms around each other's waist with Dru in the middle.

"I've never felt so good yet so weak."

I handed him a health-bar. "No one has ever exerted so much energy as you did, or for such a long time. It took two of us to jump-start you; you might not recover for months."

"Yeah, now it's my turn to be head-blind." He sighed then looked up under his brows. "But you got yours back."

I shrugged. "I just steered and channeled."

He eyed me, unconvinced, but lacked the gumption to challenge. All of us used the dregs of our energy to return to the tent, dry and dress, untangle our hair, and rummage for food in our baggage. Dru and I wolfed down everything we found. Blanche ate or drank what I handed her but otherwise just stared at Dru, her eyes glittering, cheeks glowing, and hair standing in spikes.

Dru asked, frowning, "How long have we been here?"

"Us about a day, you going on a week."

"How did you find me?"

I groaned. "It's a long story. Let's leave the catching up for later. We need to get to the village and find some help."

Blanche pleaded, "Can we rest a bit first? The minute we show up anywhere, it'll be consequences, consequences all the way home."

"Can we go home?" Dru's voice rose in hope.

"If you accept the conditions."

I recited what Colin had told me. Dru pursed his lips and listened with unfocused eyes. Nodding, he said, "I can live with that," when I finished. He looked at Blanche. She nodded, too. Both looked at me.

I dodged their gazes. "I'm not making any decisions until we get out of here and I get Kit back." I described the message trail I had left. "If we're lucky, he'll be waiting for us. And even luckier if he hooks up with that pilot or takes the next snorkeling tour. I'm willing to wait until noon to see if any choppers show up. If not, then present ourselves to the village and beg, barter, or steal a ride back to Kauai."

"If the villagers don't find us first," Blanche said, "and toss us in jail for trespassing!"

"We can deal with that," Dru said with his old confidence. Yeah, I thought. One phone call announcing Dru's Montclair's return would get us airlifted pronto.

Decision made, we piled together like a litter of puppies and fell into slumber. The physical contact; the release of fear; exhaustion; for whatever reason, we also fell into the same dream, which took us back to Atlantis. The original one . . .

In a scene blurred and sparkling around the edges, Dru and Blanche faced each other clasping both wrists but their heads turned toward me and Buck at the far end of a grassy plateau. He and I stood on the pediment of a roofless temple, which rose in marble columns from a promontory above the surf. We all wore white and gold belted garments that lifted in the breeze.

Buck opened his mouth to speak but only water flowed out. Or flowed in. The sea rose and surged around us, salty and gritty and cold. His eyes held mine—two desperately glinting chips of blue—before we were swallowed.

I woke to find myself truly immersed in water, scouring and tumbling me like a fire hose inside a washing machine. Blanche and Dru shrieked inside my head. The tent adhered to our faces and limbs, trapping a vital gulp of air while trussing us in nylon and poles and punching us with camping gear. Before I could think *tsunami!* we were swept up the beach.

42
The Wheel of Karma

Tent, clothing, hair, and skin shredded during the journey. Just as my lungs were about to burst, and I accepted that everything had been in vain, my head popped into air. I inhaled in a roaring gasp. No chance to clear my eyes before water shoved me down again, up again, down, up, then the whole in reverse as the wave sucked back to where it had come from. I landed yards off shore on mud where surf had earlier pounded. Everything went abruptly silent.

I wanted to just lie there, rub the crud out of my eyes and blow it out of my nose and cough it from my throat, but instinct demanded, RUN!

Tsunami, I knew, came as either a colossal wall of water or the tidal-bore-style uprush we had just experienced. It depended on what kind of earthquake occurred how far away, plus local underwater landforms. Regardless, there was always more than one. We had to reach high ground before it struck.

I rolled half upright and dragged my eyelids open. The sea was gone, the bottom strewn with debris. Animal, vegetable, mineral, Dru and Blanche. Dru was kneeling and puking, Blanche on her back with outflung arms, half wrapped in the tent. I pulled in my legs and tried to stand. Rubber and gelatin—I tottered like a newborn foal. Then flopped backward with a splat and started over. Dru finished retching and turned toward my noise.

I lifted an arm. He followed the direction of my finger. Spotting Blanche, he scuttled across the mud and flung himself down to breathe into her mouth. I staggered after him, looking over my shoulder at a glittering line on the horizon.

Dru had revived Blanche to sputtering by the time I reached them. We each grabbed a pair of limbs and hauled her up the beach, stumbling up the foothills until the water roared in. It erased our tracks but stopped short of our feet. We crawled a little higher then watched as the sand-choked water boiled then retreated. The third came sooner, crested lower, followed by a later, lower fourth and fifth.

We stared, dazed, until the ocean stabilized. Then kept staring through puffy, slitted eyes as the sun sizzled our raw skin. Awareness grew that we were marooned on an island and help might not be forthcoming. I started craving fresh water.

Dru, gaze still fixed on the salt water, said flatly, "Ironic, isn't it, that for all the psychic power we have between us, nobody foresaw this event."

Blanche and I stayed silent. Dru looked at me and added, "We both foresaw the fire but neither imagined the flood."

"Guess that tells you something about psychic power," I answered after clearing my throat a few times. Still, I sounded like a three-pack-a-day smoker.

Dru looked blank. I hacked again then tried to explain. "The fire was human-caused. This was natural."

"Unless you and Blanche worked up so much energy last night that you caused the quake!"

We laughed lamely, then Dru and I watched Blanche cough herself purple as the last muck and water tried to eject themselves from her lungs. After she stopped, spat, and wiped her eyes, she spoke to me as if nothing had happened. "He may have a point. I mean, Raoul moved a lot of stone when he took down the ballroom!"

"True, but the smallest real quake moves a lot more material than he did. This one was real. I suppose we could have sensed the pressure release coming, like animals sometimes do . . . but that's not the same as psychically intercepting someone's intent."

"I thought tsunami could be intercepted with a warning system," Dru said. "What happened to the sirens they told about in the phone book?"

I shrugged, regretting the gesture with a wince. "There's not always enough time. Like, if the quake was local. Or maybe Niihau isn't on the system."

"They have radios, don't they?"

"Yeah, but why tell us? We still don't know if they know we're here. Your psychic shield might have been strong enough to keep us cloaked until last night. And now, anyone on the other side is pretty distracted."

"If they're even there any more," Blanche croaked from where she huddled within Dru's arm. "And our hotel on Lanai, or—"

"Kit!" I pressed both fists to my mouth and gnawed them. Had his voice been part of the chorus screaming in my head?

Dru placed a comforting hand on my forearm. "If anyone can surf a tsunami, it's Kit. Don't be surprised if he shows up in an hour with a chopper!"

My heart clenched. At that point I started feeling other pains: wrenched joint sockets, stinging skin that seeped blood, and a hot spot on my scalp, bleeding more vigorously where a hank of hair had been torn out.

Dru sported a swelling cheekbone that would probably leave a shiner, plus lacerations all over and an ugly, oozing gouge on his leg. Blanche was as abraded as I was with the added bonus of a twisted ankle and flooded lungs.

But we were alive! And I was so glad I hadn't jumped off that icy cliff that I wanted to spring up and dance.

My legs had other ideas. None of us moved for what felt like hours, other than to take turns shading each other from direct sun scald, and to daub at our wounds with what remained of our clothes. This amounted to my fanny pack and shorts; Dru's shirt and money belt; half of Blanche's top and bottom.

"Now I know," she said, "how the first life forms felt when they crawled out of the sea."

"Brace yourself, we may have to crawl across the island to get help."

"That pilot who dropped us off will surely tell somebody we're here," Blanche hoped aloud. "And other people saw Dru's tent. Even if the village got it worse than we did, somebody will come out to check."

Likely true, so I didn't respond. But I wished they'd hurry up about it!

Then what?

"Dru," I said after silently rehearsing ways to broach the subject. "This is the best chance you'll ever have to start over. Assuming we get rescued, it will be a cinch to fake your death. Or play up that you've lost your power. Maybe then—"

"Forget it, Madeline. Power or not, I'm playing it straight, just like before."

"Okay, okay." I held up my hands. "Then . . . what makes you think this time will be different?"

"The fact we're sitting here. The wheel of karma has done a full turn. Fire and flood took us out in the original Atlantis; fire and flood will give us a fresh chance at New Atlantis."

He smiled at Blanche then sobered and directed his words to me. "Mere days ago, we had no options. By accepting your influence, I broke our enemies' boundaries—and yours, and my own—and opened new possibilities. And gained worldwide attention, without destroying anything. We can't jeopardize that. So many people are watching, waiting, listening . . . and their reaction will start the domino chain that will bring peace and enlightenment for all."

Blanche and I studied him with opposite expressions. I said, "You remind me of John."

Dru bit off his next remark and cocked his head.

I continued, "His absolute certainty about his role. The way he'll let himself be a cosmic doormat because it serves The Purpose. No protest. No pride. No need for personal gratification."

Dru smiled. "That's because we get it. Serving The Purpose is its own reward. Sometimes we get frosting on the cake, like what I get from Blanche. And what she gets from me, I hope."

He looked at her. She smiled. I thought, And what John got from me in New Hampshire. Frosting, whipped cream, sugar and spice, with a cherry on top.

Dru finished, "And what you get from Kit."

Who was plying his way to me across continents and oceans, I hoped, I hoped. "I don't know yet if he'll make everything worth it; I shouldn't lay that burden on him, anyway. And I won't accept him as a reward—only himself, for myself, for each other's sake."

Dru studied me then warned, "Don't deceive yourself into thinking you can choose your fate."

I snapped my head around, ignoring the pain that followed. "You said yourself there's always a choice. Free will is the one thing we've proved!"

"Technically true. But one's role in life is set. Take you, for instance."

He shifted on the rocks, oblivious to his nakedness and the sun bubbling his skin. "Your role is to counterbalance me through the transition. That's what it's been all along. Not like her." He tipped his head toward Blanche. "I need you both. That's something else we've clearly proved."

"I don't want my existence to depend on yours. I want my own purpose!"

"You've got it backward, Madeline. My existence depends on yours."

I rolled my eyes.

"It's not your karma to affect the world directly," he insisted. "Left on your own, you'd never do it. Instead, you have a bigger impact by rescuing me."

"Which I have now done twice. And I'll do it a third time by demonstrating that you're right, by living outside New Atlantis as a free citizen of the world. If the Feds and paparazzi want to follow me around, big deal! What else is new? If anything will prove that psychic power is a normal aspect of life, then it has to be a normal life."

"Your life was never normal," Dru stated. "And you underestimate how bad it will be if you leave New Atlantis. Freedom isn't free, Mad.

You will never, ever not be followed, spied on, photographed, and harassed—possibly even hurt. But by staying with the group, you'll have complete freedom inside and protection out."

"You're willing to trust lawyers and government after all that's happened?"

"Yes. They've learned their lesson. Any funny business in the future, we fry them—and they can't complain."

I brayed in laughter. Dru ignored me. "But if we persist in our goal—"

"—your goal—"

"—then there won't be any funny business. Everyone will win. We're not going to rerun the Son of God routine. That one didn't work. No, we're going to operate within the system, which means evolution. Change has to be insidious: little sparks that set tinder to smoldering. Sometimes they blow out and have to be relit. Ultimately you get a forest fire, which clears the way for fresh growth."

I flattened my lips and turned away, splitting my mind to concentrate half on mental barriers—just because we all felt like sea bottom didn't mean his power wouldn't snap back any second!—and the other half on spinning free. Those sparks he had mentioned . . . they were flaring into an idea. An understanding that had eluded me before.

Evolution. Yes.

Evolution was driven by singularities. One gene mutating. One anomalous event. One creature surviving an environment change, and thus passing its attributes to offspring. Without evolution, things chugged along until they ran out of momentum. Only chaos altered entropy.

The anomalies at New Atlantis had generated enough chaos to ripple outward for a long time, ultimately upsetting the global apple cart. If Raoul had won our private battle, the changes would ripple and pinball in one set of patterns; but because we won, those changes would take different form.

I was a key singularity in the process. Likely none of us would live long enough to see the outcome; we were merely the trigger event and trend establisher for a huge cycle of change. All I could do now was wave the free-will banner like mad while Dru beamed out his message, and scientists unraveled the mechanical mysteries of psi (how had Raoul floated that coffee mug?), and everyone else argued about what it all meant. I would keep my own power under cover until I understood the ethics and etiquette of using it. And if we ever got home, I would paint many renditions of the Möbius strip as map and symbol to help all of us understand.

These thoughts drained my last vestige of energy. I melted into the rock, no longer able to speak. Blanche and Dru sagged into each other, their eyes closed, their breathing shallow. We would have baked into dust if the beat of an approaching helicopter hadn't penetrated our fading consciousness.

From somewhere within, a reservoir of adrenaline threw us upright. We jumped and waved and hollered as the chopper hove into view.

It changed course from its beeline over the island and descended to our strip of sanctuary. A man wearing a backpack jumped out and ran, ducked over, from the rotor wash. The chopper rose and shot away toward the village.

The man swung an arm and jogged toward us.

"Kit! Kit!" I shrieked.

I barreled over the ragged brush and stone, heedless of bobbling breasts and streaming blood. He raced uphill as if his leg had never been shattered. We collided and clamped into each other's arms. Kissed so hard we bruised our lips.

"Oh Kit oh Kit oh Kit!"

"Easy, babe—it's okay, it's over."

He cupped his hands around my face to detach our lips and smile at me, nose to nose. "Fast first then slow, remember? In this case, fast means 'fix.' You look like somebody scrubbed the ocean floor with your body. Here."

He unshipped his backpack and pulled off his shirt. I tracked each motion while chewing my lip with tears coursing down my face, looking back to his eyes again and again to make sure he was still there, he was really there.

He held my gaze except when needed to direct his hands. "I was hoping," he said, tongue in cheek, "to put some whipped cream on that nice pair of strawberries you have, but if you don't cover them up they'll turn into charcoal."

He eased the T-shirt over the gooey spot on my head and tucked my limp, red arms through the sleeves. "Thank you," I burbled. He stole a kiss then turned to Blanche and Dru approaching at a shuffle, arms around each other in support. They disengaged to fall against him with exclamations and hugs.

Kit didn't flinch, even though neither had touched him before. Eyeing them clinically, he spoke in the same level tone he had used with me. "Hey guys, you look like flotsam and jetsam. All your parts in working order?" He unzipped his pack in controlled haste.

"I got drowned," Blanche told him.

"Zat right?" Out came a space blanket, first aid kit, and water. "You don't look too dead to me. Or have you reincarnated already?"

"I wish! Though if Raoul could see me now, none of this would've ever happened."

Dru scowled and helped Kit sit her down and bundle her into a wrapper. "That chopper coming back?" Dru asked.

"Yeah, as soon as they finish at the village. Since you guys were standing, they just dropped me off for triage."

He handed Dru a water bottle then pulled a radio off his back pocket and called into it. "I've got all three here okay, coming out of shock, probably need tetanus shots and stitches."

A voice crackled through the speaker. "Roger that," Kit said when it stopped.

They signed off. We stared at him while he produced a knife and sliced a second space blanket into coverings for Dru and me. "You guys are lucky," he said. "A real wipe-out in some areas, not bad in others. Spotty casualties around the islands. I can't believe you took it right on the beach and survived!"

I gazed at his face, so crisp and carved in the sunlight. His eyes burned a water-clear, sky-intense blue.

"We didn't make it by much," Dru said. "What happened?"

"It was a local. Submarine landslide off Big Island. Your hotel got flooded but they rebuilt it sturdy after that last hurricane so there I was opening your door to empty rooms when the tide came in."

"I love you," I said.

He smiled and sketched a wink. "I got back late after a long day searching Volcanoes, got your message and grabbed the first flight over. The guy at the desk said you'd gone on the snorkel tour yesterday but he hadn't seen you come back. A new message asked me to wait and left a key for me, so I went upstairs."

He sat and slung an arm around me. I clung to him, believing at last that anything was possible. He continued, "I ran down at the ruckus and helped people in the lobby. Panicked and asked a bellhop if he knew where the MacRae sisters had gone, hoping it was just out for breakfast—real far inland. No, he said, the LaRue sisters were last seen on this island ten feet from the waterline. He'd heard about it from his buddy, the chopper pilot you hijacked. Who got pressed into service for airlifts. I nearly hijacked him myself."

He broke off to kiss me more thoroughly. I drank him in. Blanche and Dru busied themselves with water, first aid cream, and bandages.

"You're not in disguise," I realized when we came up for air. Already I felt stronger.

He sat back in the sand. "Didn't need it. Hat and sunglasses did the job. Thanks to Dru, I assume, my guards got slipped a Mickey at the clinic. Somebody drove them to a nearby mall and left them snoring in the car. I was carrying the New Atlantis company card I always use, which is in Mark's name, then at the clinic I got handed an envelope with five grand and four addresses inside bus range. A note said, 'Pick one and wait 'til somebody contacts you.'"

"They would have . . ." Dru began.

Kit shut him up with a glare. "I wasn't gonna pin my life on that! I called a racing buddy from a pay phone and he picked me up. We dug out Mad's car—bit of a delay there, with people thinking we were stealing it. All that and lucking into a flight out of Albany, I got out of sync with your calls."

"Did you get our message?" Blanche asked, glancing at Dru.

"That volcano?" Kit said. "I couldn't sleep without that damn thing blowing in my head! In reality, that's probably what triggered the quake. But you weren't kidding when you said we wouldn't be able to miss your signal! It came so late, I wasn't sure what to do until I saw a news report about Kiluea waking up after being quiet for a while. It looked just like my dream. So I went for it. I mean, I've been invaded before by someone I didn't know, so I figured someone I did know, who's just as powerful, could get through if they were screaming loud enough."

"Not bad," Dru said, "for someone who scored all negatives on the psi tests!"

Kit ignored him and turned to me. "Where did you go?"

I sucked in my gut. "Dru knocked me out and had John Powers take me north to the original rendezvous point. When I got the volcano dream, I stole your Land Rover back from him and pretty much retraced your steps."

He nodded and moved on to Blanche, who described eluding Rosalind Burke and heading to the correct rendezvous while Dru went off course. I concentrated on holding myself up when relief undid my muscles.

When Dru didn't follow with his own report, Kit said, "How in hell did you get here?"

"I'm not sure. A weird form of sleepwalking, I guess. It took all my energy to hang a veil between me and anyone looking. Gave them a phony name and a phony image to go with it."

"You traveled across the country behind an illusion? Jeez, that's a Raoul trick!"

Blanche shot him a dirty look. Dru shrugged. "Same thing Buck did when he left the hospital. I only hope he survived the strain. It blew me out completely. I would wake up now and then, figure out where I was, then blank out again for the next leg. My target was some sanctuary in Hawaii, but I went for a present sanctuary, not one from the past."

An image of Atlantis flickered in my mind, long enough for me to wonder why I never saw Kit there. It worried me into wondering if my Atlantean "memories" were just fantasies I had peopled with Dru, Blanche, and Buck. More than anything, they had tempted me to believe in reincarnation. I began a fast review of all the books I had read, movies I had seen, in search of images my mind could have borrowed to invent a lost continent. Then the helicopter arrived, drawing all thought to the present.

I leaned into Kit's arms and let him steer me through recovery. Just as Dru had sleepwalked across the country, I drifted unconscious but open-eyed through air and ground transport and medical treatment, occasionally popping alert to get my bearings, then falling back into somnambulance.

At the clinic, Dru gave our true names in order to navigate the bureaucracy already upset by the tsunami. Nobody blinked, but we were discreetly culled from the public, attended in private rooms, then driven back to our hotel around sunset.

The hotel had gotten its feet wet but otherwise stayed open for business. Our belongings remained undisturbed, including the cars rented by me and Kit. Dru, however, possessed nothing beyond his money belt and coverings provided by the clinic. While he did a fast lap through the hotel gift shop, the rest of us took turns scrubbing ourselves clean.

I emerged from the bath to find Blanche zonked out on one bed, Kit sitting stiffly in a chair beside the other, and Dru on the phone with Colin. My brother was shouting so loud I could hear him across the room.

"Stay right where you are! We can get a private jet to you faster than you can get a commercial flight back to the mainland. I'm coming with a doctor and an attorney—don't you dare leave the hotel. Get the bellhop or someone to return your cars, and live off room service. Don't move!"

Dru mumbled some response, but I didn't hear it. A thought had skewered me to the floor: *I'm not ready to go back!*

Nobody heard my protest. Kit, however, reflected my sentiments in his eyes.

Dru hung up and rubbed his face, dragged his hands through his hair, like any other exhausted mortal. For once, perhaps the only time, he could not sense my emotions or read my mind. I had no doubts his power would return once he was safe and rested at New Atlantis. That left the time between now and Colin's arrival as the only chance to stand my ground.

I almost blurted out my thoughts then gulped them back. Dru, unfocused, relayed Colin's decree. I asked only, "Can we get separate rooms while we're waiting?"

Dru looked down at Blanche. "Absolutely."

Kit stood, holding my eye. "I've got stuff to get out of my car."

I offered, "I'll walk down with you and arrange the room."

Dru was already reclining beside Blanche, who slept without twitching. "While you're at it," he mumbled, "arrange a pickup of those rental cars and order some food." He closed his eyes without waiting for a response.

Kit and I ducked into the corridor, then halted and looked at each other. I put a finger across my lips and led him into the stairwell, stopping when the door sealed behind us.

"What's it gonna be," he demanded, standing a yard away from me.

I sucked in my breath and exhaled, "Just me and thee in the real world."

His eyes flared. We held gazes until he said, "You'd better mean it."

"Then you'd better believe me if I spell it out!"

He crossed his arms and waited. I leaned forward in my intensity. "Colin told me that no decisions would be made until everyone was back at New Atlantis. So that leaves us three choices. We can go back and let others decide our future. Or get out right now and start our own life from scratch. Or wait until everyone gets here and have a really big argument about you and me staying on another week—"

"Good luck!"

"—so we can have the space we need to figure out what to do. Just you and me, in as neutral and safe a place as we can find. Like, a little grass shack in some gated resort where we can make love until we can't stand up and talk until our voices fail. Then take breaks for perspective, like touring Volcanoes to watch the Earth being born, and the observatory on Mauna Kea to look at the stars. All of us should take that perspective, but you know the others won't do it. You and I have got to, for our own sakes as well as theirs. But if we go home with them tomorrow, we'll never get the chance."

Kit, unblinking, digested this. I stepped closer. Before allowing me to close the distance, he said, "What about Buck?"

I felt tears prickle but held them back. This was the bottom line. I sucked in my breath and plunged into the future. "Buck and I said goodbye during the Debacle while you were signing off with Julia."

Kit flinched. "So if he shows up, you're still with me?"

"Yes. When we get back to New Atlantis and she's still there, are you with me?"

"Yes," he pronounced.

I grinned at him. "In that case, I've gotten all the magic signals I need."

Kit shut his eyes and took a deep breath. Upon reopening them, he smiled and stepped forward, reducing our gap to inches. "Much as I'd like a free ride home, I'm tempted to just hop an interisland right now. It would take 'em a while to find us!"

"Great idea." I took the final step and slid my arms around his waist. "Except the airport will be gridlocked by tourists freaked out from the tsunami."

"Whatever." He closed the discussion with a kiss.

We necked in the stairwell for a long time, until I said against his lips, "Mmmm, maybe we should just get our own room here tonight."

"I dunno, if I sit on this step and you get on my lap . . ."

"Uh, let's get a room."

We detached and started down, but Kit balked. "You really think you can win that argument tomorrow?"

I stopped on the stair beside him and gave a cryptic smile. "I know so."

As he cocked a head at my tone, I pivoted and pulled him back to me, pouring an energy into him that he had never felt from me before. It must have tingled him, or thrown a visual, for he opened into his brightest smile—the expression that still caught my heart, and which I still hadn't captured on canvas. Maybe during breathers next week I'd do some painting . . .

For now, we clasped hands and went downstairs to launch another variable X into destiny's equation.

About the Author

Carolyn Haley lives and breathes books as a writer, editor, reviewer, and contest judge. Along with novels, she writes a mix of articles and commercial copy for magazines, corporations, and blogs. She also helps other authors with fiction and nonfiction projects through her editorial services business, DocuMania.

She lives in rural Vermont and when not writing enjoys outdoor pursuits—gardening, paddling, walking, riding, birdwatching—along with autosports and aviation.

Learn more at Carolyn's website:

https://carolynhaley.wordpress.com/

www.ingramcontent.com/pod-product-compliance
Lightning Source LLC
LaVergne TN
LVHW050914080826
845145LV00001B/81

9780988719163